MAGNIFICAT

MAGNIFICAT

< A NOVEL BY >

JULIAN MAY

BOOK THREE
OF THE GALACTIC MILIEU TRILOGY

ALFRED A. KNOPF

New York

1996

THIS IS A BORZOI BOOK
PUBLISHED BY ALFRED A. KNOPF

ISBN 0-679-44177-8

Manufactured in the United States of America

For Emy and John Harris
avec mes amitiés

Magnificat anima mea dominum, et exsultavit spiritus meus in deo salutari meo.

LUKE 1:46–47

God said: It is necessary that sin should exist, but all will be well, and all will be well, and every manner of things will be well.

JULIAN OF NORWICH

Love is the only thing that makes things one without destroying them.

PIERRE TEILHARD DE CHARDIN

REMILLARD FAMILY TREE

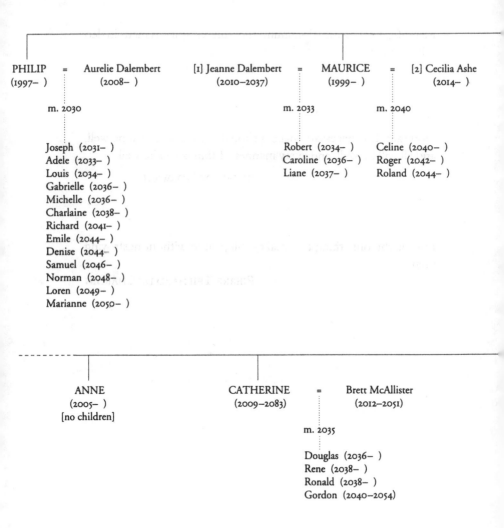

PHILIP = Aurelie Dalembert   [1] Jeanne Dalembert = MAURICE = [2] Cecilia Ashe
(1997–)   (2008–)   (2010–2037)   (1999–)   (2014–)

m. 2030   m. 2033   m. 2040

Joseph (2031–)   Robert (2034–)   Celine (2040–)
Adele (2033–)   Caroline (2036–)   Roger (2042–)
Louis (2034–)   Liane (2037–)   Roland (2044–)
Gabrielle (2036–)
Michelle (2036–)
Charlaine (2038–)
Richard (2041–)
Emile (2044–)
Denise (2044–)
Samuel (2046–)
Norman (2048–)
Loren (2049–)
Marianne (2050–)

ANNE   CATHERINE = Brett McAllister
(2005–)   (2009–2083)   (2012–2051)
[no children]

m. 2035

Douglas (2036–)
Rene (2038–)
Ronald (2038–)
Gordon (2040–2054)

DENIS   =   Lucille Cartier
(1967–2082)   (1968–)

m. 1995

[1] Genevieve Boutin   =   SEVERIN   =   [2] Galya Miaskovska   =   [3] Maeve O'Neill
   (2004–2045)   (2003–2083)   (2006–)   (2013–)

              m. 2027   m. 2030   m. 2035
              div. 2029   div. 2033   div. 2046

          Gregory (2028–)   Yvette (2031–)   Suzanne (2036–)
                               Natalya (2032–)   Quentin (2040–)

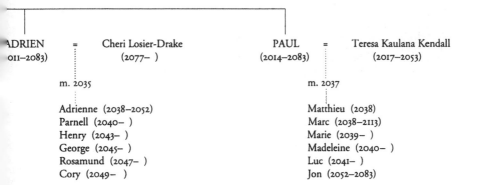

ADRIEN   =   Cheri Losier-Drake   PAUL   =   Teresa Kaulana Kendall
011–2083)   (2077–)   (2014–2083)   (2017–2053)

         m. 2035   m. 2037

     Adrienne (2038–2052)   Matthieu (2038)
     Parnell (2040–)   Marc (2038–2113)
     Henry (2043–)   Marie (2039–)
     George (2045–)   Madeleine (2040–)
     Rosamund (2047–)   Luc (2041–)
     Cory (2049–)   Jon (2052–2083)

MAGNIFICAT

[PROLOGUE]

KAUAI, HAWAII, EARTH
27 OCTOBER 2113

It was dawn in the islands. In the ohia thickets of the highland forest, apapane birds and thrushes gave a few drowsy chirps as they tuned up for their sunrise aubade. Inside a rustic house on the mountainside above Shark Rock, the old bookseller called Uncle Rogi Remillard yawned and stopped dictating into his transcriber. He looked out of the big sitting-room window at the dark, choppy Pacific nearly a thousand meters below, pinched the bridge of his long, broken nose, and squeezed his eyes shut for a moment while he gathered his thoughts. The adjacent isle of Niihau was just becoming visible against the rose-gray sky and a few lights in Kekaha village sparkled down along the Kauai shore.

Uncle Rogi was a lanky man with a head of untidy grizzled curls and a face that was deeply tanned after a three-month stay in the islands. He wore a garish aloha shirt and rumpled chinos, and he was dead tired after an all-night session of work on his memoirs, so close to finishing this volume that he couldn't bear to break off and go to bed.

Now only the final page remained.

He picked up the input microphone of the transcriber again, cleared his throat, and began to record:

> *I stayed on the planet Caledonia with Jack and Dorothée for nearly six weeks, until they bowled me over (along with most of the rest of the Milieu) by announcing that they would marry in the summer of 2078. Then I finally reclaimed the Great Carbuncle, which had done a damn fine job, went back to my home in New Hampshire, and tried to decide what kind of wedding present to give the improbable lovers.*
>
> *I was feeling wonderful! Le bon dieu was in his heaven and all was right with the Galactic Milieu.*

Rogi studied the transcriber's display. Not bad. Not a bad windup at all! He yawned again.

His ten-kilo Maine Coon cat Marcel LaPlume IX stalked into the room and uttered a faint, high-pitched miaow. Rogi acknowledged the animal's telepathic greeting with a weary nod. "Eh bien, mon brave chaton. All done with this chunk of family history. Only the worst part left to tell. One more book. Shall we stay here on Kauai and do it, or go back to New Hampshire?"

Marcel levitated onto the desk and sat beside the transcriber, regarding his master with enormous gray-green eyes. He said: *Hot here. Go home.*

Rogi chuckled. Hale Pohakumano was actually situated high enough to be spared the worst of the tropical heat and humidity. But the cat's shaggy gray-black pelt and big furry feet had been designed by nature for snowy northern climes, and even the joys of chasing geckos and picking fights with jungle cocks had finally paled for him.

Home, Marcel said again, fixing Rogi with an owl-like coercive stare.

"Batège, maybe you're right." The bookseller picked up the silver correction stylo, tapped the display, and dictated a final word, changing "the planet Caledonia" on the last page to "Callie." Then he hit the FILE and PRINT pads of the transcriber. "Yep, I guess it's time to get on back to Hanover—make sure the bookshop's okay, enjoy the last of the autumn leaves. And put my goddam stupid wishful thinking in the ash can where it belongs. There's no reason to stay here. I've got to stop acting like a sentimental sap."

Marcel inclined his head in silent agreement.

"She's just not going to show up. Haunani and Tony must have let her know I was staying in her house. If she'd wanted to see me, she had plenty of chances to drop in, casual-like."

Rogi looked out the window again, letting his inefficient seekersense sift through the human auras glimmering far downslope. The residents and holidaymakers in Kekaha village were mostly still asleep, their minds unguarded so that even a metapsychic searcher as clumsy as he was could sort through their identities quickly.

None of those minds belonged to Elaine Donovan, the woman he had loved and lost 139 years ago.

The farsensory search was a futile gesture, bien sûr, and he didn't bother to check out any of the other towns. Elaine was probably nowhere near the Hawaiian Islands—perhaps not even on the planet Earth.

Borrowing her house while he wrote the penultimate volume of his memoirs had been a bummer of an idea after all, even though the Family Ghost had colluded in it and mysteriously made all the arrangements. Rogi really had thought it wouldn't matter, sleeping in Elaine's bed, cooking in her kitchen, eating off the tableware she'd used, mooching around the garden of tropical flowers she had planted.

But it *had* mattered.

Rogi had seen her image on the Tri-D and in durofilm newsprint rather often in recent years, for she was a distinguished patron of the arts, both human and exotic. The rejuvenation techniques of the Galactic Milieu had preserved her beauty. She retained the same silvery eyes, strawberry-blonde hair, and striking features that had left him thunderstruck at their first meeting in 1974.

He had no idea whether or not she still wore Bal à Versailles perfume.

Long ago, his pigheaded pride had made marriage impossible and they had gone their separate ways. He had loved other women since their parting but none of them were her equal: Elaine Donovan, the grandmother of Teresa Kendall and the great-grandmother of Marc Remillard and his mutant younger brother Jack.

The Hawaiian couple who served as caretakers for her house told Rogi that Elaine hadn't visited the place for over three years. But that wasn't unusual, they said. She was a busy woman. One day she'd return to Hale Pohakumano . . .

The transcriber machine gave a soft bleep and produced a neat stack of infinitely recyclable plass pages. Like most people, Rogi still called the stuff paper. He riffled through the printout, skimming over Dorothea Macdonald's early life, the challenges she had overcome, her great triumph, her eventual recognition of a very unlikely soul-mate.

"Gotta go into that a tad more thoroughly," he said to himself. "C'est que'q'chose—what a bizarre pair of saints they were! Little Diamond Mask and Jack the Bodiless." He thought about them, smiling as his eyes roved over the final page.

But his reverie evaporated as he reached the last line. He was suddenly wide awake with something horrid stirring deep in his gut.

"No, goddammit! I can't get away with a happy ending. I'm supposed to be telling the whole truth about our family." He grabbed the mike, barked out a concluding sentence, then reprinted the page and read what he had produced.

Pain tightened Rogi's face. He slammed the durofilm sheet down on the desk, mouthed an obscenity in Canuckois dialect, and sat with his head lowered for a moment before looking up toward the ceiling. "And you say you didn't have *any* idea who Fury was, mon fantôme?"

Marcel the cat flinched, skinning his ears back, but he held his ground. Rogi wasn't talking to him and he was used to his master's eccentric soliloquies.

"You really didn't know the monster's identity?" the old man bellowed furiously at the empty air. "Well, why the hell not? You Lylmik are supposed to be the almighty Overlords of the Galactic Milieu, aren't you? If you didn't know, it's because you deliberately chose not to!"

There was silence, except for the dawn chorus of the birds.

Muttering under his breath, Rogi pulled a key ring from his pants pocket and lurched to his feet. A gleaming fob resembling a small ball of red glass enclosed in a metal cage caught the light from the desk lamp as he shook the bunch of old-fashioned keys provocatively.

"Talk to me, Ghost! Answer the questions. If you want me to finish up these memoirs, you better get your invisible ass down to Earth and start explaining why you didn't prevent *all* that bad shit! Not just the Fury thing, but the Mental Man fiasco and the war as well. Why did you let it happen? God knows you meddled and manipulated us enough earlier in the game."

The Family Ghost remained silent.

Rogi crumpled back into the chair and pressed his brow with the knuckles of his tightened fists. The cat jumped lightly into his lap and butted his head against his master's chest.

Go home, Marcel said.

"Le fantôme familier won't talk to me," the old man remarked sadly. He tugged at the cat's soft ears and scratched his chin. Marcel began to purr. Rogi's brief spate of wakefulness was fading and he felt an overwhelming fatigue. "The Great Carbuncle always rousted the bastard out before. What the hell's the matter with him? He hasn't been around prompting me in weeks."

He's busy, said a voice in his mind. An' not feelin' so good. He come back laytah an' kokua when you really need 'im.

"Who's that?" Rogi croaked, starting up from the chair.

It's me brah. Malama. I got da word from yo' Lylmik spook eh? Somet'ing you gotta do fo' you go mainland.

"Oh, shit. Haven't I had enough grief—"

Hanakokolele Rogue! Try trust yo' akamai tutu. Dis gonna be plenny good fo' da kine memoirs. Firs' t'ing yo' catch some moemoe den egg on ovah my place. Da Mo'i Lylmik wen send special visitors. It say dey gone clarify few t'ings li' dat fo' yo' write summore.

"Who the hell are these visitors?"

Come down in aftanoon fine out. Now sleep. Aloha oe mo'opuna.

"Malama? . . . Malama?" Rogi spoke a last feeble epithet. Why was his Hawaiian friend being so damned mysterious? What was the Family Ghost up to now, using the kahuna woman as a go-between?

Sleep, urged Marcel. He jumped down from the desk and headed out of the room, pausing to look back over his shoulder.

"Ah, bon, bon," the old man growled in surrender.

Outside, the sky had turned to gold and wild roosters were crowing in the ravines. Rogi turned off the desk lamp and the transcriber and shuffled after the cat. The key ring with the Great Carbuncle, forgotten, lay on the desk looking very ordinary except for a wan spark of light at the heart of the red fob, reminiscent of a similar, more sinister object buried in Spain.

Rogi slept poorly, plagued by dreams of the Fury monster and its homicidal minion, Hydra. Roused by the pillow alarm at 1400 hours, he slapped shave on his face, showered, put on fresh slacks and a more subdued shirt, and went out to the egg parked on the landing pad at the edge of the garden.

Tony Opelu was trimming a hibiscus hedge with a brushzapper. He waved. "Howzit, Rogi! Goin' to town? Try bring back couple E-cells fo' da Jeep, eh? She wen die on me this mornin'.'"

"No trouble at all."

"T'anks, eh? Howza book goin'?"

"Just finished the chunk I was working on. I'll be taking off for the mainland tomorrow, leave you and Haunani in peace. It's been a real pleasure being here, but I've got a hankering for home."

"It happens," Tony conceded.

"I'll leave a note for Elaine. Give her my best when you see her again." Rogi climbed into the ovoid rhocraft, lit up, and lofted slowly into the air under inertialess power.

Rainclouds shrouded the uplands, but the lower slopes of Kauai were in full sunlight. He flew across Waimea Canyon, a spectacular gash in the land that Mark Twain had compared to a miniaturized version of the Grand Canyon of the Colorado. Beyond were dark lava cliffs, gullies carved in scarlet laterite soil, and lush green ridges with glittering streams and the occasional waterfall. He flew on manual, heading southeast, descending over lowland jungles that had once been flourishing cane fields. Some sugar was still grown on the island, but most of the local people now earned a living catering to tourists. There were also colonies of artists and writers on Kauai, enclaves of retired folks who scorned rejuvenation and intended to die in a paradisiacal setting, two cooperatives dedicated to the preservation of island culture that staged immersive pageants, and a few metapsychic practitioners who specialized in the huna "magic" of ancient Polynesia.

Malama Johnson was one of those.

Her picturesque house, deceptively modest on the outside, was in Kukuiula Bay, a few kilometers west of the resort town of Poipu, not far from the place where Jon Remillard and Dorothea Macdonald had resided when they were on Earth. There were no other eggs on the pad behind Malama's place, but a sporty green Lotus groundcar with a discreet National logo on the windscreen was parked in the shade of a silk oak tree next to her elderly Toyota pickup.

Rogi disembarked from his rhocraft and tried farsensing the interior of the house. But Malama had put up an opaque barrier to such spying, and his mind's ear heard her scolding him in the Pidgin dialect that Hawaiians loved to use among their intimates:

Wassamatta you peephead? Fo'get all yo' mannahs o' wot? E komo mai wikiwiki!

With a shamefaced grin, he knocked on the rear screen door and came into the empty kitchen. "Aloha, tutu!"

Malama Johnson called out in perfectly modulated Standard English. "We're in the lanai, Rogi. Come join us."

He passed through the cool, beautifully appointed rooms to the shaded porch at the other end of the house. It was dim and fragrant, with a fine view of the sea. The stout kahuna woman bounced up and embraced him, kissing him on both cheeks. She wore a royal blue muumuu and several leis of rare tiny golden shells from Niihau. "Cloud and Hagen flew in last night from San Francisco," she said, indicating the two guests.

Rogi swallowed his astonishment. "Hey. Nice to see you again."

The fair-haired young man and woman nodded at him but remained seated in their rattan chairs, sipping from tall tumblers of iced fruit juice. They were immaculately attired, she in a snowy cotton safari suit and high white buckskin moccasins, he in a white Lacoste shirt, white slacks, and white Top-Siders. Rogi knew the visitors, all right, but no better than any other members of the Remillard family did. They were still very reclusive and reticent about their early lives. Their presence here on Kauai under these peculiar circumstances came as a considerable shock to the old man.

He took a seat at Malama's urging. On the low koawood table was a tray holding an untouched dish of pupus—Hawaiian snacks—and two beverage pitchers, one half-empty and one that was full. Pouring from the latter, the kahuna offered a glass to Rogi. The drink had a sizable percentage of rum and he gulped it thankfully as he eyed the young people. They were in their early thirties. A remote smile touched the lips of Cloud Remillard as she looked out at the sea. Her brother Hagen was blank-faced, making no pretense of cordiality.

Rogi ventured an awkward attempt at heartiness. "So the Family Ghost put the arm on you two kids to collaborate in the memoirs, eh?"

Hagen Remillard's reply was chill and formal, and every aspect of his mind was inviolably shielded. "We were bespoken by a Lylmik wearing the usual disembodied head manifestation. He ordered us to come here and talk to you about certain events that took place during our exile in the Pliocene Epoch."

"That . . . should be mighty interesting." Rogi's grin was wary.

"You know that our entire group was debriefed by the Human Polity Science Directorate when we first came through the time-gate." Hagen did not meet the old bookseller's eyes. "At that time we were instructed not to publicize details of our Pliocene experiences, and we complied scrupulously. Even now, very few people know that the two of us were among the returnees."

"It was a relief, having an official excuse to keep quiet about our identities," Cloud said. "We knew that if the public were spared the more gaudy details of our prehistoric adventures, there would be less likelihood of our lives becoming a media circus. In most of the Milieu, our group was just a nine days' wonder. You know: *Time-Travelers Return!* Whoop-dee-doo . . . then on to the next bit of fast-breaking news. My husband, Kuhal, had a harder time of it, but at least he's humanoid and so he adapted. We've been kept busy doing certain work connected with our conditional Unification and we've managed to live more or less in peace—until now."

Hagen said, "The entity who countermanded the Directorate's gag order told us that he was Atoning Unifex, the head of the Milieu's Supervisory Body. Cloud and I were properly overawed at first. But as the Lylmik spoke to us we both experienced a shocking sense of déjà vu. After Unifex vanished we were confused—no, we were terrified!—and we wondered if we had experienced some shared delusion, a waking nightmare. Not long afterward, the Lylmik's orders to us were reconfirmed by the First Magnate of the Human Polity and also by the Intendant General of Earth. Both women took some pains to tell us what an extraordinary communication we'd been honored with." The young man's face was sardonic. "That was a considerable understatement."

"We agreed to come here and talk to you only after it became evident that we would be coerced if we refused," Cloud added. Her voice was low-pitched, but warm and without rancor. "We've had quite enough of that already in our lives."

"Did you recognize Unifex, then?" Rogi asked softly. "Do you know who he really is?"

"I knew almost immediately," said Cloud. "I was always closer to him than my brother. The realization was . . . shattering. Hagen didn't want to believe it."

"Unifex is Marc Remillard," Rogi said. "Your father."

"Damn him!" Hagen exploded to his feet and began striding about the lanai like a caged catamount. "We were so relieved when the time-gate closed after us and the Milieu authorities obliterated the site! Cloud and I and all the rest of us thought we were finally free. Papa was trapped six million years in the past along with that madman Aiken Drum, and he could never hurt us again."

"He never meant to be cruel," Cloud murmured.

Hagen rounded on her. "He never thought of us as thinking, feeling human beings at all. We were nothing but subjects in his grand experiment." He turned to Rogi and Malama. "Do you know what his gang of decrepit Rebel survivors called him behind his back? Abaddon—the Angel of the Abyss! At the end almost all of them repudiated him and his lunatic plan for Mental Man."

"Papa gave it up, too," Cloud insisted. "Or he would never have sent us back through the time-gate."

Hagen's rage seemed suddenly extinguished, leaving hopelessness. He slumped back into his chair. "Now we discover that our father won out after all. Not only did he miraculously survive for six million years, but somehow he also managed to transmute himself into the Overlord of the Galactic Milieu! God help us and our children." He lifted hate-filled eyes to Rogi and Malama. "God help all of you."

"Unifex atoned," the Hawaiian woman said serenely. "During all those endless years he tried to make restitution for his crimes. He performed his penance not only in this galaxy but in the other one—where the Tanu and Firvulag people came from. I know almost nothing about his Pliocene activities and his later accomplishments in Duat, but everything that he's done for the races of the Milky Way has been for the good. He founded the Milieu and guided it every step of the way. Thanks to him there are six coadunate racial Minds secure in Unity— and thousands more nearly ready to join the galactic confederation."

"Too bad he didn't do a better job shepherding his old home planet," Hagen said bitterly, "preventing natural disasters, plagues, famines, wars—to say nothing of the Metapsychic Rebellion. His Lylmik self just stood idly by while his earlier self nearly destroyed galactic civilization."

Malama only smiled. "The greatest spatiotemporal nodalities are immutable and the past, present, and future form a seamless whole. It is impossible to change history. Unifex acted as he must act—and yet his actions were and are freely done. Our own actions are free as well, contributing to and formulating the mystery of the Great Reality."

Hagen gave a scornful laugh. "And 'God's in his heaven and all's right with the world'?"

"Perhaps," Malama said.

They sat in silence for several minutes. Then Hagen spoke again. "Something's just occurred to me. The Lylmik race is the closest thing to Mental Man that our galaxy has produced, but it's decadent and headed for extinction. What do you want to bet that Papa tried to modify *Lylmik* evolution just as he wanted to modify ours—and failed!"

Rogi shrugged. "Nobody knows a damn thing about Lylmik history."

"Maybe," the young man continued slowly, "Papa plans to return to his original scheme now that he's six million years wiser after the fact . . . and he has his original experimental subjects back in hand."

"Don't talk like a fool,' Cloud cried out to her brother. "The Galactic Concilium would never permit the Mental Man project to be revived—not even by the arch-Lylmik himself."

"Would you bet your life on it?" Hagen shot back at her. "Again?"

"I can think of one sure way you two can help prevent it," Rogi said suddenly, "in the unlikely event that Hagen's right."

"How?" the brother and sister demanded.

"Tell me all you know about Marc's scheme, and I'll publish it in the fourth volume of my memoirs. The full story of Mental Man has never come out. Most of the details of the plan were suppressed by the Galactic Concilium—supposedly to preserve the tranquillity and good order of the Milieu."

"You were on the brink of the Metapsychic Rebellion then, weren't you?" Cloud asked.

"Right. Officially, the Rebellion was fought to liberate humanity from the Milieu and its Unity. But the main reason Marc decided to declare war was because he was so pissed off at having his great dream condemned. He caused a monumental uproar when the Mental Man project was cancelled, charging that the exotic magnates and their loyalist human confederates were conspiring to deprive our race of a great genetic breakthrough. He said that the Milieu was afraid humanity would become mentally superior to all the rest of creation, and the only solution was breaking away, as the Rebel faction had advocated for so long. A lot of normals believed that the Mental Man project would insure that all their children would grow up to be metapsychic operants. But Marc and his people never did explain to the general public exactly how this miracle was going to be accomplished."

"He didn't dare," Hagen muttered. "They would have lynched him."

Cloud said, "It was years before Hagen and I finally discovered what Papa had planned. When our mother found out the truth . . . well, you know what happened."

"No, I don't," Rogi said. "Not really. Tell me! Help me tell the story to the whole Galactic Milieu. That's got to be the reason why you two were sent here to talk to me. I don't understand why Unifex doesn't give me the information himself, but he must have his reasons."

"It was his worst sin," Malama Johnson stated in her calm voice. "Worse than leading the Rebellion into violent conflict and causing the deaths of all those people. Deep in his heart, Marc thought the war against the Galactic Milieu and its Unity was justified, as his followers did. But the Mental Man project was quite different. He knew it was wrong, and yet he couldn't resist the awful elegance of the concept—the opportunity to personally engineer a great leap forward in human mental and physical evolution."

The three others stared at her wordlessly.

"Don't you see, dear grandchildren?" Malama spread her hands, embracing all their minds in huna healing. "Unifex is too ashamed to talk about it. Even now."

[1]

FROM THE MEMOIRS OF
ROGATIEN REMILLARD

I flew home to New England on auto-Vee the next day, sleeping most of the way with my cat curled up beside me on the rear banquette. Oddly enough, I didn't have bad dreams after the interview with Marc's son and daughter, for which I suppose I can thank Malama Johnson. God knows, I would never be able to think of Marc—or the Family Ghost—in the same way again after the horrors that poor Cloud and Hagen disclosed to me back on Kauai.

I woke up, feeling fairly decent, as the egg announced that we were nearly home and demanded further navigational instructions. We traced a leisurely holding pattern 1200 meters above Hanover, New Hampshire. It was a lovely morning and the old college town by the Connecticut River was at its most charming, spread out below like a patchwork quilt of bright colors thanks to the autumn foliage.

I discovered that I was ravenously hungry. Half a dozen congenial campus eateries lay within strolling distance of my apartment, and I had opened my mouth to give the command to descend—when suddenly a completely different notion on where to break my fast occurred to me.

Sheer serendipity.

Right.

I programmed the aircraft for Vee-flight to Bretton Woods, and a few minutes later we'd whizzed 90 kilometers northeast and descended into the egg-park area of the old White Mountain Resort Hotel. It crouched at the foot of Mount Washington, a gargantuan white wooden confection with bright red roofs on its gabled wings and quaint towers. As the rhocraft landed, I announced myself over the RF com and confirmed that the establishment would be delighted to accommodate Citizen Remillard for breakfast.

I opaqued the egg's dome for decency's sake, used the facilities, freshened up with a Beard-Wipe, combed my hair, and donned my old corduroy jacket. Then I opened a pouch of cat food for Marcel and thrust him into his carrier-cage. He bespoke telepathic indignation as he realized I was about to go off and leave him behind.

"Sorry, old boy. No companion animals allowed in the hotel dining room. Old Yankee custom."

Marcel gave a bitter hiss of betrayal as I exited the rhocraft. Silly brute. When were the goddam cats going to admit that the raison d'être of the human race was not humble service to felinity?

I came through the gardens, where chrysanthemums and dahlias and winter pansies still bloomed, and ambled into the hotel's main entrance, giving my nostalgia free rein as I sopped up the familiar Edwardian ambiance. I hadn't been here in thirty years, but the old place, beautifully restored, subtly tricked out now with high-tech innovations to allow year-round operation and adapted to accommodate other races besides humankind, looked almost exactly as I remembered it. The lobby was crowded with tourists, both human and exotic, many of them preparing to ascend Mount Washington via the antique cog railway.

I went out on the veranda, where there was a gorgeous view of the Presidential Range, not yet touched by snow. The lower slopes were a blazing mosaic of dark evergreens and gold-and-scarlet sugar maples.

Memories overwhelmed me like a psychic avalanche. The wedding of Jack and Dorothée had been held here in 2078, and I'd been the ring-bearer and killed a man for the second time in my life. And in 2082, the last time I had stood on the mountain, my nephew Denis had been with me.

Denis. And the other.

But I dared not think of that yet. So I went in and had a fine breakfast, then returned to my egg, where Marcel had retaliated against my perfidy in the time-honored catty fashion. I didn't even bother to chide him, only turned on the aircraft's environmental deodorizer full-blast and flew home. It was time to begin writing again, with or without the Family Ghost's help.

It was more than happenstance that brought me back to the White Mountain Hotel.

In my younger days, before opening the bookshop, I worked at the place as a convention manager. My nephew Denis, who adopted me as his father figure when my twin brother Don let him down, first visited the hotel in 1974 when he was seven years old. We rode the smoke-belching cog train to the summit of Mount Washington together, and it was there that the boy and I first met Elaine Donovan and made the joyous discovery that there were other people on Earth with operant higher mindpowers besides ourselves.

Fifteen years later, as I attended mass in the Catholic chapel in nearby Bretton Woods, I heard my wretched brother's telepathic death-scream. Even worse, I experienced Don's last burst of furious hatred for me—and also, mysteriously, for himself. At his funeral I received disquieting news from Denis, who was then a professor at Dartmouth College in Hanover and one of the most famous metapsychic researchers in the country. My nephew blamed himself for not preventing his father's death. Denis also told me that Don had been murdered, and that I myself was in deadly danger. He urged me to come live near him—so that he could protect me and also help me to attain my full metapotential.

I didn't want to leave the White Mountain Hotel. I had a job that I was good at and thoroughly enjoyed, and nobody in the place knew I was a metapsychic operant—which suited me just dandy. In the end, however, Denis did convince me to join him. I moved to Hanover and became an antiquarian bookseller, sole proprietor of the shop called The Eloquent Page; but from then on the relationship between Denis and me was more ambiguous and troubling.

I loved my foster son dearly. But deep in my heart I was afraid of him and his tremendous mindpowers—as I was also afraid of my own metafunctions. The fear was entirely irrational, rooted deep in my unconscious, and I never have managed to shake free of it.

Like many geniuses, Denis Remillard was a man of unexceptional appearance. He was fair and slightly built, with a manner that seemed gentle and self-effacing—unless you happened to look directly into his electric blue eyes and feel the strength of the coercive power lurking there. Whereupon you might be excused for thinking that your skeleton had suddenly liquefied and seeped out through your paralyzed toes.

Denis's intellectual achievements were even more prodigious than his metapsychic talents. His research earned him a Nobel Prize in psychiatric medicine, and his books and monographs are classics, still highly respected thirty years after his death. As is Denis himself.

The 2013 Congress on Metapsychology was held at the White Mountain Hotel at his instigation, and its fateful climax was largely his doing. Prominent metas came to New Hampshire from all over the world for what was supposed to be their last annual convocation. They were a beleaguered minority in those early days of the twenty-first century, weary of being assailed and misunderstood by hostile normals, discouraged by the apparent inability of our race to live together in peace and fellowship, but still hopeful that they might somehow be able to use their higher mindpowers for the good of all humanity.

On the last night of the Congress, the operants were scheduled to dine at the spectacular Summit Chalet atop Mount Washington . . . and there they were also supposed to die. Other historians in addition to myself have told how the operant madman Kieran O'Connor conspired with Denis's younger brother Victor to murder the Congress delegates. The failure of the plot has been ascribed by some people to fortuitous coincidence—by others to the aggressive use of metaconcerted mindpower by numbers of the delegates under attack.

In these memoirs, I have told what actually happened. Some of the besieged operants did use their mindpowers as weapons. But then, rallied by Denis, they resisted the temptation to strike back mentally at their enemies. It was Denis who integrated their minds—and the minds of countless other human beings of good will, both operant and non-operant—into a benevolent mental alliance that extended worldwide. That unique, loving metaconcert, foreshadowing the greater one forged by Jack and Dorothée in 2083, lasted only for a few moments. But it was sufficient.

The planet Earth had shown the watching Milieu that its immature, quarrelsome Mind was worth saving. The sky above Mount Washington—and above every major population center in the world—filled with exotic starships, and the human race was inducted willy-nilly into a galactic confederation.

I also had a hand in it, and so did a certain Lylmik. But the Great Intervention would never have happened without my nephew Denis.

Et maintenant la leçon touche à sa fin.

[2]

HANOVER, NEW HAMPSHIRE, EARTH
2 FEBRUARY 2078

The rudalm-composer MulMul Ziml landed its rhocraft across the street from The Eloquent Page bookshop, climbed out, and stood in the snow for some time absorbing the local telluric aura and giggling in unashamed rapture at the heady stimulation of it all. Earth in winter! The veritable heart-nest of the Remillard clan! It was inimitable. Sublime. Very nearly inenarrable!

The hermaphroditic exotic had feared that Rogatien Remillard's place of work and residence would have been tarted up and modernized by now, sixty-five years after the Great Intervention. But no—there the exquisite old three-storey building stood, Federal-style clapboards gleaming in the thickening snowfall, windows cheerily alight (the upper ones had green shutters), and sloping metal roof softly blanketed. So evocative. So *human*! One might readily compose a worthy rudalm on this enchanting scene alone. (But, alas, if one expected to sell the work to the lucrative Human Polity market as well as to one's own, more aesthetically sensitive Gi race, the leitmotif required more interspecies appeal and pizzazz.)

The planet's sun had long since set. Increasing numbers of crystalline flakes danced in the frigid atmosphere, glistening as they drifted through the beams of streetlights and the headlamps of passing groundcars. Melting grids were working full tilt to keep the sidewalks and streets clear for pedestrians and vehicles, but fresh snow was already thick on the bare branches of the trees and other unheated surfaces. It lay nine cents deep on the little patch of frozen lawn in front of the bookshop and whitened the concrete footing and the evergreen shrubs around the building's central vestibule steps.

The Gi musician's tall quasi-avian body was clad in a rented environmental suit, and its enormous yellow eyes peered out through a transparent protective visor. The creature found the nocturnal townscape to be almost unbearably ravishing, especially when savored through the pla'akst sensory circuit, but it now began to shiver and feel incipient chilblains in its feet and hypersensitive external genitalia. Turning up the suit's thermostat didn't seem to help. Reluctantly, the Gi decided it had accumulated enough outdoor imagery. It was time to get on with the interview and the full-sensory extraction.

MulMul Ziml tripped off heedlessly across Main Street, only barely managing to dodge a scannerless, aged groundcar full of Dartmouth students that skidded on the wet pavement trying to avoid it. The reversed turbine whined and a horn blared furiously. The near-disaster had been entirely the Gi's own fault and it prayed forgiveness from the Cosmic All as it scrambled clumsily onto the opposite sidewalk. Fortunately, the human occupants of the vehicle weren't metapsychic operants, so MulMul's excruciating telepathic cry of terror had not distressed them unnecessarily.

The door of the bookshop opened and an operant human male peered out, broadcasting emanations of anxiety. "God! Are you all right?"

"Quite safe, quite safe," the Gi fluted. "How kind of you to inquire! It was *so* silly of me not to calculate the velocity of the approaching vehicle before attempting to cross the street, but I'd forgotten how fast you Earthlings drive."

"Well, come inside before we both freeze our bizounes off," the man said rather tetchily. "I suppose you're the one Dorothée said was coming."

"Yes, the Dirigent most kindly—" The Gi broke off, did a double take, and shrieked in delight. "It's *you*! Uncle Rogi!"

The bookseller sighed and shut the door behind the exotic visitor. "That's what everybody in town calls me. You might as well, too. Take off your things and come sit by the stove with me and my buddy. Tell us about this opera or whatever it is you're writing."

An antique cast-iron heating device and several chairs occupied one corner of the bookshop. There were also reading lamps and a small table with a coffee-making machine. Another male human, weakly metapsychic like Rogi, was sitting there quaffing from a mug. His mind-tone was amiable and a species of small domestic animal rested on his lap.

MulMul hesitated. "You're sure you won't mind if I divest? Some Earthlings feel uncomfortable in the presence of unclothed members of my race."

The bookseller laughed. "Hell, no. Go right ahead. Me and Kyle need more than a buck-nekkid Gi to shock us. Just hang your suit on the clothes-tree there and kick off your boots. I know you folks can't abide coffee, so I'm going to make you a hot toddy. You look like you need one."

Rogi went off to the back of the shop and MulMul shyly undressed, shaking out its compressed filoplumage and untangling its testicular peduncles and accessory mammillae. "The rental agent at Anticosti Starport assured me that this garment would keep me comfortable in the coldest weather," the Gi remarked, "but I fear it may be defective. My toes have turned quite blue with cold and just *look* at my poor phallus."

The second man seemed to choke slightly on his drink, but he recovered quickly and gave a sympathetic nod. He was a robust specimen with abundant brown hair and a ruddy complexion. "Aweel now, Citizen, that's truly a scandal. The stuff they hire out these days just can't be trusted. You be sure to raise a stink when you return it and likely they'll cancel the fee."

"Oh, I'd never *dream* of complaining!"

"By damn, of course you will," Rogi said, returning with a steaming cup, which he thrust into the Gi's elongated, near-humanoid hands. "When on Earth, you gotta do as the locals do. Stick up for your rights! Sit down there now and toast your tootsies and let's get on with whatever it is you want from me. I'm planning to close the shop early because of the snow ... Oh, by the way, this is my old friend Kyle Macdonald. You won't mind if he sits in?"

"Not at all!" MulMul Ziml burbled. "The Dirigent's grandfather! What a signal honor to make your acquaintance." The exotic flopped into the indicated chair and extended its large four-toed feet toward the stove. What a relief it was to be warm again! And the hot drink was truly delightful, its generous alcoholic content enhanced with butterfat and a large helping of maple sugar. The Gi expressed its gratitude after belatedly introducing itself.

"As Dirigent Macdonald may have explained, I am a composer. My specialty is the rudalm—a musical artform that some critics have called a cantata virtuale. Recently, rudalma have enjoyed considerable favor among human music-lovers. They are not true operatic works, but rather full-sensory impressions of a significant event or scene, virtually realized for operant attendees, accompanied by a Gi choir."

"And you're doing the deliverance of Caledonia," Rogi said.

"Precisely! The inherent excitement of the event—together with the participation of distinguished beings such as Jon and Marc Remillard—make it what you humans deem a 'natural' for both Gi and human audiences."

"My granddaughter Dorrie and a few other folk had a wee hand in saving Callie, too," Kyle Macdonald put in, flashing a chilly smile.

"Yes, of *course!* Oh, dear—I didn't mean to imply otherwise. Most especially since Dirigent Dorothea Macdonald and the Caledonian geophysical team have been so cooperative in sharing their own memorecall of the averted catastrophe. Unfortunately, I've been unable to secure the memories of Jon or Marc Remillard. They seem to be occupied with other affairs just now. The Dirigent suggested that I come to you instead, Uncle Rogi, since you *were* there during the incident and you enjoy such a close rapport with the heroic Remillard brothers."

"Umm." The old bookseller looked dubious.

"What a singular challenge it must have been!" the hermaphrodite caroled. "Using metaconcerted mindpower to defuse an ascending magmatic plume that threatened to destroy the colony!"

"Not a plume," said Rogi. "A diatreme. Different kinda thing. With plumes, you don't get diamonds in the eruption."

The Gi's huge eyes glazed in ecstasy. "And what a climax that fantastic shower of gems will provide in virtual experience! I've viewed the media recordings of the event, of course, but *you* were a sensory witness—"

Rogi shook his head. "Only viewed the blowout on monitor equipment in the observers' bunker. Still, it was quite a show."

"If you would consent to share your impressions, you'll provide invaluable input on the entire sequence of events. The Dirigent said that you *did* witness Marc Remillard's arrival on Caledonia, and you also persuaded him to intervene in the geophysical operation. That occasion is *crucial* to the exposition of my work."

The Gi took something small from its feathered armpit orifice and held it out to Rogi. The device looked something like a badminton shuttlecock with a narrow, spongy tip. "This full-sensory extractor will absorb your perceptions of the entire episode in short order. The process is quite painless. All we do is insert the soft end into your ear, and I ask you questions—"

"Now, just a damned minute, you!" Rogi barked, starting up from his seat. "Nobody mind-probes me. Nobody!"

The Gi fell back in confusion. "But—"

"You won't coerce me, either! I can put up a damn strong mind-shield if I have to. And I don't care if Dorothée sent you or not. To hell with this virtual operetta, or whatever it is, if it means fucking around in my brainpan!"

The hypersensitive exotic uttered a heart-wrenching soprano wail and sank slowly to the floor in a disheveled heap of plumage and quivering primary and secondary sexual organs. "I never meant . . . I never intended . . . Oh, forgive me!" The melodious voice coarsened to a rasp, the saucer eyes rolled up into the Gi's head, and it swooned away.

"Now you've done it, you great clumsy gowk." Kyle Macdonald dumped the cat Marcel from his lap and knelt beside the collapsed exotic. Unable to locate any of the Gi's hearts in the mass of fluffy body feathers, nipples, and ovarian externalia, he felt for a pulse in its stringy neck. "Could y'not have been more tactful? The big birdies are ower delicate things! Sometimes they drop dead just to emphasize a point."

"Aw, shit." The dismayed bookseller helped his Scottish friend lift the Gi into a chair. Its eyelids were beginning to flutter. "I didn't mean to hurt its feelings. But dammitall, I don't even let members of my own family past my mindscreen nowadays."

"It wasn't going to probe, ye steamin' nit. Yon wee gadget just records memories as a man thinks 'em. There's no ferreting or forcing as with mechanical mind-sifters . . . Uist! I think the critter's coming round."

"Hey, I'm really sorry about that," Rogi said to the exotic composer. "I didn't mean to knock you for a loop."

MulMul Ziml opened its eyes and managed a tremulous smile. "You are quite blameless, dear Uncle Rogi. We Gi have a psyche that is unfortunately a trifle fragile. One does realize *objectively* that overly emphatic discourse is commonplace among humans and not *necessarily* charged with mortal hostility, but—"

"I misunderstood you," Rogi said. He retrieved the fallen full-sensory extractor. "I'll be glad to do what you want if you promise to stick to matters concerning the diatreme." He gestured to Kyle. "My friend will make sure that your memory requests are on the up-and-up. Okay?"

"Excellent!" The Gi bounced to its feet, miraculously recovered. Its pseudomammary areolae, which had gone waxy pale when it fainted, engorged to an enthusiastic cerise and its intromittent organ became tumescent with anticipatory joy. "Just relax in your chair—splendid! Let me help you with the extractor. Now, as I announce successive events, just close your eyes and try to relive them briefly in a daydream. Don't worry about the details—the device will capture them. Ready?"

"I guess." Rogi's expression was resigned.

"Now!" The Gi crouched in front of Rogi and spoke with soft coercion. Kyle Macdonald, grinning fiendishly in the background, made twiddling motions with his fingers, parodying a symphonic conductor. "Think about when you and Jon Remillard first landed on Caledonia and learned details of the imminent seismic peril to that planet."

"Wake up, old son," said Kyle. "It's all over and your fine feathered friend is gone, floating on cloud nine. It promised to send you a special presentation fleck of the rudalm just as soon as the thing is produced."

Rogi groaned and stretched. "Putain! Wait till I get my hands on that chit Dorothée, siccing that oversexed turkey on me . . . Look at that rug! It was just back from the cleaners."

"Och, don't be such a cranky old fart. So the Gi did get a wee bit transported. The music the birdies make is glorious and their virtual vision's unique. Fascinating the way they manage to put an erotic luster on everything. I can hardly wait to see what they do with the Callie diamond shower."

"Three guesses." Grumpily, Rogi rolled up the rag rug with its fluorescent pink cum-stain. "For God's sake, Kyle, grow up. Virtual-reality porn was old hat before you were even born."

"The Gi rudalma are nothing like that. No tickle-suits or buzz-hats or other paraphernalia. I caught a show once on Zugmipl with Masha. Very tasteful and all done through the unencumbered mind."

Rogi grunted dismissively and peered out the bookshop window at the thickening snow. "That Gi didn't . . . try anything funny with my other memories when it was rooting around in me, did it?"

"Nary a bit. I stood by every minute guarding your mental integrity. The only memories it called up were the ones relevant to the diatreme. What're you fashed about, anyhow? Who'd give a rat's ass about the rubbish in your skull?"

"You'd be surprised," Rogi said darkly.

"Nobody cares if you're a Rebel. Any more than anybody cares that I write my little fantasy novels pissing in the eye of the Milieu. We're small fry, laddie, beneath the notice of the Magistratum and the Concilium. Or . . . is it the Fury thing that's got your knickers in a twist?"

Rogi whirled around and seized the lapels of the Scotsman's rough tweed jacket. "Now you listen to me, haggis-breath! I was shitfaced last week when I blabbed to you about that. You gotta swear you'll never tell a soul!"

Kyle Macdonald's eyes shifted. "Turn me loose, man. Are you daft? You and your fewkin' skeletons in the family closet."

Rogi let go of his friend, but he spoke quietly now and in deadly earnest. "I betrayed a family confidence when I shot my mouth off to you about Fury. The Galactic Magistratum knows all about the bastard—including the fact that it's probably one of the Remillard Dynasty—and so do the Lylmik Supervisors. But they've sealed the evidence of the crimes and intend to keep quiet about them to save the reputations of the Remillard magnates."

"And I say that's a sin and a scandal! Why the cover-up?"

"They want Paul and Anne and the other strong pro-Unity members of the family to remain in office."

"Oh, aye?" Kyle plucked his winter coat from the clothes-tree and shrugged into it. "I don't see why we shouldn't put a spoke in their loyalist wheels and give a leg up to our Rebel cause."

"Don't talk like a simplistic asshole. If word gets out that an unknown Remillard is a murdering nutcase, *all* the family will be discredited—Rebels and loyalists alike. Even Jack and Marc. There'd be the mother of all flaming flaps."

Kyle leered. "And maybe that'd be all for the good, watching your hot-shit relatives scatter like cockroaches when you turn the kitchen light on!"

"You know it wouldn't," Rogi said quietly. "A scandal of that magnitude touching the Remillards might turn the exotic races against humanity as a whole. They might kick us out of the Concilium—or even out of the Galactic Milieu."

"Speed the day!" Kyle chortled.

"Be serious. Throwing the Human Polity into turmoil over a Remillard scandal won't help our cause. The Rebel magnates have to persuade other top human minds that the anti-Unity position is morally valid and logical. We can't win this fight with only normals and low-powered heads like you and me. We need the real longbrains on our side—the Remillards, goddammit, with their reputations intact! We need Marc. We need Jack. We need the First Magnate and the loyalist members of the Dynasty."

"Some hope you have of converting that lot. Marc doesn't give a flying fewk about Unity, and the loyalist members of your family are adamant in favor."

"Now they are. But given time, who can say? We've got Adrien and Sevvy already, and there's a strong chance that Catherine is leaning in our direction, too. Just ask Masha."

"Arrr." Kyle growled in disgust. "Her nibs and me aren't speaking this week." He pulled a heavy wool tam-o'-shanter down over his ears and hauled on a pair of gloves. "You want to come along with me to the Sap Bucket for a wee dram or five or six?"

"Kyle. This is important. Will you keep quiet about the Fury thing?"

The Scotsman flung up his arms. "Oh, losh, I'll be keeping your bloody secret, I suppose. Not to save the skins of the high-and-mighty Remillard Dynasty, mind, but for my granddaughter Dorothea's sake. The poor lass has enough on her plate already, saying she'll marry that freak of a Jack the Bodiless."

"It's especially important that no whiff of this gets to Davy MacGregor."

Kyle was nonplussed. "Why? What's the Earth Dirigent got to do with a potential scandal in the Galactic Concilium?"

"Davy has a personal vendetta against Fury and its creature, Hydra. They killed his wife back in 2051. Her death seemed to be suicide and the Magistratum didn't disabuse the public, but MacGregor knew the truth—and he also knew that a Remillard was probably responsible. The Lylmik forced him to butt out. He's only stayed off our case because he thinks Fury and Hydra have been dormant since then. But if he found out about the other killings and the attacks on Dorothée there'd be the devil to pay. The family doesn't think the Lylmik would risk another grand-scale whitewash. Too many exotic members of the Concilium were opposed to Earth joining the Milieu in the first place."

Kyle gave a solemn wink. "And they were quite right about us disreputable humans, weren't they? I'll bid you good evening, then. And be sure to keep a sharp eye out for things that go bump in the night."

The bookshop's little door-chime rang and Kyle Macdonald slouched away into the storm.

"Ah, chite de merde." Rogi heaved a sigh. Kyle would probably keep his word. And in a few months, when Ti-Jean and Dorothée tied the knot, the rejuvenated old Scotsman would be an honorary part of the Remillard clan, too, with a stronger motive for keeping his trap shut.

Locking the door, Rogi programmed its little sign to read CLOSED. Marcel, the Maine Coon cat, came padding out from among the bookshelves and suggested telepathically that the two of them retire to their cosy upstairs apartment and eat.

"Pretty soon, Greedyguts," the bookseller said, flicking off the lights in the front of the shop. "I still have a little work to do sorting out the last of the stuff that came in while I was off gallivanting on Caledonia."

He went to the back room and worked for more than an hour, unpacking the newly arrived copies of rare old science-fiction and fantasy books that were the stock in trade of The Eloquent Page bookshop. Some choice items had shown up in response to his circulated want-list: Several R. A. Lafferty paperbacks in good condition, a first of Hugo Gernsback's *Ralph 124C41+*, a fine set of Michael Moorcock's Jerry Cornelius novels in the original British edition, and an excellent *Flowers for Algernon* by Daniel Keyes. He smiled and laid them out carefully on the worktable. Best of all, a New York dealer had managed to find mint copies of the 1943 Knopf edition of *Donovan's Brain* by Curt Siodmak and the 1946 Viking edition of Franz Werfel's *Star of the Unborn*. Along with a pair of bookends of polished New Hampshire granite, those two evocative volumes would be his wedding presents to Ti-Jean and Dorothée.

Marcel uttered a chirping cry and projected urgent vibes—and at the same moment someone began to rap loudly on the front door. Rogi looked up in annoyance and decided to ignore the interruption; but the caller, a powerful metapsychic operant, was not to be denied:

UncleRogi Iknowyou'rethere LETMEIN I *must* talk to you.

He reached out with his seekersense, recognized the person standing outside in the blizzard, and said: I'll be damned!

With the cat galloping ahead, he hurried to the front of the shop and unlocked the door. A tall figure swathed from head to heels in a hooded gray woolen cape came in, stamping slush from her boots. The storm was overwhelming the capacity of the sidewalk melting grids.

"Annie! What in God's name are you doing out on a night like this? I thought you were still in Concilium Orb."

"So do the other members of the family." The Reverend Anne Remillard, S.J., took off her cape and shook it over the entry mat. "I just egged in from Kourou Starport and I'm here on Earth for only one reason: to talk to you. But first, I'm starving and desperately in need of a drink."

"Why, sure—but howzabout I tell Denis and Lucille that you've arrived? With a little luck, we can nip around the corner and have a really decent dinner at their place. All I got is leftovers I was planning to nuke."

"I—I don't want to see Papa tonight." Anne's voice broke and Rogi saw to his amazement that there were tears in her eyes. Her mind was unassailable. "He's the one I must talk to you about. And you'd better brace yourself for bad news."

"Let's go upstairs to my apartment, then," Rogi said gravely. "Is Denis ill?"

"In a manner of speaking." The tears vanished and Anne's fine-boned face, almost gaunt in the shadows of the darkened shop, became a grim mask. "I'm still not absolutely certain about this, but I think Papa is suffering from a dissociative mental disorder."

"What in Christ's name is that?"

"In laymen's terms, a split personality. I may be mistaken." *I hope to God I am you're the only one I dare talk to about this—*

"Annie, will you stop beating around the bush and *tell* me?"

"Denis is Fury," she said.

SEATTLE METRO, ORCAS ISLAND, EARTH
2 FEBRUARY 2078

When he knew it was hopeless, when his sleep-deprived body was beyond metaredaction and his paramount mind stumbled and flagged despite the utmost self-coercive press, he reluctantly set the analysis aside and took off for home.

The weather was terrible. A winter storm with near-hurricane-force winds pounded Puget Sound and the Strait of Juan de Fuca, raising mountainous waves, closing the submarine tubeways, suspending skim-ferry service, and clearing Seattle Metro's lower airways of all but the most powerful private rhocraft. His big black Lear-Hawkins laughed at atmospheric turbulence and ordinarily he would have enjoyed free-flying through the raging night. Instead he programmed the egg to fly to Orcas Island on full auto. He had labored for over eighty hours without a break in the crucial systems compatibility analysis and he was exhausted to the point of collapse.

Weakling mortal immortal!

Too tired to do the remaining four or five hours of work that would have completed the job. Too tired to pilot his rhocraft on manual a mere 170 kilometers from CEREM to his home in the San Juan Islands. Too tired to keep vagrant thoughts and memories from plaguing and distracting him.

Jack, the lucky bastard, wouldn't have succumbed to simple fatigue so readily. He could stay wide awake for weeks on end if necessary, living on photons of light and the occasional PK condensate of atmospheric molecules and fucking dust-bunnies.

And to think that I once felt sorry for him poor little brother poor grotesque mutant genius . . .

If Jack had been here to help, the knotty brainstem adaptation problem that had frustrated and infuriated him would already have been either validated or deep-sixed, the Keogh proposal judged *GO* or *NO-GO*. But ever since the Science Directorate inquiry into the Caledonian incident, Jack had disclaimed interest in cerebroenergetic enhancement technology. All he seemed to care about was meddling in galactic politics, promoting Unity, and mooning over his bizarre love affair with Dorothea Macdonald. Jack squandered his unique life on irrelevancies, while the important work he had once shared with his elder brother went begging.

Jack is a fool. He doesn't appreciate how special he is how lucky how superior to ordinary humans he has no drive no fire no élan his vision is mediocre puerile fribbling. It should have been me God WHY couldn't it have been me?

The full-body CE rig would be a step in the right direction—if he could only build it. If he could verify that the E18 SIECOMEX system was compatible with the arcane cerebellar/stem unit of the Keogh design. Four more hours of work with the simulator and he'd know whether or not he would finally be able to lay his betraying flesh aside, setting his metacreativity free to achieve its ultimate magnification.

Finally free! Free as Jack the Bodiless free as a Lylmik free as an angel . . . if the reactionaries don't hamstring me.

The ethics of artificially enhanced mindpowers still deeply perturbed the other five races of the Galactic Milieu. From the very beginning of CE research the exotic members had expressed strong reservations about any form of brain-boosting—an unprecedented human scientific innovation. His own work, involving the creative metafaculty, was even more suspect in exotic eyes than amplification of the other higher mindpowers "because of the potential for abuse."

THEY said. Liars! But the inquiry had caught them out forced them to confess the real reason for their opposition.

The spectacular triumph of the CE-equipped geophysical team on the Scottish planet last November had finally drawn the debate from the cloistered Concilium into the public arena of humanity. Numbers of other Earth colonies besides Caledonia were at risk from seismic disaster, and those worlds, some settled for over fifty years, could not readily be abandoned without wreaking enormous hardship. Now, with a CE remedy to crustal instability at hand, any attempt to outlaw the new technology would cause an uproar among humanity.

The cat is out of the bag and we're not putting it back just to soothe the vague qualms of jealous exotics.

All the same, it was galling that he might have to keep the new fullbody rig secret in order to forestall any renewed onslaught from the hand-wringers. Who lately included both Jack and the First Magnate of the Human Polity.

I might have known Papa would oppose me. He has a vested interest in appeasing the exotics. But Jack—!

Immediately after the successful CE modification of the Caledonian diatreme, the Human Polity Science Directorate convened an inquiry intended to quell exotic misgivings. CEREM's Chief Operating Officer, Shigeru Morita, testified that the most powerful brain-boosting device, the E18 helmet, could be utilized only by highly trained grandmasterclass metapsychic operants. It went without saying that the Milieu's careful training and monitoring of all such gifted individuals should preclude any possibility of reckless or even criminal activity among them. The knottier question of whether high-end CE presented an unacceptable hazard to the operators remained open. There were certainly grave personal risks; but they seemed to be at an acceptable level compared to the benefits derived. Even the Dirigent of Caledonia, who had nearly lost her life in the diatreme operation, concurred on that point.

A majority of the Science Directors had been prepared to give metacreative CE their unqualified stamp of approval—until fresh opposition surfaced from an unexpected direction. The First Magnate of the Human Polity entered the dispute (as was his right, ex officio) and testified to the real reason behind exotic apprehensions about CE:

The nonhuman races of the Galactic Milieu feared that *any kind* of cerebroenergetic enhancement would skew the evolution of the human racial Mind, making it incompatible with Unity, the coadunate mental state that formed the very foundation of the benevolent galactic confederation.

Unity! That damned bête noire . . .

The exotics' thesis was totally unprovable. But it had impressed many of the Science Directors—including Jack, who was also a member of the Panpolity Directorate for Unity. By a scant three-vote margin, the Directorate decided that the E18 CE helmets and other, less powerful mind-enhancers might continue in use without restriction. But the Directors also overwhelmingly endorsed a motion calling for a floor debate at the next Concilium session, proposing a moratorium on further metacreative CE research. Paul Remillard, the First Magnate of the Human Polity, and his son Jon went on record favoring the moratorium.

Imbeciles! Creative CE had proven its vital importance. Could the same be said for Unity?

Thus far, the Milieu had failed even to define the Unity concept satisfactorily, and it remained a troubling abstraction to the majority of the human race. The nonhuman races had not yet made an outright declaration that an unUnified humanity would be expelled from the galactic confederation; but Milieu-loyalist humans feared that such an announcement would inevitably come as the human population attained its critical "coadunate number" of ten billion, sometime in the mid-Eighties.

They can't expel us and put us in some galactic quarantine it's too late we're too strong for them why can't the damned exotics accept that?

But they wouldn't. So while Milieu scholars redoubled their efforts to demonstrate Unity's potential benefits to humanity, the Rebel faction of the Human Polity viewed with alarm the potential loss of human mental autonomy Unity might entail, and spoke more and more openly of a draconian solution to the controversy. And pro-Unity human Magnates of the Concilium waffled and weaseled.

A parliament of assholes!

At this critical time, the human Milieu loyalists would do anything to forestall a premature Concilium debate on Unity. His own CE research would merely be an incidental casualty in the Unification battle.

Damn them damn them DAMN THEM I've got to find a way to shoot down the research moratorium they can't be allowed to stop me now not now when—

Exotic opposition to CE had been somewhat ameliorated by the general belief that the E18 helmet represented the upper limit of creative brain-boosting technology. Enhancement of the creative metafaculty much beyond the 300X factor yielded by the E18s was supposedly impossible because of natural constraints imposed by the human condition. Above 300X, the energized brain in creative mode was quite capable of incinerating the operator's body.

But the Milieu was wrong about 300X CE being the ultimate creative boost for metapsychic humanity. It was merely the upper limit for helmet-based CE design. The way to circumvent the barrier was obvious: dissociate the energized brain during mental enhancement by freezing every body part except the self-fortified cerebral cortex to near absolute zero. A full-body CE rig would simultaneously protect the operator's extraneous flesh and bone and turn them into useful superconductors of mental energies.

Jackforming.

It went without saying that this radical new concept, already in the planning stage at CEREM when the Caledonian inquiry was convened, would be anathema in excelsis to the exotic magnates. They would pressure their human colleagues to vote the moratorium.

Let them try.

The notion that he should back off from this crucially important work in order to reassure exotic misgivings about human mental evolution was not only ridiculous, it was also contrary to the very philosophy of science. The human race had a right to achieve its maximum mental potential.

And so do I!

The artificial enhancement of creative brainpower was no more immoral than the augmentation of human muscles by levers and other machines. When they were backed into a corner, the exotics would have to give in—or finally admit that their Unified minds were afraid of human mental superiority.

I'll continue research on the full-body rig and in time I'll demonstrate its practicality in some overwhelming fashion and they won't dare to suppress it.

The radical new technology had had a difficult birth.

His CEREM organization included no workers who were expert in the advanced cryonics needed for the revolutionary design. And so Jeffrey Steinbrenner, his Director of Bionics, had suggested that they secretly approach Dierdre and Diarmid Keogh, the shining lights of Du Pont's Cryotechnology Division. Overcoming his personal distaste for the eccentric lifestyle of the talented pair, he had requested a private feasibility consultation at an astronomical fee. In a surprisingly short time the brother and sister presented CEREM with a credible "barber-chair" full-body CE rig proposal that was everything he had ever dreamt of.

Provided that it could be made compatible with the operating system of the E18.

He thought it could. So did Jordan Kramer and Gerrit Van Wyk, the hotshot psychophysicists he had lured away from Cambridge University, who had helped him to modify the SIECOMEX system for the ultra brain-booster. Steinbrenner, a brilliant neurologist as well as a specialist in bionics, had been less certain of success.

But I'm certain now.

Because of the need for perfect security he was doing the systems compatibility analysis himself. Shortly before fatigue cut short the marathon simulation session, his efforts finally seemed to be pointing to a positive resolution.

The full-body CE rig would be built and he would use it.

And nobody is going to stop me—not Jack, not the First Magnate, not the Science Directorate, not the whole Galactic Milieu . . .

He was home. The doors of the subterranean egg-bay opened, a welcoming haven of light on Orcas Island's western flank. The rhocraft docked and he hauled his aching frame out and trudged to the lift.

Perhaps if my body wasn't so damned big it would require less sleep.

But he was 196 cents tall and weighed more than a hundred kilos, having inherited the massive frame of some ancestral French-Canadian voyageur. In the North Woods of the eighteenth or nineteenth century his powerful muscles, big hands, and bull neck would have given him a decided survival advantage; in the Galactic Milieu, A.D. 2078, a heroic body was very nearly an embarrassing anachronism.

The elevator door opened on the second floor and he stepped out. His imposing multileveled house, built of cedar and native stone, was maintained by a single nonoperant houseman named Thierry Lachine, assisted by an extensive array of domestic robotics. Thierry had long since retired and the premises were silent except for the muted tumult of the storm outside. There was a spectacular view of the San Juans and Vancouver Island from the glass-walled corridor leading to his bedroom, but he lacked the energy to exert his farsight and banish the darkness.

Sleep. All I want to do is sleep.

He was so fatigued that the thought of food was repellent, but he knew he required nourishment. Yielding to a nostalgic impulse, he called up from the bedroom snack unit a fortified version of Grandmère Lucille's favorite Franco-American comfort food, remembered from his early childhood: Habitant pea soup, thick and golden and aromatic. He downed it unceremoniously, drinking from the bowl, then stripped off his clothes and fell into bed naked. Exhausted as he was, his mental and physical safeguards remained adamantly in place. No one could harm him while he slept.

He had made certain of that.

. . .

<My dear Marc.>

So it's you again.

<I'm surprised that you remember me.>

I don't ... when I'm awake. I thought you were long gone. Go away!

<Not yet. We must talk.>

No. You're full of the most incredible shit you're a REMsleep dream I don't want to listen to you I don't *have* to—

<That's true. But I think that you will listen just as you always do. I have more suggestions that you'll find valuable.>

I doubt it damned sex-obsessed dickhead.

<Ironic laughter. Now you're talking about yourself not me!>

I've abolished my sexual urges. They're an irrational distraction. Useless.

<You still dream of her [image] allow her to enter your mind and when you wake up ...>

I ... I can't help that. No one can control dreams. Especially wet ones.

<It's nothing to be ashamed of. Your dreams are symptoms of your need. You think you've nullified your sexuality but it's merely suppressed ready to erupt when you least expect it. What you have done to yourself is psychologically damaging. And dangerous.>

Bullshit. Human beings have practiced celibacy sublimated sex in favor of a greater good for ages.

<You are not a man who can do so safely. You must accept this part of your nature and make creative use of it.>

Like Paul does? Plant my superior germ plasm in every other presentable grandmasterclass female in the sector? [Revulsion.]

<You are a different man from your father. But like him you should engender children in order to propagate your extraordinary genetic heritage: your paramount operant mentality and the self-rejuvenating gene complex you call immortality.>

The other members of my family have increased and multiplied enough to satisfy the most fanatical eugenicist. God—I've lost count of the number of cousins I have!

<None of your brothers and sisters have reproduced in spite of the fact that you are the genetic culmination of the most remarkable family humanity has ever known. And you yourself possess a

supradominant mental heritage. Your paramount mindpowers would be passed on to your children provided that you take the appropriate mate.>

Merde et mon oeil . . . Go away.

<Your offspring would be the true Homo summus if you mate with this woman [image] who already attracts you subconsciously.>

No God damn you I won't look at her—

<Do you know why the two of you are so ideally suited why you feel an irresistible affinity of mind and body? Look! [Genetic diagram.]>

!!!Jesus!!! You perverted swine.

<The prejudice against such a mating is a cultural artifact that is quite irrelevant now that the human genome is subject to analysis and manipulation. Consider the redoubtable Dierdre and Diarmid Keogh and their six magnificent children—>

Get out of my mind! GET OUT!

<Not until I leave you with one last morsel to ruminate over. You are on the brink of succeeding in your personal goal of Jackforming. In time you will be a Star Mind with the uttermost secrets of the universe within your mental grasp. But unless you accede to my proposal you will be all alone.>

It doesn't matter.

<It does. You are no lone wolf you are a foredestined leader a social being. New goals will present themselves to you splendid visions requiring the assistance of likeminded entities loyal to you.>

? . . .

<Listen: If you should beget even two offspring of increased homozygosity with this ideal woman and do this . . . [IMAGE] . . . then you would be able to sire uncounted numbers of exceptional progeny! You would become the father of Mental Man.>

. . . Mental Man?

<A new race superior to any in the galaxy. I assure you that I speak the truth.>

It's nonsense. The Milieu would never permit such a scheme. Besides it wouldn't work.

<Laughter. It would! I could help you make it so—whether or not the Milieu gave its approbation. To prove my good will allow me to assist you with your little brainstem compatibility problem: [Profoundly esoteric image].>

My God. Of course! . . . But—you tantalizing shit!—I'll forget the solution when I wake up.

<By no means. You will remember this (and this alone) when you awake. The rest of our conversation will abide in your unconscious for the time being.>

You . . . who are you? What do you want from me?

<You know who I am what I am my goals are your own. Au revoir. We'll speak again.>

[4]

FROM THE MEMOIRS OF
ROGATIEN REMILLARD

Anne's stunning announcement put my brain on HOLD.

I rejected what she had said and ceased processing input, passing into a state that the shrinks call profound denial. I saw, I heard, I smelled, I felt every aspect of the pleasant old bookshop all about me. I even grinned idiotically at the grieving priest who had placed both her hands on my shoulders to steady me. I was no more capable of rational thought or response than a chunk of firewood. I stood there, sickened to the depths of my soul, while Marcel anxiously stropped my legs and Anne tried in vain to redact my barricaded mind.

She finally took me by the hand and opened the door leading to the building's small lobby. The little coffeeshop opposite my place was dark, shut up early because of the snowstorm. Anne and I and the cat climbed the creaky old inner staircase and I felt the carpeted treads under my feet and the age-smoothed wood of the banister beneath my fingers. The people in the insurance agency that occupied the second floor of the old Gates House building had all gone home and the wind whipped around the dormers of my third-floor apartment. Outside, the Great White Cold walked abroad, and my heart was lost somewhere in the blizzard along with it.

I didn't speak until we were in my kitchen, me sitting at the oak table with an untasted Wild Turkey triple before me, she—having checked out the leftovers and rejected them—scratching up the makings of a decent meal for us while she sipped a Scotch rocks made with Bruichladdich.

"Denis can't be Fury," I said at last. "You're full of shit, Annie."

She found a packet of Nova Scotia lox that I had been saving for a special occasion, a heel of Vermont cheddar, butter, and six eggs in the refrigerator. In the pantry was a flute of gamma French bread and some ready-to-zap Turkish apricot pastries. Tying an apron over her chic black wool pantsuit, she began to grate the cheese.

"I can't prove my contention, Uncle Rogi—which puts me up the proverbial fecal watercourse without a paddle. But I am morally certain that my father is the malignant entity we call Fury. He doesn't realize it, of course. That's what's so abominable about this situation."

"I don't believe it," said I. "I know Denis better than any of you. He's like a son to me. Pour l'amour de dieu—he bonded to me when he was only a few days old!"

"I have only circumstantial evidence to support my belief. But it's strong. Very strong."

I took a tentative lap of the whiskey, found it good, and swallowed a sizable belt. "Tell me."

"The first clue involves the single occasion when I'm positive that the Fury persona actually took over its host's physical body. That was in 2054, when someone went to Baby Jack's room in Hitchcock Hospital at Dartmouth and started the fire that was intended to kill him. A living entity was truly there in the flesh. It wasn't merely a metacreative 'sending.' The hospital security monitors proved that, even though the intruder creatively fuzzed his image so it was unrecognizable, and the operant guard at the scene had his mind wiped."

"But we thought one of the Hydras did it."

"They couldn't have. The timing is wrong—but I only proved it much later. Just before the fire, the four Hydra-children were at Paul's house. They'd killed the housekeeper, poor Jacqui Menard, and were trying to do a snuff-job on you. You told me so yourself."

"It was kinda confusing," I mumbled, pouring myself another stiff snort. I was actually half-sozzled at the time. "I'm certain all four of the Hydras were there, ready to fry my brain. I'm still not too sure how I got away from the damn brats, but I did. Then they escaped in a red egg that looked like yours, and there was this sonic boom—"

"They stole my rhocraft earlier in the evening. The time of their take-off at illegal velocity was precisely noted by a curious college student living in one of the houses nearby. Unfortunately, he never thought to notify the authorities. It took me a long time to track down that witness. The Hanover police and the Galactic Magistratum weren't especially interested in *when* Hydra decamped. They just wanted to know where the children had gone. No one bothered to compare the time of the sonic boom with the time-code on the monitor recording of the intruder in Jack's room. When I finally found the witness, I discovered that it was impossible for the Hydra-children to have started the fire. Ergo, Fury did it personally."

"And you're certain . . . that it was Denis?"

"Every one of my siblings had a verifiable alibi for that time except me—and I know I'm innocent! There was no way you or Marc could have done it. Lucille had gone to comfort Catherine after visiting Marc in the other hospital south of town, but Denis went home alone after dropping off Lucille at Cat's house. You remember how my sister collapsed after her son Gordo's death. Mama was going to spend the night with Cat and the other children. Papa has no alibi from the time he left Mama until nearly an hour later, when he came to the hospital after the fire was put out."

"Why didn't anyone else think of Denis?"

"The Dynasty never seriously considered him to be a Fury suspect. I didn't myself. We thought the monster was one of ourselves, or perhaps Marc. That our own father could be the controller of Hydra was inconceivable. You must remember that all of the Remillards—including Denis—passed the test on the Cambridge lie-detector machine after Jack's rescue. The mind-probe reaffirmed that none of us was Fury. We knew about the possibility of Fury being an aspect of a multiple-personality disorder in one of us, which wouldn't register on the machine, but there was also the faint hope that the monster might not be a family member after all."

"My head ached for a week after the Cambridge ream-job." I poured myself some more booze on general principles. "What are you going to do about this mess? Tell the Lylmik?"

"I went to the four Supervisors in Concilium Orb and asked for their help. They said they could do nothing and justified themselves with the usual mystical gobbledygook. They further declined to put the matter to Atoning Unifex, their chief. Apparently, since we Remillards produced this family demon, we're the ones who will have to exorcise it."

So the Family Ghost had washed its invisible hands of us! Even as I was cursing the thing inside my skull, a useful idea obtruded, no doubt spawned by the liquor's lowering of my misery quotient. "We can count on help from Jack and from Dorothée, too. She'll be part of the family soon."

Anne considered this without much enthusiasm. "At least it's worthwhile taking both of them into our confidence. Fury can never probe their paramount minds and learn we're on its tail. But I'm not at all sure about the other members of the Dynasty. Or Marc."

"He told me he's had dreams," I admitted. "And not harmless ones like mine, unless I misunderstood him. Fury's trying to tempt him into joining it—like it once tempted Dorothée."

"And me," Anne confessed.

"Toi aussi? Ah merde—ça, c'est le comble!" And the first hint that Anne might be lying came tiptoeing into my mind on icy little pygmy crampons.

"That was when I first started to suspect Denis. When Fury tried to convert me to its cause in a series of elaborate dreams." She replenished her drink. "It happened late in 2054, right after humanity was finally enfranchised in the Galactic Milieu."

"That's eighteen years before Dorothée had her encounter," I said.

"Perhaps she and I share some attribute that made us suitable candidates for Fury's scheme. In my case, Fury took the form of the goddess Athene and tried to recruit me. I was going to be far superior to Hydra, it said—a kind of sacred vessel of election, but a mind-slave all the same! At the culmination of my dream-temptation I had this sudden devastating insight that my temptor was Fury, not Athene. I rejected the goddess and her plan for a Second Galactic Milieu, but I nearly lost my mind as a consequence. Later, when I had recovered, I recalled that the goddess was Zeus's favorite, his daughter who had sprung full-grown and fully armed from his own brow, the wise, powerful virgin who sat at his right hand and even used his sacred shield and lightning bolts to administer justice."

"You used to have a little statue of that goddess on your desk," I recalled.

"Quite right. In my conscious life I had always seen *myself* as an Athene-figure. And my Zeus, the beloved father-god whose mind I most admired—"

"Was Denis," I concluded. "There's a certain Jungian plausibility."

"And no logic—but it was then I first became convinced that Papa was the only possible candidate for Fury."

"Do you have any other evidence?" I was staring into my empty glass, trying to make sense out of all this unwelcome data.

"It derives from Denis's psychology. The disease that laymen call multiple-personality disorder is brought on by some hideous trauma that probably occurred very early in the patient's life. The instigating mental injury or injuries are often painfully sexual and involve someone very close to the victim. A person he wanted to love, who betrayed his natural childish trust and devotion. The trauma would have been reinforced later by other damaging experiences associated with this evil person and by intense guilt, eventually resulting in the emergence of the dyscrasic persona. The only living Remillard who can possibly fit this scenario is Denis. And his victimizer—"

The awful light dawned. I looked up and our eyes met. "Donnie!" I blurted. "Oh, God, my own twin brother! From the time Denis was born Don was afraid of him and resented him. But Don could never have . . . not to his own little boy . . ." I broke off, too appalled to put the accusation into words.

Anne's face was bleak. "Don probably would have been drunk the first time it happened, perhaps half out of his mind with frustration and anger because of his wife's inaccessibility during the later months of her pregnancy with Victor and the postpartum recovery. As I understand it, Donatien Remillard was an insecure man who never managed to come to grips with his metapsychic potential. He was self-centered, susceptible to attacks of depression, and physically aggressive."

Near tears, I agreed. "We were fraternal twins, not identical. Our temperaments were miles apart. He and Sunny . . . Don took her away from me. I don't think he really loved her at all. He wanted her because she'd been planning to marry me. She was his most valued possession."

Under Anne's gentle questioning, I told her about my brother's early life and his oddball relationship to me. Then I shut up and tried to get hold of myself. Anne could still be mistaken. On the other hand, all this made a horrible kind of sense.

Anne unwrapped the loaf of gamma bread and freshened it briefly in the microwave. She slivered the lox and put it in the IR-oven to warm, set the table, poured us glasses of milk, and got butter sizzling in the omelet pan. She wasn't wearing her priestly rabat and dog collar. A small silver cross with a central cabochon of green jade hung from a thin chain on the breast of her white blouse. Her blonde hair was cut short and she was thin to the point of being haggard, with a wan face and eyes that were deep-sunken and dark.

I asked her how the split-personality thing worked. How lunatic Fury took over from quiet, unpretentious Denis.

"Every case is different," she said. "But this is the way Denis's mental illness seems to manifest itself: Most of the time, his core persona is in control and he's himself—Emeritus Professor of Metapsychology at Dartmouth College, Nobel Laureate, respected theorist and writer, loving husband, your own dear foster son, papa to Phil and Maurie and Sevvy and me and Cat and Adrien and Paul. But sometimes—there's no telling what sets it off—his dyscrasic personality seizes the ascendant and takes over his mind and body. His rational everyday self is transformed into a thing so filled with pain and hatred that its only release seems to be in violence, murder, and megalomania. This second persona is completely separate from the core. Neither one knows the thoughts of the other. The abnormal persona seems to have goals diametrically opposite to those of the benevolent core. It may even have more powerful metafaculties, drawing upon areas of Denis's mind that are ordinarily latent."

"Fury!" I cried. "It named itself Fury. I was right there when it was born . . . *inevitably*, it said. I never understood what it meant by that."

"The dyscrasic aspect of Denis calls itself Fury for an excellent reason. He had a classical education, and in Greek and Roman mythology the Erinyes or Furies were avenging spirits who tormented and destroyed *those guilty of violating the natural order*."

"Sacré nom d'un chien," I muttered, letting the tears flow at last. I had all but accepted Anne's judgment on my poor foster son.

She broke eggs into a bowl and began whisking them. "Can you think of any incidents in Papa's early life that might confirm my diagnosis?"

I mopped my face with my handkerchief and reluctantly tried to cogitate. "I remember one time when Denis was tiny—after I'd told Don and Sunny about his strong metabilities and they both agreed to let me teach him how to use them. It must have been about 1970. Denis would have been around three. Don came home plastered and in the mood to play a nasty practical joke on me. He slipped LSD into some cocoa he gave me, but baby Denis innocently blew the gaff and Don was mad enough to shit bricks. He came at Denis, ready to belt him or something, and the kid coerced him. It was spooky. One second Don was a bull on the rampage, and the next he was helpless and scared out of his mind. Denis said, 'Papa won't ever hurt me.' And my brother just said, 'No.' "

"Perhaps the child had only recently learned to focus his coercion. What Denis was really saying, was: 'Papa won't ever hurt me *again*.' "

She seasoned the eggs with salt and pepper and tipped them into the pan. The hot butter smelt wonderfully nutty. She stirred with a fork, then added the small amount of grated cheese. A quick flip folded the omelet. When it was ready she slid it onto a plate and gave it a last swipe of butter to make it shine. She cut it in half and sprinkled it with the warm shredded smoked salmon.

Anne spoke an abbreviated grace (Jesuits are ever practical) and we fell to. I was surprised I had an appetite, but she'd prepared the omelet perfectly—soft but not runny, with the cheese completely melted and the lox adding a perfect garnish. For a time we concentrated on the food. Marcel came to the table, plume waving, and I spared him a hunk with plenty of fish. Outside the double-glazed kitchen window the snowstorm hissed and howled.

"Victor," Anne said at length. "The second child of Don and Sunny who grew up to be an overt monster. Did you have any idea he might have been abused?"

"Not at the time. Vic was born later that same year, 1970. He looked just like his papa and Don was crazy about him. He wouldn't let me teach the little guy about operancy, wouldn't hardly let me near him. Don said he'd take care of this kid's education himself."

"And evidently he did just that . . ." Anne looked away for a moment, her lips tight. "You know, there was a passage in the Gospels that always struck me as particularly apposite—where Jesus uses a little child as an exemplar for his followers and then says, 'But whoever scandalizes one of these little ones, it would be better for him that a millstone should be hung around his neck, and he should be drowned in the sea.' Psychologists know now that Jesus was speaking a profound truth. When young children are badly injured by those who should love them, their minds are almost always irreparably damaged. Victor became a sociopath, and I can recall Denis himself conjecturing that Don might have been the source of his son's viciousness. But Denis never seems to have considered that *he* might also have been one of Don's victims."

"Don was eaten up with self-hatred," I whispered. "As he died, he told me I should have hated him, too. But I thought he was talking about his alcoholism and shiftlessness, the way he'd failed Sunny and the kids."

"Did you ever have hints that something might be seriously wrong with Denis himself?"

I thought about it. "Maybe. For one thing, I was always afraid to let

Denis into my mind. I love him so much, but it always terrified me to put myself in his power. After a couple of experiences, I wouldn't permit it at all and he was unable to force his way in."

Anne nodded. "It's a thing operant parents and their children seem to agree on unconsciously: The child is almost always incapable of coercing the parent." She reached across the table and took my hand, a glint of excitement in her eyes. "And you stand in loco parentis to Denis . . . That's the reason why I came to you, Uncle Rogi, rather than to any of the other older members of the family. *Fury can never forcibly read your mind or coerce you.*"

"I think Denis did coerce me a few times," I said.

"There may have been an unconscious element of permissiveness on your part, then. But now, when your opposition is firm, it would probably be impossible."

I mulled over my recollections of our early relationship. "In hindsight, I can see other things about Denis that troubled me. He blamed himself when Vic killed Don. He also knew that Vic deliberately suppressed the operant mindpowers of their younger brothers and sisters, but Denis never did anything about it—not even when Vic murdered three of the girls who defied him. And their mother, poor Sunny . . . when Denis finally did get her out of Vic's clutches it was too late. She'd gone out of her mind with grief and she died not long afterward."

I broke up again, knuckling my eyes. When I pulled myself together I added, "The strangest thing of all was Denis's insisting on keeping Vic alive when he was mind-zapped to a vegetative state. The bastard hung on for twenty-six years. Denis said he kept him on the machines so he'd have time to repent his sins. Fat fucking chance! But not even Lucille was able to talk Denis out of his foutue idée fixe. Every year on Good Friday, the Dynasty had to join Denis in metaconcert and pray for Vic. That last year, in 2040, Denis even tried to rope *me* into the mind-prayer. Thank God I was able to wiggle out."

"Can you tell me any other details about Fury's birth? It's highly significant that the thing managed to take overt control of Denis just as Victor died. This might suggest that Denis's shadow persona unconsciously approved of Victor's crimes, or even abetted them. I think it's also important that Fury was forced to manifest itself only after Victor was gone forever."

I said, "Fury was all set to make me its slave when it was born, there at Vic's deathbed. I heard it say so. But another entity—a good one—showed up suddenly and saved me."

Anne's eyes widened. "Who could it have been? Denis's core persona?"

I beat around the bush, deciding this wasn't an auspicious time to introduce her to the Family Ghost, then said, "I guess Fury took the five fetuses instead of me and turned them into Hydra."

"Their seduction and manipulation is more complex than that, but I suspect you've got it in a nutshell." Anne got up and put the apricot pastries into the microwave. "Have you been conscious of Fury attempting to invade you at other times?"

"Not really. I've felt it lurking and I've dreamt about it—but the dreams always seemed to be real nightmares, if you get what I mean, and not coercion-inspired. The one other time I was strongly aware of Fury's presence was at Ti-Jean's birth in 2052. The baby was having a hard time of it and the monster tried to take advantage of the situation and get to him. Somehow . . . I was able to help. Fury went away and Baby Jack was all right."

"But you recognized the entity positively?"

"Damn straight." I winced at the recollection.

"This may be very important." Anne studied me with uncomfortable intensity and I felt the tentacles of her grandmasterly coercive faculty fingering my good old bombproof mental shield. "You're an untrained head, Uncle Rogi, but I've always suspected there were depths to you that the rest of the family might not have appreciated."

I gave her a cool look. "Denis always said my suboperant creative faculty might have a few surprises. But I wouldn't let him measure it—and I'm damned if I'll let *you* fossick around in my skull either, ma petite."

She laughed rather uneasily, got the pastries, and set them before us. We ate and drank while she regrouped, and her next remarks were almost clinically objective. "All bullshit aside, Rogi—if you were able to furnish details of Fury's metapsychic complexus, it might help immeasurably in the treatment of Denis. Success would depend upon fine-tuning a coercive-redactive course that would safely integrate the antisocial shadow persona with Denis's benign core—his true self."

I gave her the fish-eye. "But you'd have to mind-ream me to find this data you need?"

"Essentially, yes. It might not be there. But there's a chance that Fury's birth made an exceptionally powerful engrammatic impression on you. Without any volition on your part, you could have stored the profile of the metafaculties Fury attempted to exert upon you. Especially the coercion."

"The way young Dorothée stored the Hydra's mental profile?"

"Exactly. Any therapy for Denis would have to break through Fury's coercion before redactive healing could begin. You can see why your input could be extremely important."

"I'll consider it," I said ungraciously. But behind my screen, I was thinking: What if she's wrong about Denis? What if Anne *herself* is Fury? By letting my guard down, I could be making her a present of my metawhoozical ass! I'm no genius and no Paramount Grand Master— but this old Canuck isn't a fucking idiot either.

Anne said, "Denis's core persona is completely innocent of the crimes committed by Fury. But he can never control or integrate Fury to harmlessness unassisted. I'll concede that your psychic reaming will probably be painful. But we members of the Dynasty will have to gamble our lives and sanity attempting to treat Denis in metaconcert. There's no certainty that the seven of us will be able to succeed—especially with our own father."

"You mean, the parent-kid thing would get in the way?"

"I'm afraid so. And there's something else. Remember the grandstand play that Fury wreaked on the database computer at Concilium Orb when it helped Hydra escape from Scotland? That piece of work demonstrates that the entity almost certainly has paramount metacreativity. This gives it a formidable weapon against any minds who dare threaten it."

"You mean, it could zap the lot of you to cinders with a mental laser if it thought you were out to kill it." A question popped into my mind. "I wonder why it's held back using its mind as a weapon? It's always worked through Hydra, except for setting Jack's fire."

"I have no idea. Perhaps it has something to do with the structure of Papa's disorder. Fury's metapsychic complexus may be distorted, limited in any number of ways. On the other hand, the forbearance may simply be strategic."

I pushed my dessert plate away. In spite of my shock and dismay, I'd somehow managed to eat every morsel. I got up from the table and started a pot of coffee.

"You know, Denis has never had a really comprehensive metapsychic assay," I observed. "Just half-assed tests in the early days. He evaluated the bejesus out of his associates and subjects—except me—but he claimed he wasn't *interested* in the calibration of his own mindpowers, just in their theoretical aspects. So he was never assayed using Milieu technology—and who'd ever give the Grand Old Man of Metapsychology a hard time about it? Another thing: By continuing to turn down being appointed a Magnate of the Concilium, he neatly sidestepped the obligatory Lylmik mind-sifting. For all we know, Denis could be paramount in every damned one of his faculties."

"I considered the possibility." Anne leaned forward, turning the coercion on to me again. "This is why your own mental data on the Fury monster could be crucial, Uncle Rogi."

"How about you and Dorothée? Wouldn't memories of *your* Fury dreams provide better dope?"

"We'll try to obtain those data, too, of course. But—forgive my frankness—the Dirigent and I have minds that are enormously more complex than yours. Once you open up that bloody invulnerable mindscreen, your repressed memories should be rather easy to get at. The stuff Dorothea and I have stored may not be." She paused and delivered the zinger. "If you really love Denis, I don't see how you can refuse."

I gave the sly Jesuit female a twisted smile, but said nothing.

When the coffee was ready I suggested we take it to the living room. Outside the windows was a weird luminous glow, New Hampshire's winter answer to the gray limbo of hyperspace. The blowing snow was so thick that you couldn't eyeball a thing aside from fuzzy streetlamps and the creeping twin blobs of light indicating cautious groundcars navigating on full auto.

We settled down, me in my old armchair and Anne on the couch with Marcel, who was now purring from a surfeit of cat food and table scraps. I had turned on the fire, programmed a John Coltrane album, and found some Rémy Martin to liven up the coffee. For quite a while we just sat. "There's something I might as well confess to you, Rogi," she said eventually. "I'm no metaconcert designer, but my best calculations show that my brothers and sister and I probably won't be able to crank the watts to overcome a paramount Fury through coercive redaction—even if we do manage to work out the proper program."

"There's Ti-Jean," I pointed out, "and Dorothée, of course. Surely they'd be willing to join in the concert. Two paramount minds would give you the edge you need."

"I don't think we have the right to ask them to risk their lives. They're both so young."

"Balls! They'd jump at the chance. And what about Marc?"

"I don't trust him. He's too self-centered. Too—" She shook her head. "He's such an arrogant, calculating bastard. I guess I'm half afraid he'd side with Fury . . ."

"Now *that's* the most ridiculous thing I *ever* heard!"

"I'm not joking, Rogi. I know Marc very well. Better than any other member of the Dynasty does. Even better than Paul, his father. Marc's a monumental egotist with a deficient affect, and unless I miss my guess, one of these days he's going to cause the Galactic Milieu a shitload of trouble. There's no way I'd let him participate in the treatment of Denis."

"Well, you may have a point," I conceded. "But you don't really have to use Marc in the metaconcert. Just get him to lend you some of his E18 CE brain-buckets. Solve your mind-wattage problem in one swell foop."

Anne frowned, but understanding was gleaming in her eyes. "Are you suggesting that we use cerebroenergetic enhancement equipment in Papa's healing metaconcert?"

"Why the hell not? Jack and the rest of them used those gonzo hats in creativity mode to chill the diatreme on Callie. Curing Denis couldn't be any more humongous than that little caper."

"Dorothea nearly died from a dysergistic flashover during the Caledonia operation," Anne noted grimly, "and none of the Dynasty are experienced in the use of CE. I've always had my doubts about the safety of mechanical brain-boosting and so have Paul and Philip and Maurie. To say nothing of the majority of the exotic Magnates of the Concilium."

"Tout ça c'est des foutaises! The Dynasty can muzzle its precious principles until poor old Denis is back on line and Fury-free. You could learn to use the CE hats. Other grandmasterly operants have."

I could tell Anne was weakening. "I don't think Marc has ever considered augmenting coercion or redaction through his CE designs. There's been no practical application."

"Until now," I said. "It could be your answer. With metaconcerted CE and help from Ti-Jean and Dorothée the Dynasty could either cure

Denis, or—" I broke off, appalled at the direction in which my thoughts were heading.

"Or we could execute him, as a last resort, using the flip side of the healing metafaculty, and be rid of Fury that way. The creature has already been summarily condemned to death by Paul, just as the Hydras were."

"But the good part of Denis's mind is innocent!" I protested. "You can't kill him!"

"If there's no other course open to us, we *can*." She toyed with her coffee cup, rotating it in the saucer with one finger pushing the handle. Her face was devoid of expression. "Both moral theology and the laws of the Milieu would give us the right to execute Denis if the First Magnate deputized us. But with God's help—and yours, Uncle Rogi!—it will never come to that. We'll cure Denis at the same time that we exterminate Fury."

I didn't say anything for a long time. Anne was bound and determined to go ahead with the redactive exorcism, and I was going to have to cooperate. But I was damned if I'd give her free rein to rummage in my brain—even to save Denis. Then a notion occurred to me, a perfect way to do my bit without laying myself open to her. I took a deep breath.

"Okay. Let's get started as soon as possible. I'm willing to let *Dorothée*—no one else—probe my mind for repressed Fury memories anytime you like."

"I should have thought of that myself," Anne said approvingly. "She's the most talented redactor in the Human Polity. Even better than Jack . . . Very well. This will all take some organizing, Uncle Rogi, and we're going to have to be very careful not to tip our hand to Fury. We know the thing's farsensory faculties are extraordinary."

I shrugged and quoted an old metapsychic cliché. " 'The whole operant world could be spying on us this very minute—but it probably isn't.' "

That was true for as far as it went. Unfortunately, it didn't go far enough . . .

We drank our cognac and coffee and listened to the music. Anne may have been checking the aether for metapsychic snooping, but there wasn't a hope in hell she'd detect anything if the eavesdropper was a paramount.

I finally said, "How in blazes do you plan to get Denis to submit to your therapy? I can't see Fury lying meekly doggo while a squad of CE-equipped Remillards politely asks for permission to unbutton its host's mind."

"I'll talk the matter over with Jack and Dorothea, but I suspect we've got no choice but to take Denis by surprise."

I mulled that over. "If Marc builds coercive-redactive brainboards for your therapy session at the CEREM facility, word of it will almost certainly leak out. There are too many Rebels in his corporation who'd really prick up their ears about something as outré as CE redaction. Before you knew it they'd spread the news all over the Orion Arm."

"I think you're exaggerating—"

"Listen to me: The one person who *could* build the hats in secret is Ti-Jean. The crafty little bugger's got unlimited resources."

"Jack!" Anne exclaimed. "What a great idea. And he could do the metaconcert design, too. You're brilliant, Uncle Rogi."

I flapped one hand modestly.

"My greatest fear," Anne went on in a low voice, "is that an alerted Fury might find some way to subjugate Denis's core persona before we're ready to attempt the therapy. If Fury took over Denis's body and then went into hiding, we'd never be able to track him down—any more than we've been able to trace the two surviving Hydra-units."

I was aghast. "Do you really think Fury might snatch Denis's body permanently if it gets the windup?"

"I think it's distinctly possible. That's why I'm going to stay away from Earth until we're ready to roll. I'll work out of my office in Concilium Orb so Fury has no chance to probe me. It can't do it at a distance. Fortunately, Denis hates star-hopping."

"But you'll miss the wedding!" I exclaimed.

"It will break my heart not to be able to marry Jack and Dorothea, but I'll survive. I'll brief the newlyweds on the entire situation when they attend the next Concilium session in Orb. That'll be late July, Earth time. We'll get things started then. In the meantime, I don't intend to mention a word of this to the other members of the Dynasty—and you won't either. No one in the family must know about the plan until Jack gets the modified CE equipment and the metaconcert program ready and we're set to begin practice."

"You won't even tell the First Magnate?"

"Especially not Paul. Heaven only knows what tangent he'd fly off on if he discovered the truth and had months to brood about it. He might decide that the lot of us had an obligation to turn ourselves and Denis in to the Galactic Magistratum or Davy MacGregor—just to make a grand gesture. He'd certainly insist on resigning the First Magnateship, and that would jeopardize our pro-Unity agenda."

I kept my subversive opinions about that to myself. "How long before you'd be ready to act?"

"That will depend entirely upon Jack and Dorothea. Don't worry, Rogi. You'll be safe enough from Fury-probes if you don't get smashed and start shooting your mouth off."

I cringed, remembering my indiscretion with Kyle Macdonald. It looked like I might have to forgo overindulgence in bottled delights for the duration. Bon sang, c'est emmerdant, ça!

We sat there for another hour or so, killing the rest of the cognac and listening to moody selections from my music-fleck collection. Then I lent her spare pajamas and fixed up a bed for her in my little study, which doubled as a guest room, and we both retired, intending to sleep in until the foul weather was over.

[5]

FLEET SECTOR BASE, HUMAN POLITY
SECTOR 12: STAR 12-340-001 [NESPELEM]
PLANET 2 [OKANAGON]
16 CHEWELAH [9 JUNE] 2078

<Are you ready my dearest little one?>

Yes. I took over one of the unmanned maintenance craft from Chopaka Moonbase. I'm now in position docked against one of the meteorsweeper satellites. When the Orb courier exits the hype into c-space I'll be well within metacoercive range.

<Are you certain that your presence has not been detected?>

Give me credit . . . I've been working on the operation night&day for nearly a week.

<Please do not take that tone with me.>

I'm sorry. I've experienced a certain amount of emotional tension.

<But there is a high chance of success?>

My coercive power will be more than adequate to control the cerebroenergized pilot. But if the target herself should discover the source of the malfunction before the point of no return and abort the maneuver she may not only survive but also be able to identify me. I wish to hell Parni were here! If we could do the job in metaconcert I'd feel more confident.

<Parnell has his own important work on Earth eliminating the other target and this unique opportunity was not to be missed. You know how she has kept herself isolated in Orb out of our reach. I couldn't believe our luck when I discovered that she was coming to Okanagon on Unity Directorate business.>

Right. Well this plan of mine is the most effective one I could come up with but it's not a total lockup. Even if she can't prevent the sneetch&splat there's still a remote possibility that she'll pull some creative stunt [image] and stave off death.

<You must not fail! This woman is a threat to MY LIFE as well

as your own . . . and so is the other one that Parnell is coping with.>

!!!You didn't tell us that!!!

<I am telling you now.>

But . . . you are the invincible one.

<I was and I will be again when both targets are dead.>

If the deaths are truly imperative you should think again about letting Parni act alone. He's strong but he's dangerously overconfident and too fond of bizarre stunts.

<He is not as intelligent as you. But his target is a laughably puny mentality well within his capabilities.>

I'm not so sure about that. Remember how—

<Silence! Your new contentiousness disturbs me. Do not forget that without me you are NOTHING. You are an amputated limb. You are dead.>

Yes . . . Forgive me. But I worry. Single units utilized in vital tasks such as these leave no margin for safety. Even the Hydraentire would be inadequate to deal with a metaconcert of three or more Grand Masters or an alerted paramount mind.

<The probability of such a metaconcert forming during the current operation is vanishingly small. And no paramount can interfere unless you act with abysmal stupidity.>

But this brings up an important point: You promised that I/we would soon have help. New Ones. Subordinate minds to amplify Hydra's energy.

<And you will! Be patient my darling. A long period of preparation was necessary but now that phase of my great scheme is coming to fruition. Soon there will be a hundred New Ones working with you and later there will be millions. Millions.>

And I will control them! You promised.

<If your love and loyalty do not falter Hydra will rule the New Ones and the Second Milieu as I have said. But do not distract yourself from the task at hand. Eliminate this mortal threat to us both.>

Will you be able to continue your surveillance and assistance?

<I will try. You know that I am under . . . certain constraints.>

Yes. Well the time is getting short. I must withdraw.

<Farewell my dearest Hydrachild my dearest Madeleine.>

Goodbye Fury.

. . .

The Commander-in-Chief of the Twelfth Fleet and his fellow Rebel, the Dirigent of Okanagon, stood side by side in companionable silence on the observation deck of the Space Needle, awaiting the arrival of their mutual nemesis, the head of the Panpolity Directorate for Unity.

Under different circumstances, Owen Blanchard would have enjoyed looking out over his bailiwick on a cloudless winter afternoon. The Pasayten high plains region where the Sector Base was situated enjoyed a light breeze, and the air temperature was mild enough to make extra clothing unnecessary. Most of the facilities were underground, but the physical plant of the starbase extended farther than the eye could see, a vast conglomeration of circular landing pads, landscaped artificial lakes, docking facilities, service buildings, and ground transport and supply stations.

The peaceful Galactic Milieu had no warships, but a myriad of other superluminal craft belonging to five races were parked at the pad perimeters or trundling to or from the massive elevators that gave access to the infrastructure. Occasionally a starship took off or landed with majestic slowness. Among the Human Polity vessels were small, high-df government couriers, research and survey ships of every description, cruisers equipped with modest photon weaponry that policed the human star systems within Sector Twelve and succored vessels in distress, and even enormous colonization transports serving pioneer planets.

Owen Blanchard's idiosyncratic variant of the starfleet uniform reflected his nonmilitary mindset and was so simple as to be virtually indistinguishable from civilian garb. He wore a blouson of classic midnight-blue worsted with six pencil-thin golden stripes circling the lower sleeves. A small badge with the Twelfth's insignia was fastened above his breast pocket. His shirt was white and his cravat an old-fashioned dark four-in-hand. Although he had reluctantly accepted rejuvenation, the Fleet Commander had chosen to retain the snowy hair and weathered countenance he felt he had earned.

In his youth, prior to the Great Intervention, Owen Blanchard had been an outstanding concert violinist. But the nonhuman Simbiari Proctors who supervised humanity throughout its long probation took note of his formidable intellect and higher mindpowers and denied him an artistic career. Instead he was forced to become a dynamic-field physicist. As the Proctors revised the course of Owen's life for what they believed was the greater good of the Galactic Milieu, they unwittingly created one of the principal architects of the Metapsychic Rebellion.

The frustrated musician became a brilliant designer of hyperspatial drive mechanisms. In time, Owen Blanchard was chosen to head the Human Polity's first Academy of Commercial Astrogation on the planet Assawompsett. Later, after humanity was fully enfranchised in the Milieu, he became Commander-in-Chief of the Polity's first Sector Fleet, the Twelfth, based on Okanagon. He had now held that position for twenty-four years, during which time the Thirteenth Fleet was established on the planet Elysium and the Fourteenth on Assawompsett; but the Twelfth remained the Human Polity's largest and most important interstellar flotilla.

In his leisure time, Owen Blanchard still played the violin . . . when he was not secretly working on ways and means of extricating his race from a galactic confederation dominated by exotic beings.

As they waited, the rugged old man and the handsome younger woman idly exerted their farsight, watching a huge cosmic exploration vessel slowly descend for a rare landside docking. Ordinarily such starships were serviced from one of the three orbital stations encircling Okanagon rather than on the planetary surface. Owen told the Dirigent that this particular explorer was scheduled to undergo a complete refit before heading out on an extended tour of potential human colonial worlds located in the Perseus Spur of the Milky Way, ten thousand lightyears distant. Following the scandal involving inadequate Krondak surveys of certain Twelfth Sector worlds, the Human Polity had insisted upon doing its own inspections before new colonies were established.

The enormous starship was over two kilometers long, composed of dozens of disparate modules connected by a crazy network of struts. To Dirigent Patricia Castellane, who had been educated as a chemist, the craft looked more like a gigantic model of a polysaccharide molecule than an astrocarrier. Because of their size and peculiar shape, cosmic explorers lacked sigma shielding of their antigravity rho-field envelope, a modification that was now mandatory on other fleet starships, and had to land "hot." For safety's sake (and to spare the landing-pad surface) the explorer descended into one of the large artificial lakes at the northern perimeter of the base. A great cloud of steam ballooned skyward as the burning purple rho-field touched the water. Then the ship's generators shut down and a minnow-school of tugs popped out of lakeside bunkers and prepared to haul the explorer to its subterranean refitting bay.

"I should be blasé by now," Patricia Castellane remarked, "but the sight of one of those monstrous things hovering in the air still gives me the shivers. Look at it—a good-sized city full of scientists and their equipment, weighing millions of tons—but it floated down as lightly and silently as an autumn leaf. A hundred years ago we would have called that a miracle. Now it's just another working example of dynamic-field engineering, courtesy of the generous exotic races of the Galactic Milieu. On our own, we might not have developed dy-field technology for another century—if at all."

"The point is moot," Owen said, a surprising bitterness in his voice. "We took off and ran with Milieu science and we left the nonhumans in the dust. We're made of superior stuff and we know it, and so do the exotics. But the human race is also flawed and immature, and therein lies the crux of our Rebel dilemma: Are we better off inside the Milieu or out of it?"

"You know my answer, Owen, and I don't mind telling you that I'm getting damned sick and tired of the question." Patricia gave her long chestnut hair an emphatic flip. She was tall, dressed in a trouser suit of forest-green faux leather ornamented with trapunto work. Her blouse of ecru lace was pinned at the throat with an antique Spanish sardonyx cameo.

"I think we're wasting time on philosophical debates and shilly-shallying," she said, "and so do most of the other younger Rebel magnates. The exotic races are holding us back, stifling us! The way the Concilium is currently structured, the Human Polity is continually being reined in by exotic restrictions. The Krondaku are stodgy archconservatives, the Simbiari are jealous of us, and the Gi are a gang of sex-crazed loony-tunes. But their combined voting bloc adds up to forty-four hundred, while ours is only a tenth of that. Even if all the friendly Poltroyan magnates vote with us, we still have no chance to win any important floor fight. This Unity controversy is the last straw! Secession is our only option."

He smiled at her vehemence and his reply was mild. "Are we really ready to abandon the Milieu for the sake of human sovereignty? I can tell you this for certain, Pat—if we tried to secede tomorrow, we'd fail.

The exotic minds in metaconcert could overpower us, force us to retreat back to our own solar system, and keep us there in quarantine forever."

"I wonder if they'd really be able to do that?" the Dirigent said softly, turning away from him to look down at the crowded plaza below the Space Needle. "Even if they took away our starships and other high technology, we'd still have our brains. We could build it all again. They'd never slaughter us outright—it's contrary to their damned Unity ethic. Whatever means of mental or physical interdiction they used, we could eventually overcome."

"Perhaps," the Fleet Commander admitted. "But it might take generations."

"We can't compromise on the Unity question," she said urgently. "We can't let the exotics force us into this—this pacifistic mental intercourse of theirs. We have a right to evolve in our own way, flaws and all."

"I agree. But they've said they won't coerce us into Unity . . ."

"No. They're more insidious than that, with their talk of mutual love and perfect civilization! They're setting a trap, reminding us how morally deficient we still are, promising cosmic harmony, an end to aggression, paradise in the here and now." She turned back to him, her expression stony. "But the exotics are deceivers, Owen. They'd make us docile slaves of the Milieu, destroy human individuality, and subordinate our superior minds to their own stunted view of reality."

The Fleet Commander pretended to wince. "I hope you won't make the point too emphatically with Director Anne Remillard and her people when they haul me on the carpet for neglecting to suppress disloyalty."

The Dirigent of Okanagon smiled contritely. "Well, maybe not this time around. I came here today hoping to make things easier for you and the Fleet in Remillard's inquiry, not to stir up a fresh hornet's nest. I promise to be ever so mealymouthed and smarmy."

"That'll be the day." Owen consulted his wrist chronograph. "The Directorate courier ship is due to break through the superficies into c-space just about now. It'll do a VIP docking right here at the Space Needle in less than five minutes. I really would appreciate your support, Pat. But remember: De la diplomatie, et encore la diplomatie, et toujours la diplomatie!"

She embraced him lightly and kissed his cheek. "You betcha, mon cher commandant. Together we'll bedazzle the inquisitors with our arsenal of good and worthy shit. We'll prove that Rebellion equates with virtue—and that we don't *really* mean it when we skulk and plot and mutter about seceding from the Galactic Milieu."

Owen threw back his head and roared with laughter.

"Seriously," Patricia said, "my image is just as smutchy as yours in the eyes of the Concilium. I welcome this chance to defend Okanagon against critics who view us as a cesspool of sedition."

"I doubt that this inquiry will be that stringent. I have a feeling we're all going to be terribly decorous and nice. The Unity Directorate has no official mandate to purge Rebel elements of the Fleet. At worst, they can require that the operant officers submit to attitude readjustment courses."

Patricia rolled her eyes and began to chant in a mocking falsetto. "Thou shalt not mistrust nor despise thy inhuman neighbor! Thou shalt not impute that Teilhardian Unanimization is a crock of shit. Thou shalt not worry thy silly little head about getting into a permanent mind-meld with exotics when sweet Unity eventually prevails . . . And thou *especially* shalt not contemplate the inconvenient fact that humanity has greater mental potential than the coadunate races, and would be better off outside their damned confederation."

"Time is on our side, Pat. The Concilium backed off on outlawing us Rebels for a very good reason: The action would have alienated most of nonoperant humanity and a fairish proportion of the metas. But the day will come when we can compel the Milieu to let us go our own way."

"Maybe. But you'd still better pray that we manage to get the CE hats built without getting caught." She turned away from him, took out a small compact, and touched up her lip gloss. "Well, I'm as lovely as I'll ever be. Bring on the Inspector General, and we'll—"

The external annunciator said: "Vessel emergency. Vessel emergency. Space Needle personnel prepare for sigma cover."

"Oh, shit," Owen muttered. His mind farspoke Ground Navigation Control: ThisisCommanderwhatemergency?

A laconic telepathic reply came from the chief controller: Incoming courier HU 0-652 ex NAVCON in uncontrolled full-power inertialess descent severe atmospheric ablation precludes RF com or mental hail NAVCON unable trigger emergency upsilon translation and tractor-beam retrieval of impacting craft unfeasible deploying ground-defense sigma.

Frozen with horror, Patricia asked Owen: Isit AnneRemillardship?

Yes.

Abruptly, the sky above the headquarters stratotower darkened to ultramarine blue and the structures and landing pads surrounding it faded into ghostly insubstantiality. The Space Needle and everything within a radius of three kilometers of it had been enclosed within the protective hemisphere of an enormous sigma-field. A moment later smaller sigmas, dimly visible to Owen and Patricia as mirrored half-bubbles, shielded every building and parked spacecraft within the estimated impact area.

"Can you farsee the ship, Pat? I'm damned if I can make it out through the sigma."

She nodded grimly, her face tilted toward the sky. "It's vectoring in vertically. A flaming broad arrow."

"No tumbling?"

"Straight down, like it's on rails."

"Then the situation must involve more than rho-field generator malfunction. It could be that the pilot is deliberately augering in, overriding the approach control backups. Come on!"

He seized her hand and pulled her into the observation platform's lift. As they whisked down to ground level the car vibrated to a faint ground tremor.

"That's it," Patricia murmured. Her eyes were unfocused, her ultrasenses concentrated on the accident site. "Ground Control has cut the big sigma . . . The debris is right at the bubble tangent, almost due east. There's no crater. The ship hit the shield and slid on down."

The elevator door opened and the two of them ran across the broad main lobby. Appalled humans and exotics, most of them in uniform, had gathered into small groups, listening to audible and telepathic announcements of the disaster.

The Fleet Commander and the Dirigent dashed outside. Sirens of emergency ground vehicles wailed in the distance. Because of the danger of residual ionization or anomalous dy-fields shorting out their generators, rhocraft were prohibited from approaching the scene of a superluminal carrier crash until their safety could be assured.

At the edge of the Needle's east plaza was a rank of staff eggs. Their drivers stood together gaping at the thin column of smoke in the distance. Owen's coercion scattered the bystanders and he hauled open the door to one of the rhocraft. "Breaking regulations," he said. "But to hell with it. The courier's burnt and blasted to bits. There's no danger of field-suppression or explosion."

Moments later he and Patricia were in the air, hovering over the scene of the crash. They were the first ones to arrive.

"My sweet Lord," the Dirigent whispered. "Is that a *body?*" Then she cried, "There! Do you see it?"

Cursing, Owen Blanchard maneuvered the egg to set down as close as possible to the thing Patricia's farsight had indicated. They climbed out and stumbled through smoldering grass littered with shattered cerametal and half-melted fragments of nameless detritus. The courier wreckage had fallen into a landscaped area near the edge of a pad. Some of the ornamental trees were still on fire. Others were blackened skeletons.

What they found was incredible.

The body of a woman, mutilated and frightfully burned, with lidless eyes wide open. The eyes moved. She was alive.

Awestruck, Owen knelt beside her. "Unbelievable! Somehow she must have managed to generate a partial protective envelope."

"It's the Director," said Patricia. "I recognize her mental signature." Ground vehicles were approaching and sirens blared. "The paramedics are almost here."

"Anne!" Owen called. He dared not touch the woman's ruined corporeal shell, but his mind reached out to hers with coercive strength. "Can you tell us what happened?"

Anne Remillard's last vestige of metacreative screening winked out. Suddenly a rush of pain hit Owen and Patricia with a force that was almost physical. The victim's thoughts were broken, indecipherable. She seemed to be on the brink of death. Hastily, the Dirigent added her own quotient of grandmasterly redaction to Owen's powerful coercivity. Mentally conjoined in a rough metaconcert, they sustained the injured Director's flickering lifeforce until the medical crew arrived and swiftly connected her to their sophisticated machines.

Exerting all her willpower, Anne spoke telepathically: *Dying?*

"It's all right," the chief medic reassured her. "You're going to live. The regen-tank will take care of everything."

Anne's mind said: Good. I'm going down now . . .

"That's right," another technician said. "Let go. No more farspeech. No more thinking."

But in the last minute before she lost consciousness, Anne Remillard transmitted a single thought to her rescuers:

Hydra.

"Hydra?" The paramedic was mystified. "What the hell does that mean?"

Owen Blanchard and Patricia Castellane exchanged glances.

"It means trouble," the Fleet Commander said quietly. He turned away and began to walk back to his own rhocraft. "Come along, Pat. We'll have to notify the Galactic Magistratum . . . and the First Magnate of the Human Polity."

<You failed.>

I warned you that she might save herself. But she'll be a floater for months—maybe as long as a year. Incommunicado.

<Can't you get to her and finish her off?>

Certainly not while she's on Okanagon. Castellane and Blanchard must suspect that Hydra shot Anne down, even if the medics haven't a clue. All of the senior Rebels know about Hydra and Fury, thanks to that damned Adrien Remillard. The Dirigent has very good reasons to make certain that nothing else happens to Anne on her turf . . . and you can bet she'll be hot on *my* trail too.

<Is there a chance of ODO tracing the Hydra attack to your cover identity?>

I doubt it. But I'll be on the alert.

<Contemplation. It would be a great setback if you should be forced to give up your influential position in the Office of the Dirigent of Okanagon. Especially now when the Rebel element is so strong in the planetary government. *But you must not compromise your safety.*>

Don't worry. I'll get myself assigned to the crash investigation team. Castellane will need someone from ODO liaising with the Galactic Magistratum. I'll muddy the waters when I can, and if it looks like my cover's blown I'll flit. But I'm confident no one can tie Hydra to me. Just *you* make certain that bloody idiot Parni doesn't screw up his assignment. If any members of the Dynasty get on to him, old Parn's toast. He does well enough when you need mental muscle but he can't think his way out of a plass Baggie. Has he told you his plan for eliminating the old man?

...

Fury?

...

Damn. Offline again. *Damn!*

[6]

SECTOR 12: STAR 12-337-010 [GRIAN]
PLANET 4 [CALEDONIA]
NEW GLASGOW, CLYDE SUBCONTINENT
25 AN SEACHDMHIOS [10 JUNE] 2078

Niall Abercrombie, Executive Assistant to the Planetary Dirigent of Caledonia, made no apology for stonewalling the distinguished caller on the subspace communicator.

"I'm sure it's a verra important matter, Director Remillard, and under ordinary circumstances I wouldnae hesitate to interrupt the Dirigent. But she's deliberatin' an appeal of a capital sentence the noo, and ye understand why I can't break in on her."

The display showed the pleasant, rather ordinary face of a dark-haired man in his mid-twenties. Jack and his fiancée customarily alerted each other on the SS com when intending to project a telepathic message on the intimate mode over interstellar distances. The ultrasenses were not easily focused across the lightyears. Even paramounts could do it only with difficulty unless the recipient of the message was alerted to "tune in" ahead of time.

"I'll bespeak her later then," Jack said. "When do you think she might be free?"

"Let me take a wee keek at her sked." The assistant consulted a plaque on his desk. "She has a simple adjudication followin' this, and some trade quotas for avizandum and other special export-import documents to ratify and seal. We're verra careful aboot such things on Callie. And then there's a penciled-in luncheon appointment with her dad if there's nae early vote in the Assembly. If ye bespeak her in aboot forty-five minutes, she'll surely be available for a moment."

"A moment . . . You're working her to death!"

"Oh, aye," Niall admitted cheerfully. "Our Dirigent Lassie's insisted on slavin' night and day ever since the big blowoot. And this week ODC's been in a rare carfuffle wi' her tryin' to get urgent matters taken care of afore she takes the regular flight to the Old World for the wedding. On Di-h-aoine—och, sorry, that'd be your Friday—two days from noo."

"Thanks for telling me. I think I'd better fly her to Earth myself in my own starship. I'll make sure we bunny-hop nice and slow so she has time to unwind before our big day."

"A fine idea! The staff here at ODC wanted to throw a ceilidh for her but she wouldnae hear of it. It'd be grand if both o' ye came back to Callie taegither for a bit later on, so's we could have a proper planetary bash. After the grief this world's had coping wi' the diatreme, we've unco' need for a celebration."

"I promise we'll both come after the honeymoon," Jack Remillard said.

"If ye'll pardon my sayin' so, Director, don't let the lass haver on about having to cut the honeymoon short because she's indispensable. She *is*, o' course! But Callie has a perfectly competent Deputy Dirigent, Orazio Morrison, to deal wi' things whilst she's away. Take a guid lang holiday. Laird knows ye both deserve it."

Jack laughed. "We'll try—if the media vultures leave us in peace. And now, goodbye to you, Niall." The screen of the subspace communicator went dark.

Abercrombie sighed and flicked the instrument onto STANDBY. He scanned the outer reception room with his farsight and was relieved to see that no unscheduled petitioners had arrived. Only the two Magistratum agents who had brought in the recidivist felon and his wife were there, patiently awaiting the outcome of the clemency hearing.

It was time to see how matters were progressing. Niall pulled up the garters of his socks, tucked his sgian dhu into the right one, put on his tweed jacket, and smoothed the fake fur of his sporran. Then he slipped into Dorothea Macdonald's office from a side door and stood where the petitioners could not see him.

The room was simply furnished with a broad desk and armless chairs of local daragwood, so deeply violet in color that it was almost black. Matching wall units contained communication and data-reference equipment. One entire wall was a polarized window overlooking the city of New Glasgow and the surrounding countryside. On another wall directly behind the Dirigent's desk hung a golden representation of the nine-pointed star and cross saltire of the Great Seal of Caledonia, with its motto *Is Sàbhailte Mo Chaladh*—Safe Is My Haven.

The condemned man, one Geordie Doig, was a former hop-lorry driver and a nonoperant. He was below average in height but broad across the shoulders and well muscled. Dressed in orange prison garb, he sat before the Dirigent's desk with his young wife, Emma Ross, who was also a normal. As he spoke his last plea for commutation of his sentence, his strong, restless hands kept straying to his temples, fingering the freshly shaved places where the docilator electrodes had been fastened to his scalp.

Since his legal representatives had exhausted all other avenues of appeal, Geordie Doig's only hope now was to have his sentence commuted by Caledonia's highest executive, who represented the central authority of the Galactic Milieu. The clemency hearing involved both a personal interview and a mandatory mental examination of the prisoner. Most Planetary Dirigents had the ream-job done in advance by redactive specialists, but Dorothea Macdonald was unique in performing the probing herself. Her paramount metafaculties gave her the ability to work with a virtuoso swiftness and subtlety that spared examinees the usual pain caused by the procedure.

The Dirigent of Caledonia stood casually before the two petitioners, leaning against the desk, listening with her head deeply bowed and her arms folded. As usual, she conducted the hearing without having any guards or legal advocates present. She wore a loose-fitting cowled coverall of azure metallic fabric that was belted tightly at her slender waist. Panels of gauzy midnight-blue silk dotted with tiny sparkling gems hung from a deep collar intricately adorned with faceted blue and white stones.

"So you cooperated in rehabilitation therapy?" she prompted the prisoner.

"I did whatall the damned shrinks wanted," Geordie replied in a querulous voice. "They blethered on at me for months, analyzing me mind, they said. Then there was the aversion therapy. They zapped me till I skreiched and even passed out from the pain of it. But I didn't miss a session. Is it my fault that the bloody treatments didna work?"

Emma Ross dabbed at her eyes with a pocket kerchief. "The therapists said Geordie was doin' guid. Even let him take off the wristband eight months ago, they did. He was just fine. Kind to me and the two bairns and staying off the liquor. I let him do me abed as often as he said he had to, and he didna hurt me like before. But—but then after the big blowout things were so wild and rambailliach with our building crashing down and the car smashed and fires all around and people so scared and the looting and all—and—and Geordie just lost it. I tried to stop him, but he wadna tak tellin'. He went out stravaiging with the mob and that's when it happened. But he really couldna help it, ma'am."

"I couldna, Dirigent!" the prisoner said. "I just come over strange. It happened in spite of meself, and that's God's ain truth. It wasna my fault."

"It truly was not," the wife reiterated.

Dorothea Macdonald lifted her head and regarded the pair steadily. She was a woman of small stature, only twenty-one years old. Wavy brown hair framed her face within the gleaming blue hood. Her eyes were hazel, rather closely set, and below them her face was covered to the chin by a half-mask entirely encrusted with diamonds—some star-white, others a more brilliant blue than any sapphire.

Ever since her participation, five planetary months earlier, in the mitigation of the potentially world-wrecking diatreme that had ruined her face and nearly cost her her life, Dorothea Macdonald had insisted upon wearing diamonds produced by the great eruption. For reasons she refused to explain, she declined to spend months in a regeneration-tank having her facial injuries healed and wore a prosthetic mask instead.

Her eyes, above the glittering façade, seemed to look into the soul of the man before her. He flushed and averted his gaze.

"I've examined your record carefully," the Dirigent said. "You've done over eight thousand hours of public service as punishment for battering your wife and children. After your first aggravated rape conviction, you served three years at hard labor, followed by three more years of work-release with intensive counseling and behavior-modification therapy. In spite of this, you committed a second aggravated rape in the aftermath of the diatreme eruption, for which you were duly tried and convicted. Psychologists of the Caledonian Magistratum have declared you mentally competent—"

"He couldna help it!" Emma cried, and she would have continued but the Dirigent's metacoercion silenced her.

"—to withstand my redactive examination of your mind. Do you freely consent to the procedure, and do you agree to abide by my decision based upon it?"

"Aye," Geordie said. He clenched his big fists and stiffened in his chair.

The Dirigent came close to the prisoner and put one hand on the crown of his head. "Please sit still. It won't hurt."

He braced himself, screwing his eyes shut, and then gave a galvanic start. His head lolled and his body went limp. His wife uttered a whimper of apprehension and watched curiously during an interval of silence.

It was not necessary for the Dirigent to probe deeply into the mind of Geordie Doig to find what she needed to know. Her eyes above the mask narrowed and she withdrew her hand. A moment later the prisoner was fully alert. "Is that all?" he asked.

"Yes."

"What—what d'ye say, then?"

"After examining your mind redactively, I regret that I can find no reason to commute the sentence passed upon you."

"But I swear I wadna do it again! I swear!"

The Dirigent only said, "But you would."

"Geordie!" Emma Ross wailed, and burst into hopeless tears.

"Belt up, you silly cearcag!"

"Haud yer wheesht, mon!" Niall Abercrombie admonished the prisoner sternly.

Geordie deflated. He threw a disgusted look at Emma. "Och, can't we just get on with it?"

"If you wish," the Dirigent said, "my assistant will escort your wife outside before you make your choice of sentence."

"Aye, take her away." Geordie seemed impassive now, staring at the floor while Niall led the distraught woman out the door.

The Dirigent took a reader-plaque from her desk and handed it to the prisoner, speaking formally. "George William Doig, since you have been adjudged by a jury of your peers counterproductive to the ultimate harmony of the Galactic Milieu, you are offered the three options inscribed on the sentencing plaque you hold. One: permanent incarceration in the Caledonian Correctional Institution on Caithness Subcontinent. Two: psychosurgical implant of a docilization unit and release to the custody of your wife, Emma Ross. Three: euthanasia . . . Please make your choice now by touching one of the numerals firmly with your index finger."

"This implant," Geordie said. "It's the same as yon headset thing they clamped on before they brought me here?"

"Not quite. You would have a smaller device placed permanently within the limbic system of your brain. Its effects would be the same as those you experienced with the temporary docilator. You would feel easygoing and peaceful, without any inclination to perform independent actions. You would obey any legitimate command given to you without question. You would be capable of coherent speech, but it would be slow and labored."

"I'd be a bloody zombie, right? I've seen those poor dossie sods picking up highway litter and restocking supermarket bins."

The eyes above the diamond mask were steady. "Caledonia has only a few hundred docilates thus far. The program is still somewhat experimental. But you should give it serious consideration. With the implant you would remain free, do useful work, live at home, and help to support your family. You would no longer pose a danger to the community because of your inability to control your anger and sexual aggression. Instead you would feel a quiet contentment. You would still be able to experience love."

"You mean sex with my wife?"

The Dirigent shook her head. "The docilator modifies the brain's hormonal output, making erection and orgasm impossible, as well as suppressing other strong emotions such as anger and fear."

Sweat had broken out on the prisoner's brow. He stared at the options listed on the plaque. "Jesus God—some bloody choices! Turn me into a no-ball retard, lock me up for life in the chokey, or feed me to the worms!"

Dorothea Macdonald said nothing. She was standing straight now, with her arms at her sides, a shining, seemingly aloof figure.

Fiery rage welled up in Geordie Doig and he sprang from his chair. He would have flung himself at her, bludgeoned her with his big fists, torn off her fancy clothes, and fucked her senseless—

But he was paralyzed. Stiff as a plank, he overbalanced and crashed to the floor. The Dirigent's coercion forced him to climb to his feet and stand still, trembling in every limb with impotent wrath.

"Choose," she said.

He gave a hysterical giggle. "Oy, Diamond Mask! Is it true what they say about you? That your face is such a godawful mess it'd make a maggot puke to look at it?"

"Choose."

"Eat shit, you rotten cunt!"

She only stared at him.

"Okay! Right, then!" He jabbed his finger at option number one. "I choose the goddam fewkin' Devil's Island slammer. Caithness. At least I'll still be a man out there."

Niall Abercrombie reopened the office door to admit the uniformed agents of the Magistratum. As they led Geordie Doig away, he cursed the Dirigent at the top of his voice, piling obscenity on obscenity until they clamped the docilator on him again.

Dorothea Macdonald went back to her desk and sat down. She took up a refreshment flask with a drinking tube and drank some water. Niall handed her a sheaf of durofilm documents and the official seal.

"A rough one, eh, lassie?"

"A rough one," she agreed, and for a moment her artificial voice, generated by psychokinetic manipulation of air molecules, wavered. "But then, they all are."

"That scunnersome swine! 'Twas all I could do not to fetch him a guid belt in the gob, hearin' him snash ye like that." Niall was a holdover from the administration of the late Graeme Hamilton, as invaluable as he was overfamiliar. In spite of this, and his incorrigible addiction to trite Scots dialect, the Dirigent was extremely fond of him.

She took the papers without commenting on his indignant outburst and swiftly read the first one. "I'm denying this descent-and-distribution appeal from the Cairngorm probate court. Even if the man died intestate, the inheritance rights of nonborn second-degree kin clearly supersede those of the state." She scribbled a few words and added her initials. "When are those Cairnies going to concede that nonborns have exactly the same rights in law as biological offspring? This is the Galactic Milieu, for heaven's sake—not nineteenth-century Aberdeen."

"They're a dour and conservative ilk out there in Cairngorm," Niall observed with a shrug.

She frowned as she read the next document. "What's this? An import quota extension request for two hundred C240 mind-interface units? What in the world are these people building that requires premium brainboards like that? Who owns this company—this Muckle Skerry Bionics—anyway? I've never heard of them."

"I can find oot. Could be they're some adult amusement outfit with a hot new line in expensive erotic perjinkities."

She set the document aside. "With boards like this in their tickle-suits, the customers would risk gonad meltdown . . . Have an ODC interstellar commerce agent go to Beinn Bhiorach and do a quiet investigation. This is the second shipment of sophisticated glom components somebody's tried to import ex-quota within the past three months. It may be perfectly innocent. But I've heard a rumor about offensive metacreative CE equipment—mental lasers—being built on Satsuma. I want to be certain it's not happening here."

Niall nodded. "Will do, and I'll bid our lad gang warily. By the bye, there was a subspace call from Director Jon Remillard, came in whilst ye were dealing with sweet Geordie. He'll be giving ye a farshout in ten minutes or so."

"I should be finished with these soon. Check with the Sergeant-at-Arms at the Assembly, will you? See if there's any likelihood of a vote delaying Dad."

"Aye, that I'll do." Abercrombie left the room, closing the door.

All of the other documents were routine, and she initialed those that were ratified and zapped them with the small laser seal. When the work was done she rose from the desk and went to look out the window at the capital city. There was a fine view of the Firth of Clyde from her office on the three-hundredth floor of the Dirigent House stratotower. Vessels crowded the waters—container ships bringing goods from the outlying small continents, tugboats hauling barges filled with grain, produce, and forest products from upriver, skim-ferries zipping between the suburban islands, smaller watercraft of every description. It was too overcast to see the Vee-ways overhead, but her ultrasenses perceived the intricate computer-controlled streams of commercial and private rhocraft moving in dozens of different vectors above New Glasgow.

For a moment she concentrated, savoring the deeper aura of Caledonia itself. It was a world having precious little dry land, with jagged mountains, strings of volcanic islands, and forests that were as bravely multicolored as the tartans of old Scotland. Its population was only just over a million, even though it was one of the earliest settled of the ethnic planets. An Earthling didn't earn a living easily on Callie, but the stubborn colonists had persevered in their "safe haven." The Scottish world had been both self-sufficient and prosperous until the blowout of the diatreme.

New Glasgow was heavily damaged by earthquakes and fires following the eruption, as were many other cities and towns on the populous Clyde Subcontinent. The stratotowers housing the government, the university, and the principal business offices were buttressed by inertialess fields and had gone unscathed. But the older parts of the capital, the twisting lanes and closes along the waterfront that were crowded with quaint jerry-built structures dating back over fifty years, had been hard hit. Most of the devastated areas were lower-working-class neighborhoods, long overdue for urban renewal for all that they were picturesque and evoked memories of the earliest days of Callie's colonization.

Dorothea's late predecessor, Dirigent Graeme Hamilton, had always had a soft spot in his heart for the rickety waterfront with its flourishing grog-shops, flea markets, resorts of dubious amusement, and ever-useful junkyards, and he'd balked at renovation. (It would also have cost a lot of money, which the colony couldn't spare.) Now, thanks to the diatreme and a subsequent influx of no-strings Milieu disaster relief funding, New Glasgow could be tidied up without depleting the planetary treasury or raising taxes. There'd be a difficult interim, but reconstruction was well under way. The most serious problem involved the nearly forty thousand displaced residents who had been housed by the Human Polity Red Cross in temporary towns set up in the Clyde hinterlands. Despite the government's best efforts, most of these settlements were little more than collections of cheerless barracks, decent enough shelter from the weather but sadly lacking in privacy. There was already grumbling that the Milieu and the Old World weren't doing enough to help the diatreme refugees, and politicians were exploiting the situation both on Caledonia and in the European Intendancy back on Earth.

Musing over her planet's problems, the Dirigent wondered if it was really possible that criminal elements were manufacturing potentially lethal CE equipment somewhere on Callie. The Japanese ethnic world of Satsuma, located in a star system not far away, had a persistent problem with operant yakuza mobsters, but there had never been organized crime on the Scottish planet. On the other hand, Beinn Bhiorach, where the suspicious components were to be shipped, was the most remote and thinly populated of Caledonia's continental landmasses. BB had been her own childhood home, and she knew well enough that its steep glens and abandoned mine workings were capable of concealing any number of crooked enterprises.

But a Scots mafia in embryo? What a stone daft notion!

There was a more chilling possibility—one that the lofty-minded, altruistic exotic races of the Milieu had scarcely yet begun to address. What if the illicit cerebroenergetic equipment wasn't intended for criminals at all? What if the faction of anti-Unity humans, the so-called Rebels, were arming themselves in order to secede from the galactic confederation by force?

It was a far-fetched idea that had come into her mind out of nowhere—perhaps because of the upcoming lunch with her father, about which she was feeling qualmish—and she gave it small credence. Callie wasn't yet a hotbed of anti-Milieu sentiment as cosmop Okanagon and some of the "planets of color" were; but its Celtic-heritage denizens were prickly and antiestablishment by nature, and hardship caused by the diatreme eruption had exacerbated the groundswell of political discontent that had long flourished among the plaidie hills.

One of the most vocal of Caledonia's Rebel stalwarts was Ian Macdonald, Beinn Bhiorach's sole Intendant Associate and the Dirigent's own father . . .

Diamond.

Jack!

Her troubled mood vanished as she responded to his telepathic hail. For a few minutes they shared special thoughts on the intimate mode of farspeech. Persons other than young lovers would doubtless have found their mental conversation cloying and sentimental, to say nothing of hackneyed; but to Jack and Dorothea the ideas were new and precious and important, dealing as they did with the wonder of each other.

At last, however, his mental nuances reluctantly revealed that he had another reason for bespeaking her:

There's bad news, sweetheart. I'm on Okanagon. My Aunt Anne was involved in a serious accident here. Her starship crashed.

Oh, no! How is she?

Anne's alive but badly hurt. Unfortunately, her three exotic companions and the human pilot died.

I'm so sorry, Jack.

The worst part is, we think the crash was no accident.

Oh, God. *And it happened on Okanagon?*

Yes. Anne and some of her associates from the Panpolity Directorate for Unity had come from Orb to confer with the Commander-in-Chief of the Twelfth Fleet, Owen Blanchard. There have been recent allegations by loyalist Magnates of the Concilium that the Twelfth is top-heavy with officers belonging to the Rebel party.

Yes, I know. And the allegations are true.

Anne and her colleagues were going to look into it. No big thing. She didn't want to get the spacers all torqued and testy. It was to be a discreet sampling of sentiment, to find out how the anti-Unity misunderstandings that seem to be so prevalent in this Sector might be corrected. In the case of the Fleet, Anne had considered revising the curriculum at Chelan Academy, plus instituting mandatory reeducation of the commissioned officers. The Directorate discussed all this months ago.

What did Blanchard think of that idea? I've heard that he's one of the top Rebel leaders. He and Annushka Gawrys were once lovers, you know. Some people say that the concept of an anti-Milieu political party originated with the two of them.

Anne never talked to Blanchard. Her courier ship went down the very morning that the first conference was scheduled. There's no doubt that the pilot deliberately caused the disaster. He might have been a suicidal anti-Unity fanatic—but there's another possibility. The ship was an express courier, and the pilot was a low-ranked adept-class operant, wearing a conventional CE control helmet. The hat could have been sneetched, coercing him to fly the ship into the ground. The passengers had no inkling that anything was wrong until it was too late to do anything about it. Anne only survived because she spun a crude metacreative cocoon around herself at the last minute. It didn't protect her completely, but it did the job. She'll be in a regen-tank for at least a year.

The poor woman . . . What will happen to the Unity Directorate? Anne was its prime mover. It won't be the same without her. Who will take over the chair? You?

I don't think I'm right for the job, sweetheart. But never mind that. There's one last bit of info I haven't told you. Before Anne went switch-off, she made a last heroic effort and managed to bespeak a single intelligible word: *Hydra*.

!!! OhdearGod.

The Okanagon authorities notified the First Magnate. When Papa found out about the Hydra thing he told me, and I came zorching to Oky like a bat out of hell. Dirigent Castellane bent over backwards to cooperate with us and the Magistratum investigators.

Small wonder. Nobody's forgotten that earlier mystery accident on Okanagon that conveniently wiped out Pat's predecessor . . . And now the First Magnate's pro-Unity sister is nearly killed and talks about Hydra! A very suggestive coincidence. Especially when one recalls the Alvarez flap six years ago.

How could I forget? It happened the very night we first met—more or less face-to-face—at Marc's Halloween party.

Yes . . . you wore that adorable clown suit, and I picked your giant brain like an overripe muskmelon.

And *you* conceived the idiotic notion of going to Okanagon with Uncle Rogi to interrogate Alvarez.

It wasn't idiotic! I had good evidence that the man was a Hydra.

Your idea was shit-for-brains stupid . . . even though you were right about the Hydra. Fortunately, I found out about your scheme and had Alvarez framed with a felony hit-and-run charge to put him temporarily out of circulation—and beyond your reach.

You *what?*

Diamond, you were only fifteen years old then! I couldn't let you endanger your life by playing clumsy detective games with a potential Hydra.

. . . Uncle Rogi! That damned old stool pigeon—*he* told you!

He did what he thought was best. What if the other Hydra-units had been there, backing up Alvarez when you tried to interrogate him? They would have nailed you to the wall.

Well, they weren't on Okanagon. They were on Earth, stalking me in Hawaii!

Yes. [Chilling recollection.]

I presume that the Remillard Dynasty snuffed Alvarez.

They had nothing whatsoever to do with his death. Actually, it was a very nasty surprise. I had hoped to mind-ream him for information about the identities of the other Hydra-units and Fury. After Alvarez died so mysteriously in his cell, Krondak evaluators from the Galactic Magistratum took over the phony hit-and-run investigation at the First Magnate's request—allegedly because Alvarez held such a high position on the Okanagon Dirigent's staff. The exotics managed to do superficial redactive examination of Patricia Castellane and her top people without their knowing it, but the lightweight probes failed to find proof that she or any of the others at Dirigent House on Okanagon were aware of the Hydra's real identity. They didn't find any other Hydras living on the planet, either. The Lylmik Supervisors and the First Magnate eventually put a lid on the entire Alvarez affair.

I'm not surprised. But now it seems that there *is* at least one other Hydra hiding on Okanagon. After all this time.

We really don't have the foggiest notion why the pilot crashed the starship, or what Anne meant when she said "Hydra." There's no way of questioning her until she comes out of the tank—and thank God for that. The last thing the Dynasty needs now is public speculation about a new Hydra attack.

Jack, you can't simply ignore the possibility.

Of course not. But Paul intends to keep the Hydra angle of the case sub rosa. Only the inner circle of Castellane's bureaucracy and the Fleet Commander himself knew about Anne's upcoming visit. If one or more of *them* is a Hydra-unit in disguise, we'll have the devil's own time proving it. There isn't enough evidence to justify an official inquiry of the planetary bigwigs—much less their full-scale mind-ream—and the law won't let us mount a fishing expedition. The Galactic Magistratum will continue to investigate the crash, but there'll be no Hydra hunt.

I see. Another cover-up.

For the good of the Milieu, darling.

Indubitably . . .

The real question is, why did the Hydra want to kill Anne?

She heads the Unity Directorate—and I *told* you that Fury has this daft notion of founding a Second Milieu with its own evil substitute for Unity.

Diamond, dear Diamond! Don't let your own terrible experiences with that monster color your right reason. Fury is only a single warped individual. It has just two Hydra-units left to act as its agents. The Concilium would know if any larger Fury-led cabal existed. The *Lylmik* would know! There is no such group.

There are the Rebels.

Their agenda bears no resemblance to Fury's—except that both want humanity out of the Milieu.

I've had the damned monster inside my mind and I know how seductive it can be. Fury doesn't have to coerce large numbers of people or lead them openly. All it has to do is secretly exploit human weakness and perversity. And eliminate persons who threaten its scheme.

Yes.

Jack, everybody acknowledges that humanity is still far below the Unified races in sociopolitical maturity. Compared to the exotics, Earthlings are still at the level of Genghis Khan and the Golden Horde. We still commit crimes, cheat, lie, connive, and try to better ourselves at the expense of the other guy. Believe me, I see it all from behind this desk! The Dirigent is a combination ombudsman, judicial despot, and glorified nanny—

And I love you.

Don't be facetious. And don't patronize me!

Never. I love you and I also respect your judgment and your intuition. You're right about Fury being a potential menace to the Milieu, and you're right about it being capable of manipulating humanity to its own ends. You *do* know the monster better than I do. And the human condition as well.

Don't say that, Jack.

It's true. It's so easy for me to forget what being human is. My knowledge is all academic. What does Jack the Bodiless know about human weakness, human feeling, the emotions that sway the human heart? I try to understand but I don't always succeed. You should know that better than anyone, darling.

Don't be silly.

Did I tell you that Marc thought it was absurd that a—a thing like me should fall in love and want to marry?

He would! If anyone in your family is inhuman, it's Marc, not you.

You'd better hope not, babe. I modeled my wedding tackle on his three-piece set.

Jack, it's not funny. You know as well as I do that human nature is ultimately mental, not physical. You have the mind of a dear, genuine human being. I could never have loved you otherwise. And I do love you.

Diamond . . .

I want to be with you. I want to put all of these problems aside, just for a little while, and think only about us. It's selfish—

It's not.

[Interval of mutual consolation.]

Jack, what will become of Anne? Will she be transported to Earth?

Paul will arrange it.

It seems heartless for us to go ahead with a big wedding.

Nonsense. Anne would be the last one to want to put a damper on the festivities. Now listen to me. I'm coming to Caledonia immediately. In two days we'll fly to Earth in Scurra II—slowly.

Yes. Oh, yes. It would be marvelous to have some quiet time with you. Some learning time.

Some *teaching* time! I'll be with you before you know it. Goodbye, my dearest Diamond, a nighean mo ghaoil.

Goodbye, Jack, a churaidh gun ghiamh!

Intendant Associate Ian Macdonald picked at his poached salmon and champit tatties, his dark brow furrowed in an obstinate scowl. "I still think I should stay home. There's not only Assembly business, but the harvest is on back at the airfarm and Gavin and Hugh have their hands full and call me every other day with this crisis or that. There are equipment problems, and two new flitter pilots who aren't up to snuff, and the wee plants are driftin' far to the north this season, beyond the Goblin Isles."

"I want you to give me away at the wedding, Dad."

He snorted. "As if you ever belonged to anybody but your own self, Dorrie Macdonald!"

Her eyes softened. "You know what I mean. I want you there beside me affirming my marriage. And playing those bloody pipes of yours for the sword dance after."

"Aye, well, there'll be plenty of Remillards about who could do the honors at the altar," he muttered. "That Uncle Rogi you're so fond of. Your Grandad Kyle, for a' that, if you're bound to have a kiltie relation stirrin' up a ruckus."

"It wouldn't be the same and you know it. Kyle can no more play the pipes than Rogi can." The Dirigent lifted a specially prepared container of puréed food, deftly inserted its tube into a hidden orifice behind the chinpiece of her diamond mask, and ate. Her pseudovoice continued to speak as clearly as ever. "I know you're still sulking because Jack and I are getting married on Earth instead of here on Callie. But it wouldn't have been practical having the ceremony here. Not with things still all in a flaughter from the diatreme. Saint Andy's cathedral is a pile of rubble."

"Beinn Bhiorach wasn't touched, as you know very well. We could have had the wedding at Saint Maggie's in Grampian Town, where you were christened, and—"

"—and put up forty or fifty Remillards at the farm? And heaven knows how many Magnates of the Concilium and other distinguished human and exotic guests that Jack will have invited, to say nothing of the odd Macdonald who may have a notion to attend, and a few friends and associates of my own!" She shook her head and her eyes flashed. "Be realistic, Dad. Grampian Town has one fleabag hotel and two pubs with tatty rooms on top."

Ian Macdonald banged his fork down. His massive brow was like thunder. "And perish the thought that the high mucky-muck Remillard Dynasty and their swank friends should have to demean themselves stayin' in low Caledonian dives! Never mind what's right and proper for a father to do for his own lassie's marriage. We'll let the stinkin' rich Remillards pay all the bills and do exactly as they please because *they're* the First Family of Metapsychology and darlings of the media and fawnin' lapdogs of the fewkin' Lylmik!"

There were murmurs and snickers from people at the tables nearby. The Intendant Assembly dining room was packed with legislators, senior staff members, and lobbyists, and a lot of them undoubtedly shared the Rebellious inclinations of Ian Macdonald.

The Dirigent suppressed her mortification and broadcast vibes of fond tolerance to let the operant diners, at least, know that she was unfazed by her father's tirade. Why did normals love to make scenes? If Ian had been operant, the two of them could have quarreled decently, mind to mind on the intimate telepathic mode . . .

When his daughter ignored his explosion, Ian Macdonald took a long pull from his glass of McEwan's ale and continued in a much lower tone. "That's not the whole of the matter, either. What about yourself, Dorrie? It's as though the diatreme blew away your good sense, for I swear I don't understand what's come over you since then. A Dirigent of Caledonia dressin' like a carnival queen! Graeme Hamilton must be spinnin' in his grave. And your poor face . . . Don't tell me you couldn't have it fixed if you wanted to. By God, your own paramount redaction would do the job without any regen-tank if you bade it! It breaks my heart to see you looking like that, eating invalid's slop, without even a tongue to speak with or lips to kiss—"

"Dad, we had this out before. If you really can't bear the sight of me as I am, I'll let you see me otherwise."

He gasped, for suddenly the diamond mask blurred and seemed to vanish. Her face was as it had been before—heart-shaped and solemn within the gem-studded blue lamé hood, with plain features and a mouth with a secretive little smile.

"Anytime you wish, Dad, it'll be my old face you see when you look at me. I've made it so in your mind."

The muscles of Ian's strong jaw worked and he was dismayed to feel his eyes growing moist. "But not your real face."

"No," she said, and he saw the glittering covering rematerialize.

"Why, Dorrie?" His rasping whisper was heartbroken. "In God's name, why? Is it because of *him* somehow?"

She was serene. "You've no right to ask me that, Dad. Nor to ask the other question trembling on the tip of your tongue. I love Jack. That's all you need to know. And he loves me."

"Does he love you the way you are behind the mask?" Ian hissed.

"A face is also a mask," she said, "and no more the real Dorothea Macdonald than the prosthesis is. Let me prove it."

He gave a low cry of horror and gaped at the sight across the table, feeling his gorge rise. Once again the diamond mask beneath his daughter's calm hazel eyes had faded away, but this time Ian saw hideously scarred flesh clinging to a noseless skull. The ghastly injury was visible only for a moment before sparkling blue and white gems hid it again.

"Is that the true me?" her pseudovoice asked gently.

Ian had covered his eyes with one hand. "No, lass. No." His shoulders shook. "I'm sorry. I'm a pigheaded fool with no right to question your judgment. You must live your life as you see fit and marry your uncanny Jack if that's your choice."

She reached across the table, touching his arm. "Will you come to Earth with Janet and Ellen, and give me away to him at the wedding?"

He raised his head. "I will."

The Dirigent got up from her chair. Her father was such a brawny man and she so small that even with him seated, their eyes were nearly on a level when she stood at his side. "I'll see you there, then," she said. Her masked face came close to his and he felt the cool hardness of the diamonds brush his cheek. "Goodbye, Dad."

She walked away, nodding to acquaintances and colleagues and exchanging brief telepathic greetings with some of them. Then her shining blue figure passed through the dining-room door and was gone.

Ian Macdonald tossed down the last of the ale, keyed the table-com, and demanded that the waitron bring more drink. He swept the room with a defiant glare. Nobody looked at him. They were all suddenly busy with conversations of their own or attentive to their plates. Ian grunted, then bent to his meal and finished the salmon and potatoes and peas and bread. It would have been a sin to let the good food go to waste.

[7]

FROM THE MEMOIRS OF
ROGATIEN REMILLARD

A week before Jack and Dorothée were to be married, the best man farspoke me and said he was egging in to New Hampshire from his place in the Pacific Northwest to do a little fishing before the festivities. Would I like to join him? His childhood friends Alex Manion, Boom-Boom Laroche, and Arkady Petrovich O'Malley might also show up.

I was delighted by the notion of taking a few days off with Marc. The tabloid vampires were getting bolder as the date of the ceremony approached. Stonewalled by the wedding principals, they'd besieged my bookshop in Hanover, clogging the comlink and scaring paying customers away. It was enough to drive a man to drink—but I was maintaining an unwonted sobriety just then, as well as spending a lot of time looking over my mental shoulder.

The attack on Anne by Hydra might have mystified the rest of the Remillard family, but I had a pretty fair notion what was behind it. Somehow, Fury had found out that Anne was hot on its trail. It had decided to eliminate the threat before she could set up Denis's exorcism. I figured the monster must have told Madeleine and Parnell, the surviving Hydra-units, to kill Anne. They'd made a damned good try, probably by performing some kind of mind-fuck on the pilot of her starship. Hell, the guy was even wearing a control-helmet! Marc had told me years ago that Hydra had almost killed *him* that way by coercing him to crash his CE-controlled motorcycle. It seems the brainboards of those infernal hats create a wide-open door to coercive mischief.

So far, there'd been no attempts on my own life. If Anne was right about the parent-child mental constraints (and if Fury abided by them, which was by no means a sure thing), then the monster wouldn't be able to hurt me through its own mindpower. I was still vulnerable to Hydra, though, and I knew I wouldn't be safe until I told Jack and Dorothée everything that Anne had told me.

Unfortunately, the young lovers had already taken off from Caledonia on a shallow-catenary voyage when I learned about Anne's crash. In those days, communication with a ship in hyperspace was a difficult and involved matter, undertaken only in the gravest emergencies, and had no guarantee of privacy. I couldn't risk it. Jack and Dorothée weren't scheduled to show up in New Hampshire until the last minute, the afternoon before the wedding. Then their time would be taken up by a whirl of clothes fittings, the rehearsal, and the rehearsal dinner. So it looked like I was going to have to find a way to break the bad news to the kids on the day of the ceremony itself, before they took off for their honeymoon on the Hawaiian island of Kauai.

Dandy. What a great little wedding present that would be.

It was definitely time to go flyfishing with Marc and forget.

At that time I didn't own an egg, so I threw my tackle in my old nongravomagnetic Volvo wagon and headed up to Pittsburg Township at the far northern end of the state. There, deep in the restored "primeval" woodlands west of Indian Stream, was the big lakeside cabin that Victor Remillard had built before the Great Intervention. The family had taken over White Moose Lodge after Vic was decommissioned, and the place was so pretty and the fishing and snowmobiling so good that it had no lingering evil associations. Live-in caretakers kept the lodge open all year round, and the Remillard clan felt free to drop in with their friends and recreate anytime they felt like it.

It was early evening on June 11 when I arrived. To my mind, the North Woods in mid-June are about as idyllic as New England gets. The no-see-um gnats are about finished, the mosquitoes aren't yet up to strength, and the more benign hatches of insect life that brook trout fancy are on the wing. I pulled up in the lodge's parking area next to a couple of modest vehicles that I presumed belonged to the staff. Over on the dirt landing pad stood a jet-black performance egg with the CEREM corporate logo on its door. Marc had arrived, but his boyhood pals Boom-Boom, Alex, and Arky apparently had not.

Guy Laroche worked for the Human Division of the Galactic Magistratum down in Concord and had his sights set on the top-cop position. Alexis Manion had become the premier authority on the relationship of mental lattices to dynamic-fields, and his work at Cambridge University had already begun to attract the attention of the Nobel Committee. Arkady Petrovich O'Malley was Exotic Liaison

Chief of the Twelfth Fleet, based on Okanagon. In spite of their high-powered heads and exalted positions, all three men were ideal fishing buddies, unpretentious and ready to laugh at an old man's raunchy jokes. They were also sympathetic to my Rebel leanings and concerned about the way the exotic races continued to limit human freedom.

I shut down my Volvo's whiny old turbine, climbed out, and stretched the kinks out of my bones. It wasn't dark yet. Night takes its own sweet time falling in New Hampshire as the summer solstice approaches. The pines and hemlocks were silhouetted against a greeny-blue sky and a loon warbled its spooky love song out on the lake. The still air smelt of conifer resin and fried pork sausage and the wild roses that had been planted near the rambling log house. A chipmunk chipped and song sparrows sang farewell to the day. The only evidence of the famous albino moose herd for which the place had been named was a fresh pile of olive-sized droppings that I almost stepped in as I unloaded the car.

A quick look through the lodge's kitchen wall revealed Norm and Suzanne Isbrandt, the current caretaker couple, eating the aforementioned sausages for supper. Out on the lake the resident brook trout were already rising in anticipation of the evening hatch. The mayflies weren't out yet, but there were a few caddises winging around. In the distance I perceived a fancy float-tube, gliding with suspicious speed toward Porcupine Cove nearly a klom away on the lake's northern side. Naughty, naughty! The operant fisherman was using PK—not his swim fins—to get into casting position. He had suppressed his aura, as the most powerful metas do routinely, but even my myopic farsight had no trouble identifying him. The husky shoulders and hatless head of black curly hair belonged to Marc Remillard.

He said: Bonsoir Onc' Rogi!

I said: Hi Marc. How's the lake looking?

Fair, he said, in the typical deprecating understatement that has characterized flyfishermen for two hundred years. No matter what kind of luck you're having, it's gauche to be emphatic about it. Fishing is never fantastic and it never sucks; it's "middling" or "a mite slow." If the trout are hitting on the backcast or otherwise virtually leaping into your net, the sport may be characterized as "halfway decent."

I watched as my great-grandnephew guided his U-shaped float into position, cocked his arm, and made a perfect 30-meter cast. Show-off!

He was using an ancient, perfectly preserved No. 4 split-cane rod from Partridge of Redditch, together with the newest top-of-the-line model Donner AG reel. No sooner had his elk-hair caddis dry fly fluttered to the water than a big brookie hammered it. Marc played the creature for a few minutes, then brought it to his net and carefully set it free. The trout had been what I, wedded to obsolete systems of weights and measures, would have called a helluva scrappy two-pounder.

Languidly, I said: Nice fish.

Marc said: Quit jabbering and get out here on the water.

Dusk is the best time of day for lake angling, especially if you are an operant and can see in the dark. (We heads don't talk much about these little blessings to shortbrained folks.) I had no intention of joining Marc over in the cove. Flyfishing is something you do in solitude, even if you go out with a buddy. There'd be time enough afterward in the lodge for us to gossip and tell lies about who caught and released the biggest and feistiest trout. (When the actual fishing is over, one is finally permitted to pull out all the stops.)

I put on my chest-high secoprene waders and cussed when I discovered I'd left the belt at home. But what the hell. My belly-boat had three support bladders, and the chances of all of them deflating at once were nil. A wader-belt was a necessity when you fished fast rivers, where even a good swimmer could drown if he fell into the drink and his waders filled with water and dragged him down. But a little bitty dead-calm lake like this was safe as houses.

Right?

Well, I'm still here to tell the tale, but it was a mighty close shave . . .

Since Marc was fishing his precious bamboo, I decided to use my Orvis Zipster with a miniature Hardy Flyweight reel and a threadlike No. 1 line. The streams of New Hampshire being mostly quite small, lively little brookies 20 cents or so in length are the usual thing you catch. If you use ultralight tackle these nanoids are fine sport, fighting as fiercely as a Montana rainbow. Our larger fish mostly live in lakes, and unless you are—as I was!—a snot out to prove something, you use heavier tackle when you try for heavier fish.

The zero-weight outfit is so light that any kind of breeze makes casting almost impossible unless you cheat and use your PK faculty. Tonight, however, conditions on the quiet lake were perfect. Contrary to what you might think, it's quite possible for a skilled angler to land a monster with a well-made Zipster rig such as my Orvis. If I managed to bring in any kind of decent fish I'd ace Marc on piscatorial points no matter how big a hawg he pulled in with the heavier Partridge.

Chortling in anticipation, I put on my vest and my brown Tilley hat with the flies stuck in it, gathered the rest of my stuff, and set off along the path that paralleled the southern lakeshore. Marc would watch me with his paramount farsenses; but I'd stay as far away from him as possible so I wouldn't have to see that maddening one-sided smile of his when I had my inevitable break-offs. Fishing with ultralight tackle means that you lose more fish than you net; but therein lies the challenge and the fun.

When I reached a suitable put-in spot I pinched the inflators on the float-tube, put on my flippers, and—voilà! I was ready to go. Lots of anglers—Marc included—prefer open-fronted floats because they're convenient to get into. I like my classic donut belly-boat with the high backrest because it's easier to maneuver in the water. It's a medium bitch to get yourself settled into, though. The cloth sling you sit in takes up most of the central opening and it's a tight and awkward fit to step into the thing with fins on. If you're a beanpole like me, you just put the tube on over your head, push it down until the sling hits your rump, then fasten the 'tween-legs strap. With your rod clamped ever so gently in your teeth, you grip the tube's side handles like a duchess lifting her skirt to curtsy to the queen and wade into the water backwards in the approved frogman fashion.

Then you sit down . . . and enjoy bliss! The float-tube is somehow more aesthetically satisfying than a regular boat, which your dedicated flyfisher tries to avoid using. You ride waist-deep in the water, finning silently, close to fish who don't seem to realize that you aren't one of the gang. All of your tackle is near at hand, organized in zipper pouches. Your rain jacket and snacks are in the backrest.

I knew a little bay with an outflow stream and an interesting drop-off to a springhole where sizable fish often lurked. I headed for it at a brisk rate of knots—moving backwards, of course. As it got darker the lake turned to a sheet of polished onyx with the sinking moon and the lights of the lodge reflected in it. The loons gibbered, a duck splashed in the weeds, and the little outflow stream chuckled merrily over its rocks. Tiny wisps were beginning to rise to the water's surface, floating like elfin sailboats. They were newly hatched mayfly duns drying off their first wings. I gently scooped one up, studied it, and then found a dry fly that resembled it and began to tie it onto the leader.

An incisive telepathic thought zinged my brain:

How's it looking over there?

I said to Marc: The hatch is on. I'm using a Number 12 yellow paradrake on a 7X tippet and the nought-weight rod. Eat your heart out flogger.

Big fly for toy tackle. Smile. Crazy old salopard . . . Did you come alone?

Damn right.

Then it's just you and me and the fishies tonight. Alex and Arky said they probably wouldn't be able to make it until tomorrow, and Boom is trapped in Concord indefinitely. Talk to you later.

I said: Tight lines mon fils.

Then I forgot Marc and concentrated on my aquatic prey.

You have to understand that flyfishing is a deliberately inefficient sport. Any blockhead can catch a fish with a pole, a hank of string, and a hook with a worm or marshmallow or some other organic bait. But to deceive the wily trout into striking at a pinch of fiber, feathers, or tinsel tied to a barbless hook requires a carefully conceived strategy and artful tactics. If you're a metapsychic operant, you have to handicap yourself even further to make it a fair fight. You dassn't use your ultrasenses to find the fish underwater. You can't metacoerce the critter into sampling the fly. And of course you must never use your creative faculty to conceal your presence or enhance the fly's illusion of edibility.

Sometimes I cheat.

But I didn't this night, except in harmless ways like PKing the nearly invisible tippet into clinch knots tying on the fly, and using the same homely metafaculty to resolve tangles. In the space of two hours, I caught and released a couple dozen valiant tiddlers too small to snap the half-kilo test leader.

I fairly hooked—and broke off, because I made various mistakes in playing them—five fish of respectable size. The brook trout took my flies away with them, but eventually the special-alloy barbless hooks would fall off or dissolve, leaving the critters unharmed. The moon vanished, the loon serenade continued, and I was a happy man. When the hatch came to an end, the duns that had survived greedy fish flew away to rest in the bushes. Fully mature ephemerides that had hatched a few days earlier now spun giddily in their mating dance overhead. Fertilized females bounced along the water's surface laying their eggs while the males dropped from the sky, dead of a surfeit of ecstasy.

Eventually Marc got hungry and decided to pack it in. I told him I'd stay just a tad longer, fishing the spinners.

And of course it had to happen; no sooner had Marc disappeared inside the lodge than I finally hooked the big one.

I had taken note of this fish over an hour ago, cruising well out of range in shallowish water on the right side of the springhole. It was taking spent mayflies with majestic precision: *gulp, gulp, gulp* (pause for a number of minutes to ruminate), *gulp, gulp, gulp* (time out for really serious contemplation). My mind's eye could study the stately fish without compromising angler's honor since I wasn't casting to it. It looked like the grandaddy of all brookies, a real mossback, dark greenish-blue above and silvery-white below, with pale wiggly markings up around the dorsal fin and blue-ringed yellow and pink spots on the flanks.

I didn't paddle the belly-boat over and try for him earlier because I was afraid he'd spook. Besides, with every feeding pass he got a little closer. I was willing to wait, playing my game with smaller fry.

Finally, he condescended to head my way, drawn by a shower of dying insects. I hastily tied on a rusty spinner. *Gulp, gulp—*

I cast, and my fly settled like a whisper a meter in front of the trout's abovewater snout. I gave the spinner a tiny, seductive twitch.

Gulp.

Gotcha!

I set the tiny hook in the monster brookie's tough jaw and mentally howled out a prayer: S'il vous plaît, mon doux Jésus! No mistakes this time!

The fish streaked off, making my little reel squeal like a tortured mouse. He dove to the bottom of the springhole. The line went dead slack.

God! Had I lost him already? (No fair peeking.) I lifted the rod high, reeled in with delicate caution, and met resistance. There was a vibration as the trout shook his head and darted off a short distance, but the rod—not the fragile leader—took the strain. Then the line went limp again. Had the fish broken off, or was he coming toward me? It took all my willpower not to look. I cranked in line like a madman, but the dinky reel was too slow on the uptake. Somewhere underwater the brookie was wagging his great head again. If I didn't tighten the line soon I'd surely lose him. I took hold of the line and began stripping in slack cautiously with my free left hand, catching each fresh loop with my right index finger while simultaneously gripping the rod. It's not classy flyfishing but it works ... provided the damned fish doesn't zoom away all of a sudden and half take your finger off, catching it in a bird's nest of snarled line.

Taut at last! I held my lunker ever so gently while I got the coils of loose line back on the reel. He exploded in fury—*zeeee!* went the reel— and away he ran again. He pulled me and the float-tube out into deep water. Then he jumped, a tactic that had already lost me three or four decent fish that evening. But this time I was ready, bowing the rod to the fish in the approved fashion. He splashed back and sounded again, but he was definitely weakening.

I began the end game, reeling in as much line as I could when he was quiet, but allowing him to run short distances when he wanted to. Gradually he came closer and closer to the float-tube. It was full dark with only stars to illuminate the water, but my night sight saw him darting and pausing near the surface. He had to be 125 cents long and weigh over 4 kilos, a very respectable size indeed for a brook trout.

Coaxing him in, I held my breath and prayed that he wouldn't take me by surprise at the last minute and snap the cobweb tippet. I even spoke to him telepathically (a totally useless ploy, since a trout has a cerebrum smaller than its eyeball), reassuring him that I would set him free as soon as I got him into the net and removed the hook with forceps.

I had the net in the water now, moving it slowly so the fish wouldn't panic when I eased the meshes around him. My entire attention was fixed on my prize as I brought him close to the left side of the float-tube. The net moved up to take him from behind.

He turned, saw the net . . . and laughed.

I swear that my mind's ear heard him, and the laughter was completely human. Incredulous, I tracked him with my farsight as he dove straight down, hauling line from my screaming reel, then reversed and rocketed toward the surface again, directly underneath my float-tube. Snout-first, he struck the mesh sling I sat in and delivered a fearful blow to my testicles.

I yelled. Great balls of fire popped in front of my eyes and I dropped the rod. The sudden, excruciating pain was so distracting that I failed to notice that the quick-release buckle of the float's 'tween-legs strap had popped open. I began to slide deeper into the water, too agonized to think straight. Coldness flooded around my armpits, down my body, and into my aching groin. I gripped my crotch and cursed, trying to redact away the pain.

The laughter in my mind intensified. I seemed to see the great trout, now scarcely a meter away from me on the left. His head was out of the water, his eyes glowed a spectral green, and my fly was still affixed in the corner of his grinning mouth. The fish dove and struck me a second terrible blow in the privates. When I screamed again my mouth filled with water.

It was then I realized that my waders were rapidly filling and dragging me down.

I thrashed like a gaffed shark, trying to grab the belly-boat seat and haul myself up before my head went under again, but I was being pulled down too fast. Ordinarily I'm a pretty decent swimmer and I hadn't really started to panic yet. Underwater, I pulled my fishing vest loose from the dangling float-tube strap that had snagged it, opened it, unfastened the buckles of my waders, then tried to push them down and free my legs of both waders and swim fins.

I couldn't.

Something bound my ankles tightly together and I knew what it was: not the easily broken nylon leader but WF1F flyline, as strong as steel wire. More of the stuff floated around me, writhing in the water as though it were alive. The goddam fish was circling me with unbelievable speed and I was being trussed like a rolled rib roast! I felt my knees suddenly constrained as more line wound around them. My left wrist became entangled and that arm was yanked tightly against my body. My bursting lungs now hurt more than my wounded nuts.

Again I had a vision of the homicidal trout and heard it laugh. But the voice was that of a man. An imbecilic notion came into my oxygen-starved brain: Didn't I *know* this fish?

Wasn't it Parnell Remillard, Adrien and Cheri's wayward son, one of the two surviving Hydra-units? . . .

It was at that point that I panicked.

The bizarre attack had left me so muddleheaded that it had not occurred to me until then to send out a telepathic shout for help. I tried to farspeak Marc, but the effort was pathetically weak. Precious air escaped from my nostrils. I sank deeper and deeper and my ultrasenses faded to extinction. I was enveloped in pain, darkness, and a growing lethal chill. Dreamlike visions dredged from my memories began to explode before my blind eyes. I was dying and the sadistic Parnell was greatly amused.

I refused to surrender to the Hydra. With the last of my strength I drew up my knees, then abruptly straightened my bound legs, flapping the swim fins. Again and again I performed this maneuver, trying to propel myself toward the water's surface. But something was holding me down. The flyline had snagged on the bottom. My free right hand fumbled at a pocket of my fishing vest. I had a small Swiss jackknife. If I could just get hold of it—

I was rocked by a third savage blow, this time to the abdomen. My lungs expelled their remaining hoard of air. I stopped struggling and drifted, knowing Parnell had finished me. Fury's secret was safe.

Oddly, I could see again—but the vision was detached, evidence that the terminal excorporeal excursion had begun. My body was suspended near the bottom of the springhole in about five meters of inky water, tethered to the broken branch of a sunken log by a few turns of line. The flyrod lay in the mud amidst waving weeds. There was no sign of the trout. I felt warm again. The pain had vanished and I was moving slowly away from my mortal hulk, up to the surface into marvelous, shining air.

Without emotion, I watched a swimming human figure descend and approach my dead body. This was an uninteresting development, and so I turned away and smiled into the fascinating light. I began to speed toward it—

The light went out.

After a blank interval I realized I was breathing. My lungs were on fire and my brain was a throbbing clot of agonized jelly. Two men were talking.

"He's coming around. His heart's steady, and from what I can tell, his brain function is back in the normal range."

"Thank God."

"Rogi's a damned tough old Canuck. Hard to kill."

"I don't think I could have saved him without your redactive course. Even in extremis, his mind was shut up tight against me."

"I'll bring him to the lodge in a few minutes. You'd better go on ahead. Get the egg ready and tell the hospital in Colebrook that we'll be flying him in."

I heard departing footsteps skwodging in the mud. My eyes still refused to open. Unearthly laughter rang out, and for an instant I convulsed in terror, stiffening in the arms that held me. But it was only the damned loons cackling. I groaned in relief, then mumbled, "Gonna be sick."

Strong hands turned my body and held my head while I vomited lake water. Then a dazzling dart seemed to impale my brain and I instantly felt better, zapped by redaction. My eyes opened and focused—more or less—and I processed optical input: a starry sky framed by conifer trees, branches of underbrush up close, and a face looking down at me. Deep-socketed eyes with winged brows, the aquiline Remillard nose, a cleft chin, a thin-lipped mouth smiling a lopsided smile.

"Feeling better?" Marc asked. He wiped my mouth with a bandanna handkerchief and lifted me into a sitting position.

"It was Parnell—Adrien's kid—that tried to kill me," I wheezed feebly. "Hydra disguised as a killer trout! You gotta believe me, Marco."

"We'll talk about it later." He scooped me into his arms like a child and carried me toward the lodge. I could hear excited voices.

A maudlin tear trickled down my cheek. "Thanks for saving my life. Stupid old fart . . . I didn't think to call till it was almost too late. But you heard me after all."

"I didn't hear your mind calling," Marc said. "And I didn't really save you. I came running after you were out of the water and helped with the mental first aid."

We had reached the parking area of the lodge. The caretaker couple were there with blankets and pillows, leaking anxious vibes. Marc's big black egg was open and he put me onto the rear banquette and covered me up. Somebody was already in the pilot seat. Marc climbed in beside me, the other guy slammed the hatch and started the rho generator. The egg shot up inertialess into the night sky.

Marc said, "Here's the one who heard your farsqueak, dived into the lake, cut you loose from the mess on the bottom, and pulled you ashore."

The man in the pilot seat turned around and smiled. I goggled at him, so blitzed that I couldn't utter a word. Like Marc and I, he was sopping wet. His damp blond hair straggled over a youthful brow and his eyes were the same vivid coercer-blue as Ti-Jean's.

But it wasn't Jack the Bodiless who had saved me. It was Denis.

[8]

BRETTON WOODS, NEW HAMPSHIRE, EARTH
18 JUNE 2078

The First Magnate of the Human Polity of the Galactic Milieu smoothed his striped silk tie, checked his spats, put on his pearl-gray stroller, tugged down his waistcoat, shot his cuffs just a trifle, and surveyed himself in the hotel suite's full-length mirror. He liked what he saw. Paul Remillard was a slender, striking man with a palpable air of command. The self-rejuvenating gene complex of his famous family made him appear half his actual age of sixty-four, and the archaic formal wear looked notably spiffy with his silver-streaked hair and well-trimmed beard.

All he lacked was the finishing touch of a boutonniere. Who had charge of the damned things, anyway?

He decided to farspeak Lucille. It had been her idea that the attire of the wedding party should reflect the romantic Edwardian Era when the White Mountain Resort Hotel was new. Jack and Dorothea, amused by the incongruity of the matriarch's conceit, had acceded willingly. Period clothing was optional for the guests but strongly encouraged. Even the attending Krondaku had insisted upon assuming human form and coming in fancy dress so that their normally monstrous appearance would not clash with the mise en scène.

Paul sent out a farspoken hail on Lucille Cartier's intimate telepathic mode:

Mama! WheredoIpickupflowerformybuttonhole?

Goodafternoon dear mygoodness aren't *you* the dapper boulevardier!

The posies. Where?

Flowersforgentlemen in Marc&Jack's suite just trot over pick yours up I'm inconference with cateringstaff yourPapa soothing IanMacdonald's wounded Scottish pride I suppose it *really* wasn't toowiseofme to suggest he forgo kilt for Englishstyle 1905soup&fish we'llmeetyou RooseveltParlor 1hour relax dear I have EVERYTHING IN HAND.

Super! [Passionate gratitude.]

Lucille laughed indulgently and withdrew her mind.

Paul thanked God that his mother had volunteered to oversee the nuptial arrangements. Who would have thought that the logistics would be so complicated—or that the popular media would take such an inordinate interest? Other children of the prolific Remillard Dynasty—including Paul's second son, Luc—had tied the knot without attracting any special attention. "Why," the First Magnate had grumped earlier to Lucille, "are the sensation-mongers getting into such a pucker over these two?"

His mother's response had been dry, but she charitably refrained from chiding him for his insensitivity. "Dorothea and Jack are Milieu heroes, Paul dear. Don't tell me you've been too preoccupied with your official duties to notice. And they're also quelque peu bizarres! There's the inevitable vulgar speculation about how in the world they'll ever manage to . . . do it."

Paul had frowned quizzically as comprehension dawned. "That's a good question! But dammit, it's nobody's business but the newlyweds'. I don't often take advantage of my perks of office, but I'm going to do my utmost this time to make certain that our family privacy is respected."

"Good luck," Lucille had wished him tartly. "I'm sure you're a wiz at keeping great matters of state secret. But the marriage of Jack the Bodiless and Diamond Mask is something else altogether."

Carrying his top hat and gloves, the First Magnate went out into the sunny corridor. Windows at either end of the long hallway were wide open and their lace curtains flapped in the lilac-scented afternoon breeze. He looked down into the back garden from the elevator alcove and saw neat rows of folding chairs, a red carpet leading to a flower-banked altar area with florists still fussing over it, and a giant marquee with tables all formally set for the wedding dinner. A small ensemble of musicians was playing Mozart's String Quintet in E-flat for a group of appreciative listeners. Most of the four hundred guests had been ensconced in rooms in the hotel overnight, and numbers of them were already strolling about the lawn or seated in the chairs, humans in old-fashioned finery and exotics in their own version of traditional formal attire. Paul could not help chuckling. The place was starting to look like a fantasy adaptation of the Ascot Opening Day scene in *My Fair Lady*.

The door to one of the other hotel suites opened and two gorgeous beings emerged. They were members of the diminutive Poltroyan race, less than a meter in height and humanoid in appearance except for their violet-tinted skin and ruby eyes. Their bald heads were gold-painted in elaborate designs and they wore robes heavily embroidered with precious metal thread and edged with rich green fish-fur. Following Poltroyan custom, both were decked in the extravagant pearl jewelry they had worn during their own espousal celebration years ago. The First Magnate was so taken aback by their splendor that he hardly recognized his two old friends.

"Paul!" they exclaimed in happy unison, and came bounding over to seize both his hands.

Paul embraced them in turn. "Minnie . . . Fred. High thoughts!"

"What a beautiful day for your youngling's mate-affirmation," said the female Poltroyan, Minatipa-Pinakrodin.

"And do let me compliment you on your handsome costume," said the male, Fritiso-Prontinalin. "It's a bit different from the human nuptial garb we're familiar with."

Paul gave a humorous shrug. "Clothes like this were the height of fashion in this part of Earth about a hundred and eighty orbits ago, when this hotel was new. But my outfit won't be complete until I find a certain little bunch of flowers I'm supposed to wear right here." He thumbed his lapel. "I hope your rooms are comfortable."

"Our accommodation has a lovely view of the mountains," Minnie said. She added playfully, "The furnishings are just the least bit lackluster, but perfectly adequate to our needs."

Paul affected to be shocked. The sumptuous lifestyle of the Poltroyan race was legendary in the Galactic Milieu. "No emerald-studded bathtub? No solid-gold clothes hangers or platinum doorknobs? I'll complain to the management."

Minnie giggled.

Fred said, "It was very extravagant of you to have rented this entire huge establishment, but I suppose it was the only way to insure against an invasion by unwelcome newsgatherers."

The First Magnate let his exasperation show. "We've blocked the entry roads and set up sky barriers, and the hotel perimeter is cordoned with stun-fencing. In spite of all that, reporters in disguise have already been detected and ejected from the kitchen staff, the corps of waitrons, and the groundskeeping crew. One brazen gentlewoman of the tabloid Tri-D even tried to substitute herself for a viola player in the orchestra. Her AV recorder was hidden in the fiddle."

Both Poltroyans laughed. Then Fred's kindly face turned sober. "How is your sister Anne? We understand you personally saw to her safe transport to Earth."

"I got in from Okanagon late last night and took her directly to the Polity Genetic Research Institute in Concord. They say she's doing well, and her complete recovery is only a matter of time. But having Anne out of the picture for nearly a year will play merry hell with the Unity Directorate, and it's going to have to contend with a tricky matter of moment during the next Concilium session. You probably haven't heard the news yet, but metapsychologists from the Sorbonne in Paris are going to announce officially that they've detected the initial stages of emergent coadunation of the human racial Mind. I'm not familiar enough with autocatalytic set theory to understand the details, but it seems that a distinct phase transition is taking place."

"But that's wonderful!" Minnie exclaimed. "What is the difficulty? I should think you Earthlings would be overjoyed."

"There are certain human magnates who'll use the announcement as an excuse to inflame anti-Unity sentiment among our people. Anne was a past master at dealing with these loose cannons, but unfortunately the other Directors aren't nearly as handy in a brawl. Theoreticians, most of them."

"There's your son Jack," Fred suggested. "Wouldn't he be the logical chairman pro tem? His paramount mind—"

"Is only twenty-five years old," Paul said dismissively. "It's true that the majority of the Unity Directors are prepared to approve his interim appointment, but I'm afraid that he lacks the experience—and the authority—to deal with this impending crisis. The top guns among the Rebel magnates, people like Annushka Gawrys and Hiroshi Kodama and Cordelia Warshaw, would eat the boy for breakfast during a no-holds-barred debate over the protocols of Unification. It's not that Jack isn't brilliant. I'm just afraid he's not tough enough to be our principal spokesman on this issue."

"He might surprise you," Minnie said.

Fred asked, "If not Jack, then who?"

"I was thinking," Paul said, "of appointing Davy MacGregor."

The two Poltroyans were shocked into silence.

"I believe that the Lylmik Supervisors would agree if Davy would." Paul flashed an ironic smile. "You have to admit that MacGregor is tough enough to take on the entire Rebel contingent with both hands tied behind his back."

"Indubitably," Minnie agreed. "But it surprises us that you would consider a person who is so . . . conspicuously uncongenial in his relationship to yourself and the other members of your family."

The First Magnate lifted his beautifully tailored shoulders. "Davy is the perfect one for the job—not only because of his temperament and superior mindpower but also because of his great prestige as Earth's Planetary Dirigent. He's here at the ceremony, you know. A distant relation of the bride. I plan to sound him out later today. He may tell me to take a flying leap, but I hope not."

"If this plan of yours is for the best," Fred murmured, "then may the All in all speed its happening." He added telepathically: Paul mydearoldfriend can you afford to risk it? Deliberately bringing MacGregor into close association with Remillards enhances possibility of his discovering that Fury+Hydracreature are still alive&active.

Minnie's mind said: Davy has it in him to destroy you+yourfamily in order to avenge his wife . . .

Paul said, "He's a just man. If he takes the job he'll give it everything he's got. And to hell with the risk to my family! The Human Polity needs Davy MacGregor for the Unity debate. This issue is going to be crucial to the future of our race. If the Rebel faction ever gains the upper hand in the Human Polity, you know as well as I do that the exotic members of the Concilium will write us off as a bad job and rescind the Great Intervention."

The two little purple people nodded their gold-painted heads solemnly. "The Amalgam of Poltroy would cast its vote against you with the greatest reluctance," Fred said, "but we would have no other option. An unUnified humanity intent on cutting itself off from our confederation would present an unacceptable risk to the survival of the Milieu."

"Oh, please!" Minnie pleaded. "Let's not talk of such things on this day of joy for Dorothea and Jack."

Paul agreed and they said goodbye. The Poltroyan couple took the elevator down to the garden level while the First Magnate continued along the corridor and knocked on a door.

Come in Papa, said Marc.

Paul entered the suite occupied by the groom and the best man and found four Gilded Age dandies lounging about drinking champagne amidst the scattered remains of a lavish lunch. Uncle Rogi was still sitting at the table, clearly feeling no pain. Paul's sons Marc and Luc and Luc's spouse Kenneth Macdonald stood near the window, checking out the scene below. All of them were dressed in the same elegant gray formal wear as the First Magnate.

"I've come for my boutonniere," Paul said. "Where's the bashful bridegroom?"

Rogi hauled himself up. Swaying a little, he declaimed: "Waiting for his dear papa to arrive and impart a few last words of paternal wisdom before he marches down the aisle . . . Ti-Jean! Tire ton cul de là!"

The inner bedroom door opened. The four gallants tried to keep straight faces as a disembodied brain sailed slowly out, suspended in mid-air. It was wearing a pearl-gray top hat.

"Good God!" said Paul.

Marc kept his composure but the others fell about laughing. Uncle Rogi thrust a glass of champagne into the First Magnate's hand and helped himself to more.

"I couldn't resist it," said Jack the Bodiless, wreathed in mental smiles. "Can you believe that Uncle Rogi tried to talk me into going down to the ceremony like this?"

"Wrong!" Rogi declared in ringing tones. "I said Ti-Jean should go on his *honeymoon* like that." He went into a fresh fit of laughter, delivering salacious toasts to the floating brain in broken Canuckois.

"Uncle Rogi," Luc Remillard observed redundantly, "is as sozzled as a boiled owl."

"You lie, mon cher fagot," the old bookseller said sweetly. "I am as drunk as a skunk in a trunk!"

Paul grimaced in distaste. "Couldn't you boys have kept an eye on him?"

Luc shrugged. "It's a wedding, Papa. Rogi has a right to celebrate."

"I guess somebody'd better redact him sober," Ken Macdonald said. "Can't allow a swacked ring-bearer, can we? My sister the exalted Planetary Dirigent would have our balls for bidet-swabbers." He turned to Luc. "What say we two give it a try, luv?"

"Nobody touches my mind!" Rogi yelled. He dodged nimbly away from both men, simultaneously tossing down the last of his bubbly, and headed for the outer door.

Marc Remillard casually reached out and touched his fleeing great-granduncle's shoulder. Rogi froze in mid-skitter, paralyzed by coercion. Without effort, Marc frog-marched the skinny old man toward the bathroom. "We won't have to redact him. Black coffee and a modicum of simple emetic therapy will do the trick."

"Don't mess up his clothes," Jack said.

Luc and Ken cackled heartlessly and followed along to watch the fun.

The levitating brain doffed its topper and said: "Will you help me get ready, Papa?"

Paul slammed his strongest mental shield into place. "If you like." Uneasily, he followed the thing that was his youngest son into the bedroom and shut the door behind them, muffling the pitiful offstage noises.

"I have a confession to make," Jack said.

"Oh?" Paul pretended to inspect the groom's clothing, which was laid out neatly on the antique colonial bed.

"I'm responsible for Uncle Rogi's overimbibing. I coerced the poor old guy into guzzling too much champagne in order to distract him. You see, he'd got it into his head that it was his solemn duty to give me my prenuptial sex instruction. He's been trying to get me alone ever since he arrived."

Paul barely suppressed a snort.

"You know how close we've always been, Papa. I didn't want to deliberately hurt Rogi's feelings, and I confess that I do need certain information. But not the kind of thing he had in mind. I hoped . . . to get the data from you."

"I see." The First Magnate smiled tightly at the hovering mass of cerebral tissue. "Well, I'll certainly do the best I can—under the circumstances."

Jack's psychokinesis opened the cherrywood wardrobe door and a considerable quantity of thick, grayish-pink liquid matter flowed out like a colossal glistening amoeba. Paul stood motionless and his eyes widened as the amorphous blob moved across the fine oriental rug without leaving a trace and gathered into a large spheroid directly beneath the suspended brain.

"Didn't you know, Papa?" Jack's pseudovoice was good-humored in the face of his father's evident repugnance. "I usually keep the artificial plasm now when I disincarnate. It saves a lot of time if I don't have to regenerate a new body from scratch—to say nothing of averting wear and tear on my surroundings from molecular scavenging."

Paul *hadn't* known. If truth be told, he had not lived with his mutant son or otherwise shared the ordinary day-to-day domestic intimacies with him for over twenty years. When Jon Remillard was five years old, the widowed First Magnate had given him and his older siblings into the care of their grandparents, Denis and Lucille. Paul's work, which took him to every human-colonized planet in the Galactic Milieu, to Concilium Orb, and to hundreds of exotic worlds as well, had made any kind of normal family life impossible for him. In later years, when the First Magnate's heavy responsibilities finally eased, he discovered that his meager parental instincts were almost completely atrophied. His children matured into adulthood without him.

Paul had convinced himself that he loved his offspring dearly (except, of course, for the prodigal Madeleine, who was hiding God knew where, plotting God knew what). His relations with his four other children were amiable but rather formal; but that could hardly be helped, since they saw one another so seldom.

The oldest, Marc, was the most estranged of the lot, a quirky, self-centered genius who neglected his duties as a Magnate of the Concilium in favor of dubious researches into the cerebroenergetic enhancement of the human brain. Marie, the second-born, a quiet and circumspect woman who often seemed embarrassed by the antics of her more colorful brothers, was a Professor of History at Dartmouth College who wrote popular gothic novels under a pseudonym. She had recently moved into the old farm out on Trescott Road where Denis and Lucille had lived before returning to their original home on South Street. Luc Remillard had completely overcome the physical disabilities of his youth and now enjoyed robust good health. He and his life-partner Ken Macdonald were consulting metapsychologists at the research institute headed by Paul's older sister Catherine.

And then there was Jack the Bodiless . . .

The soupy ball of organic matter slowly elongated and rose, becoming a misty, turbulent column. The upper part engulfed the floating brain and the vapor swirled eerily, generating a faint, not unpleasant odor that Paul's perfect memorecall recognized as the scent of a very young baby. Within moments the reincarnation intensified to the point that the ectoplasm assumed substantial human form. Beginning at the feet and continuing up the legs to the trunk and arms, it solidified into an accurate representation of living human flesh. All that was lacking were the scars, blemishes, and other irregularities of natural bodies. The head and face appeared last of all, and Jon Remillard finally stood before his father like a normal man. He was of medium height, having dark wavy hair, blue eyes with a disturbing luminosity, and the high-bridged nose and square jaw characteristic of most of his family. He struck a statuesque pose and smiled shyly.

"This body design is something completely different from the usual run. Usually I only do a detailed job on my head and arms because clothing hides the rest. How do I look?"

Paul kept his voice level. "Fine, son."

"Are the sex organs proportional? I modeled them on Marc's, but he's twenty-three cents taller than I am and outweighs me by more than twenty kilos."

"They're appropriate for your build," Paul said heartily. "They're perfect. *You're* perfect. You look like the goddam Apollo Belvedere without the fig leaf."

Jack began to dress. "Funny thing about me and Marc. I suppose he's my closest male friend, besides being my older brother. Intellectually, we're ideal colleagues. When we work together our minds sometimes slip into metaconcert with no effort at all, like a pair of musicians playing an intricate duet in precise tempo. But . . . he tried to talk me out of becoming a sexual entity. He thinks it's a waste of time and vital energies. He called me a fool for wanting to experience that part of human nature."

"Sometimes," Paul said briskly, "Marc is a paramount grandmasterly ass. Just you wait: One of these days he'll fall head over heels and make a fucking idiot of himself."

Jack laughed as he slipped into his shirt and installed the cuff links and studs. "I sincerely hope so. But his celibate mindset left me with a nice personal problem. Up until now, the bodies I've fashioned for myself have been little more than hollow shells activated by my creativity and PK. Their rudimentary internal organs merely imitated natural function to enhance the overall realistic aspect. I never bothered with things such as extracephalic endocrine glands at all."

"I didn't know." Paul sat down on the edge of the bed.

Jack began to put on his stockings and garters. "This particular body took me quite a while to design. It's still far from being a faithful replica of the real thing, but it does have a fairly complete set of sensory equipment, nerves, and blood vessels. The male organs are as perfectly constructed as I could manage to make them and the gonads produce the appropriate hormones. I got most of the function data I needed from reference materials—including Denis's book on operant sexuality. But I still have to fine-tune the imaginative programs for male erotic stimuli response. And for that I need help."

"Uh—would you say that your brain structures and sensory network are typically human?"

"Reasonably so."

"I asked because normal human sex is largely mental. The data you seem to require are concerned with integrating the ancient limbic system of your brain—the part responsible for the sex drive and emotion—with the more highly evolved neocortex that thinks and exercises imagination. My redactive metability's not in the same class as Marc's or your Uncle Severin's, but I'm willing to give it a shot."

"I'm afraid I haven't made my needs clear, Papa. Actually, the integration process you mentioned is already well established in me. So are the hormonal patterns, the mechanisms for erection and ejaculation, and the pleasure pathways. But I'm . . . still lacking in libidinous spontaneity. What I need help with are the more subtle aspects of eroticism in both the male and female. My new body reacts to physical stimulation, but not to imaginative images or fantasies. I'm still incompletely human."

Paul frowned to cover his apprehension. Surely this creature didn't expect him to—

"I'd like my first act of intercourse with my wife to be as transcendent as possible for both of us. As Uncle Rogi's was, with Elaine Donovan. When he told me about their experience, I knew I'd somehow have to find a way to emulate it with my own lover."

Paul's silvery brows shot up. "Rogi? Transcendent? Well, I'll be damned! The old roué never compared notes with me."

"Rogi also told me that he fell in love at first sight," Jack added quietly. "And he's never stopped loving Elaine, even though he's tried to put her out of his mind. My own experience with Diamond was nearly instantaneous, too—except that the initial attraction was cerebral in nature, an immediate apprehension of spiritual affinity. Rogi says that his falling in love with Elaine Donovan was irrational. That seems to be a common phenomenon. But I understand that other natural human beings such as Grandpère Denis have experienced intellectual love first, then achieved mutual sexual passion later."

"It can work that way. I wouldn't know from personal experience."

"Would it be tasteless or impertinent of me to ask how you and Mama fell in love?"

Paul stared straight ahead. "As a young man I was rather inhibited sexually. Much like Marc—although I had an occasional unsatisfying adolescent affair, while he seems to have kept himself pure for science."

Jack grinned.

"I first saw Teresa on the stage at the Metropolitan Opera in New York in 2036. I was twenty-two, a wet-behind-the-ears politician with an excessive metaquotient and a fine reputation for running rings around the Simbiari Proctors. She was only nineteen, and that night she made her debut singing the title role in *Lucia di Lammermoor*. At the end of the opera the audience got to its feet and screamed and stomped and applauded for nearly fifteen minutes. A new superstar was born—but she was more than that to me. When I first heard that extraordinary voice of hers I was . . . overcome."

"Do you mean libidinously stimulated?"

Paul winced. "Let's just say that it took all my self-redaction to keep my poor body under control. It was my first experience with an aphrodisiac, and the magic was all in Teresa's voice. Denis claimed it had something to do with her incredible creativity. I don't know about that. I did know that I'd die if I couldn't have her."

"And so you were married."

"Five months later, right there on the stage at the Met. The next four years were the happiest of my life. We had Marc, Marie, and Madeleine, three magnificent operant children. Then Luc was born with terrible physical deformities, and there were other babies with lethal genetic traits that were stillborn or aborted. It was a terrible time for Teresa. She lost her voice and her entire personality changed. Tests showed that your mother's germ plasm had mutated—probably sometime just before the birth of our third normal child in 2040."

"But Madeleine *wasn't* normal."

"There was nothing wrong with her genes," Paul said tersely.

Jack now stared at his pair of antique lace-up shoes and spats in momentary bafflement.

"Better put the pants on first," Paul suggested. "The spats go over the shoes and button up the sides, with the strap underneath."

Neither of them spoke for some time. Then:

"Papa . . . why did you and Mama stop loving each other? Was it because she tricked you into conceiving me, and made you a party to a crime against the Proctorship Repro Statutes?"

"Not really. I forgave her that. We had drifted apart long before because . . . she no longer aroused me. Our falling in love was irrational and so was the falling out. Perhaps what we had together wasn't real love at all—at least, not for me. Perhaps what I felt for her was only sexual magnetism. A kind of enchantment. I never tried to analyze it deliberately at the time. One doesn't do that . . ."

"But you've thought about it since."

"Oh, yes. At this late date I've come to believe that true love has to be more clear-sighted and unselfish than I ever was with your mother. If I'd really loved her I would have been more accepting when she changed. I would have tried to evolve myself. Instead, when Teresa's erotic appeal faded there seemed to be nothing I could do to save the marriage. I found myself attracted to other women. Never to a singer, though! There were all kinds of new aphrodisiacs: a lovely face, perfect breasts, an alluring body, eyes with a provocative light in them, tantalizing movements, the promise of sexual excitement that certain women can't help projecting . . . My God, Jack! There must be a thousand reasons why a man is attracted to one woman and not another. Each of my women has been appealing in a different way."

"Your women . . . but you didn't love any of them."

"I enjoyed having sex with them."

"And your enjoyment wasn't diminished by the knowledge that you were betraying your wife and the religious values you'd been brought up in?"

Paul exploded. "Goddammit, Jack! Don't you judge me!"

"Papa, I'm not. I'm only trying to understand. But it seems so illogical."

The First Magnate's anger drained away, leaving only distaste and a terrible pity for this innocent, cerebral being, this prochronistic Adam just a few steps below the sexless Lylmik on evolution's ladder, still determined to sample the forbidden fruit.

And who, Paul asked himself, am *I* supposed to represent in this weird little biblical scenario?

He stared at the floor. "Sex is often illogical, just as your brother Marc maintains. It's part of our animal nature, but it's also evolved into more than that. We don't just do it in order to reproduce. We do it for solace and the relief of nervous tension and fun and even for the hell of it. Sometimes sex is only mindless fucking. But it can also be sacramental." He paused. "At least that's what they say."

"I'd like sex to be that way for Diamond and me. Perhaps not every time, because that would make it too solemn. But numinosity should definitely be a part of it. How does the old marriage prayer put it? 'With my body I thee worship . . .' "

The First Magnate laughed without humor. He still had not met his son's eyes. "The wedding vows also say that the bride and groom are supposed to forsake all others until death parts them. But that's an ideal some people can never live up to. I couldn't, after I stopped loving your mother. The basis for erotic attraction is obscure and capricious and it can vary over the years. I know I've hurt a lot of my sexual partners by rejecting them—particularly Teresa. But I didn't act callously, in cold blood. I'm truly sorry that your mother's heart was broken. But I couldn't stay with her when our love ended, and I don't consider myself culpable in the matter of her death."

"I don't either, Papa."

"You know my reputation as a galaxy-class womanizer. I'm not proud of it. Objectively I realize that promiscuity and an unwillingness to commit to a stable sexual union are psychological flaws. But it's the way I am. I need sex and I'll have it and I'll do my best not to be deliberately cruel to my partners. And that's that."

Jack finished fastening his spats. "I think I know why most metapsychic operants are monogamous," he said. "Opening one's mind to a lover at the start of a relationship either strengthens the mutual attraction or destroys it rather quickly when incompatibilities become obvious."

"In theory," Paul said, "that's true. But a marriage or a love affair can never be a linear system. They're chaotic harmonies, like all of biological nature. Both lovers have to adapt continually to each other's changing needs to keep the truth and beauty alive. But that's not easy. Especially when there's important work to do . . . and you must agree that my work *is* important."

Jack said nothing. He had moved in front of the mirror to attack the tricky knotting of his silk cravat. Psychokinetic manipulation would have done the job in a trice, but like all well-bred operants, Jack felt that the casual use of that faculty while he was embodied would be déclassé.

Paul lifted his head and spoke calmly. "Can you understand me when I say that the sexual part of my life is completely irrelevant to what's most meaningful to me—to my real passion?"

Jack nodded slowly. "Your true love is the Galactic Milieu, isn't it. Not any human being. Not even yourself."

"I've dedicated my life to the Milieu, and the consensus seems to be that I've been a good First Magnate. I'm damned proud of what I've accomplished. But . . . "

Jack waited.

Finally, his father said in a low voice, "But sometimes I wonder if I'm not the biggest fool in the galaxy. You see, Jack, I've never known the kind of sexual transcendence Uncle Rogi talked to you about. I'm the last person you should take as your role model and adviser. Find someone who knows what real love is."

"I have." Jack's voice was gentle. "But I want to have a genuine sexual relationship in my love life, too. You could make it possible."

"How?" Paul asked warily.

"I need your memories of sexual arousal. With them I'd have a truly human male paradigm. A foundation to build my own sex life on."

The First Magnate was stunned to speechlessness. Share the most intimate aspects of his sexual fantasies with this grotesque mutant?

But he's human, Paul told himself. Perhaps more human than I, because he has the capacity to love a woman without reservation.

This creature.

This son of his.

Jack eyed Paul obliquely as he put on his waistcoat of silver brocade. "I know it's asking a great deal. The sexual part of a parent's life is an intensely private thing. Leviticus even says, 'Thou shalt not uncover the nakedness of thy father or mother.' "

Paul's mind cried out: It's not Old Testament morality or inhibition or squeamishness that makes me deny you God help me I begat you by accident without love I would have prevented your birth I was revolted to the depths of my being at what you became I failed you even when you conquered the mutation rejecting you avoiding you letting Denis and Lucille and Rogi and Marc raise you I know I owe you reparation but—

NoPapaNO I don't need that I don't want to defeat or humiliate you it would be all WRONG if what you gave me was only recompense for your guilt.

The First Magnate stood up. After a moment he regained his poise, but his face was ashen. Jack was entirely dressed now except for his formal suit coat. Paul took up the garment and held it so that Jack could slip his arms into it.

Paul said, "Can you show me a mental précis of exactly what you'd require?"

"I could try. But the problem is, I really don't know what data I'm lacking. All my theoretical knowledge of erotic response is virtually meaningless without the mnemonic and imaginative framework that would enable me to personalize it. A normal human formulates his individual style of sexuality all throughout life, beginning in early childhood. I wasn't able to do that. I have the pieces of the jigsaw puzzle, but no hope of putting them together without help from a generous, thoroughly experienced man. One that I respect and trust. One that I love."

"Your Uncle Rogi . . . " Paul began.

"He'd *tell* me anything I asked. What he won't do is lower his mindscreen of his own free will so that I can absorb the body of specialized data that I must have. And of course it would be unthinkable for me to invade him and steal his memories, even though I could do it without leaving a trace."

"Your brothers . . ."

"Marc was willing to open that part of his mind to me—but he told me quite frankly that his libido is anomalous, and I believe him. Luc said he'd gladly volunteer if I thought Diamond would be happy with a homosexual husband."

Jack inserted a tiny spray of white miniature roses and baby's breath into his lapel, then reached into the flower box and held out another boutonniere to Paul. "Please, Papa—help me know what it is to be a sexual being."

The First Magnate stared at the flowers, then at his son.

"If you can't," said Jack the Bodiless, smiling, "I'll understand."

"Give me that." Paul took the small bunch of roses and poked it into his buttonhole. Then he surveyed the young bridegroom with a critical scowl and made a minute adjustment to Jack's tie. "There. You look pretty damned good, if I do say so myself."

"Shall we go?" Jack was calm. He picked up his top hat and gloves and began to move toward the door. In the shadowed room his aura was visible to Paul's mind's eye—a halo of gold and blue with twelve flamelike interior petals of star-white. It was more intense than any other vital-energy field the First Magnate had ever seen.

"Wait," Paul said. Unaccountably, his eyes were stinging.

Jack turned. His father took a tentative step toward him, then enfolded him in a sudden, crushing embrace.

"All right, son," he whispered. "Go for it. Your wedding gift."

[9]

FROM THE MEMOIRS OF
ROGATIEN REMILLARD

I had two good reasons to be crocked on the day of the wedding: I was scared out of my wits and at the same time dizzy with newfound hope.

Frightened because Hydra had attempted to do me in and would undoubtedly try again; giddy because Denis had saved me from the monster and there really seemed to be a chance that he wasn't Fury after all.

Anne might have been wrong . . . or she might have been lying. A niggling notion had already prompted me to briefly consider the latter contingency during the course of her revelations back in February. I began to think about it a lot more seriously as I recuperated from the attack of the homicidal brook trout.

By Anne's own admission, the only two members of the family without alibis on the night of the Hitchcock Hospital fire that nearly killed Baby Jack were Denis and herself. And she had admitted being tempted by Fury. I'm no psychologist, but it doesn't take Sigmund Freud to figure out that Anne's Athene-temptation might not have had an *external* source at all. She said she had identified with the goddess. What if her own submerged Fury persona had tried to seduce her "good" core personality, hoping to integrate the dissociated duo into a single, more efficient mind?

But why would an Anne/Fury order Hydra to kill its host body?

Ah, but she hadn't died in the starship crash! She'd just been put on hold for a year or so, and eventually she'd emerge from the regen-tank as good as new. The accident might have served Fury's evil purposes in a number of ways.

This was my reasoning: If the Dynasty—sans Anne—performed their exorcism of Denis and discovered that he was innocent, they'd be thrown back to square one, clueless except for my hysterical babbling. But if Anne were there on the scene and Denis was proved not to be

Fury, her good core persona would surely tell the other Remillards that Fury therefore had to be part of *her*. And she'd demand that they nail it, whatever the cost to herself.

Anne's crash could have been arranged in order to preserve Fury from this threat of detection. Fury might even have figured out some way to take over Anne completely before her healing was completed!

I could take scant comfort now in the fact that Anne was switch-off down in Concord, guarded day and night by the operant security personnel Paul had arranged for. If Fury did reside in her brain, it might *not* be sunk in the usual state of tank-induced oblivion. It might still be fully aware and able to use its farsenses or even other metafaculties, actively egging on its slave Hydra to perpetrate assorted nefarious schemes— including the engineering of my demise before I manage to blow the gaff.

As I lay in Upper Connecticut Valley Hospital, getting checked out after the drowning attempt, I knew that I would have to transmit to Jack and Dorothée not one improbable piece of unsavory intelligence but two—and to do it, I'd have to keep out of Hydra's clutches at least until the day of the wedding ceremony, a week away. Marc certainly would have been able to protect me, but God only knew how he'd react to my assertion that either Anne or Denis was certainly Fury. Most likely, he'd just laugh. He was highly skeptical about my fish story (he also doubted that Anne's crash on Okanagon had involved a Hydra), and too wrapped up in his own private affairs to humor a drunken old geezer afraid of bogeymen under the bed. That left me with only one other surefire refuge from Hydra.

When the doctors decided I would survive the dunking, I got Marc to put me on an express flight to Kauai in the Hawaiian Islands. The egg-bus didn't crash en route—although I expected it to, momentarily—and dear old Malama Johnson met me at Lehue Skyport as I'd requested. She asked me no questions but just took me home with her.

"Don' worry, Rogue," she said, hugging me. "I gonna spin a kahuna cocoon roun' you, make you kapu to aihamu, akua mano, an' da kine monsters so long as you heah. Nothin' gonna off you kokole while I'm aroun'."

Even top metapsychic researchers concede that certain kinds of ancient "magic" are mysteriously efficacious. Whatever—no Hydra came prowling while I stayed in Malama's house. After an interval of peaceful tropical days punctuated with mango coolers and mai tais, we both flew back to the White Mountain Hotel in New Hampshire in time for the rehearsal on the eve of Dorothée and Jack's nuptials.

When I was a young man it would have been inconceivable for a wedding party to have a 133-year-old ring-bearer or a roly-poly Hawaiian flower "girl" who was definitely of a certain age. Nowadays the roles might still be filled by children, according to the old custom; but one is just as likely to see a superannuated relative like me, an amiable ex-spouse, a special friend—human or non—or even a beloved companion animal carrying rings and flowers.

Malama was serene and regal at the rehearsal in a green-and-white muumuu with antique shell leis. I had a bad case of the heebie-jeebies until she calmed me with her loving coercion, whereupon I acquited myself like a champ. When the practice session was over Malama said that she had scanned the hotel premises and detected no lurking fiends. She told me I was now on my own, kissed me aloha, and went off to party with Tom Spotted Owl, the President of Dartmouth College, and his wife Socorro Ortega.

I wanted to believe I was safe, but I couldn't shake the realization that neither Marc nor Denis had managed to detect the presence of Hydra up at White Moose Lodge—which meant that the thing must be a crackerjack at mental disguise. It could be in the hotel, biding its time before taking another shot at me.

What to do? There was only one reasonable course of action. I went down to the hotel bar and got shitfaced. Then, enveloped in a comforting haze of Kentucky corn-squeezings, I shuffled off to my bed in the suite I shared with Marc and slept like the proverbial log.

Damn good thing, too, considering what was going to happen to me the next day.

When Marc and the others finished wreaking their wicked will on me in the bathroom of the groom's suite, I was rendered sober enough to be freshly terrified; but on second thought, it seemed unlikely that Hydra would try to scrag me hereabouts, surrounded as I was by most of the mental stalwarts of the Remillard Dynasty, along with a mob of guests that included nearly a hundred Magnates of the Concilium and enough heavyweight grandmaster operants to stagger the Earth in its orbit. I still had my trusty flask tucked in my hip pocket, but I decided to hold off drinking until after the ceremony. Once I had cornered Ti-Jean and Dorothée and unburdened myself, Hydra's motive for killing me would be negated and I'd have real cause for celebration. If the rumors were correct, Paul had laid on beaucoup cases of Taittinger Blanc de Blancs '71 to toast the happy couple. A magnum of that would go a long way toward restoring my usual sunny disposish.

Toting the little lace-trimmed cushion upon which the wedding rings would rest during the procession, I descended in the elevator with Jack, Paul, and the groomsmen and went to the Roosevelt Parlor on the garden level where Denis and Lucille were waiting with the priest and the rest of the bridal party. Only Dorothée herself was missing, and I was still skittish enough to be alarmed.

"Where's the bride?" I whispered to Marie Remillard. "She's all right, isn't she?"

Mentally, Ti-Jean's sister indicated an inner door of the parlor and said: Of course she's all right. It's an old tradition for the bride not to let the groom see her just before the ceremony. She's waiting in the next room with Malama. Praying, actually! *I* certainly would under the circumstances . . .

We were a decorative bunch. Except for Ian and Kyle Macdonald—who wore full Scottish fig, including Balmoral bonnets with rakish feathers, kilts, fancy shirts with lacy jabots at the neck, and black velvet Prince Charlie coatees with square jeweled buttons—the gents were a muted symphony in dove gray. Ti-Jean's suit was a bit darker than those of the others, and he was the only one wearing a silver brocade waistcoat. The priest, a genial Jesuit named George Duval, who had been Jack's favorite teacher at Brebeuf Academy, had managed to find an antique black cassock, one of those funny little clerical hats with a pompon on top, and a white linen surplice edged with fine old lace. He had been talking with Denis when the groom's party arrived, and now he took a minute or two to shrive us all so our souls would be squeaky clean for the upcoming ceremony. All I had on my conscience were a few venial sins of frivolous fornication, plus an uncharitable wish to do Marc and Luc grievous bodily harm because of the cruel way they'd sobered me up.

The ladies were a pastel chorus of Gibson Girls, swanning grandly about in the latest mode of 1905. I discovered (not by peeking: see below!) that none of them went so far as to wear authentic corsetry—

which would have compressed their waists to near-lethal waspish-ness—but otherwise their outfits were typical of the romantic Edwar-dian Era, and amazingly attractive. Because the wearers were still self-conscious about the impression they'd make, their minds involun-tarily leaked subliminal details of couture that were fairly easy to pick up. I found it amusing to do so, rather than listen to Lucille's hectoring as she organized the procession.

The three bridesmaids were Dorothée's foster sister Ellen Gunn, an old school chum named Cicely Duncan, and Jack's elder sister Marie. They wore high-collared princess gowns of fine batiste linen, formfit-ting to the hips, with swinging gored skirts and long, narrow sleeves. The lightweight fabric had multitudinous tucks, simulated hand-embroidery, and innumerable inserts of white Point de Paris and Cluny lace. Marie and Cicely were in pale apple-blossom pink, while young Ellen Gunn, the nonborn maid of honor, had a gown of dusty rose. Their hair was upswept, augmented with wiglets, and crowned with huge mushroom-shaped straw hats gussied up with ribbons and masses of pink and white flowers.

The bride and groom had chosen to have their grandparents, as well as their surviving parents, as part of the procession. Masha MacGregor-Gawrys, Dorothée's formidable Rebel grandmother, wore a dress and semifitted coat of pale apricot linen, edged and inserted with natural Point de Venise lace. Her auburn hair was topped by a hat heaped with silken daisies, wallflowers, and poppies.

Lucille, the self-appointed mistress of ceremonies, was awesomely chic in a gown and fitted Directoire jacket of réséda green silk with tiny gold buttons. A dark, softly curled wig replaced her usual French bob and bangs, and she wore a towering chapeau wound about with folds of ecru and moss-green chiffon and decked with satin foliage, silk mignonettes, velvet pansies, and a single enormous lavender rose. She carried a folded green parasol, which she used like a marshal's baton as she got us all properly lined up.

The bride's stepmother, Ian's second wife Janet Finlay, had chosen a rather simple honey-colored batiste princess dress in a style similar to that of the bridesmaids, with champagne lace inserts and trim. Her hat, in contrast, was a huge confection piled with creamy ostrich plumes and fake aigrettes. Over her shoulder she wore a taffeta sash of the Far-quharson tartan (Finlay being a sept of that clan), fastened with a canary diamond brooch handmade by the bride.

Paul's sister Catherine was standing in for Jack's deceased mother, Teresa Kendall. Cat was also a close friend of Dorothée, who had been her student at the Metapsychic Institute. Her tailleur (which went wonderfully well with her blonde hair) was periwinkle-blue silk with a lace-trimmed cutaway coat, embroidered in ivory and navy. The saucy brim of her hat was upturned on one side, confining a mass of light blue plumes and azure satin rosettes.

I gawked at the monumental assemblage of historically correct feminine headgear and asked Lucille, "Aren't those big hats awfully heavy?"

"Of course not," she snapped. "Do you think the women of 1905 held their chins up with psychokinesis?" She raked me with her eyes from top hat to spats. "Well, you *seem* to be compos mentis and properly dressed. Do you have the rings?"

I fished out a tiny white velvet box, opened it, and showed her two starkly plain golden bands about half a cent in width. "Good." She made me hold out the pillow, then poked a depression in its center and tipped the rings into it. "See that you don't drop them, and stay close to Marc when it's time for him to pass them over . . . Oh, by the way. Brother Duval's wife the deaconess couldn't make it, so you'll be assisting him as acolyte during the mass."

I opened my mouth to protest. After all, the last time I'd been an altar boy was in 1957! But Lucille turned to the others and announced, "We're almost ready, everyone. I'll just go out in the garden for a final check and cue the musicians and then we'll begin." She was off in a swirl of long petticoats and embroidered silk hosiery.

I peeked outside with my farsight and saw that most of the four hundred guests were in their seats—the humans and the exotics, the Edwardian and the Galactic, the friends and relatives of the bride and groom happily mingled in the modern casual fashion, leaving only the front rows empty for the wedding party.

Lucille reappeared, the orchestra struck up the solemn "Trumpet Voluntary" by Angus Hayakawa MacGillivray, and the slow parade began. Brother Duval led the way. Then came the grandparents, Kyle and Masha, Denis and Lucille; the groomsmen, Luc Remillard and Kenneth Macdonald; Marc, the best man, walking alone (as was symbolically apropos). The groom stepped out next, Paul on his left hand and sweet-faced Catherine on his right.

When Jack was safely on his way up the aisle and the bridesmaids were poised to begin their march, Janet Finlay opened the mystery door and out came Malama with Dorothea Macdonald.

All brides are beautiful, but this one was smashing. She'd designed the outfit herself and would have stitched it up as well if the press of her official duties hadn't made it impossible. The gown was shining white silk with a high neck. The skirt had no train, but it clung to her narrow hips and flared widely at the bottom like a calla lily, making her petite form seem taller. The lace that covered the bodice and was appliquéd over the sleeves and skirt had been lavishly reembroidered with Caledonian seed pearls; tiny diamonds from that planet flashed among them. Over the bride's left shoulder, fastened by a pearl brooch with a single huge central diamond she had cut and faceted herself, was a long sash of Macdonald of the Isles tartan, matching her father's kilt. Dorothée's veil was almost like a Spanish mantilla, densely figured white lace that hid her entire face and extended nearly to the floor behind her. Over it she wore a narrow tiara of pearls. Her bouquet was small white roses with satin ribbons.

Ian, stiff and solemn, offered his right arm to his daughter and Janet took her place on Dorothée's other side. The bridesmaids, walking single file, had already gone out, followed by Malama with the bridal leis of maile leaves. Then it was my turn. I ceased my mental eavesdropping, settled my top hat, and hurried into the late-afternoon sunshine.

Jack and his best man were already standing in front of the little table-altar with the priest, toppers doffed. An enormous bank of multihued blossoms was behind them, and beyond that loomed the profile of the White Mountains. I marched down the aisle, bearing my cushion before me. The aether brimmed with amiable vibrations, and the air was filled with music and the perfume of flowers. Hardly anyone looked at me; all eyes (except my own) were on the gorgeously dressed bride and her father and stepmother following behind me.

Surreptitiously, I searched the grounds for Hydra.

The guests all seemed to be kosher, as were the musicians in the orchestra. My seekersense roved to the adjacent marquee over on the left where the food and drink were going to be served after the ceremony. Most of the waitrons were standing quietly outside, watching the spectacle.

He was right in the midst of them, arms folded across his burly chest, a triumphant smile on his face.

I saw him for only an instant before I was forced to wheel about and take my place with the other attendants. As the priest spoke his first words of greeting and Ian Macdonald gave his daughter's arm to Jack, I farspoke Marc on the intimate mode, nearly incoherent with fear and desperation:

He'sHEREhe'sHEREthegoddambastardis **RIGHT HERE!**
Rogi you sillyoldfool—
No Marco listen it's Parnell HYDRA he's here one of the waiters overthere by the tents lookforyourself LOOK!
. . . I've scanned the lot NONEofthem have Hydra sig you're batshit if you fuck up Jack's wedding I'll wring your scrawny neck NOW PULL YOURSELF TOGETHER!!!
I'm not drunk I'm not imagining things he's THERE [image] the big guy right in middle of pack—
There's no one like that standing there. Every one of those waitrons is nonoperant&harmless.
Marco—
SHUT UP! Or I'll zap your brain to oatmeal I swear UncleRogi and work you like a puppet.
I'll ask Malama to help me.
No you won't t'es frappadingue espèce d'oeuf toi and you won't harass Jack&Dorothea either I'm putting a BLOCK into you *there* now for God's sake behave yourself!

He'd muted my farspeech with his paramount coercion. The block would dissolve all by itself eventually, but until it did I would be unable to converse telepathically with anyone except him.

Softer music was playing. Ian and Janet had withdrawn to their seats, along with Paul and Catherine. The attendants now also moved back, leaving Jack and Dorothée side by side on a prie-dieu as Brother Duval began the nuptial mass. Marc's coercion forced me over to the left side of the outdoor sanctuary, where there was a little kneeler for the server and a stand with carafes of water and red wine and a crystal bowl of unconsecrated communion wafers. I sank down, numb and resigned to my fate. With my back to the marquee I'd be spared the sight of Hydra waiting for me with that damned grin on his face.

Fortunately, there was nothing for me to do in the first part of the ceremony. The priest concluded the brief opening rites and began the Liturgy of the Word with a powerful quotation from the Song of Songs.

My Beloved lifts up his voice and says to me:
"Come then, my love, my lovely one, come.
For lo, the winter is past, the rains are over and gone,
the flowers are all in bloom,
and the voice of the turtledove is heard in our land.
My little bird, hiding in the clefts of the rock,
show me your face and let me hear your voice,
for your speech is sweet and your face is beautiful.
Your eyes behind your veil are soft,
your breasts are two fawns that feed among the lilies.
Till the day break and the shadows flee away
I will go unto the mountain of myrrh,
To the hill of frankincense."

[Thus says the Bride:] My Beloved is mine and I am his!
Awake, north wind; come, wind of the south,
Breathe over my garden and scatter its fragrance,
welcome my Beloved and let him taste its precious fruits.
My Beloved is radiant and bright,
he stands out among thousands.
His locks are black as the raven,
his eyes are like doves beside running waters,
his lips are red blossoms,
his body carved ivory adorned with sapphires.
Such is my Beloved, and such my friend.
And he says to me:

"Set me like a seal on your heart,
for love is strong as death
and jealousy relentless as hell.
The brilliance of love is a flash of fire,
a flame of the Lord himself:
this love that no flood can quench,
that no torrent can drown."

       This is the Word of the Lord.

We all stood for the familiar Gospel According to John:

       Jesus said to his disciples:

"As the Father has loved me, so I have loved you.
Remain in my love. If you keep my commandments

you will remain in my love, just as I have kept
my Father's commandments and remain in his love.

"I have told you this so that my own joy may be in you
and your joy complete. This is my commandment:
Love one another, as I have loved you.
No persons have a greater love
than those who lay down their lives for their friends."

Ça ira, ça ira! Saint Jean le Désincarné, Sainte Dorothée Masque-des-Diamants, priez pour nous.

The nuptial rite itself began. The witnessing attendants (including me) left their places and stood on either side of the bride and groom, who had joined hands. Malama draped the long strands of fragrant maile leaves around their necks. The priest made a little speech that began with "Dearly Beloved." Then Ti-Jean and Dorothée began to pronounce their vows.

Marc said to me: NOW. The rings dammit! To me!

I proffered the pillow. Marc handed one ring to his brother and gave the other to the bride. Faintly, I heard the couple speaking.

"Dorothea, my wife, take this ring as a sign of my love and fidelity . . ."

"Jon, my husband, take this ring as a sign of my love and fidelity . . ."

Both of them prayed together. "Father of Light, you brought us together, you helped our love grow, and at this moment you are with us in a special way. We ask that you stay by our side in the days to come. Protect us from harm and give us courage to face whatever difficulties lie ahead of us."

I no longer heard them. Stupefied with fear, I had barricaded myself inside my own cranium. Like a robot, I went through the proper motions as the witnesses once again withdrew and the priest celebrated the Liturgy of the Eucharist with my wooden assistance. In my battened-down state all my farsenses were useless. Several times I attempted to peer over my shoulder at the marquee to see if the monster was still there, but my neck muscles refused to obey me.

After the consecration the bride and groom recited the Lord's Prayer and the priest delivered the nuptial blessing, ending with, "Let us offer each other the sign of peace and love."

Jack lifted Dorothée's veil to kiss her.

I heard a soft gasp from the operants present, drowned almost instantly by the orchestra beginning "Jesu, Joy of Man's Desiring." The diamond mask was gone and the promise of the Song of Songs was fulfilled momentarily in the bride's face. Jack kissed Dorothée on the lips, then lowered her veil again. Brother Duval, a nonoperant who had not been privy to the transfiguration, came forward beaming. He embraced the couple, shook hands with me, and went down to the seats to extend the sign of peace to the wedding party.

Marc (or somebody) made certain that I performed the rest of my altar-boy duties with precision. I even assisted the priest in giving communion to all the guests—exotics included. Weird, isn't it, that bread is the one foodstuff that all entities in the Galactic Milieu can extract nourishment from?

All entities with bodies, that is.

The mass was nearly over. Brother Duval blessed the bride and groom and all the people, who responded with loud applause. I was expecting a recessional march from the orchestra (and so was almost everyone else), but something entirely different was on tap. Ian Macdonald seemed to materialize out of nowhere, splendid and barbaric in his Highland garb, playing a rousing bagpipe tune from the "Orkney Wedding and Sunrise" by Sir Peter Maxwell Davies. The big Caledonian led the recession with the priest close behind him, and then came Jack and Dorothée. She had thrown her veil back and the lower part of her face was a blaze of diamonds. Malama and I followed the newlyweds. I had my little satin pillow clutched in one hand and a glassy smile on my chops.

Marc said: That wasn't so bad was it Uncle Rogi? I've farscanned the entire hotel grounds and there's no Hydra here. I know its mental signature and I'm absolutely positive.

I said: Did you try scanning out your Cousin Parnell?

No. But—

Fact is you don't even *know* Parni's adult sig! Nor your sister Maddy's for that matter. Last time you touched minds with them they were little kids now they're both Grand Masters maybe even paramount in some of their faculties like you and they're SAFE even from Dorothée or Ti-Jean none of you can do an MP ident unless they combine in Hydra metaconcert and they're not stupid enough to do that anymore!

Marc said: Rogi you're acting like a nutcase there's *no danger.*

I laughed out loud.

We'd reached the big terrace behind the chairs, just outside the door of the Roosevelt Parlor. Guests were already leaving their seats and surging toward us. Lucille bustled about trying to organize a receiving line, an effort that wasn't helped at all by Ian continuing to play the bagpipes at a lusty fortissimo. The bride and groom were right in front of him, doing some kind of stately Scottish minuet while Janet and Kyle and Masha and Davy MacGregor and a bunch of others clapped in rhythm. Marc was nearly ten meters away from me, still encumbered with his recession partner, Ellen Gunn. The young maid of honor clutched his arm in a steely grip and gazed up at him in adoration. Having the Human Polity's most eligible bachelor in hand, even momentarily, she was not about to give him up meekly.

My one chance had come. I said to Malama, "I've got to have a quick word with Jack and Diamond."

In a trice I seized the dancing newlyweds by their free hands. While Lucille spluttered furiously and the pipes skirled, I waltzed the couple back inside the hotel and slammed and locked the double doors of the parlor. They laughed and thought it was some kind of prank until they saw my face. Then both of them sobered.

Dorothée said anxiously, "Uncle Rogi, what is it?"

I sagged into a handy chair. People were pounding on the doors, yoo-hooing and laughing and calling out arch witticisms.

"I wish there was another way to do this," I said, "but there isn't. Read my mind, for God's sake! As quick as you can. Then laissez le foutu bon temps rouler."

With that I cancelled my mindscreen and opened the relevant thoughts about Fury's identity to them.

The sense of liberation I felt after they'd drained me was overwhelming. Leaving the poor lovers stunned and incredulous (the bashing on the outer door and yelling was approaching riotous dimensions), I fled into the corridor of the hotel's lower level, intent on summoning an egg-limo and getting the hell out of there. They could send me my piece of wedding cake via UPS.

As luck would have it, I passed the open entry of the Cave Lounge on my way to the main staircase. Given my state of imminent mental collapse, it was a dim and appealing sanctuary and I said to myself: "Why the hell not?" I'd survived the wedding ordeal and successfully passed on the crucial intelligence to Ti-Jean and Dorothée. Who was now more deserving of an altered mood than moi?

I lurched inside, draped myself over a barstool, and took off my slightly mashed top hat. The place seemed deserted. "Hello?" I croaked. "Are you open?"

From somewhere in back a soothing voice replied, "I'll be right there, sir."

It was very dark in the bar and almost quiet. The bridal couple had evidently unlocked the door of the parlor and escaped, and the tumult had subsided. The orchestra was playing "In a Sentimental Mood." I heaved a great sigh, ran a shaky hand through my sweaty silver curls, and let my eyes close. Safe! I'd told the great secret and now the Dynasty would have to take responsibility for the fates of Denis and Anne. The matter was out of my hands.

"What will you have, sir?" Still bemused, I heard the disembodied voice of the barkeep.

"Wild Turkey. Double. Straight up."

"Right away."

I felt myself drifting away on a tide of overwhelming release. No more worry, no more fear. The sensation was almost as delightful as the terminal excorporeal excursion I'd experienced while drowning. Limp as a dishrag, I rested my eyes, breathed deeply, and enjoyed Duke Ellington's music.

I heard the faint sound of a glass being set down before me. "Was it a nice ceremony, sir?"

I cracked an eyelid wide enough to let me home in on the 101-proof elixir of life. "Peachy. Just peachy." Imbibo, ergo sum!

The bartender went away, his footsteps tapping on the stone flags of the floor. I heard him moving some chairs around over by the entrance to the lounge. Then the sound of music cut off abruptly and it got darker. He'd closed the doors. I straightened, finally back among the living, and turned toward him to ask for a refill.

Parnell Remillard was standing there.

"I'm in a lot of trouble because of you, Uncle Rogi," he said casually. "But before I get the hell out of here I figure I might as well even the score. Just for my own personal satisfaction."

I tried to yell and my vocal cords came unstrung. I tried to farspeak a warning to Marc, but the grim smile on the Hydra's face told me that my telepathic ability had also been coercively squelched.

He took a single step toward me, still disguised in his waitron's outfit. His eyes were dead. And so, I realized in a shocked instant, was he. Whatever had once been human in Adrien and Cheri's lost son had died long ago, surrendered to his almighty god and controller, Fury. Parnell's mind was self-aware, the vital lattices still animated his body, and his aura burned bloody crimson; but he was a dead man by some awful choice of his own. He had died even before he was born.

I slid off the barstool. He was less than three meters away, poised momentarily to enjoy my terror.

"No metacreative shit this time, old man," he said in a friendly fashion. "Too bad I can't drain your lifeforce properly, but I'll give you a few good lessons in pain before I break your neck with my bare hands. They'll find your drunken bod at the foot of the lobby stairs. A tragic accident! And so inconsiderate of the old lush to spoil the wedding reception."

I squeezed my eyes shut and tuned the Hydra out. There was only one thing that might save me now, and it would require every bit of concentration I could muster.

As a young man, I'd experimented with yogic exercises called pranic spirals. The inspiral was supposed to help concentrate the mind's creativity, and the outspiral . . . did the opposite. I'd only half believed in the archaic discipline then, as I'd only half believed in the entire concept of metapsychic power; but the outspiral thing had twice saved my bacon, surprising the hell out of me.

Perhaps there was a chance I could surprise Parni, too.

I am not normally operant in creativity. But every normal human being possesses a considerable latent store of the metafaculty, and I prayed I could extract enough energy from my mind and body to defend myself against the Hydra. With my eyes still tightly shut I lifted my arms and spread my feet, assuming the posture I'd called Leonardo's X-Man.

Parni let out a coarse guffaw. "You trying to surrender or something? Too late for that, asshole!"

Ignoring him, I summoned my body's creative power, bending the vital lattices pervading me, squeezing them like a sponge until the essential lifeforce began to pool and glow golden-hot in the region of my heart, my center. I urged that energy clot into motion, making it trace a flat spiral through the middle of my body—first downward, curving through my solar plexus, then back up to my trachea and the thymal remnant. I opened my eyes. A swelling radiance illuminated the dark room—not Parnell's bloody aura but a new clear amber light moving inside my thorax. I had become as transparent as glass, a kind of human lantern.

The Hydra froze in its tracks, dead eyes wide, unbelieving.

I made the golden comet of life-energy accelerate in its spiral path. It dove downward to my spleen, traversed the suprarenals, left my body for an instant, and then swung back through the thyroid gland in my throat.

"What the *fuck?*"

I barely heard Parnell's astonished shout. Every bit of my willpower was focused on keeping that shining ball of gold within its controlled outspiral. It illuminated the root chakra at my tailbone and grew, soaring up in an ever-expanding blaze to my thalamus, dazzling my eyes, racing faster and faster, touching the left elbow of my upraised arm, the left knee and the right, my right elbow, the crown of my head, left hand, left foot, right foot—

Yes, Hydra, it's for you. A part of my life.

As the golden ball of energy spiraled into my right hand I lowered my arm and pointed my finger straight at Parnell Remillard's distorted face. Every nerve in my body seemed to discharge in an orgasmic explosion that momentarily stunned me witless and left me blind.

[IMAGE: Transparent skull sunlit from within jaws wide before dissolving jewel bones in centripetal whorl crumble chiming golden corona devouring red flame-ball fading . . . fading to white ash.]

I felt myself tumbling down to the flagstones, meeting them so softly and painlessly that I might have been a scarecrow stuffed with feathers. My ears rang with a colossal reverberation. There was a peculiar wooden clatter. I fought to stay conscious, won the contest, hoisted myself up on hands and knees, opened my eyes.

The Hydra was gone. So was approximately half of a stout oaken tavern stool that had been close to him when my metacreative bolt hit. Where Parnell Remillard had stood was a scattering of gritty stuff that looked more like spilled white sand than ashes. The truncated stool lay in the middle of it. No steam, no smoke, no charring. No other evidence of any incinerating heat. Except for the ruined stool, the lounge was undamaged. I seemed to know instinctively that the gong-tone still echoing faintly in my ears had been heard by no one but me. The end of my nose, the tips of my fingers, my toes, and another cherished portion of my anatomy experienced an odd lingering warmth, but otherwise I felt righteous, fit, and chipper—better than I had in weeks.

I'd killed a man for the second time in my life, and I really hadn't the least notion how I'd managed it. I experienced not a shred of remorse. Both Hydra and Fury had been condemned to death in camera by the First Magnate of the Human Polity, and I had simply acted as his terrible swift sword.

On one of the tables lay a discarded durofilm printout of the *Boston Globe*. I knelt and carefully scraped Parni's mortal remains onto a sheet of the newspaper and folded it up. He measured less than three cups full, and some of that had to be oak ashes. Humming along with Duke Ellington, I took the small package into the handsomely appointed gentlemen's restroom adjacent to the lounge. Fortunately, there was no one there.

I dumped Parni into one of the old-fashioned water closets, made the sign of the cross just in case, and flushed. Then I spruced myself up, retrieved my top hat, and went off to get some champagne and dance at the wedding.

[10]

KAUAI, HAWAII, EARTH
18 JUNE 2078

Let me try *please* let me try! Look at them silly besotted young idiots they'll be so distracted at the Moment that their defenses will be down I'm SO close it would be easy—

<No! I cannot risk your life my darling you are the last until the New Ones are engendered I must keep you safe until then.>

—not a mental attack no something purely physical laserweapon or firearm longrange or obliterate with micronuke or even purée them with sonicdisruptor—

<Imbecile! The Great Enemy cannot be killed that way. I have not yet discovered *any* sure means to destroy him. It might require heliogenetic energies. And now that they are one he will share the defensive secrets with her.>

Despair. If I had only arrived in time to assist that fucking idiot Parni! If only YOU had helped him kill Rogi before the secret was passed on.

<I was not able to do so. I do not even know exactly how Parnell perished . . . except that the old man was somehow responsible. I underestimated Rogi badly. He is an enigma a buffoon a coward a bungler but possessed of formidable latent mental power. You must promise me that you will stay away from him my only darling my last sweet living Hydra.>

I will do whatever you command. But how will you avoid detection now? How will you avoid extinction?

<I have thought of a way. But it can be implemented only as a last resort. Do not concern yourself my dearest little one. I shall not die but triumph and you my Hydra will be with me ruling the Second Milieu.>

Beloved Fury I put my trust in you . . . Shall I return to Okanagon then and resume my work among the Rebel leadership there?

<Not yet. Marc must now be drawn actively into my plan for the New Ones. I laid the groundwork for it in his unconscious years ago

but the concept must now be reified. He will return to his home in the Pacific Northwest tomorrow. You must visit him again in a dream but while provoking him in the usual fashion you must also be sure he assimilates *and remembers* [image].>

!!! Fury is THIS the great plan?

<Yes. And not only for the New Ones. Marc thinks he is invulnerable because his mind and body are guarded from conventional forms of assault but in time he will be ours . . . one way or another.>

I want him. Not as another Hydra but as a slave.

<His place in our future is not clear to me. Use all your skill in coercive allurement and your wish may be fulfilled. Soon you'll leave Okanagon and begin new important work on the planet Astrakhan. Seduce Marc in his dreams and then wait for my instructions. Farewell now my beloved Hydra my sweet Madeleine.>

Goodbye dear Fury.

They timed it to perfection, reaching the Hawaiian Islands just as the sun touched the sea in the west, descending in a cloudless sky, hovering just above the light-painted water until the dazzling solar globe slipped down, down, into the horizon's coin-slot. And as the last bit of it vanished—

Green flash.

"Wonderful!" she exclaimed, bouncing up and down in her seat like a delighted child.

"Make a wish," Jack said.

Dorothea squeezed her eyes comically shut, then popped them open. Her mind smiled. "Do I have to tell?"

"Not if you want the wish to come true."

So she kept silent, knowing that he would never come into her mind without her explicit invitation. Her wish was *Let me love him more.* For in every nuptial pairing, one of the partners has a passion greater than that of the other, placing a heavier burden of love-sustenance on the one less engaged . . .

They were silent for a time, side by side in the cabin of the little starship, hands joined. He had changed into plain khaki pants and a loose puananala shirt for the honeymoon flight, and she wore denim shorts, sandals, and a blouse of soie-argentée with the sleeves rolled up.

"I'm glad we saw the green flash together," she said. "It's bound to be a good omen and we Scots are very keen on such things. I've heard about the sunset color-flash phenomenon, but on Caledonia the atmosphere is too full of moisture and volcanic dust for them to occur. When I came to Kauai before, I was too distracted by other things to think of watching for it."

Jack put his arms around her and held her tightly. "You'll never have to worry about Fury and the Hydra again. One of the things I'm going to teach you is the way to create an invincible shield—the kind that protects me from every type of physical and mental harm. It'll take a little while, but you'll find that I'm a pretty good kumu."

Shyly, she probed the vestibulum of his inviting mind to find the meaning of the Hawaiian word. It meant not only "teacher" but "lover." She lifted one of his hands to her masked face and he felt a kiss. "I'm glad this island will be our home on Earth," she said. "New Hampshire is beautiful, but it's a little too much like Callie: stern and rugged and indomitable. Not that I don't love my planet and expect you to love it, too. But it'll be good to have a gentler place to come to now and then, when things become especially difficult."

And they will, their minds conceded. As the pressures of our work distract us, as the Rebellion intensifies, and as the deadly paradox of Fury is forced toward a final resolution.

"Damn that Rogi," Jack said in a low voice. "Why did he have to pick our wedding day to spring his nasty surprise? . . . Did you notice that I redacted you to keep you from becoming too upset?"

She uttered a sly laugh. "No more than *you* noticed that I redacted you for the same reason! Poor old Uncle Rogi. He didn't set out deliberately to spoil things. It was really the first chance he had to talk to us privately." Her tone became somber. "Do you think his mind was recalling actual events in the case of the Hydra attacks?"

Jack hesitated. "He believed in the murderous fish just as he believed in Anne's story about Denis being Fury. There's no easy way that you and I can determine whether or not Rogi psychozapped Parnell in the hotel bar as he said he did, but I've told Paul about it and left it to him to investigate the matter or ignore it."

"And the Denis/Fury theory?"

"It could very well be true. I'm afraid we'll have to proceed as though it *is* true."

"Rogi could be suffering from delusions."

"No. He's a strange old duck, but he's far from delusional. He *does* possess extremely strong latent creativity, so it's perfectly plausible that he might have zorched Parnell. And there's something else about Rogi that you should know: He believes he has some sort of peculiar relationship with the Lylmik. Both Marc and Denis have commented on it in passing—disbelievingly, of course—but I think Rogi may be telling the truth. There's the Great Carbuncle, for instance. For years he's joked that the Lylmik gave it to him. Did you deepscan the thing when he lent it to you for good luck during the diatreme event?"

"Why, no . . ."

"I did. And right at the center of the red diamond sphere is a sizable molecular anomaly that could be an infinitesimal natural flaw—but is more likely an artifact. The Carbuncle is some kind of machine: maybe a subspace transmitter, maybe much more. No conventional Milieu science I know anything about could have produced it. But the Lylmik could have."

"Jack, this all seems incredible. I've rooted around in Rogi's mind myself, you know. He's a borderline neurotic, uncomfortable with his operancy. His habitual overindulgence in alcohol is certainly a symptom of personality imbalance—"

"Rogi's not a true alcoholic. He abuses the booze when it suits him and lets it alone when he's of a mind to. The man is an atavism, Diamond. An old-fangled type we don't see very often in the Galactic Age."

"He's a gormless auld whaup!" But her Scots insult was overlaid with grudging fondness. "And I don't see how we can commit ourselves to this Fury integration project solely on his unsupported mnemonic data. I really think we should wait until Anne comes out of the tank. Then you and I can deep-probe her in metaconcert. We'd not only corroborate or refute Rogi's picture of the situation, but we might even be able to determine whether or not Anne herself is Fury."

"It would mean waiting at least a year," Jack said, shaking his head.

"Could we complete the preliminaries for Denis's healing operation in less time? I've got to ream the Fury sig out of Rogi without damaging his dilapidated psyche, you've got to design a brand-new kind of CE brainboard and a self-contained power supply for the E18 helmet, and both of us have to work out a unique and untried metaconcert involving both coercion and redaction."

"We could do all that in less than six months. The only tricky part is roping the Dynasty into the project and training them to use the CE hats."

Her eyes, fixed on the fading sunset glow, were full of misgiving. "The procedure with Denis will be extremely dangerous. Some of the metaconcert participants could be killed unless we build special safeguards into the program."

"All the more reason for dealing with this thing as soon as possible. Before the other troubles the Milieu is facing come to a head—and are aggravated by Fury. Weren't you the one who told me that the monster might exploit the Rebels, or foment God knows what other kind of mischief?"

"Jack, we're proposing to endanger the lives of nine important Magnates of the Concilium—including the First Magnate himself—all on the say-so of a bibulous old gaffer!"

"I've known Rogi since I was in the womb. I still can't predict when he'll play the fuddleheaded eccentric and when he'll do something noble and unselfish, but I do know that he's dead honest. He loves me and I love him. Marc feels nearly the same way about Uncle Rogi as I do—and I suspect that Denis does, too."

"So do I," she admitted, turning away from him, "most of the time."

They sat side by side in silence. Dusk was falling with tropical suddenness and both Venus and Jupiter were visible as evening stars. It was going to be a clear, moonless night.

"We must go ahead on this, sweetheart," Jack said quietly.

"I suppose you're right." Her pseudovoice took on a resigned tone. "And Rogi's probably right, too. About all of it. Except . . . what do you think about his notion that Denis saving his life proves he's not Fury?"

"A complete non sequitur. Denis's legitimate core persona would have no knowledge of its homicidal alter ego."

She sighed. "That's what I thought, too." She paused. "An interesting thing, the theory that Uncle Rogi might be immune to Denis/Fury's coercion because he's Denis's foster father. The flip side—that Denis/Fury might be immune to coercive redaction by his own children—could pose a serious problem in any healing metaconcert design."

"We'll have to try to work around it. Your probe of Rogi might help us to understand and counter the parent-child coercive constraint. We might also find a useful clue studying the love that sometimes must condone pain in the beloved . . . The Dynasty *does* love Denis, thank God, and I doubt that that love would be diminished if they knew their father harbored the Fury persona within him."

"No. Their prime concern would be to heal him."

"The only one of Denis's children who would definitely be unsuited to the metaconcert is Anne. If she's Fury, her dyscrasic persona could conceivably emerge during the operation and kill all the rest of the concert participants through the CE helmets. But with luck, we'll have everything taken care of long before Anne gets out of regeneration."

"And if Denis turns out *not* to be Fury?" she said.

"We can redact Anne when her body has healed, while she's still in the tank and her mindpowers are below par."

"Denis or Anne . . ." Dorothea spoke the names softly. "Which one do you think is the monster?"

"I don't know," he admitted. "I've never tried to deep-probe either of them—unlike a certain nervy female with a titanic redactive faculty whom I could mention."

She was visibly troubled. "When I did my mind-sifting investigation of the Dynasty six years ago, my methods were pretty crude. And I didn't obtain irrefutable data, only a probability analysis based on temperament and overall metapsychic potential. Based upon my limited criteria, Marc was the one most likely to be Fury: a probability of 74 percent."

"Darling, that's utter codswallop!"

"He has the most alien mindset of the lot," she insisted, "and the strongest metapsychic complexus."

"Well, I won't disagree with that . . ."

"Anne was the second most plausible Fury at 68 percent. Then came Paul at 64. The others were all much lower in probability. I was able to obtain only incomplete data on Denis and Lucille. The only time that I really got into Denis's mind was at Marc's Halloween party, when Denis and I danced."

"And?" Jack prompted her.

"Of all the Remillards I examined, Denis was the most complex—and surprising. I couldn't begin to analyze him in the brief time I was inside. His mind was vast! Do you know he's a subfunctional paramount in every metafaculty?"

"I was afraid he might be."

"I'm sure he doesn't realize it himself. He seems to be a fully integrated personality—without any of the obvious quirks and defects of Paul, Anne, and Marc. But the intricacies of Denis's mind are so profound that they actually terrified me. When I tried to dig deeper to illuminate them—*pow!*"

"Denis found you out?"

She nodded. "He was very kind and forgiving of my intrusion . . . and very firm in booting me out and slamming the screen door behind me. So my analysis was inconclusive. I had no impression of a resident second persona, however."

"You haven't tried to probe any Remillards since then?"

"Marc knew what I'd been up to at the Halloween party, just as Denis did. Rogi also found out that I had probed his mind. I presume one of those three told the others about my prying. At any rate, Marc and the Dynasty all set up alarm barriers specifically designed to counter my brand of imperceptible redaction. I was never able to sneak inside any of them unawares again."

The little starship free-flew toward the southern Kauai shore, coming in only a few dozen meters above the calm, darkening water. Dorothea watched the approach with interest. She had never seen Jack's house. Their decision to marry had been sudden, a notable shock to their relatives and associates, arrived at back on Caledonia in the aftermath of the diatreme eruption.

He had stayed with her for several weeks after the blowout, not only helping to heal her injuries but also assisting her as she personally inspected the disaster sites, coordinated relief efforts, and supervised plans for rebuilding. Their relationship had been warm but not overintimate. The fervent moments in the deep-driller following her injury, when he had declared his love, were never mentioned.

Finally, when he told her that he was overdue in Orb, where the Unity Directorate was in session, she simply agreed to his going, apparently still distracted by her planet's troubles.

They had gone to Killiecrankie Starport together. And it was there, in the entryway of the departure concourse, that she seemed to realize at last that he was actually leaving her. An inexplicable panic seized her, an emotion totally alien to her normal grave competence.

"But what am I going to do without you?" her pseudovoice had cried. She was wearing the diamond-encrusted flying suit without its helmet. Her brown hair flew wild in the blustery wind and her eyes above the jeweled mask were suddenly wide, fearful, and unbelieving. "I need you. I don't know why. It's not the disaster or anything to do with my injuries. It's me. It's you. Oh, Jack, I don't understand what's happening to me—"

"I do. It happened to me a long time ago." He took her hands, standing close to her to shelter her slight figure from the rain that had begun to pelt down. Other travelers entering the building recognized the illustrious couple and with typical Scots reticence and courtesy gave them a wide berth.

"But what are we going to *do?*" she asked him desperately.

On that amazing day, he had laughed and told her.

The burdens of her duties as Dirigent had prevented her from visiting Earth before the wedding. Jack said that he was having his house on Kauai prepared for their honeymoon, and she had looked forward to being surprised . . .

"There's Lawai Kai, between those two headlands." He pointed ahead to a small bay. A beautiful crescent beach lay inside, bordered by coconut, pandanus, and umbrella-shaped tahinu trees. Further inland they flew slowly over a lush little river valley encompassing a string of picturesque lagoons and extensive groves of tall palms and flowering tropical trees.

"Two hundred years ago," Jack said, "Lawai Kai belonged to Queen Emma, the wife of Kamehameha IV. Later on, it became a private estate and a botanical preserve, until Hurricane Palapala devastated it early in the twenty-first century. The valley reverted to jungle after the population exodus to the colonial planets. The Remillard Family Trust bought the place in 2073 and deeded it to me when I decided I wanted to have my permanent Earth residence on Kauai. I built a house and started restoring the ornamental plantings and the Lawai River pools. You'll find that the place is quite modest, except for a rather snazzy lab in the basement that I use for special projects."

"Is that where you intend to work on the special CE equipment?"

"Yes. Here and in Orb. The prototype for the coercive-redactive brainboard will be easy enough to carry around with me, but I'll keep the modified CE helmets here. After we break the news to the Dynasty, this will be a convenient and secure place for the practice sessions."

He landed the ship on a small pad near one of the lagoons and they climbed out. Stars were beginning to spangle the deep blue sky. A mass of waterlilies floated in the black waters, including an enormous species with pads over a meter in diameter and fragrant flowers nearly half as wide. Along the banks were plantings of bamboo and wide-leaved shrubs with curiously shaped blooms.

"How lovely," she said. "Everything looks so natural—but I suppose you had to work very hard to make it that way."

"Well, yes. I have more spectacular things to show you in the gardens than this, but it's part of my big surprise. First let's go up to the house."

Their bags, sustained by his PK, floated along after them as they followed a stone walk. On either hand grew gorgeous heliconias, anthuriums, red ginger, bird-of-paradise plants, and proteas, mingled with many varieties of ferns. The house, framed in flowering poinciana trees, crepe myrtles, and silk oaks, at first seemed to be little more than a quaint old wooden plantation residence with a screened porch and a couple of rambling extra wings. It stood on rising ground overlooking the lagoons.

"Why, Jack!" she exclaimed as the realization struck her. "You're a romantic! I never would have suspected it."

"Few people do," he admitted, making a wry face. "And imagine *my* surprise when I finally figured out the awful truth."

The porch was full of potted orchid plants. "Those are mostly gifts from Denis," he said, keying the state-of-the-art thoughtlock and opening the front door. "Would you like to be carried over the threshold? I don't want to spoil my surprise, but you might care to postpone the tradition for just a bit."

"Hmm! All right."

The door closed behind them with a faint hiss, shutting out the perfume of the gardens, and she suddenly realized that the rustic appearance of Jack's house was a sham. The place was a stronghold, made not of wood, glass, and stone but of artfully textured cerametal, clear sheets of laserproof boron perboride, and indestructible high-molecular plass. The air was cool, filtered, and humidity-controlled. In the tiny front hallway was a wall control station for programming aerial and terrestrial alarm systems and a double-ply sigma shield.

"Good heavens," she murmured, "Is all this for Fury and Hydra?"

"Among others. I'd prefer to talk about it later . . . This is the living room." He stood aside politely so she could enter first.

She did, and stood speechless.

Table lamps and standards had switched on automatically, giving soft illumination. The place was about nine meters square, with tall windows along the side overlooking the back garden. Hung on the walls in museum-style shadow boxes were a precious tapa cloth from Tonga, a nineteenth-century Hawaiian quilt, and an intricate feather-work cloak of modern vintage. Carvings, masks, bowls, fiber-art constructions, and framed collections of shells from all over the South Pacific were wall-mounted, displayed in niches, or scattered about on tables or on the polished teakwood floor. There were scores of paintings, including one by Paul Gauguin, three by Madge Tennent, and a set of exquisite native bird studies by Marian Berger. In the place of honor above the fireplace, subtly lit, was a James Goldenberg portrait of Teresa Kaulana Kendall costumed as the Queen of the Night in *The Magic Flute.*

Several old Chinese rosewood cabinets had been modified to hold a stereo, a Tri-D, and impressive communications and reference equipment. There was also a tall case full of paged books. Near the room's center a crystal container that resembled a globular fishbowl rested on a lau-hala floor mat. The furnishings, of native woods, rattan, and quietly colored hand-screened fabric, looked brand new and rather homely, considering the awesome collection of artwork surrounding them.

"This room and the lab in the basement used to be all there was to the house," Jack said. "But I've made some additions. Kitchen and indoor dining area through there in the south wing."

She nodded. It went without saying that a naked brain had no need of the usual domestic amenities. They inspected the new rooms briefly. Both were small and cheerfully appointed. The kitchen was equipped with every conceivable laborsaving device, including an automatic food-delivery system. As they returned to the living room she pointed to the mysterious empty fishbowl.

"I hope that's not the bedroom."

"Not while you're in residence," he said, grinning. "I think we'll use it for a flower vase instead. The new sleeping chamber is across the hall. Let's see if it meets Madam Dirigent's requirements."

The room was large, with an adjoining lanai and bathroom. The walls were white-painted, adorned with a few pieces of artwork. In one corner hung a little old crucifix carved of koawood. At its foot was a bracket with a tiny red light. The bed was of fancifully wrought brass, covered with an intricate green-and-white patchwork quilt in the classic Hawaiian style that had been Malama's wedding present. Gauzy draperies hung at the tall jalousied windows in the French doors leading to the lanai. The other furniture was sparse: a lovely old mahogany chest of drawers and a framed mirror, a couple of ladder-back chairs, and a pair of pickled-pine nightstands with glass-shaded lamps.

"These things are only temporary," he said. "I wanted you to decorate this room in your own way. And the rest of the house as well, if you like."

"It's quite lovely the way it is. I'll just add a few things here and there. We can play turnabout when we fix up our house on Caledonia."

He hesitated. "Would you like to see the laboratory?"

"Tomorrow," she said gently. "It's been a very long day."

He opened the sliding doors to a walk-in closet. "If you don't mind, I've got us some special things to wear. And then my surprise!" He turned, his face composed but his mind radiating nervous hope. "The weather is going to be perfect. I thought we might spend our first night in a grass shack I've built out on Pu'u Kiloia, one of the promontories beside the bay. It's . . . very pretty there. The air is cool and you can hear surf beating on the rocks, and there are special flowers."

He shook out a folded piece of soft golden cloth imprinted with a scarlet pattern. "I know how you love to make clothing. I thought I'd try it, too. This is a pa'u, a kind of Hawaiian sarong, the traditional women's garment of the old islands. I made it from the bark of the wauke, the paper mulberry tree."

Her eyes lit up as she took it. "It's marvelous! As soft as silk. Thank you, Jack."

"I have a malo for myself, cut from the same length of kapa cloth." He gestured toward the bathroom door. "If you'd like to get ready, I'll see to a few things and then come back and take you to the shack."

She nodded.

He scanned her masked face anxiously. "It's all right, isn't it, Diamond? I mean . . . in traditional human sex, the male is the initiator. But if you'd rather—"

She placed two fingers against his lips to silence him and her mind suffused him with warm approval. "I'd like to be a traditional bride. I think your idea of spending our honeymoon night in a grass shack is incredibly romantic and I love you."

He smiled his relief. "I'll be right back."

She went into the bathroom, taking both the native garment and her wedding lei of maile. They had brought the garlands of sacred Hawaiian leaves with them from New Hampshire. She stripped off her traveling clothes, took a quick shower, and prepared her body. There were many jewel-bright flagons of tropical oils lined up on a tiled shelf, but she seemed irresistibly drawn to the delicately scented pikake jasmine. After the anointing, she wound the pa'u around herself in the way that Jack's mind had indicated and studied the effect in the full-length mirror.

My hair should be longer, she thought.

Well—why not? On this night above all they could defy the conventions of "correct" operant behavior and please themselves. She made the hair grow until it cascaded down nearly to her hips, brown and shining and slightly waved, concealing the sides of the diamond mask. For good measure, she augmented her small breasts just a bit and enhanced her eyelashes. Then she was ready.

When she went out into the bedroom Jack had not yet returned. She dimmed the night-lights almost to extinction and stood for a moment before the crucifix, where the tiny votive light cast eerie shadows on the carved face of Christ.

Help us, she prayed. Send a real angel to watch over Jack and me and bless our marriage. It's going to be so hard, Lord, being separated for so much of the time. Our minds can bridge interstellar space, but not our bodies. We're human and we need to be more than soul-mates. Both of us . . .

They would be together only when the Concilium was in session, or on the rare occasions when their duties otherwise permitted it. From this bright beginning they would learn more and more about each other while their devotion either grew stronger or faded: Jack the Bodiless and Diamond Mask, two grotesquely atypical human persons who had improbably found love.

They would have no children. Even though Jack's male organs were functional, not even his paramount creativity was capable of fashioning the intricate DNA strands that would make his sperm germinal. Nor could such DNA be derived from his brain cells for a quasi-clonal nuclear transfer through artificial means. Not without having their baby share the "bodiless" fate of its mutant father.

They had discussed this and other intimate matters during the voyage from Caledonia to Earth. Jack had also informed her then that he

lacked the self-redacting "immortality" gene complex that characterized other members of his famous family. His naked, self-sustaining
brain, favored as it was with near-godlike mental capabilities, was nevertheless genetically programmed to age and eventually die, just as a
normal human body would. No one held out much hope that genetic
engineering would provide a way to rejuvenate him, any more than it
could provide him with germ plasm. He was unique, a being less
evolved than the insubstantial Lylmik but more advanced than the
human race.

If he dies, so will I, she thought. Without him I have no real life. His
love is the stronger, but I need him more . . .

The bedroom door opened.

He came in, wearing the golden kapa loincloth and his own maile
garland. Draped over his left arm were dozens of fragile leis made of
pikake buds, while his right arm bore heavier chains of white dendro-
bium orchids. Before she could question him he hung the ivory jasmine
solemnly about her neck, lifting her hair to let the scented flowers
touch her skin.

"I wed thee again, my sweet Diamond," he said, "in the old way of
these islands."

Tears welled up in her eyes. She took the orchid leis and adorned
him. "And I wed thee, dear Jack. Forever."

At a gesture of his hand the doors leading to the lanai flew open. He
drew her outside into the open air, onto a patio surrounded by pale-
flowering shrubs. Overhead the sky was black, scattered with uncountable stars.

" 'You have ravished my heart, my sister, my bride. You have pierced
my soul with a single glance . . . My sister, my spouse is a garden enclosed, a fountain sealed up. The rarest of perfumes are hers, and the
well of living water.' "

She whispered, " 'Awake, north wind; come, wind of the south.
Breathe over my garden and scatter its fragrance, welcome my Beloved
and let him taste its precious fruits.' "

Hand in hand, they went up and out. The stars were so many that
they silvered the leaves of the trees, reflected in the lily-pools, and
caused the poinciana trees to cast faint shadows on the frosted grass.
The trees' blossoms, which would be flame-bright in sunlight, were the
color of polished jet under the stars. A wind from the sea rattled the

leaves of the halas and coco palms down along the beach. Waves, surging under the invisible moon's pull of the tide, hissed as they lapped the sand.

He drew her higher into the air, up the bluff on the western side of the bay, above a dark lava reef where the surf creamed, past ravines with liana-hung trees. She smelled a new fragrance borne on the rising wind, saw a great tangle of heavy stems scattered with huge white blossoms. The thicket covered the entire tip of the promontory except for an open space at its center, where the land was highest. A small thatched hut stood on the eminence within the living curtain wall.

They drifted down, their feet touching the ground near the seaward mass of tangled plants, which reached to nearly twice Jack's height. She saw now that the thick twining stems were studded with sharp spines. Spectacular white flowers, nearly as wide as dinner plates and intricate in form, seemed to open wider even as she looked at them.

Her mind posed a wordless question and Jack replied: Night-blooming cereus. They last only twelve hours.

And they have thorns, she said. To guard us and to remind us . . .

He lifted her into his arms and carried her toward the little hut. It stood on low stilts, with a crude door made of framed matting and wide window openings that could be closed by unrolling lengths of woven dried grass. A fat candle in a hurricane lantern burned on a bamboo table that held food and drink. The bed was a simple platform covered with a thick kapa pad. It had coverings of the same soft natural fabric.

They undressed each other slowly, carefully setting aside the leis. He kissed her forehead, her eyelids, and the adamant gems sealing off her lower face. She guided his hands to her tender breasts, reaching down to caress him, feeling him grow.

Their minds opened to each other and she saw the aching pleasure glowing within him, matching her own melting neural fires. His arousal was more than mere physical stimulation. The desire for her, fully nurtured by imagination, swelled into an urgent hunger. He lifted her onto the bed, speaking her name.

"Diamond. I want you. I want your dear self more than anything in the world." And the wanting is real my darling finally real just as we hoped. I'm human. I'm a man."

He began to kiss her entire body.

"You did find it—the part of you that was missing! Oh, Jack. Thank God. Thank God . . ."

As his lips and tongue savored the sweet anointing, her mind cried out in pure ecstasy. Then he was in her, breaking the maidenhead with a delicious brief stab of pain, filling her, moving slowly so they could first know the simple ignition of their human flesh. Then would come the special things they had planned for each other, the lovemaking fantasies that nonoperant couples could only dream about.

Tendrils of her long hair awakened the nerves in his skin. Her small form molded to his in perfect rhythm, breasts crushed against his pectorals. Their nipples had become erect conduits of vital energy. She let hers expand and seek his smaller mammillae like creatures with minds of their own, intent on some outrageous conjunction. Yes—the breast-to-breast merging was possible. It happened and they shouted together as the fresh source of sexual pleasure fed their passion.

He kissed the hollow of her throat, the lobes of her ears. "The mask," she said, her voice strangely muffled. "Darling, take it off. Now."

It never occurred to him to hesitate. With a single powerful movement he pulled the thing from the anchor-studs embedded in the bones of her face and flung it away. Its faceted gems caught the candlelight and sprayed the ceiling thatch with tiny rainbows.

She smiled.

"I knew it." His whisper was triumphant. "I knew it!"

"Only for you. Kiss me, my dearest love."

Your lips, my wife, drip wild honey. Honey and milk are beneath your tongue. I am come into my garden, my sister, my bride. I gather myrrh and balsam and drink sweet wine . . .

The third neural pathway formed as their mouths united. They fell away together into thundering incandescence, complete.

CONCORD, HUMAN POLITY CAPITAL, EARTH
19 JUNE 2078

The weather reporting unit in David Somerled MacGregor's apartment command post was a high-tech marvel. On request, it would provide an instant précis of meteorological conditions anywhere on Earth—or a forecast for the major population centers of every inhabited planet of the Galactic Milieu.

Ignoring it as usual, Davy drew the drapes, cracked open the balcony door, and ascertained that this particular Sunday morning in New Hampshire was muggy and already pushing 30 Celsius. Right. Forget the stroll along the Merrimack River bottoms. It was down to the promenade for the two of them.

He ordered up a durafilm copy of *The New York Times,* sans Sunday bumf, and scanned it briefly. Aye, there it was. Yesterday's wedding-of-the-century hadn't made the front page, but *his* turndown of Paul's offer to head the Unity Directorate had. The First Magnate was quoted as being "very disappointed." There was no mention of Jack as second choice.

Davy MacGregor chuckled. No political mileage for Paul when another Remillard acceded to high office. Just the reverse, actually!

He folded the news, tucked it under his arm, and gave a sharp whistle as he headed for the elevator door. When nothing happened, he called out in a raspy voice, "Hamish, come! Get a move on, ye lazy auld bugger!"

The measured clicking of toenails on the tiles of the back hallway and a throaty rumbling noise announced Torridon's Zodiac Hamiltonian, an aged Scottish terrier. The dog shot a challenging glance at his master.

Impatient? he inquired loftily.

"Damn right," snapped David Somerled MacGregor, Planetary Dirigent of Earth, "and wanting breakfast, you slugabed dinky brute. So get your bones into yon lift or I'll leave you behind." He stepped into the small private elevator that served his flat, the only special perk he had requested when he decided to move his private quarters out of Dirigent House and into Cynophile Tower.

Maybe I don't want to go out today, said Hamish, suddenly sitting down on the wrong side of the elevator door.

They glowered at each other through dark eyes hedged by wiry black brows. The faces of man and beast had nearly identical stubborn expressions. The old Scottie's muzzle was steel-gray and so were Davy's face-framing Dundreary side-whiskers, even though he had been twice rejuvenated. He was a rangy, slightly stooped figure dressed in jeans, a maroon mesh polo shirt, and loafers without socks.

"Too bloody bad." The Dirigent hit the DOWN pad. "You'll just have to miss your Sunday banger, then." The door began to slide shut.

Today is Sunday——?

The little black dog streaked into the elevator and settled at his master's heel.

Davy smiled with dour satisfaction. "Silly tyke, I thought that'd rouse ye."

Hamish gave that comment the disdain it deserved, and in a moment they stepped out onto the promenade floor of Cynophile Tower.

The residence was only two years old and it had proved extremely popular with dog-loving legislators and bureaucrats in the capital. Every apartment had a private exercise run, but most tenants and their animals preferred the social atmosphere and natural beauty of the extensive indoor promenade.

Joggers and strollers moved along designated pathways among the trees, accompanied by four-footed companions. The dogs could play fetch in the open meadows, amble through gardens where interesting things were buried, or romp in fountains and pools. Some areas featured realistic mechanical prey to entertain terriers and other hunting breeds, and there were real sheep that allowed themselves to be herded. If a dogfight or other inappropriate activity broke out, operant human monitors adept in creature coercion restored public decorum. Mobile sanitation modules, resembling large turtles, kept everything exquisitely clean. Après sport, and when other necessary business had been taken care of, canines and their humans could relax and take refreshment at one of the five informal eating establishments. The promenade also had doggie boutiques, grooming salons, and a well-appointed veterinary clinic.

Run? Hamish requested, tail wagging madly. *Look for vermin? Please?*

Davy said, "Off with you, laddie. I'm still tired out from dancing at the wedding yesterday. I'll order food for us and read the paper at Charlie's Place while you have your exercise."

The Scottie dashed off and Davy MacGregor headed for his favorite eatery. Its umbrella-shaded tables were ranged along the shore of a pleasant artificial lake. An ornamental fence kept recreating water dogs and the wily hybrid geese they chased—who happily chased the dogs in return—at bay. Some of the restaurant patrons nodded to the Dirigent, but the majority politely ignored the chief executive of Earth. He was about to sit down when someone called out to him on his intimate far-speech mode:

Care to join me Davy?

He saw Cordelia Warshaw (née Warszawska) smiling at him from a table half-screened by pots of blooming fuchsias. Her comical Polish Lowland sheepdog, Ignacy, caught sight of him and said: *FriendofMaster hello come come!*

Davy ambled over and greeted the pair of them.

"It's been a while, Cordelia. You look smashing. And how's the PON?"

"Full of the devil as usual. But he makes me laugh, so he earns his keep."

She was a tiny woman, nearly as old as Davy himself but much more extensively rejuvenated and cosmetically enhanced. Her ash-blonde hair was styled in a modish pageboy cut and she wore a short summer walking suit of iris lumasheen with a white silk singlet. White patent-leather cothurni called attention to her excellent legs. Cordelia Warshaw was no longer the Intendant General of Earth. Her open avowal of the Rebel cause had cost her the office in the election of 2076, but she was still an influential Intendant Associate for Europe, a Magnate of the Concilium, and a Visiting Fellow in Cultural Anthropology at Oxford's Jesus College. She and Davy had been platonic friends for over fifty years.

Her medium-sized shaggy dog grinned as the two humans exchanged casual chitchat. The Polski Owczarek Nizinny had twinkling dark eyes that peered through a thick fringe of biscuit-colored hair. His mind said to Davy:

Sit sit! Eat ***{FRESH STRAWBERRY BLINTZES} *** like Master!

"Well . . ." The Dirigent hesitated. A male waitron appeared with a second place setting and a menu.

"Have your breakfast with me," Cordelia invited, indicating her empty plate. "The blintzes are very good today. I'm going to have some more because a certain greedy rascal ate most of mine."

Save you from [image of bloated fat Cordelia], said the PON.

Ty chujku, odpierdol sie! she scolded. "Go find Hamish. Go play!"

Flashing another black-lipped smile, the sheepdog said, *Friend is nice male. You have [explicit image] fun.* Tail awave, he trotted off.

Davy burst out laughing at the outraged expression on Cordelia's face. He sat down and ordered the blintzes, a pot of Spiderleg tea, and a dish of Canine Crunchies No. 3 with a grilled frankfurter garniture for Hamish.

"I knew you'd moved into the Tower," Davy said. "I'm surprised we haven't run into each other here before. But I suppose you were in England while the Assembly was in recess."

"Yes—helping to cook up a fresh batch of ammunition for the anti-Unity push at the next Concilium session with Valery Gawrys and the rest of the Oxbridge outlaw gang." Her tone was satirical but the mental overlay of her words was deadly serious, with an invitation to discuss the matter further.

The tea arrived, saving Davy from having to respond immediately. When the brew was satisfactory he added milk and sugar, sampled it, and sat back with a sigh. "So our meeting here this morning wasn't just a happy coincidence."

"No," she admitted. Her eyes flicked to the newspaper he had laid on the table. "It's a direct consequent of that."

Davy's smile became glacial. "My turning down Paul's invitation to head the Unity Directorate doesn't mean I've gone over to your side, Cordie."

She cocked her head quizzically. "No? The *Times* article reported you'd declined because of philosophical reasons. And I know you, Davy MacGregor! You've been half a Rebel for years—and not just because of Milieu pussyfooting over Margaret's murder. You're not blinded by the glories of the Galactic Milieu like Paul Remillard and his kurewskie Dynasty."

"No, I'm just an Earthman, plain and simple, and I intend to stay that way." He stirred the tea and stared into it, scowling. "I'm afraid of Unity's possible effect on the Mind of Humanity, and I'd be overjoyed to see us out of the Milieu . . . but I'm damned if I'd ever resort to force in order to resolve the issue."

The waitron came up with their food and they were silent until he had gone away. Cordelia delicately cut up one of the cheese-stuffed rolled pancakes and ladled strawberry sauce over it.

"Whether you're with us or not," she said carefully, "we'd like you to reconsider your refusal of the First Magnate's offer."

What? Woman are you bloody daft?

His vehement thought-blast didn't faze her. While she consumed the blintz with evident relish her mind said:

As head of the Panpolity Directorate you would be privy to every aspect of the Unity controversy. You'd know the antiRebel strategy of the exotics and the human loyalists the planetary troublespots that most concern them the schemes they plan to implement as our population approaches its coadunate number. In time you'd certainly uncover the truth about the Unification process itself.

Cordie you're incredible you want me to be a *REBEL SPY* inside the most sensitive Concilium body simultaneously promoting Unity and trying to undermine it—

No. I want you to be the only member of the Directorate who is still objective. Who still puts the needs of the human race ahead of the needs of the Milieu. Whether or not you chose to *share* the data you uncover is entirely a matter for your own conscience.

"Hah!" said Davy MacGregor out loud. "You're so confident, aren't you, which way I'll lean."

"Your food's getting cold. Eat." Of course I'm confident, because I know where your sympathies lie. The reason you're not wholeheartedly with us now is because you still have honest doubts about the validity of the Unity concept. You're also afraid that we Rebels wouldn't scruple at destroying the Milieu if it tried to impose Unity on us by fiat or if it threatened humanity with severe sanctions for rejecting Unification.

Yes dammit *yes!*

"Then reconsider the appointment," she said. "Dithering and brooding won't help the Human Polity decide what's best for its future." But your objective scrutiny inside the Panpolity Directorate might.

How the hell can I head the Directorate pretend to be in favor of Unity when I'm *not?* Would you have me violate my moral principles?

Paul Remillard doesn't expect you to be a yes-man.

No—but he was counting on me to steamroller the opposition taking the place of his sainted Sister Anne in the skirmishes HE thought I'd have my doubts resolved in favor of Unity YOU say I should retain my objectivity but you expect me to be a pipeline of intelligence to the Rebel cabal— "And my answer to you both is no. No!"

He pushed away from the table, rose, and signaled the waitron with his credit card. "I can't stay after all. Give me a doggie bag for the tyke's crunchies."

"Certainly, Dirigent." The man went off to fetch one.

Hamish came trotting up in response to a farspoken command and sat at Davy's heel.

Cordelia regarded her old friend calmly. "Will you report this conversation to the First Magnate?"

Davy leaned down, hands on the tabletop, and spoke softly. "To hell with the First Magnate! . . . No, I've no intention of discussing your ploy with Paul. Let him do his own spying. But here's a wee bit of sensitive data to share with your fellow connivers: The Fury monster's back, and so is its stooge, Hydra. And I'm going to see both of them polished off no matter what Remillards get caught in the crossfire— Rebels or loyalists. You have my word on it."

Cordelia said nothing.

The waitron came up with the bag, and Davy dumped Hamish's meal into it. "As for Unity," he said, "I'm keeping my mind open. I'll neither oppose it nor promote it. Tell your fewkin' Oxbridge associates they'll get no joy from me. But neither will Paul Remillard."

The Dirigent of Earth, Scottish terrier at heel, strode off in the direction of the elevators. After a few moments a hairy, broadly smiling head rose up across the table from Cordelia Warshaw. She gave a rueful laugh.

"So, Ignacy! Have you come to console your master for her abject failure as a diplomatist?"

The Polski Owczarek Nizinny said: *Blintzes for me?*

"I might have known."

Cordelia Warshaw put Davy MacGregor's plate on the ground. Then, after a moment, she also set down her own.

At a table not far away, the four Lylmik Supervisors rose, summoned their dogs, and set off down a tanbark track toward the shady Bone

Garden, where they would await the arrival of Atoning Unifex. They had done as their superior had instructed, observing the small drama of Cordelia and Davy from a safe distance, and now they mused over its significance.

"The event, although interesting, was clearly neither cuspate nor nodal," said Homologous Trend.

"One is mystified," said Noetic Concordance, who walked beside him, "at Unifex's insistence that we come here to observe it in person. It has been aeons since It required us to physically excurse from Concilium Orb."

"Even more bewildering," said Eupathic Impulse, "was Its request that we wear these awkward human bodies once again rather than simply watching the proceedings invisibly. One might have thought that the usefulness of a tangible disguise had expired some time ago."

"One does not lightly question the dictates of Atoning Unifex," Asymptotic Essence remarked rather prissily. Her straight black hair was cut in a fringe above her brows and done up in a chignon held with carved ivorywood sticks. She wore a striking cheongsam of sky blue.

"One must demur," said Noetic Concordance reluctantly, "for intuition seems to adumbrate that challenge is not only permissible in the current situation but perhaps even required."

The other three entities pondered this uncomfortable notion in silence.

"It is to be hoped that there will be an eventual clarification," Concordance said.

"And that it comes sometime before Omega," Impulse muttered.

The forms that temporarily housed the negligible Lylmik material substance represented four different human races. Except for their unusual eyes, which had the appearance of backlit aquamarines, and their mindscreens, which were wondrously opaque, the Supervisors seemed to be youngish men and women dressed (except for the gorgeous Asymptotic Essence) in unobtrusive casual clothing. Arriving at the Bone Garden, they sat down on wooden benches beneath a chestnut tree while their dogs explored the little glade.

"Whatever else may be going on, one is simultaneously gratified and made apprehensive by Davy MacGregor's reaffirmation," Homologous Trend remarked with ponderous gravity. He was incarnate as a hawk-nosed, physically impressive Native American. His dog, a standard Xoloitzcuintli, hairless and attractively spotted, began digging zealously beneath a bridal-wreath bush.

Trend's fellow male, Eupathic Impulse, repressed a snort of impatience. "Would one care to explain one's emotional dichotomy?"

"MacGregor's refusal to cooperate with the Rebels is praiseworthy," Trend said, "while his persistent doubts about the future of the Human Polity within the Milieu provoke serious worry. How have we failed in our explication of the Unity prospect, that an intelligent being such as MacGregor cannot see its overarching merits?"

"Humans are funny that way," said Impulse. He wore a pink-skinned, blue-eyed body with dishwater-brown hair. His canine companion was a Kavkazskya Ovcharka, a massive fawn-colored guard dog of the Caucasian Mountains that set about marking every tree trunk in the vicinity. "In their present immature stage of development many humans place an inordinate value upon rugged individuality and absolute mental autonomy. Unfortunately for us, this recalcitrant segment of the human population includes some of their finest minds."

Noetic Concordance, the gentle poet, said, "It's a pity that Unity, like love, cannot be casually sampled, analyzed, or demonstrated."

"Its manifest benefits can be perceived easily enough in the other coadunate races," Asymptotic Essence pointed out with a touch of asperity, "provided one has mental eyes to see with!" She snapped her enameled fingers and delivered a reproving coercive tap to her Chinese Shar-Pei puppy, which was poised to pounce upon the tail of Noetic Concordance's dignified Azawakh gazehound.

The copper features of Homologous Trend clouded with melancholy. "One must ask whether humanity is merely obtuse when it fails to appreciate Unity's exemplars, or whether the race is perhaps fundamentally incompatible with the ultimate form of socialization."

"They're bloodyminded, for sure," said Eupathic Impulse.

"Only the dear little Poltroyans are deemed fully congenial entities by humankind," Concordance noted. Her tall African body, elegant even in simple white Levi's and a red bandanna-print shirt, was complimented by the regal hound that now reposed beside her, resting its narrow head on her knee. "Humans think of our earnest Simbiari friends as cold, cloddish, and lacking in humor—"

"It's hard to appreciate your ex-proctors," Impulse put in, "especially when they're prone to drip green on the carpets and furniture."

"Humans do appreciate Gi aesthetics," Concordance continued. "But they tend to deplore the giddiness and flamboyant sexuality of that race. And the estimable Krondaku, for all their mental brilliance, are viewed by humanity as alien and fearsome merely because their invertebrate bodies and tentacular appendages fail to meet human standards of beauty. As for ourselves . . ." She gave a wry, expressive shrug, and the other entities laughed appreciatively.

"Humans are paradoxical," Eupathic Impulse insisted, "and when one resides in a human body, reality takes on unfamiliar and even disturbing nuances. Haven't you felt it, colleagues?"

"Certainly not!" Asymptotic Essence retorted, with suspicious vehemence. The skirt of her cheongsam was slit nearly to the thigh and she had arranged her slender legs in a graceful pose. Unfortunately, the effect was marred by her puppy's insistence upon chewing on her shoes. The Shar-Pei, a droll little creature with loose, folded skin that seemed much too large for its body, had an obstinate nature. Essence was having a hard time controlling it without coercing it to the point of stupefaction.

"Davy MacGregor has proved to be an exceptional Earth Dirigent," said Homologous Trend, returning to the original matter under discussion. "He is possessed of both wisdom and empathy—although he often hides the latter beneath a curmudgeonly façade. One must respect his motive for declining the position, but one still feels he would have made an outstanding head of the Panpolity Directorate for Unity. One is quite certain that in time, he would have modified his present skeptical views and become a doughty apologist for the Unification of the Human Mind."

"MacGregor would certainly have kept the Directorate on its toes," Asymptotic Essence said. She firmly bespoke her Shar-Pei to divert it from an overenthusiastic inspection of another dog's droppings. "He is even more incisive than Anne Remillard. One might have hoped he would lead the nonhuman members of the Directorate to do a better job defining the Unity concept, thus encouraging human acceptance."

Noetic Concordance was surprised. "Does not one feel that Jon Remillard will also pursue this goal when he heads the Directorate?"

"One suspects," said Essence, "that Jack the Bodiless already partakes of the Unified state—at least in spirit—and thus he fails to understand why humans of a less exalted mindset would find the prospect unappealing." She uttered a small sound of disgust and firmly coerced her wrinkle-skinned puppy to abandon its fascinating find.

"Where are the mobile sanitation modules when one needs them?" she complained.

"I'll get a poop-robo right away," Impulse said. "Don't be distressed, colleague." There was a soundless flash of light. One of the turtle-shaped MSMs materialized in the glade and set about its business.

Asymptotic Essence gave a fastidious sigh. "These canine creatures are appealing companions, but one might wish they were not quite so . . . animalistic."

Homologous Trend chuckled. "They are animals, after all." His hairless Xoloitzcuintli had dug up a bone and proudly brought the treasure to be admired. "Good boy," said the Lylmik absentmindedly. The Mexican dog looked slightly disappointed, but settled down at its master's feet and began chewing.

The Shar-Pei puppy suddenly became tired and whimpered to be taken up by Asymptotic Essence. "Poor baby," she said, lifting it into her silken lap, where it promptly fell asleep. Only Impulse's huge Caucasian Mountain dog continued to pace about the glade restlessly, sniffing every rock and shrub.

Then suddenly it stiffened and gave a soft growl.

A very tall man with curling white hair and a short beard, wearing Cazal sunglasses and dressed in a crisp pale tan seersucker suit, came strolling into the Bone Garden. He was accompanied by a foxy-looking reddish dog.

"High thoughts, colleagues!" said Atoning Unifex.

The other Lylmik Supervisors greeted the Overlord solemnly. Impulse hastily compelled his animal to stop growling and lie down.

"I hope you've found the dogs entertaining," Unifex said, seating himself. "Mine is a New Guinea Singer. The breed is alleged to be very close to the canine foundation stock. I call him Caruso. He doesn't bark. His voice is a kind of yodel."

The little animal had its eye on the much larger Caucasian dog. Its body stiffened and the hairs along its spine rose ominously.

Unifex laughed. "Keep your beast under coercion, Impulse. Caruso gets feisty if he thinks I'm likely to be attacked. We've bonded, you see."

"Fascinating," said Impulse. He patted his own dog and it subsided after giving his hand a quick lick.

"Caruso really does love you, Unifex." Noetic Concordance was awestruck after a brief examination of the New Guinea canine's mind. "That's amazing! I must confess I have detected the beginning of a similar devotion to me in my own Azawakh hound. I thought at first I was imagining things . . ."

"What's her name?" Unifex inquired.

"Name?" Concordance was taken aback. "But that would imply personhood."

"Yes." The Overlord waited.

"I—I shall call her Samira," said the poet suddenly, stroking the dog's silken ears and smiling.

The other three Supervisors gasped at her daring.

"Don't be silly," Unifex reproved them. "Even though these animals aren't completely sapient, they're certainly persons. They want your approval and love. Give it to them. It's good practice."

"For what?" Eupathic Impulse asked apprehensively. But the Overlord did not reply.

Asymptotic Essence cradled her sleeping puppy. "One admits to being astonished at the warm emotions provoked by these creatures. This immature specimen is a continuing nuisance—and yet one cannot help but feel tenderness when it surrenders itself, completely trusting. One wonders if a human maternal parent might experience a similar satisfaction caring for her own dependent, pestiferous young."

"Oh, a human mother would feel even happier," Unifex assured her. "Even human fathers get all mushy about sleeping babies."

"Would you like a summary of the meeting between Davy Mac-Gregor and Cordelia Warshaw?" Eupathic Impulse inquired. When the Overlord nodded he presented the data. "We had been discussing Mac-Gregor as an example of a highly intelligent entity who still has serious reservations about Unity with the Galactic Mind."

"The unspoken question," said Homologous Trend, "involves Mac-Gregor's suitability to continue as Dirigent of Earth during the perilous future, given his demonstrated lack of wholehearted loyalty."

"Oh, he must certainly remain in office," Unifex declared. "Davy's the only man for the job." He bent down to scratch the small triangular ears of his dog. Caruso appeared to smile adoringly. He wagged his bushy, white-tipped tail and uttered an odd musical cry.

Noetic Concordance said, "Now that the first evidence of their mental coadunation has been detected by the humans themselves, the Unity controversy is bound to escalate. The probability lattices show a truly dreadful prognosis unless the Quincunx undertakes stringent preventative measures."

"Yes," Unifex said. "Awful things will happen, because we will not intervene to prevent them." He took off his sunglasses, folded them, and tucked them into an inside pocket.

The four Supervisors looked into his cavernous gray eyes, aghast. After a moment of silence, Trend spoke.

"Will the Milieu survive?"

"One may hope so. The impending disaster is as inevitable as it is necessary."

"Surely not!" cried the scandalized Asymptotic Essence. "By the Prime Entelechy, one demands that you clarify that statement!"

But Unifex only said, "We have such high hopes for humanity. The Lylmik race is moribund, and humans are the only ones fit to succeed us as guides and guardians of galactic mental evolution."

"We have accepted this asseveration of yours with reluctance, even though the truth of it is arguable." Eupathic Impulse said. "However, the necessity for a hostile confrontation between humanity and the Coadunate Milieu is a hell of a lot tougher to swallow."

Unifex inclined his head in appreciation of the Supervisor's use of idiom. "One knows for a certainty that humanity will not soon accept Unification as an evolutionary inevitability, as the other races did. Left to itself, the Human Mind would not fully coadunate until some twelve galactic millenaries had gone by—at which time we Lylmik would have already passed into extinction, with a concomitant decay of the Milieu social structure and a distinct possibility of spontaneous dissolution. To prevent this fatal calamity, it is necessary that we allow the predicted events to take place, introducing the Percruciate Progressive Principle into the probability equation." [Data.]

"Ah!" said the four Supervisors.

The Overlord's voice was quiet, almost weary. "Again and again in human history, this principle has paradoxically accelerated and enhanced evolution—and not only physical advancement but also mental and moral growth. There is even an apposite human proverb: 'Things will get a hell of a lot worse before they get better.'"

"Is one certain," Essence asked, "that the conflict will have a felicitous outcome?"

"No," Unifex admitted. "The past, present, and future *are,* but my own prolepsis—or what I might call my prolepsis—is imperfect, just as my atonement is still imperfect. What I do know is that this confrontation is fast approaching, and we of the Supervisory Body must stand aloof from it, giving no warning, vouchsafing no aid to either side. We may only coerce the All in all, praying for a happy dénouement."

"And if it is not forthcoming?" Noetic Concordance inquired.

"Then, given your gracious consent, we fall back on Plan B." The Overlord smiled his mysterious smile. "Tell me: How are you getting along in your bodies?"

"Fairly well," said Homologous Trend, not bothering to conceal his perplexity.

"Good. Do you think you could wear them from now until the next Plenary Concilium Session begins? Could you live quietly here on Earth in this place with your canine companions?"

"For *thirty-two days?*" Impulse murmured in horror.

"That'll do for starters," Unifex said.

Noetic Concordance kept her eyes downcast. Of all the Supervisors, only the poet had begun to suspect what Unifex was up to. "Does one truly believe that mere residence of the psyche in a corporeal envelope has the potential to reinstate atavistic behavioral patterns?"

"Yes. And the pets will help, too."

"What are you talking about?" Eupathic Impulse demanded.

"Everything in your bodies works," Unifex said to Concordance. "I'm a much better creator than Jack. You're under no compulsion, of course, and one doesn't expect instantaneous success. Still, if you don't find incarnation totally repugnant, it's worth trying. As I said, it might provide the first step toward a backup if the worst should happen during the Metapsychic Rebellion."

Comprehension was also dawning in Asymptotic Essence's almond eyes. She held her puppy close. "But is such a thing possible?"

"Ensoulment is ensoulment," Unifex observed airily. "Trend and Concordance did manage it once before, way back in Fa-Time."

"Yes," the two of them agreed. But they still exuded doubt and incredulity.

"I'll be going now," Unifex said. "There are things I must see to."

He got up from the bench. Caruso came to heel and the two of them disappeared among the trees.

"Will anyone condescend to tell one what's going on?" Eupathic Impulse demanded with some heat.

Noetic Concordance explained.

Impulse stared at her openmouthed, his expression of consternation only partially mirroring a mental turmoil so profound that it perturbed the very mental lattices in the immediate vicinity. The aetheric warpage was beyond human perception, but suddenly all of the canines in the promenade began to howl, including those temporarily assigned to the four Lylmik.

Concordance damped the inharmonious vibrations. The dogs fell silent.

Perspiration had broken out on Impulse's pale forehead. "It's unseemly," he muttered. "Grossly indecorous! This time, Unifex has gone too far. Surely you can see that, colleagues! Surely . . ."

Asymptotic Essence smiled at him enigmatically. The other two Lylmik studied the grassy ground.

After a time Homologous Trend looked up at Noetic Concordance. "Unifex did say that everything works."

"Yes," she said. Her startling eyes shone in her ebony face like inset jewels.

"One could take the word of Unifex," Trend went on, "since It has never evinced demonstrably false data. On the other hand, it would be prudent to check matters out personally."

"I agree," said Concordance. The two of them arose, nodded to their colleagues, and strolled off with their dogs.

"This is madness." Eupathic Impulse's voice was a husky whisper. His breathing had accelerated and the human heart within his rib cage thudded at an elevated tempo. Asymptotic Essence put her puppy down onto the ground and stared at her colleague wordlessly.

She was really very beautiful—according to limited human criteria, of course. The curve of her cheek was harmonious and her lips were moist and soft. Her breasts swelled the blue silk dress in piquant contrast to her narrow waist. The slit skirt hinted at delicious hidden attributes that Impulse recalled from the first occasion when they had donned their bodies, before Unifex had given them clothes . . .

"Madness," he said, less confidently. His human body, which had embarrassed him once before, showed fresh signs of willfulness.

"That's the spirit," said Asymptotic Essence. She pulled him to his feet and threw her arms around him. "One has observed certain precoital maneuvers among humans that might prove pleasurable. Shall we experiment?"

"I—I shall submit," Impulse said faintly. "Submit to the Percruciate Progressive Principle. Under protest."

Essence's laughter bubbled up as she molded herself against him and drew his face down to hers. "Whatever it takes," she said, and kissed him, probing with her tongue.

Again, all the dogs began to bark.

[12]

FROM THE MEMOIRS OF
ROGATIEN REMILLARD

I didn't quite get off scot-free in my eradication of the Hydra.

Around noon on the day after the wedding, Marc shook me awake in our suite at the White Mountain Resort Hotel and ordered me to get dressed. I had a hangover clanging like the bells of hell, but I was damned if I'd ask Marc to cure it and he didn't volunteer. Creeping out into the sitting room in search of caffeine and stronger analgesics, I discovered that we had company: The fuzz had arrived in the person of Guy "Boom-Boom" Laroche, who was at that time a Chief Inspector for the Galactic Magistratum, based in Concord. Official business had kept Laroche from attending the wedding ceremony. I was too wretched and woolly-headed to wonder why he had shown up now.

The two bruisers sat at the table eating lunch, neither one offering a femtoerg of sympathy for a poor suffering old man. Funny thing, though, the looks they gave me were neither condescending nor pitying. In fact, both their minds leaked intimations of puzzlement, touched with something very close to awe.

In my misery, I didn't give a hoot, nor did I bother to speak. The coffee on the sideboard was hot and strong. I chugalugged a liter of it black, which soothed my pounding head not a whit. Then I called up a double Bloody Maria with extra Tabasco sauce from the suite's bar and sat myself down at the table with extreme care, so that my throbbing skull would not accidentally part company with the first cervical vertebra. While the healing potion was scorching its way toward my stomach, I caught sight of Exhibit A.

A mutilated oak tavern stool.

Oops!

Instant recall.

"Yes," said Marc with ominous gravity. "And Boom-Boom recovered white ash from the crevices in the hotel barroom floor. An off-the-record forensic analysis confirms that the stuff is human-body residue, consonant with incineration at a couple of thousand degrees Celsius."

"But how did you manage it, Uncle Rogi?" Laroche asked softly. He had on civilian clothes, and his sincere, ugly-cute kisser with the soulful eyes made you want to trust him with your life. He was a top-notch interrogator and the scourge of upper-echelon operant crooks. "You zapped your victim in a rather special way. No scorch marks anywhere in the room, no gaseous or particulate traces in the furnishings. Just the ashes and the barstool neatly cut in half. That means you must have dispersed the energy of combustion and the residual chemical odds and ends into the dynamic-field lattices via a sexternial aperture. We never suspected you of such metacreative finesse."

"I didn't do a friggin' thing." I feebly clawed apart a sourdough roll and slapped butter on it. It was the only food on the table I could contemplate without ralphing.

"Don't lie," Marc said evenly. "You were so pleased with yourself last night and so smashed on champagne that you would have babbled about killing the Hydra to the entire wedding reception if I hadn't reinstalled the mind-block. You told me, and you told Jack and Dorothea, and they told Paul, and Paul asked Boom-Boom to get the truth of the matter. Now tell us exactly what happened."

"Why don't you just use your paramount redaction and screw it out of me?" I sniveled.

"I would if I could," Marc assured me. "But there's some kind of new barrier in place that I'm unable to penetrate. You're just chock-full of surprises this morning, Uncle Rogi."

Well, well! Had the Hydra pulled a fast one? Or was there some other reason Marc was suddenly unable to pry open my conk? . . . Ooo! Thinking was too painful.

Boom-Boom said, "Will you give *me* permission to examine your mind?"

Just in time, I stopped myself from laughing in his face. In my present condition, it might have been fatal. I told him, "Go ahead and arrest me, tu gros connard, toi! Then you'll have a legal right to ream my mind as much as you please."

The two of them just stared at me.

"Huh. I thought so! You've got no probable cause except my drunken boasting. No body, no weapon, no nothing."

Boom-Boom showed me one of his dazzling, understanding smiles.

His teeth were enormous, and white as sugar cubes. "Now, Uncle Rogi, be sensible. You've already confessed the killing to Marc, Jack, and Dorothea."

"You know I was sozzled last night. The confession's useless. Now that I'm sober, I recant." I drank some more of the Bloody Maria. "You can't prove the ashes are from Parnell Remillard, either, can you!"

"True," the galactic cop admitted. "And the zapped chair—c'est une situation bizarre à l'extrême, but it's hardly evidence of homicide." He heaved a great sigh, then suddenly speared me with his dark and compelling eye. "But let me tell you what we do know for certain. One of the hotel's resident waitrons reported for work this morning thinking that today is *yesterday*. He apparently has perfect twenty-four-hour amnesia. Somebody else substituted for him during the wedding reception. Of course, the interloper might have been just another determined tabloid reporter. But if we knew for certain that the fake waitron was a Hydra—and that you killed it—it would help the First Magnate's continuing inquiry into the Fury affair. Why do you think Parni was trying to murder you?"

Slick! But I didn't fall for it. My lip remained zipped, as did my mind-screen. On the intimate mode, I told Boom-Boom: Fous-moi la paix flicaillon!

But he continued his cajolery. "You have nothing to lose by talking to me, Rogi. The Lylmik have sealed the Fury files and made them accessible only to the highest level of the Magistratum. Absolutely nothing will happen to you if you confess to killing Parnell Remillard. Hell, if we could, we'd give you a medal! But if you have evidence of recent activity by a Hydra, we have to know about it."

Shaking my head, I snarled another denial and started up from my seat to get more coffee.

Marc's PK took hold of me and slammed me back down with a force that rocked the table and exploded stars of agony behind my swollen eyeballs.

"Stop acting like an old fool! No one's interested in charging you with murder. Talk, damn you!"

"All we want to do is confirm that it was really a Hydra that you zapped," Boom-Boom said, his coercion as sweet as maple syrup. It was the old game of good cop/bad cop. They'd play it until my head cracked like a peanut shell.

Oh, what the hell . . .

"All right, all right!" I cried. "I killed Parnell Remillard. It was self-defense."

"Atta boy." Laroche bestowed an encouraging smile. "Tell us more."

I eyed Marc apprehensively, but he was making no effort to breach my mindscreen and confirm the truth of what I was saying. "When Parni came after me in the bar it was his second attempt to put out my lights. I have no idea why. He'd already tried a week earlier up at White Moose Lodge and nearly drowned me. Marc was a witness, but he didn't want to believe me. Then Parni showed up here at the hotel, wearing the waiter outfit. I told Marc about it and he *still* didn't believe me."

"Marc scanned the man you were suspicious of," Boom-Boom said. "He detected no anomalous mental pattern."

"Hydras are talented. You should have caught Parni's lunker brook trout gig." I closed my eyes, chewed the bread very slowly, and tried not to groan. Even my teeth hurt. This was definitely one lulu of a crown fire. "Either of you boys got any aldetox?"

Marc went into the bathroom and called some up from the hotel shop, then clapped the minidoser against my temple with unnecessary firmness. The ghastly headache began to abate almost immediately.

"Why didn't you use your mental laser on the fake fish?" Boom-Boom persisted.

"I was too kerflummoxed to get my brain in gear. The zap isn't something I can conjure up instantly. Most of the time, I can't do it at all. I have to be scared shitless."

"And you're certain that the—the person who attacked you in the lake and the man who threatened you in the hotel bar were the same? Your identification of Parnell is positive?"

"I knew him as a kid. It was Parni. He wanted me to recognize him, the vicious bastard."

"Have you ever killed anyone this way before?"

"No. But I nearly wasted Vic Remillard the night of the Great Intervention, when he tried to blow up the chalet on Mount Washington with the delegates of the last Metapsychic Congress inside. Worse luck, my mind-zap only put the fucker into a coma for twenty-six years."

Laroche gaped at me. "*You* were responsible for that?"

I shrugged, precipitating another small explosion of pain behind my eyes. The aldetox shot was fighting the good fight but the hangover still wasn't out for the count.

Boom-Boom continued the interrogation for another half hour, going over and over the details. I was frank about everything except the Hydra's motive for wanting me dead. Then Marc farspoke the First Magnate, who was at his home down in Concord, and passed along the news. He also asked if Boom-Boom should bring me in for a mechanical mind-ream. Fortunately, Paul decided that nothing was to be gained by subjecting me to the Cambridge machine ordeal. Surprise surprise. *He* believed my story.

Paul said he would break the news to his brother Adrien about the death of his prodigal son. Boom-Boom promised to have the forensics lab send what was left of the ash sample to the First Magnate, who could pass it on to the bereaved parents.

The secret dossier on Fury and Hydra was eventually amended by Chief Inspector Guy Laroche to read that Parnell Remillard was "probably deceased." This left the Fury monster with a single remaining confederate—Paul's younger daughter, Madeleine.

Marc's sister.

In late July, just after their honeymoon and shortly before they were scheduled to travel to Orb for the Concilium session, Dorothée and Jack came secretly to Hanover, metacreatively disguised, and stayed in my apartment above the bookshop. An attempt by me to demonstrate the outspiral mind-laser to them failed utterly, but they were fascinated by my unorthodox chakra-revving technique and decided to experiment with it themselves later.

Then, with Jack's assistance, Dorothée sifted my mind for mnemonic data that might be useful in designing the metaconcert program for Denis's exorcism. The redactive process was horrendous, just as the young folks warned me it would be. I was in bed for a week afterward, more or less numb from the neck up, and they cared for me like I was an infant. Marcel wouldn't come near me; my discombobulated mental vibes must have convinced the cat I was one of the Living Dead.

When I was finally on the mend, the newlyweds prepared to leave Earth. They told me that my ream-job had provided valuable data on Fury's mental signature, among other things. While she was inside my head, Dorothée had also done a careful assay of my creative metafaculty and found it almost "normally" puny. If I did possess a talent for mind-zapping, it was so deeply latent that it was damned near extradimensional.

I was instructed to take it easy for the next couple of months until my violated memory bank's NMDA receptors got back up to snuff. They ordered me to lay off alcohol entirely, because booze would further "insult" the little wounded brain-cell thingies. A mild postcoercive suggestion, planted in me by Ti-Jean, would subtly prompt me to shut up in case I was inclined to say anything imprudent about the upcoming exorcism. Jack and Dorothée were particularly emphatic about me not spilling the beans to Marc.

That reminded me of the puzzling thing that had happened during my grilling by Marc and Boom-Boom. I asked Jack if either he or Dorothée had meddled with my mindscreen, making it impossible for Marc to ream me. They said they hadn't.

"Then why," I asked, "couldn't he break into my head? He's done it before."

Jack thought for a moment. "Marc was very close to you during his early childhood, wasn't he, Uncle Rogi?"

"Well, I suppose so. He was always hanging around the bookshop when he was real small. Not saying much—except now and then coming up with a zinger of a question that'd rock me back on my heels. He was proud as the devil even then, pretending that he didn't really care when Teresa didn't have time for him. He and Paul never did get along, so I guess he kinda latched on to me by default. It was easy, with the family house on South Street just around the corner from my shop."

"That might explain Marc's inability to probe you," Dorothée said. "He could have an inhibition based upon his view of you as a quasi-parental figure. Similar to the one Denis must have."

"But Marc's drilled my brain in the past," I reiterated.

"The inhibition could come and go, influenced by any number of psychological factors," Jack said, "such as the continuing integration of Marc's deep unconscious with his conscious mind, the current state of his metapsychic complexus, and particularly his changing emotional orientation in relation to you."

"Emotional orientation?"

"How he feels about you," Dorothée said gently. "The intensity and tenor of one's feelings toward an authority figure can and often do change as a person gets older. Marc may not consciously realize that he loves you more in his maturity than he did as a young man distracted by the struggle to master his paramount mindpowers. When you nearly drowned, his repressed feeling for you might have been shocked into full realization."

"Oh," I said.

Marc, the quintessential cold fish, capable of love? Pas de danger!

"Emotional factors like these will also complicate the Dynasty's attempt to heal Denis," said Jack. "It won't be easy for them to get into their father's head. The data that we gleaned from you provided useful details of Fury's mindset—but we hope the information will also help us to analyze the parent-child coercive relationship as it appertains to Denis and the Dynasty."

"Anne talked about that, too." I hesitated, then asked, "When are you going to do it? The exorcism?"

"We should have the metaconcert design finished some time in September," Jack said. "We'll work on it during our spare time at the Concilium session. I'll also be able to complete most of the brainboard design for the new CE helmets while we're in Orb. Once I get back to Earth and build the hats, we come to the really dicey part: practicing the energized metaconcert with the Dynasty."

"Do they know yet?" I asked.

"We informed the First Magnate," Dorothée told me. "It's up to him to break the news to his brothers and sister."

"We'll require at least a solid month of metaconcert practice, for safety's sake," Jack said. "In order to keep the operation secure, we'll do the prep work at my place on Kauai. The Dynasty should have no trouble coming there incognito. I've asked Papa to arrange it."

"Will you . . . do it to Denis on the island?" I asked.

"No. He almost never leaves home these days, and we can't afford to arouse his suspicions by insisting that he come to Kauai. Diamond and I have already decided on an ideal place for the procedure: my sister Marie's farm just outside Hanover. She'll be taken into our confidence when everything is ready. We can set up the equipment out there without attracting any attention."

"Marie's farm?" I repeated numbly. "Where Denis and Lucille used to live?"

"The place is perfect for another reason," Jack said. "This year,

Marie will be hosting the réveillon after midnight mass for the first time. We'll do the coercive-redactive procedure then, when Denis—and his Fury alter ego—will be least likely to suspect that anything unusual is in the air."

They were going to do it on Christmas.

[13]

SEATTLE METRO, EARTH
27 SEPTEMBER 2078

Rory Muldowney, Dirigent of the "Irish" ethnic planet of Hibernia, shifted uncomfortably in his seat in Manion's antiquated old beater of a rhocraft and thought black rebellious thoughts about the Rebellion. The others on the Executive Council of the movement, God blast them, had committed themselves firmly to this new, disturbing course. Now, barring a miracle, they were stuck with it. His own opposition had been halfhearted because it was irrational and he knew it—just as he knew why most of the others were so enthusiastically in favor. He hadn't dared to tell them the real reason why he opposed their choice for a new leader. They were determined to have one, and all that remained was to see if the candidate was willing to accept.

Muldowney's florid face twisted in a bitter little smile. And if Marc did accept, he thought, then wouldn't I give my soul to see the look on the face of Paul Remillard—may the devil roast the prick off him!—when he finds out what his darling son has done.

The egg said, "ETA five minutes CEREM NAVCON," and began the descent from the ionosphere. It was nearly midnight.

"Display CU terrain proper CEREM plant," Alexis Manion commanded.

"Proper CU option unavailable," said the rhocraft. "Shall I show three-kay overview analog?"

"Go," said Alex. His passengers were leaning forward to study the chart that had come up on the navigation unit display. "Sorry, folks. No real-world picture of Marc's bailiwick. It seems that he's beefed up security since I was here a couple of years ago."

"How intriguing," said Hiroshi Kodama. His gaze was unfocused as he exerted his ultrasenses. "It is also quite impossible to perceive CEREM with farsight, although the surrounding region is quite clear. I conjecture that some device such as an S-450 fuzzer is in operation."

"Here's a how-dee-doo," Alex sang softly. He posed a rhetorical question: "Now what do you suppose Marc is hiding down there?"

"Something valuable?" Cordelia Warshaw suggested.

"Something illegal," said Rory Muldowney, who knew all about such things.

The screen showed a labeled chart of an industrial park at least 120 hectares in extent. The South Fork of the Snoqualmie River ran through it, and more than a dozen sizable buildings were scattered among groves of evergreen trees.

"That is CEREM?" Professor Anna Gawrys exclaimed. "All that? Why, it's enormous—bigger than IDFS! I never dreamt that Marc Remillard had such resources at his command."

"I suppose this is just one more branch of the Dynasty's far-flung commercial empire," Patricia Castellane remarked.

Alex Manion shook his head. "Not by a long shot. Marc might have had a bit of help from the family trust back in 2072, setting the thing up, but he's been independent of the Remco conglomerate structure for over five years. CEREM is Marc's private fief. It turns a tidy profit manufacturing conventional mental interface systems—besides providing him with almost unlimited facilities for his more unorthodox enterprises."

"I'll bet there are some lovely fish in that little river down there," Rory said.

"Rainbow trout," Alex confirmed. "Marc bought this particular site for CEREM so he could go flyfishing right outside the back door of his lab when he needed a break."

Rory gave a snort.

Professor Gawrys seemed bemused by the huge establishment shown on the display. "I had not realized that commercial CE was so . . . lucrative."

"Better say expensive and be done with it, Annushka," Patricia Castellane said. "It would be splendid to have Marc Remillard lending his paramount metafaculties and charismatic presence to our Rebellion—but even better to have his lovely E18 hats and brainboard components for free if it turns out that we have to fight our way out of the Milieu."

Hiroshi Kodama said, "Good point, Pat. Satsuma's Geophysical Modification Unit has already coughed up more than four hundred and fifty million dollars for CEREM equipment. I dare say Okanagon has spent even more."

"Six hundred mil thus far," Castellane admitted. "And we've budgeted another hundred megabux for the next fiscal year. Poor old Oky is just coming apart at the seams. Nothing as spectacular as the Caledonian diatreme, thank God, but enough all-around crustal instability to keep us hopping. I don't know how we find enough spare time and money to foment Rebellion on the side."

"At least," Hiroshi said, "you don't have yakuza gangsters to cope with in addition to the earthquakes."

"Rope your local rascals into our grand cause!" Rory Muldowney said, tipping his colleague a wink. "You might just find them to be very helpful in the procurement of certain vital commodities."

Hiroshi received the suggestion in cold silence.

"Now there's a real Irish proposal for you," Patricia drawled.

Rory's face purpled with indignation. "And what's *that* supposed to mean, Madam Dirigent?"

"Read my mind, Mister Dirigent. And recall your ethnic history—to say nothing of certain major suppliers of the toys in your basement."

"And why shouldn't I get the stuff wherever I can if it helps the cause in the long run? Rebellion's not for the squeamish!"

"Children, children," said Cordelia Warshaw. "Let's save our energies for the conversion of Marc Remillard."

"We must still decide who will be our spokesman tonight," Professor Gawrys said.

The five other minds immediately responded: YOU Annushka.

"Oh, no!" she protested. "I am not at all suitable. I've been thinking how unfortunate it is that Adrien declined to accompany us on this mission. He would have been the ideal one to approach his nephew. I still recall his prophetic comment about Marc and our Rebel movement, made so many years ago."

"You are the appropriate spokesman," Hiroshi Kodama said. "It's fitting that the present head of our cause should offer the leadership to the chosen successor."

"But what if he declines? Coercion is my weakest metafaculty!"

"There's not a head in the galaxy who could coerce Marc," Alex said. "We'll persuade him to join us by demonstrating that it's in his best interest—or we won't persuade him at all."

Rory Muldowney said, "Never fear, Annushka. If we're bound and determined to have the man, he's ripe for the plucking. After his narrow squeak with the Polity Science Directorate at the last Concilium session, the only way he'll be able to continue his research is with the backing of the Rebel bloc. The vote defeating the moratorium this time was a flamin' fluke. It won't happen again unless the party lends a helping hand. Marc's only chance lies in keeping opposition to his work bottled up in committee, and we can deliver the votes to insure that. So just put it to him plainly. The bastard's a natural Rebel anyway. He belongs on our side."

Unspoken was Rory's additional thought: But not as our leader.

The professor appealed to Alexis Manion. "But surely you would be the better choice to make the proposal to Marc. You have known him since you were schoolboys."

"No one really knows Marc Remillard," said Alex starkly.

There was an uncomfortable silence. Then Hiroshi Kodama said, "Even so, Alex, do you think he would have bothered to meet with us at all if he were *not* sympathetically inclined to the Rebel viewpoint?"

"Beats me," said Manion. "I was surprised all to hell when he invited us to come and make our pitch—and to CEREM, at that."

The egg continued its descent through the clear night sky. At lower altitudes the lights of Seattle Metro delineated every island and coastal feature of Puget Sound, spreading short glittering tentacles of habitation westward into the Olympic Peninsula and longer shining arms up the river valleys toward the eastern Cascade foothills.

"I must tell you," said Professor Gawrys in a quiet but firm voice, "that I still have deep misgivings about this mission."

"You agreed with the rest of the Executive Council that the movement needed more forceful leadership," Cordelia said sharply, "and that Marc Remillard was the one who could give it to us."

"Yes. That's true. Nevertheless, I am obliged to tell you what I feel in my heart. This man that we will meet tonight has the potential to transform our Rebel cause . . . for better or for worse. I will admit that he seems sympathetic to the principles of human freedom that we have dedicated our lives to. But as I listened to his brilliant rebuttal during the Concilium session, staving off the attempt to stifle his research, I was deeply disturbed. In the Concilium, all minds are supposed to be transparent and free of any trace of artifice or duplicity. But we humans, being unUnified, still veil the innermost secrets of our hearts from each other and from the exotic magnates—"

"We do it," Patricia Castellane said, "because we must."

"Yes, because we Rebels have sincere doubts about humanity's role in the Galactic Milieu," the professor agreed. "But it seems to me that

Marc Remillard's mental reservations differ from our own in an important respect. I fear that his primary concern is not humanity's right to mental freedom, but rather the defense of his own sovereign ego."

"The two things aren't incompatible," Alex said mildly.

"Perhaps not," the professor conceded. "You know Marc much better than I. Nevertheless, I wish that we had not come here. At least, not yet."

Cordelia Warshaw rolled her eyes in exasperation. "The timing is perfect, Annushka. We've needed the man on our team for years—and now we finally have an opportunity to offer him quid pro quo by forestalling any future moratorium on creative CE."

"If we invite Marc Remillard to lead us," the professor said, "I am afraid that we renounce any hope of a nonviolent solution to our Rebel dilemma."

"You can't be certain of that," Hiroshi said.

"No. It is only a feeling I have. An intuition."

"Most of us," said Patricia Castellane, her steel-colored eyes dangerously narrowed, "believe that a peaceful withdrawal of humanity from the Milieu is impossible under *any* circumstances. Given that, Marc and his resources are—"

"Attention! Attention!"

With shocking abruptness, a computerized voice blared from the speaker of their egg's navigation unit. The console display began blinking a cautionary icon.

"Attention, rhocraft UK LPZD 44926. You have breached the restricted airspace of CEREM Limited, a privately held corporation with citizenship status in the North American Intendancy. Your vehicle has been inserted into a holding pattern. If you are not authorized to land, you are herewith ordered to exit this airspace within one minute. If you have access authorization, enter the appropriate code now."

Their inertialess egg had come to a complete stop in mid-air, 3000 meters above an area of dead-black ground impenetrable to the mind's eye.

Alex Manion began to fumble in an inner pocket of his jacket. He had put on his best outfit for the great occasion, a natty dark green nebulin townsuit, a high-collared sark, and shoes with chased-silver buckles. Unfortunately, since he had felt a chill in his chest when he, Annushka, and Cordelia flew from Cambridge University to the Shetlands to collect the other Rebel leaders at Unst Starport, he had augmented the finery with an extremely long (and slightly grubby) striped woolen scarf that he had wound several times around his neck.

"Now what did I do with that key-fleck Marc sent?" he muttered.

"Attention, LPZD 44926! Failure to exit airspace or failure to enter access authorization code will result in your vehicle being enveloped in a sigma-field and taken in tow by a CEREM security force tractor. Enter access code now."

Alex squinted at the handful of little transparent plass squares he had pulled out. "Damn. I should have sent this paper to *Nature* last week."

"Attention, LPZD 44926! You are cautioned that the CEREM corporate entity is licensed by Area 360 Air Traffic Control and the Cascadia Zone Magistratum to repel trespassers with deadly force if necessary. Enter code now."

"Bozhye moi!" exclaimed the professor.

"For Christ's sake, Alex," Rory Muldowney said. "Feed the friggin' fleck!"

"Here it is." Alex delicately inserted one of the little squares into a slot on the navigation console and touched a data-transfer pad. "No doubt about it, Marc's yanked the old welcome mat to the general public."

The computerized voice dropped its belligerent tone. "Authorization code accepted. Entering CEREM NAVCON auto landing option. Please do not attempt to take manual control of your aircraft."

The egg resumed its smooth descent. As they passed through the attenuated dynamic-field barrier, the featureless area below was suddenly transformed into a spangled expanse of lights in a narrow valley. A network of driveways and walks spread among crowded car parks, rhocraft pads, and more than twenty sprawling buildings with windows blazing. In a few minutes they hung above an opening iris-door in the ground immediately adjacent to one of the smaller structures in the industrial campus. Most of the CEREM buildings were beautifully constructed of natural materials that harmonized with the landscaping, but this one was a nearly featureless monolithic cube some 30 meters on a side, lacking doors and windows. The egg descended into the underground docking area and all of its systems shut down. The overhead door closed and the rhocraft began to move through a dim tunnel on a conveyor.

Hiroshi said, "There's a very hefty internal sigma-field permeating this entire area."

"This cubic building is new," Alex noted. "My old bud's definitely up to something."

"Well, at least we won't have to worry about security at our meeting with the man," Rory Muldowney said.

"Marc's private offices in the main executive block are perfectly thoughtproof," said Alex. "I suspect he's meeting us in this high-tech fortress for another reason altogether."

"What could that be?" the professor asked uneasily.

"We'll find out pretty soon," said Patricia Castellane. "We've arrived."

Their craft had come to a halt in a parking bay and its hatch rolled open. They had been conveyed into a reception dock with wood-paneled walls and a carpeted floor. Brass urns held ornamental foliage plants, and in spotlit niches were pieces of Dale Chihuly glass sculpture and ancient wooden dance-masks of some Pacific Coast native tribe. The battered old Mitsubishi egg that Alex refused to part with looked woefully out of place compared to the luxurious executive flying machines parked in the bays on either side of it.

The dock appeared to be deserted. As they climbed out of the rhocraft Annushka Gawrys looked about with a touch of apprehension and said, "The aetheric vibrations in this building are most peculiar."

"Now don't start fretting again," Cordelia said. She had on a maroon zenil skirtsuit with matching thigh-high boots and a pert white beret.

"I am a very old woman," the professor told her curtly, "and I've earned the right to fret when the situation warrants it." But then she gave a wry shrug, took a small mirror from her handbag, and began to tuck a few wayward strands of hair back into place.

Anna Yurievna Gawrys-Sakhvadze, youngest child of the metapsychic pioneers Tamara Sakhvadze and Yuri Gawrys, had been born in 1980. Thanks to two courses of rejuvenation she appeared to be in her mid-forties, a near-contemporary of her younger companions. Her blunt features were softened by lustrous auburn hair confined in a fashionable coil at the nape of her neck. She wore a classic Chanel costume, a pleated navy blue skirt and a jacket trimmed in white braid. At her smooth throat was a strand of lapis lazuli beads.

The Council members from offworld were more casually attired. Patricia Castellane was dressed in a somber narrow poncho and leggings of black crushed velvet, and a gray cashmere turtleneck sweater. Hiroshi Kodama and Rory Muldowney, who had arrived on separate starships that morning from their home planets, had on simple warm-up gear and Romeo shoes.

"Marc's not an ogre," Alex Manion said to the professor. "You have nothing to worry about."

Annushka switched to declamatory mindspeech: I know Remillard is not an ogre. He is worse: He is a charming enigma and I have learned through long experience that such lifeforms can be dangerous!

Alex said: A lot of that Byronic façade is compensatory. It's not easy being a paramount and it's even tougher being a member of a family that's pressured you to do things their way from the time you were a little kid.

"Ochón ó," Rory murmured in mock sympathy. The poor lad! I suppose it was his mean old dad—the devil hoist him!—made him what he is today.

Alex threw the Irishman a glance of pity and said: Marc's feelings toward Paul are probably an echo of your own—and for a similar reason.

Rory seemed taken aback by the idea, then he frowned and said aloud, "Y'know, I never thought about it quite like that before."

"Start thinking, then," Patricia Castellane suggested. "For a change of pace."

"Please!" Annushka begged, before Rory could deliver a furious riposte. "We must not wrangle." I insist that we present a united mind to Marc Remillard. If there is anyone who cannot do that then I entreat that person to withdraw from the delegation.

Alexis Manion smiled coolly at the Dirigent of Hibernia and said: You can take the egg back to Seattle and wait for us at Jazz Alley if you prefer.

"Aw, shite," muttered Rory Muldowney. You know damn well I'm with you. I'll kiss the spailpín's bum if you want me to.

Hiroshi Kodama said: One hopes that will not be necessary. But if it is we should certainly make a video for posterity.

Everyone else, including Muldowney, roared with laughter.

Then Cordelia said, "I wonder how much longer Remillard is going to keep us waiting here?" With the closing of the conveyor tunnel gate there seemed to be no way out of the subterranean reception area and no indication that they were expected. "Alex, don't you think you'd better give a farshout and let these people know we're here?"

Hang on! said a telepathic voice. *I'm on my way.*

Before any of them had a chance to trace the communication, which had certainly not come from Marc Remillard, a nearly invisible door in the far wall slid open and a dapper individual of small stature, exuding surplus creativity and hyperkinesis, bounded out. "Alex!" he cried. "God, it's been too long, mon bonhomme!"

As a youth, Peter Paul Dalembert, Jr., had been the ingenious enabler who always found ways to implement the extravagant schemes cooked up by Marc, Alex, and their other bosom pal, Boom-Boom Laroche. In maturity, clever and indefatigable as ever, Peter had become the Chief Executive Officer of CEREM and Marc Remillard's right-hand man.

Alex greeted Dalembert with restraint and introduced his Rebel colleagues.

"May I present Professor Anna Gawrys, Chairman of Cambridge University's Institute for Dynamic-Field Studies . . . Cordelia Warshaw, Intendant Associate for Europe and Visiting Fellow in Cultural Xenology at Oxford . . . Patricia Castellane, Planetary Dirigent of Okanagon . . . Hiroshi Kodama, Planetary Dirigent of Satsuma . . . Rory Muldowney, Planetary Dirigent of Hibernia."

"Wonderful to have you here at CEREM," Dalembert said. Forgoing the more discreet open-palm operant greeting, he vigorously pumped the hands of the visitors. Alex rated a fond punch in the biceps. "You folks sure picked the perfect time to drop in on us! The new CE rig shell was about ready for its preliminary run and Marc decided to push the test up a couple of days so you could see it."

Alex looked startled. "He's got the new brain-booster working already?"

"Not quite. We're only testing the cryogenic shell components, and they're still in a much bulkier protoconfig than the ultimate design called for in the Keogh specs." Peter Dalembert paused significantly. "Marc hired them away from Du Pont, you know."

"The Keoghs?" Alex's amazement was frank. "That must have put a nice dent in the corporate dividend."

Dalembert chuckled. "We can afford it. Having the Keoghs personally in charge of the shell project probably halved this first phase of development. Of course, they're cosmic-class wackadoos, but Marc manages to cope . . . This way, everybody."

The CEREM executive led them through the doorway and into a fully enclosed transport capsule. In less than thirty seconds they reached their destination, a glassed-in observation chamber overlooking a hangarlike area crowded with a confusing array of equipment. Dozens of technicians were in attendance. In the center of the big room, brightly spotlit, was an elevated platform holding a hulking, matte-black piece of apparatus attended by acolytes in white coveralls.

"Please sit down," Dalembert urged his guests. "The test will begin in just a few minutes. Marc timed it to your arrival."

"How very thoughtful of the dear man," murmured Rory Muldowney.

Immediately adjacent to their balcony chamber, and clearly visible through a transparent wall, was an elaborate command center. Inside, four men and a woman, wearing comsets, were busily speaking to computers and studying expanses of monitoring equipment.

"The guy nearest to us is Doctor Jeffrey Steinbrenner, our new bionics chief."

As Dalembert spoke, Steinbrenner looked up and regarded them coolly. His gaunt frame had not a gram of excess flesh on it. They felt his ultrasenses flick over them in a brief, disdainful inspection before he turned back to his work.

"Lovely congenial sort of chap," said Rory Muldowney.

Dalembert grinned. "And talented! Next to Jeff are Jordan Kramer and Gerrit Van Wyk, Professor Gawrys's former colleagues. Inventors of the mechanical mind-probe."

They were also prominent Rebels, which Dalembert forbore to mention.

"I know them well," Annushka said, "although they were not exactly my academic associates. The Department of Psychophysics is not part of IDFS. It was . . . a considerable surprise to me when Jordan and Gerry left Cambridge University to work in the private sector."

"We made them an offer they couldn't refuse." Peter Dalembert said.

Completely absorbed, neither of the psychophysicists in the command center favored the guests with telepathic greetings. Kramer was a pleasant-looking man with large features and sandy hair. Van Wyk, scuttling from one bank of diagnostic monitors to another as he muttered into his comset, bore an unfortunate resemblance to an irritable, flaxen-headed frog. It was possible for the visitors to farsense what the people in the command center were saying, but the comments were so loaded with dismaying technical jargon that they were nearly unfathomable.

"I suppose those are the precious Keoghs," said Patricia Castellane, indicating the two other workers. A young man and woman of strikingly similar appearance, handsome and ginger-haired, were engrossed in the displays on the consoles before them.

"Wait until you meet them," Dalembert said. "You'll want to keep your mindscreen at max if you know what's good for you . . . Ah! Looks like we're just about ready to begin."

On the main floor below, a tall, splendidly muscled figure had emerged from a side corridor and was striding purposefully toward the central platform where technicians waited. He was attired from neck to toe in a tight black suit studded with monitoring receptacles and having a neck-ring seal. As he climbed onto the platform he raised a gloved hand in casual salute to the visitors in the observation booth. Their farsight showed a face with lofty cheekbones and a high-bridged nose, framed by jet-black curly hair. Gray eyes, compelling and luminous, were set deeply into shadowed orbits. The mouth was wide, lifted in an attractive one-sided smile.

Marc Remillard said: *Good of you all to come!*

Even in those few brief words, his mental voice had an extraordinary effect, projecting warmth, kindliness, and an overwhelming, almost seraphic authority. Rory Muldowney found himself wondering how he could ever have tarred the man with the same brush as his rakehell father. Why, he was magnificent! He was an ideal candidate for leader of the Metapsychic Rebellion! He was—

A Paramount Grand Master in metacoercion.

Annushka Gawrys also found herself battling to resist Marc Remillard's magnetism. Get a grip on yourself, old woman! she thought. Remember what happened at the last Concilium session. Are you going to let this enchanter bamboozle you again? Chyestnoye slovo, ya yemu etog ne spushu!

A few months earlier, Marc Remillard had formally addressed the galactic governing body for the first time since his scandalous accession speech in 2063. As he defended his right to continue his CE research, both the human and the exotic Magnates of the Concilium had been utterly mesmerized by him. Objectively, they suspected that they were being swayed by the wiles of a paramount coercer rather than by the logic of his argument; but they could not help responding positively to him in spite of it. The moratorium on metacreative CE research was voted down and returned to the Human Science Directorate for further study in committee. Marc was left free to continue his work—at least until the next Concilium session.

Marc's rebuttal speech had been a stunning ploy that was especially effective because it had been so unexpected. In the fifteen years since his nomination to the Concilium, he had served unobtrusively, almost negligently, as a simple magnate-at-large. His superlative metafunctions were common knowledge, but he had been careful not to parade them. After the upset vote on the moratorium, the buzz among the magnates in the corridors of Concilium Orb contained equal amounts of fervent approval and an appalled sense of having been well and truly flim-flammed.

But Marc would not be able to play his coercive trick twice. Unless those Science Directors with Rebel leanings voted en bloc to avert it, the Directorate would try to shoot him down again. And next time it would probably succeed . . .

"That mass of dark cerametal machinery on the central platform is the prototype of our new cerebroenergetic enhancer," Peter Dalembert said. "We call it the clamshell. It's still rather bulky, but we'll pare the mass down in time. The techs will help Marc get into it, then—"

Patricia Castellane interrupted, astonished. "Surely he's not going to act as his own guinea pig in this experiment!"

"He always has," Dalembert replied matter-of-factly. "Every CE device CEREM has produced had its initial human test on our glorious leader. Marc says it's a great incentive for the engineers to get things right the first time around—and of course his paramount faculties give him a safety edge no other test subject would have. This particular run-up won't involve boosting cerebral output per se. It's only a test of the refrigerated full-body armor for the rig."

"Full body?" Rory Muldowney's brow creased in bafflement. "I don't understand. You mean this new brain-revver involves more than a CE hat?"

"Helmet-style cerebroenergetic enhancement has an upper limit of about three hundred times normal metapsychic output," said Alex Manion. "If you try to energize much beyond that, the brain's hyped creativity burns up the operator's body. It's a variant of the flashover effect that almost killed Dorothea Macdonald during the Caledonian diatreme."

"And to prevent this infelicitous outcome," Hiroshi Kodama said, "the body is refrigerated?"

"Frozen to near absolute zero," said Dalembert cheerfully.

Below, Marc had reclined on the lower half of the fantastic clamshell and the technicians were hooking up his suit connections. Then the hinged upper portion swung closed, leaving his bare head still exposed and resting on a broad shelflike protrusion. The apparatus was nearly as bulky as a standard groundcar. Innumerable cables and lines sheathed in shiny metal flex connected it to several other pieces of equipment surrounding it.

"Here comes the headpiece," Dalembert said. "At this stage of the rig's development, it's a much-modified E18 bucket with a brainboard in creative mode. There's the usual crown-of-thorns, plus cerebellar and stem electrodes to integrate the brain with the cryonics system. Auxiliary life support and backup AV communications gear keep the op alive and in touch until the big freeze isolates his pre-energized cerebrum from the rest of the body."

A traveling hoist trundled up, poising a massive casque directly above Marc's head. The minds of the guests heard him issue a farspoken order that was computerized and rebroadcast over the observation chamber's speaker:

ENHELM OPERATOR.

In the command center, Jeffrey Steinbrenner was whispering into the mike of his comset. The headpiece lowered into place, mating with the rest of the apparatus and enclosing Marc Remillard in more than four tons of cerametal armor.

ENGAGE AUXILIARY CEREBROENERGETICS.

"Now the little photon beams in the crown-of-thorns are drilling his skull," Dalembert said. "Cerebral electrodes will sprout inside his brain in preparation for the CE phase-in. His own grandmasterclass autoredaction will maintain the vitals of the gray matter once the auxiliary CE kicks in."

ENERGIZE CRYONICS. INITIATE METABOLIC REPROGRAMMING.

"More needles into his cerebellum and medulla. Circulatory shunts in his carotid and femoral arteries draw off the blood and replace it with a cryogenic fluid. A dermal lavage formula fills the clamshell and helmet. He'd drown if he hadn't already stopped breathing. In another minute his body will be frozen to minus two hundred and sixty degrees Celsius."

ENGAGE PRIMARY CEREBROENERGETICS. ENERGIZE SIECOMEX TO LEVEL THREE HUNDRED.

"Hello!" Dalembert said in surprise. "That's not in the test sked."

Some farspoken communication passed between him and Steinbrenner. In the command center, the gaunt bionics director eyed the CEO and shrugged. Then Steinbrenner, Kramer, and Van Wyk left their own consoles and went to stand behind the Keoghs. The lighted screens before the pair cast eerie shadows on their intent faces. Dierdre Keogh's hands danced over an old-fashioned input keyboard. She was smiling. Her brother Diarmid addressed the controlling computer verbally through his comset, calling up situation analyses completely incomprehensible to the eavesdropping observers.

"What is happening?" Annushka Gawrys asked anxiously.

They waited—then delighted relief flooded out of Peter Dalembert's mind. "The test is a success! We didn't expect Marc to actually enhance, but he did it anyway. The diagnostics indicate augmented creativity function at the three hundred output level, the usual ceiling for the E18 helmet configuration. Now Marc will begin shutdown and—"

ENERGIZE TO LEVEL FOUR HUNDRED.

The people in the command center exchanged glances. Diarmid Keogh said, "Operator, say again."

I SAY ENERGIZE TO LEVEL FOUR HUNDRED. GO!

"But is that possible?" Cordelia Warshaw whispered.

Alex Manion's face was grim. "Yes. Theoretically, the E18 has an almost open-ended augmentation potential. The upper limit is in the operator's brain, not the equipment."

ENERGIZE TO LEVEL FIVE HUNDRED.

"We're not ready for this," Dalembert muttered. He called out on the declamatory mode: NegativeDiarmidnegative! DoNOTenergize!

Diarmid Keogh looked up from his control console with a sardonic expression. He said: Hisvitalsarebangonthemoney & heistheboss & hegetswhathewantswhenhewantsit.

ACTIVATE PLATFORM AREA SR-45 SIGMA SAFETY SHIELD.

Down on the main floor, the technicians retreated and a mirrored hemisphere eight meters in diameter popped into existence, engulfing the platform and the machinery on it.

ENERGIZE TO LEVEL SIX HUNDRED.

Under his breath, Dalembert said, "Oh, God. If he backflares he'll vaporize the rig. And himself." He leaned forward and turned on a small display screen. An image of the apparatus inside the shield appeared.

"Jesus, Mary, and Joseph!" breathed Rory Muldowney. "Will you look at that."

The monstrous clamshell apparatus, still tethered by its multitude of umbilicals, was slowly levitating unsupported above the platform, tilting until the casque enclosing Marc Remillard's energized brain was fully upright.

"He's doing it with his mind," Cordelia whispered.

Patricia Castellane said, "The sigma bubble's breaching at the top."

Sweat had broken out on Peter Dalembert's brow. "It's impossible. That platform sigma shield is state-of-the-art. You couldn't punch through it with a battery of X-lasers!"

"Try the creative energy of a paramount metapsychic mind," Alex Manion said quietly, "magnified six hundred times."

The massive CE rig floated up through the breached force-field, hovering on a level with the balcony containing the observation chamber and the command center. The Rebel visitors, the CEREM supervisors, and the floor technicians watched, transfixed, as the cerametal casque shimmered, brightened, and seemed to become as tenuous as mist. Their farsight perceived a ghostly simulacrum of Marc Remillard's smiling face, superimposed upon an incandescent brain.

A mind-voice echoed in the skulls of Alex Manion, Annushka Gawrys, Cordelia Warshaw, Patricia Castellane, Hiroshi Kodama, and Rory Muldowney.

THE ANSWER TO THE QUESTION YOU WANTED TO ASK IS YES . . . BUT ONLY IF YOU'RE WILLING TO DO IT MY WAY.

They said: We are. All of us are.

EXPLICIT, said the brain. WE'LL TALK MORE ABOUT IT IN A LITTLE WHILE.

[14]

FROM THE MEMOIRS OF
ROGATIEN REMILLARD

Late summer is ordinarily a very slow time for the antiquarian fantasy book business. The wares that I peddle are best savored in cosy rooms, when bad weather and too-long nights provoke a need for escapism and whet the contemplation of the outrageous. During the dwindling bright sunny days, most people prefer to be out under the open sky rather than poking around in musty old bookstores.

A good thing, too. I was in no shape to deal with customers.

I fixed my door-sign to read GONE FISHING and kept the place locked up all through August 2078, while my brain healed from Dorothée's painful excavation. When I wasn't off fly-angling or birdwatching I puttered around the shop, putting together a new E-catalog and reorganizing the stock. Early in September I took a class in bookbinding from a woman over in Lyme Center. With that under my belt, I set about repairing some battered old Fantasy Press and Shasta Publishers science-fiction titles with badly stained covers, rebinding them in morocco leather. I crafted durofilm repros of the original dust jackets, hand-marbled the endpapers, and put in cutesy-poo satin ribbons for bookmarks. The restored volumes were pretentious but appealing, and I sold them for a hefty sum to a wealthy fish-factory owner in Vladivostok.

Solvency is cheering. I reopened the shop just in time for the fall term at Dartmouth College. My regular customers returned and I tried to get on with my life.

Unfortunately, as October began to put a nip in the New Hampshire air, I found myself becoming increasingly depressed and insomniac, gripped by a feeling of impending disaster that I was unable to shake.

Thinking about Denis.

Thinking about Fury.

Denis simply *could not* be the monster. Not that quiet man I'd known from infancy. Not the loving husband and father who patiently coped with his mercurial wife Lucille and his brilliant, bewildering offspring. Not the orchid hobbyist or the lover of peaceful hikes in the New England countryside. Most certainly not the introspective scholar who often wandered into The Eloquent Page on pleasant autumn afternoons after his seminars were finished and took me out for an espresso and Danish. He and I would sit together under the Starbucks umbrella of the little coffeeshop next door to my place, sharing college gossip. Denis would smile tolerantly as I made risqué cracks about the physical attributes of comely young females passing by, and I'd pretend that I understood his learned disquisitions on the latest book he had just finished writing, *An Ontological Interpretation of Unity.*

Fury as Denis's alter ego? The idea was idiotic on the face of it. He was too kind, too guileless, too genuine. It was true that his prodigious mindpowers frightened me—but that was even more true of Paul, Marc, and Jack; and I knew none of them could possibly be the monster.

No. Anne had made a tragic mistake in judgment—or else she herself was Fury, as I'd suspected earlier, with the evil twin of her multiple personality setting up a diabolical smoke screen to confuse the good twin.

Or had Anne's Fury persona planned something even more sinister, that the starship crash had conveniently foiled?

I pondered a completely new scenario: If Anne hadn't nearly died on Okanagon, she would be one of the Dynasty participants in Denis's upcoming metaconcerted redaction. The very essence of metaconcert was openness, self-surrender, mutual trust; but if Anne was Fury, she would have had a unique opportunity to betray that trust.

All of the concert participants would be wearing CE helmets that left their minds especially vulnerable to invasion by a malignant coercer. Anne might have intended to seize control and coerce her siblings, Jack, Dorothée—and Denis, too—into becoming her slaves.

New Hydras!

This fresh hypothesis of mine presumed there had been a breach between Fury and the original Hydras. Parnell and Madeleine might not have tamely accepted the idea of being supplanted by nine more powerful minds. They might have tried to kill Anne/Fury to prevent it. They might have tried to kill me when Anne survived in order to prevent me from further muddying the waters.

Or just for the hell of it.

Shit. It was all too convoluted for my addled old mind to process. Fury might not be Anne, either. The thing could be someone none of us had ever suspected.

But not Denis. I was positive of that now. Absolutely certain.

All the same, I still couldn't shake the black depression, knowing what lay ahead.

Ti-Jean and Dorothée were already well along concocting the meta-concert that would tear Denis's mind apart—whether he was Fury or not. The mental suffering I had endured under Dorothée's probing would be insignificant compared to the agony that the Dynasty was going to inflict on my dear foster son . . . perhaps for nothing, if the real Fury was floating oblivious in a regeneration-tank down in Concord.

I had no illusions that I would be able to stave off the terrible redactive procedure by attacking Anne's theory and substituting new ideas of my own. Jack and Dorothée had accepted Anne's deduction. It was all too plausible. The metapsychic exorcism of Denis would proceed as planned.

What's more, I was going to have to take an active part in it.

Jack had agreed with Anne's original notion that I was the only one whose mind Denis would never be able to read. So I was the designated Judas-goat, the one who would somehow have to lead Denis to his fate. While the metaconcert worked him over I'd have to wait, like any anguished parent pacing the floor outside the sickroom of a gravely ill child, together with Lucille and the other unsuspecting Remillard family members who would have come to the Christmas réveillon, our traditional Franco-American supper and gift-giving session.

God rest ye merry, gentlefolk. Let nothing you dismay!

Denis's gift from us would be life or death.

By November my continual brooding (made worse by the enforced period of teetotality) had made me such a mental basket case that even my old buddy, the seditious fantasy writer Kyle Macdonald, began to wonder what was wrong. I told him it was a busted love affair, even though I'd been celibate for nearly eight months.

"Laddie, what you need is a distraction," Kyle decided. "Let me see what I can do."

Two days later, on a rainy Thursday afternoon, his egg landed on the pad behind my place and he came stomping in the shop's back door with a big shit-eating grin on his face.

"Pack your bags and fix up the moggy with food and water for the weekend," he commanded. "There's a three-day interdisciplinary symposium on the perils of Unity being held in Lyon over the Armistice Day holiday weekend. I'm tired of staying home alone while Her Nibs goes off gallivanting, so I'm going to France with her and Sally Lapidus . . . and so are you!"

"*France?* Now wait just a damned minute—"

But he paid no attention to my protests and went around putting out lights and locking the shop and programming the CLOSED sign. "Get your auld bones hopping and don't keep Masha waiting outside in the egg, or we'll both find our balls in the wringer. Shlepping you along on this wee trip was just as much her idea as it was mine."

His wife Mary MacGregor-Gawrys was a noted metapsychologist, a Rebel stalwart, and Davy MacGregor's favorite niece—by no means a female to cross lightly. She and Kyle periodically fought like fiends and vowed to go their separate ways, but their indomitable Celtic sex drives invariably brought them back together again.

"What the hell makes you think I'd have a good time at some meeting of Rebel eggheads?" I whined querulously, trying to resist Macdonald as he herded me upstairs to my apartment while Marcel the cat trailed in our wake, meowing anxiously. The kiltie bastard wasn't quite as tall as I was, but he was a hell of a lot stronger.

"The symposium is only an excuse to get out of town, dummy! While the two lassies do their panel discussions and other tosh and taradiddle, you and I will sightsee and drink and then show up for the nightly parties. There are always parties."

"But it's so far away—"

"Not in my new Formula egg. A few hours flying and we'll be there in time for a late nosh. You'll love the restaurants in Lyon: La Pyramide! Georges Blanc! Paul Bocuse! La Mère Guy! We can swill great burgundy and eat real coq au vin and truffle soup and breaded tripe. And I'll pick up your entire tab."

I unlocked the apartment door. "Tripe? Quelle puke!"

"Fake frog. So eat the pig's feet rémoulade." He hustled me into my bedroom and hauled a garment bag out of the closet. "You'll need a decent suit. And some sexy underwear. Dear little Sally broke up with that economics bloke from the Amos Tuck School she was going with, and you might get lucky."

Sally Lapidus? ... I'd seen her around Catherine Remillard's Metapsychic Preceptorial Institute, a clinical psychologist who had been one of Dorothée's early operant mentors. Sally wasn't drop-dead gorgeous like Masha—few women were—but she was a well-rejuvenated brunette with a vivacious manner, fine dark eyes, and an exquisite set of knockers. I, on the other hand, was feeling about as dashing as a pile of dog-barf, and I feared that Kyle was overly optimistic about my chances with the lady.

As I stood in front of the open armoire in my bedroom, still vacillating, Kyle put his hand on my shoulder and said quietly, "Come along, man. What have ye got to lose?"

The freeloading part didn't bother me. I'd cooked Kyle enough scratch suppers when he and Masha were on the outs, and he was currently flying high on the profits from his latest satire, *Revenge of the Weakly Interacting Massive Particles.*

I said, "Oh, hell, why not?"

Anything was better than moping around the bookshop watching the cat snooze in the front window while the last dead leaves dropped off the trees along Main Street. I gathered up my things, belted on the nifty leather stormcoat Denis and Lucille had given me for my 133rd birthday, and followed Kyle down the stairs and out into the murky back yard.

His new rhocraft was a screaming-orange Lamborghini.

As we climbed in, Masha snapped, "About time. I'd bloody well given up on you two bozos."

But Sally Lapidus gave me a sweet, welcoming smile and made room for me on the rear banquette. I began to feel better already.

We took off, and three hours later we landed in La Belle France. I'd had a nice nap, Kyle and the two ladies had jollied me out of my blue funk, and they'd filled me in on the latest poop in the Rebel community—including the mind-blowing information that Marc was preparing to announce his affiliation with the Rebel cause at the next Plenary Session of the Concilium.

As we were checking into our hotel off the Place Bellecour, we met a group of six fellow conferees from Edinburgh, former colleagues of Masha's, who insisted that we accompany them to supper at the legendary Bistrot de Lyon. The venerable eatery was crowded and noisy, full of happy people speaking heavily accented Standard English and even genuine French. The oysters, tartare de boeuf, and bouillon de poule aux ravioles were delicious (I passed on the gras-double), and the "pots" of young wine light and therapeutic—just what the doctor ordered for a recuperating old head-case. I ate and drank judiciously and listened to the shop-talk of the Rebel theoreticians with mild interest.

Up until a year or so ago, I hadn't paid a whole lot of attention to the deeper anti-Unity aspects of the Rebel cause. But then some Milieu-loyalist metapsychologists in Paris caused a furor in the media by claiming to have detected outbreaks of something called spontaneous coadunation—a sort of prelude to Unity that exotic scientists had predicted would occur when the human population in the galaxy reached a certain critical number, provoking what physicists call a phase change. Rebel theorists pooh-poohed the great news and immediately set out to prove that spontaneous coadunation didn't exist ... and even if it did, it didn't necessarily mean that Earthlings were on a sure downhill slide to Unity.

Denis (who looked forward to human Unification as though it were the Second Coming of Christ) had tried to explain the coadunation thing to me as a superior kind of mental harmony brought about by intensive interactive communication among multiple minds. He compared it to the evolution of single-cell organisms into complex, multicelled creatures, and the evolution of human society from little family-based clans into global or even galactic civilizations. He told me that Pierre Teilhard de Chardin, the canonized French Jesuit paleontologist, had discussed the possibility of this kind of global consciousness as far back as the 1930s. Mental coadunation, whatever it was, supposedly jibed nicely with what Denis called systems theory. When he had tried to explain *that* to me, my eyes glazed over.

Neither coadunation nor Unity appealed to me on a philosophical level, despite Denis's best efforts to explain them. Frankly, they scared me. I couldn't help being dubious about a phenomenon that might threaten the sanctity of my own thoughts ...

Well, all right. Maybe my thoughts weren't all that sacred. But they were mine and I wasn't keen on promiscuous sharing, not even to advance the evolution of the transcendental Mind of Humanity. I also had a suspicion that coadunation was nothing but a rehash of the romantic old notion of the perfectibility of human nature. You know: If we all just think together and strive together and achieve true mental siblinghood together—voilà!—human selfishness, contrariety, and original sin will disappear, and peace and love will rule the stars.

Sure.

Maybe the racial minds of the Gi and the Krondaku and the Simbiari and the Poltroyans and the Lylmik had evolved along those lines. But humanity was something else altogether. We were still blatant ethical primitives and a whole lot of folks like me still clung to our individuality with bloodyminded fervor. It seemed to me that we weren't ready for Unity—and maybe Unity wasn't ready for us, either.

Sitting there in the French restaurant, listening to the Rebel academics affirm in their elegant jargon the same basic conclusions my crude old mind had reached all on its own, I felt vindicated. I also felt depressed all over again, because it was plain that these people—and a whole lot of others just like them—intended to do more than debate the issue politely in sessions of the Galactic Concilium. They were going to fight for what they believed in.

And they had chosen Marc Remillard for their new leader, which meant that no matter how scintillating their theorizing was, where practical matters were concerned they were nothing but half-assed innocents.

It was two in the morning when we got back to the hotel. Dark-eyed Sally did not invite me to her room. It was just as well.

"There's this village a little west of the city," Kyle told me the next day. We had just finished a chilly and strenuous exploration of the ancient subterranean tunnels in Lyon's Croix-Rousse district and I was ready for something different. "It's called Saint-Antoine-des-Vignes. Supposed to have a great spot for lunch, and then I'd like to check out an unusual kind of country inn near it that Johnny Ludlum told me about. I'm thinking of using it in my next novel."

I was game, so we drove westward out of Lyon Metro toward a small range of mountains. The cheap groundcar that my novelist friend had rented lacked satellite navigation aids, and before long we were lost. It began to rain. Rags of mist draped themselves over the hills and obscured the inadequate directional signs. Almost by accident we finally found ourselves in Saint-Antoine, an obvious tourist trap with most of the boutiques and trumpery shops closed for the season. But the café-cum-pub, Chez Lalage, was open and its car park was jammed. Inside was a wonderful surprise, for the menu included both ordinary fare and a single plat du jour of the highest gourmet quality, with wines to match. The proprietor, a handsome young fellow named Louie, proudly told us that his wife, the chef, had headed a four-star establishment in Paris before succumbing to his charms and burying herself in les boondocks du Lyonnais.

Kyle and I lunched on the awesome blue-plate special, pigeonneaux à la Aristide Briand—fat squabs stuffed with foie gras and truffles. Then we had langoustine salad, and finished up with tiny dessert soufflés flavored with parfait d'amour. The bill was staggering—and so was I, since we had downed a couple of bottles of splendid '75 Leflaive Pucelles Puligny-Montrachet along with the meal, and my alcohol capacity still wasn't quite back up to snuff.

I was ready to curl up and go to sleep after that memorable lunch, but Kyle had other ideas. Following an earnest conversation with Louie, he drove us out of the village and turned onto a twisting, forest-bordered track that led into the cloud-shrouded mountains. Just when I became convinced that we were lost again, we pulled up at an open iron gate. On one of the gateposts was a polished brass sign:

L'AUBERGE DU PORTAIL

"This is it," Kyle said, and turned in. "The Inn of the Portal."

Tall shrub-roses with scarlet hips, nearly leafless now with the approach of winter, lined the graveled driveway. At the end of it, looming out of the mist, were three substantial buildings with balconies and mansard roofs, connected by covered arcades. They were poised above a series of landscaped terraces, and on a clear day the front rooms of the auberge would have commanded a fine view of the Rhône Valley. We drove into a parking area paved with flagstones. The main entrance to the inn had tall oaken doors shielded by a porte cochère. In the courtyard of the right wing was a rose garden, forlorn in the rain. Beyond that, tucked among pines and leafless mulberry trees, stood a quaint cottage with dark shutters and half-timbering. In spite of the lousy weather, a group of tourist types stood reverently in front of the little building listening to the spiel of a guide.

"That's where the time-gate is," Kyle said. He grabbed his camcorder, got out of the car, and began to make a video. "The equipment is set up in the basement of that cottage. The inventor was a chap named Théophile Guderian. He lived there until he died in 2041. His widow Angélique is supposed to have made a fortune shipping off well-heeled dafties and adventurers to Exile in the Pliocene Epoch, six million years in the past. Too bad we can't get inside the cottage to look over the machinery. It's off-limits except to the actual Time-Travelers and the operating techs. We'll be able to pick up some literature in the office, though."

"Time-gate?" I stood beside him on the puddled flagstones, my jaw hanging open. "Say! I think I remember hearing about this place years ago. I'd forgotten all about it."

"L'Auberge du Portail is the site of the only known temporal singularity in the galaxy. Guderian's gadgetry won't work anyplace else." Kyle did a slow 360-degree pan of the scene, finishing the shot by zooming in on the cottage. "Milieu authorities try to keep it hushed up, and there's a stiff fine if you publicize it in the vulgar media. If I do decide to use the place in my fantasy novel, I'll have to disguise the locale. The European Intendancy is mad as hell that they haven't been able to shut the auberge down, but they've tried for years without getting anywhere. The Pliocene Exile serves a useful purpose, y'see, siphoning off malcontents. I've heard that Davy MacGregor himself has given Madame Guderian permission to stay in business . . . Come on, let's tag along on the tour."

We hurried across the rose garden and joined the group that was slowly circling the cottage. It included humans, Poltroyans, and even a couple of Simbiari. The Green Leakies seemed to be enjoying the rain.

"—a period before the great Ice Age, when the hominid ancestors of humanity were small bipedal apes less than a meter in height," said the nice-looking female tour guide. "At that time, this part of France enjoyed a subtropical climate. Its open grassy savannas and woodlands swarmed with wild horses, antelopes, elephants, and many other species of wildlife. The predators included saber-toothed tigers—"

"How about T-rex?" one of the human tourists interrupted.

"Dinosaurs were extinct by the time of the Pliocene Epoch," the guide said patiently. "But there were giant crocodiles in the estuaries of the Atlantic rivers, and some authorities believe that plesiosaurs still inhabited the shallow parts of the sea."

I gawked unashamed as she continued her lecture on the flora and fauna of six million years ago, making prehistoric France sound like a Garden of Eden theme park. Kyle whispered to me that the clients of the auberge paid their extremely stiff fare, took a quickie course in wilderness survival, and stepped through the time-gate into a brave old world.

As we trailed along some distance behind the others, I said to Kyle that the Pliocene Exile sounded like heaven, and I was strongly tempted to get a ticket to ride.

"Me, too." He grinned wolfishly. "Only trouble is, the time-gate's a one-way proposition. Whatever returns through the singularity arrives six million years old."

"Tabernouche!" I groaned. "I knew there had to be a catch in it someplace."

"And no one really knows what the Time-Travelers find when they arrive in the past. Could be that they all live happily ever after like noble savages. On the other hand, even Eden had a snake—and name me one earthly paradise that wasn't fewked up sooner or later by human folly."

He was right, of course. We seem to carry the Lord of the Flies along with us wherever we go. I heaved a sigh on behalf of Paradise Lost.

The tour broke up in front of the auberge office, a small building separate from the inn proper. We rubberneckers were not permitted to mingle with the paying clientele, but there was a small selection of descriptive book-plaques about the place for sale in the office, as well as comprehensive application forms for prospective Time-Travelers. I bought one of the plaques and took a form just for the hell of it, even though I discovered quickly that no operant metapsychics were permitted to pass through the time-gate—only "normals." On the drive back to Lyon, Kyle and I joked about the fun a couple of overgrown adolescents like us might have had, living in a primitive world without rules or responsibilities.

Back at the hotel, we hung out in the bar until Masha and Sally came back from the symposium, and then we all got dressed to the teeth and went out to wine and dine at La Pyramide. Kyle didn't even flinch when the four-figure check arrived. After dinner there was a raucous party in the suite of some German psychophysicists. I got bombed on schnapps and turned maudlin, which caused Sally Lapidus to bid me a subzero good night when I sidled up to her with lascivious intent. Whereupon my old down-and-drag-ass mood swung back with a vengeance.

I don't recall too much more of the weekend, except that all the fun had gone out of it.

It wasn't until nearly a year later, long after the redactive debacle, that

Kyle told me how I had wept on his shoulder after Sally's rejection, begging him to take me back to Madame Guderian's Auberge du Portail so I could fly away to the Pliocene Exile and forget about perfidious women, mysterious mind-monsters, and the Metapsychic Rebellion.

[15]

HANOVER, NEW HAMPSHIRE, EARTH
24–25 DECEMBER 2078

Lucille Cartier studied herself critically in the dressing-table mirror and used psychokinesis to push the wings of her dark brown bangs slightly upward. The new touch of silver at the temples was definitely appropriate for a matriarch with thirty-nine great-great-grandchildren. She was glad, however, that none of them—and none of their parents, dearly loved though they were—would be at the réveillon this year. It was to be a mercifully small affair, including only the Dynasty and a handful of adult grandchildren. Later, on Christmas Day, there would be more inclusive holiday gatherings. She and Denis would drop in on the ones being held in Hanover, then end up at Adrien and Cheri's house down in the Loudon Hills for Christmas dinner.

Poking through her jewelry box, Lucille decided that a necklace of cherry-sized Caledonian pearls linked by narrow wrought-gold chains would set off her chic black wool dress to perfection.

"Let me fasten the clasp," said Denis, coming up behind her.

"Thank you." She turned toward his smiling face and their lips touched, all that was needed to kindle the familiar sweet sexual blaze in both of their bodies after eighty-three years of marriage.

"Tu es ravissante, ma biche," he whispered, "comme toujours."

They held one another for a moment, then reluctantly broke apart. She asked him, "Is it still snowing?"

He could have used his farsight, but instead he stepped to the bedroom window and looked outside. The ornamental lamps in front of the library were indistinct amber glows. "Coming down smartly. It's genuine old-fashioned New England Christmas weather."

"I'm glad." She had put on the matching pearl earrings. "This will be the first time in ages we've had Paul with us at the réveillon." And the other children except for poor Anne—

Anne will be well again in just a few more months next Christmas she'll be celebrating midnight mass for us herself she wouldn't want you to worry about her and spoil the occasion.

No of course not. "It's nearly twenty-three thirty. If we want to be sure of a seat we'd better get started. Is Rogi stopping by?"

"He said he'd meet us at the church."

They went downstairs. The big house was quiet except for the ticking of the grandfather clock in the front hall. In the darkened living room a token miniature tree with lights and plain colored balls stood on the gateleg table by the window. This year, for the first time, Lucille had loaned her precious collection of antique ornaments to her granddaughter for the tree out at the farm.

"It feels odd, not having the réveillon at our house," Lucille said. "But I couldn't say no to Marie. She was so insistent, so happy that the farm was back in the family again after years of being rented out to strangers."

Denis said, "It actually makes a good deal of sense to rotate the venue for the festivities, especially now that the family's grown so huge. I know the others always did their best to help, Luce, but most of the work still fell on you. Last year was just about the last straw: eighty-nine people!"

"I never minded. But . . . I'm beginning to realize that I've been terribly selfish, refusing to pass the tradition on to the young. Rejuvenation made me forget what it means to grow old. I see our adult children and grandchildren and great-grandchildren and I can't help thinking that I'm still the grownup in charge and they're the little ones. But they're not and I'm not."

He laughed quietly. "Thank heaven."

"No, it's really not funny at all. Old people have always tried to cling to power. We automatically assume that our greater experience equates with wisdom. And we *rejuvenated* old people think we've earned the right to be top dogs forever. I remember being so disappointed when you insisted on going emeritus at the college even though the trustees begged you to remain head of the Metapsychology Department. But you were right and I was wrong. It was time to pass the leadership on to your younger colleagues."

Denis put his arms around her. "Rejuvenation causes problems, and so will our family's immortality genes. But I expect we'll sort things out eventually. You don't really have to worry about the Human Polity becoming a stagnant gerontocracy like the Lylmik Twenty-One Worlds."

She clung to him, glad of the physical warmth. Her eyes were fixed on the small Christmas tree. "I don't want to live forever, Denis. It's unnatural. Young people are the ones who revel in the notion of immortality, not the old. There . . . have been times lately when I felt so deadly tired—not physically, but emotionally. The thought of just casting everything to the winds and letting go can be extremely appealing."

"I know."

Abruptly, she asked, "Do you think the Rebellion will escalate into a war?"

"I don't know, Luce. I pray it won't come to that."

"Do you realize that Catherine is almost ready to declare for the Rebels? I could have wept! First Adrien, then Sevvy, and now Cat."

Denis sighed. "She told me about her decision a month or so ago. It was Marc's conversion that tipped the scales for her."

"I've given up being shocked by Marc's enormities. But Cat has always been so sane and sensible! We—we had words when she broke the news to me, and I said some things I'm sorry for now. But I couldn't help it. Doesn't she realize that the Rebels are serious about breaking away from the Milieu by force? I *remember* the wars we had here on Earth before the Intervention. I couldn't bear for it to happen again. If only you would—" She broke off. Her thoughts became impenetrable, but not before he had caught their drift.

"You think it would help if I took a more active role on behalf of loyalist humanity. If I became a public champion of Unity like Paul and Anne and Jack."

"You believe in Unity," Lucille said softly. "You've assured me that it's good, that it won't destroy our individuality as the Rebel metapsychologists maintain it will. You're the premier authority on mental science and your new book will certainly help the Unity cause. But if you became a Magnate of the Concilium you'd be able to counter the influence of people like Anna Gawrys and Owen Blanchard and Hiroshi Kodama. And Marc . . ."

"He'll make a difference in the thrust of the Rebel movement," Denis admitted, his face tightening. "Taking Marc as their leader is either the smartest thing the Rebels have ever done—or the most foolish."

"You could run rings around Marc in Concilium debate. You know you could! Unity is basically about the evolution of altruism, but everything Marc does is rooted in his own ego-need and his hatred of Paul."

"Luce, I've never been a fighter—"

"This isn't about fighting. It's about moral strength. About creativity. I remember what you did on top of Mount Washington. I was there. You could do it again."

He shook his head. "The situation is completely different."

"The Lylmik keep nominating you. They know how much you're needed in the Concilium. And Davy MacGregor has urged you time and time again to accept. I know you cherish your privacy, chéri, but you aren't just an ordinary citizen. I was selfish wanting to keep my little portion of family power. Be certain that you aren't acting selfishly in a completely different way—"

He kissed her to silence:

Dear Lucille. You know me so well. And you and Davy aren't the only ones to reproach me for my greatest weakness. Another person did too a long time ago and he was right and you are right and I'll do what's right. There! Je te souhaite un joyeux Noël.

"You mean you *will*?"

"Yes. If the Lylmik ask me again."

"Merci, merci, mon amour." Her eyes glittered with unshed tears. "Mon amour seul et unique."

He helped her put on her fur coat. The Ronkomi fish-pelts were a richly shaded dark green, sewn in a herringbone pattern. She tied a white head-scarf over her hair and pulled on gloves while Denis donned a blue cashmere topcoat. He didn't bother with a hat. They were walking to midnight mass and the church was right around the corner on Sanborn Road. One of the children would give them a ride to the supper afterward.

"I forgot to tell you that Marie asked us to stay the night," Lucille said. "She's fixed up our old bedroom for us and all the overnight things are there. I told her we'd stay if you liked the idea. Then we can go on to the other parties straight from the farm."

"It might be fun," Denis said, "sleeping out in the country again in a nice little blizzard, seeing the snowdrifts pile up against the barn and the fences instead of being banished as a public nuisance. Yes. Let's do it. I'm glad the farm is back in the family. I was sorry to have to leave it."

Lucille eyed him. "You never said anything. I thought you were pleased when we moved back to South Street."

"Well, it didn't bother me that much, returning to the house where we'd raised the children. But I was sorry that Paul didn't keep the old place himself."

"So was I—but there was no helping it. You know that. I don't see how any human being can do the job Paul does. Expecting him to have a normal family life besides is unrealistic. Be glad that most of the other children were able to have good marriages."

He took her in his arms. "Not as good as ours, though."

She whispered his name, and once again they conjoined. Their bulky winter garments might not have existed, for such is the way between lovers of great experience who are also powerful operants. Without physical movement they climaxed instantly, rested in each other, then separated and went sedately outside, stopping for a moment on the porch while Denis locked the front door with an old brass key.

The snow fell thickly in the windless, curiously bright air. It did not seem especially cold. South Street and the single sidewalk opposite their house steamed gently from the action of the melting grids. Other pedestrians were heading toward the church.

"What a lovely night," Lucille said. "So immaculate and quiet."

Denis murmured in agreement. He took her arm and they crossed the street. External Christmas decorations were not customary in the college town, but most of the houses had trees in their front windows with multicolored fairy lights that twinkled through the sifting curtain of white.

The church parking area was full and cars were lined along both sides of Sanborn Road. The eggs of out-of-towners had been banished to the big lot behind the college football field across Lebanon Street. The church was a striking old building of mortared fieldstone and cut granite, almost a parody of the English perpendicular architectural style. Its boxy tower had recently been fitted out with a new muted carillon that was playing Henry Wadsworth Longfellow's carol. Denis and Lucille went inside. The choir was singing along with the chiming bells.

Lucille said: I haven't heard that song in years sentimental lyrics certainly but perhaps also uncannily apropos for our troubled times when did Longfellow flourish anyhow?

Denis said: Middle 19thcentury I suppose he was referring to the turmoil of the War Between the States plus ça change plus c'est la même chose.

Lucille said: I see Phil&Aurelie&Maurie&Cecilia [there] and Catherine [there] and Cheri&Adrien&UncleRogi [there] no Paul no Severin I hope they haven't been delayed but it would be just like them to come in after the sermon it's rather crowded do you want to sit with any of the children? We could ask an usher to squeeze us in.

Denis said: I think not. We'll have plenty of time to be with them later on. Let's just be selfish for once and sit here in the last pew and sing along with the carolers and pretend it's our first midnight mass together.

PHILIP REMILLARD: They just came in.

MAURICE REMILLARD: I saw I don't think our wives or the others have noticed yet thank God they're not coming over to mindtalk before mass starts I don't think I could bear it Phil this is monstrous how could we ever have agreed to do it on *Christmas?*

PHILIP: It provides the perfect opportunity. Papa will be completely unsuspecting and we're as ready now as we'll ever be.

MAURICE: Ready! I suppose so . . . practicing with those abominable CE helmets was a damned unsettling experience.

PHILIP: I'm glad I wasn't the only one to think so I wasn't unsettled I was appalled.

MAURICE: We take our higher mindpowers for granted and those of us who are sane come to an accommodation with them eventually but with CE that adaptation is utterly demolished suddenly one or more of the metafaculties is amplified to a godlike degree it's WONDERFUL it's TERRIBLE it's ADDICTIVE it's a satanic thrill you don't want to go back to the lower level of cerebral function where you were before—

PHILIP: You too you felt it *TOO?*

MAURICE: Oh yes.

PHILIP: Merde . . .

MAURICE: Yes indeed.

PHILIP: You know what we're going to have to do don't you?

MAURICE: We're going to have to convince the Concilium to ban CE outright. The exotics were right after all its dangers far outweigh any potential advantages.

PHILIP: We've been incredibly naive thinking mainly about the personal hazard to the CE operators. So few Magnates of the Concilium have had personal experience with CE . . . Perhaps the exotics' continual harping on CE's potential for obstructing Unity distracted us from the black heart of the matter: Our racial Mind has adapted only with great difficulty to the growing presence of Homo superior in its midst—but it CAN'T adapt to having part of its Mind aspire to Homo summus. We aren't angels Maurie.

MAURICE: We aren't even safetyvalved urlogicians like the Krondaku! CE is an unacceptable temptation even to highly trained grandmasters like you and me. In time we'd *need* it we'd mechanize ourselves we'd succumb to the ultimate addiction. Humanity will have to take another road one that's higher and slower and safer than CE refining the METACONCERT technique itself linking hundreds or thousands or billions of minds together in a cooperative synergistic structure each contributing its natural allotment of mental energy to the greater whole that's the way it should be that's the way it *must* be.

PHILIP: In time. But not yet. We have no choice but to use CE against Fury. Jack and Dorothea are right about its ambitions being galactic and God knows what damage to the Milieu it's already done. We've got to attack it with all of the redactivecoercive power we can muster.

MAURICE: If we could only be certain that this drastic procedure will work!

PHILIP: Jack thinks the chances are good all we can do is pray he's right.

MAURICE: The other option . . . I don't think I could go through with it monster or no monster knowing that Papa's good core persona still lived still watched us still hoped—

PHILIP: We'll do our best to save him try not to think beyond that.

MAURICE: There's the problem with Sevvy. It was never really resolved during the practice sessions and he could still bug out at the last minute the selfcentered coward.

PHILIP: He can't help what he is. Paul will talk sense into him—

MAURICE: I know why Sevvy's balking. He's afraid of the CE rigs he knows too much about the damned things he helped Marc with some of the intracerebral design way back in the beginning he thinks the Furymonster might get at us through the brainboards in the hats and he's right. It could.

PHILIP: We don't have to worry on that score anymore. Paul told me this morning that Dorothea found a way to quadruple the safety factor against reverse coercive invasion. There's virtually no chance for Fury to harm the metaconcert.

MAURICE: Good that leaves only the HORRIBLEPOSSIBILITY that Papa isn't Fury after all and we might kill him or wreck his mind ac-

cidentally during the procedure or the MOSTHORRIBLEPOSSI-
BILITY that Papa *IS* Fury and we can't excise the malignancy so it's
our fucking duty to put him to death . . .

PHILIP: Ferme ça Maurie! Pray for strength!

MAURICE: Don't you think I've tried? I'm burnt out Phil praying
doesn't mean anything anymore I just want it to be over I don't want
to have to think about it—

> [DENIS+LUCILLE: And the mountains in reply,
> Echoing their joyous strains.
> Gloria, gloria in excelsis deo.]

MAURICE: Et in terra pax the human race was promised pax but we
never seem to enjoy it for very long do we Phil maybe this Rebellion
is Fury's fault but I think not we've never really needed a devil to
blame for our failures we humans do very well wrecking the world
all by ourselves.

PHILIP: Remette-toi! Garde ton calme ti-frère et ton espérance surtout.

> [LECTOR: All please rise now and greet our
> celebrant Brother Bartholomew Jackson by
> joining with the choir in singing Adeste
> Fideles.]

PHILIP+MAURICE: Adeste fideles laeti triumphantes . . .

The First Magnate's rhocraft, a Saab without official markings that he
had borrowed from the staff transport pool, hurtled through the starry
sky high above the storm clouds. Paul Remillard was dressed in casual
slacks of charcoal nebulin and a bulky red-and-white cardigan that
Santa Claus might have envied. He sent his powerful farsight arrowing
ahead of the egg, scanning the farm outside of Hanover.

"Most of the others are finished eating and are getting ready to pass
out their presents. We've timed it perfectly."

"Everything you do is perfect," said Severin Remillard without a
trace of bitterness. "As for myself, I'm highly imperfect and the first to
admit it."

He was seventy-five years old, Paul's senior by eleven years, but the
family's arbitrary self-rejuvenating gene complex had given Severin an
earlier climacteric than his brother. He was a tall, blond man who might
have been in his late thirties, more muscular than Paul, with strong features that would have been attractive had he not been so haggard. A

deep vertical crease was drawn between eyes that had turned bloodshot with fatigue, and his mouth was a taut line. He had on a down vest, a blue plaid flannel shirt over a bronze polo-neck, and heavy whipcord pants stuffed into Timberline boots.

Paul said, "You have nothing to worry about, Sevvy. You were more than competent in the CE practice sessions. This flop sweat you're experiencing is distressing but it can be overcome if you'll just let me do a—"

"No," Severin said. "I'm telling you for the last time that I can't participate in the metaconcert operation. I've tried to psych myself out of this—this stupid negatory mind swamp I've fallen into, but it's no good. *I'm* no good."

"Stop talking like an idiot. Let me into your brain and I'll banish whatever horrors are eating you with a quick Band-Aid fix. Later, after we've taken care of Papa, Cat and I will do a permanent redact job on you."

"Tranquilizing me isn't the point, Paul. I'm not just yellow-bellied— I'm a weak link in the structure, a danger to all the others in the metaconcert. You don't understand . . ."

Back in Concord, faced with Severin's sudden panicky recalcitrance, the First Magnate had been obliged to coerce his brother into accompanying him to Hanover. But there was no way that he could force Severin to assist in their father's healing.

"You can't let us down now, at the last minute," Paul remonstrated. "You've got a strong grandmasterly redactive faculty that's a vital component of the program."

"You don't need me," Severin insisted. "The concert design is more coercive than redactive anyway, and with the CE hats it generates gigawatts of mindpower. My God, at full zorch you could probably coerce the whole damn population of New Hampshire to dance a jig in the snow in their birthday suits and still have enough mental energy left to shrink Papa twice over."

"Not if he's a suboperant paramount in redaction. And Jack thinks he almost certainly is." LOOK [image] how your absence would fuck up our attempt to integrate dual personae we *must* have your input!

"Postpone the operation and find somebody to take my place. Both Luc and Ken Macdonald are trustworthy and strong in redaction. Train them up and plug them in."

The First Magnate exploded. "Dammit, Sevvy, we're ready now!

We've spent four tough weeks perfecting the metaconcert using the eight of us. It's been a bitch setting this thing up without arousing anyone's suspicions and we can't start all over now because of your cold feet. We can't risk Papa finding out. We've got to go ahead."

The pinched face of the retired neurologist had begun to shine with greasy perspiration. Severin pulled out a handkerchief and swabbed his brow. He shrugged off his down vest and fiddled with the air vents on his side of the rhocraft cabin. "I tried to tell you it might be psychologically impossible for me to function in this metaconcert, but you kept shouldering my objections aside. You convinced everyone that I was just afraid of risking my own skin. But that's not the problem at all."

"Then what the fuck *is* it?"

Severin's head was bowed. "I'm vulnerable to Fury in a way you never even suspected. I've never told anyone. Ah, shit . . . I can't even articulate the engram now. Just take a look at this." [Image.]

The memory was more than thirty years old. In a shadowy sickroom, Denis and his seven adult children and their brave spouses and reluctant old Uncle Rogi gathered around a bed where a comatose figure lay. The patient was a ruggedly handsome man with dark curling hair. He bore an uncanny resemblance to Paul's son Marc. But he was not Marc.

The First Magnate was incredulous as the meaning of the vision became clear. "*Victor?* You think that Papa's dissociative persona is actually his dead brother Victor? That's preposterous! You can't tell me you're afraid of a ghost."

"I know . . . my fear seems . . . irrational to you." Severin spoke slowly, in an oddly pitched, strained tone, as though he were pulling each word past some dense mental obstruction. "But you never knew Vic when he was in full control of his faculties. I . . . did. And every time we gathered for that annual Good Friday prayer session I was . . . frightened nearly out of my mind by . . . that devil who had tried to seize control of me when I was a child . . . and afterward."

"Seize control?" Paul was stunned. "What do you mean?"

Severin plodded on, speaking more easily now, forcing himself to tell the story as he stared unseeing at the flickering position-report images on the navigation screen. "The only way I could get through those Good Fridays was by redacting myself affectless, suppressing every human emotion, turning myself into a fucking block of wood. Papa never seemed to notice what kind of shape I was in when we linked minds for the prayer—or whatever it was that he did with us. All through the years that Victor lived on in a coma, I'd go home from the Good Friday sessions and vomit my guts out from sheer relief. I was safe from Vic for another year. The bastard hadn't managed to get me."

"Get you," Paul repeated, stricken.

"He'd tried, you see. When I was just a little kid."

"Jesus, Sevvy. You should have told us. We could have helped you—"

"No. It was my battle and I had to win it. I don't expect you to understand, Paul. You were the youngest of the Dynasty, the prodigy, everyone's pet, trained from the time you were in the uterus with exotic preceptive techniques. But the three of us who were born before the Intervention had to pull ourselves up by our mental bootstraps. It was hard. Phil and Maurie were always pretty tough nuts, but I was the weak little brother. Victor must have known it and he never bothered either of them, only me. He said I was special, damn him! He pretended to know how I felt, how I chafed under the ethical restrictions our parents made us live by. Oh, he was clever—he knew what buttons to push and I almost gave in to the temptation more than once. His mind-fucks were quick and short and they only happened at the big family get-togethers like Easter and Christmas. I always managed to fend him off."

Paul shook his head but said nothing.

"I was there at the Great Intervention along with Phil and Maurie and Papa and Mama. I was ten years old. Uncle Rogi zapped Victor on the mountain and turned him into a vegetable, and the whole world was saved, and I thought my fight with the demon was over. But it hadn't even really begun yet. When Papa began that annual prayer vigil, I became obsessed with the fear that Victor would recover and begin the harassment all over again. Then, in 2040, Vic's body finally died . . . but his spirit was reborn as Fury. In some obscene coercive way he seduced my poor unborn son Quint—along with Celine and Gordo and Parni and your Madeleine. He made them Hydras. He would have made me a Hydra, too, if I hadn't resisted him with all my strength. Earlier on, I guess Vic was too inexperienced in evil to spring the trap on me properly. So he tried again when I was a full-grown man."

"Sevvy, I think I know what—"

"Victor came to me again, about five years after he died. As Fury. Trying to steal my soul. I fought him again for the last time and won."

Like Anne, Paul said to himself. Like Dorothea. *And how many others?*

Severin closed his haunted eyes. There were tears on his cheeks.

"Victor's still alive, Paul. In our poor father's brain. And I don't dare face him again. That—that last fight took the heart out of me. This time, Victor would win."

Paul let his coercive strength embrace his brother. "Listen to me, Sevvy. You're not the only one this has happened to. Fury tempted Anne, too. And Dorothea Macdonald. In both cases, it pretended to be someone else to enhance its attempt at coercion. The monster is real, but it is *not* Victor. That kind of occult transference between the living and the dead doesn't happen. Victor is gone and can never threaten you or harm you again."

Severin smiled sadly. For the first time his wavering gaze met Paul's steady one. "But if I believe he lives, it doesn't matter whether or not my belief is true. I'm vulnerable to Fury—whoever it is—because of this unresolved mental trauma from my childhood. I can't be part of your metaconcert. All throughout the practice sessions I tried to redact myself, to overcome the old fears. But I couldn't . . . You can't prove to me that Fury isn't Victor. No one will know the truth until the metaconcert enters Papa's mind and finds out for itself. But by then it would be too late for me—and perhaps for the rest of you as well if my mind gives way and leaves the metaconcert open to invasion by the monster."

"That's nonsense! I've told you how Dorothea strengthened the program design to prevent any countercoercive movement by the Fury persona—"

"If Fury is Victor, I'd be the chink in the dike. I'd crack and he'd subsume all of us. You know as well as I do that there are aspects of metapsychology that are still a complete mystery to us. Just ask that Hawaiian kahuna woman, Malama Johnson, about the unquiet dead! Ask her about your own wife, Teresa . . ."

Paul took hold of his brother's shoulders. His voice was charged with angry intensity. "Pull yourself together, man! You're a scientist and a Magnate of the Concilium—not a damned superstitious Pacific islander. It doesn't *matter* whether the Fury demon is a ghost or an aspect of a deranged personality. If it lives inside Denis's mind, we can integrate it and render it harmless with this metaconcert. Will you be able to live with yourself if you refuse to give our father the help he needs?"

"I'd help Papa if I could." Severin's voice was flat with despair. He disengaged Paul's hands. "I'm sorry. So sorry."

The First Magnate drew in his breath, biting off an exclamation of angry frustration. Severin, the onetime brain surgeon, had correctly assessed his own disability. In his present disturbed state he was incapable of participating effectively in any metaconcert operation. No quick and dirty makeshift redaction could possibly restore him.

"I'll farspeak Jack," the First Magnate said dully, "and tell him we'll have to abort."

PAUL: I never heard of such a thing.

JACK: It's been done before Papa. On the Siberian planet when the wife of one of the metaconcert participants died on the eve of a critical operation and there was no substitute available for the bereaved man. He was in no emotional state to fill an active role in the metaconcert so he was given a deep course of calmative redaction that almost completely cut off his volition. His mind remained aware and observant but incapable of exerting willpower. They plugged him into the concert and it functioned.

PAUL: A *dummy* unit in our CE metaconcert? Is that what you're proposing?

JACK: A nonparticipant mind of precalibrated metafunction that would nevertheless round out the symmetry of the original eightfold configuration and permit the release of coherently programmed energy.

PAUL: And you really think this sneetch would work?

JACK: The Yakutian concert achieved a respectable percentage of its rated output—to the amazement of one&all. Severin is right about there being a huge coercive surplus in our setup and I think the synergized redactive quotient of the seven of us should suffice to integrate Grandpère.

PAUL: And if it doesn't?

JACK: The monster could take permanent possession of his mind forcing us to utilize the lethal option. There has always been that risk. Reorganizing the metaconcert with other participants would be risky as well. It would mean a considerable delay.

PAUL: Severin suggested that Luc and Ken might sub for him.

JACK: I'm not at all certain that they would be suitable. Luc suffered from epilepsy as a child and his brain might not stand up to the strain of CE. Ken's redactive faculty is only marginally at the grandmaster level. No . . . if we decide to abort now our best course would be to wait until Anne is fit to join the metaconcert.

PAUL: But that could be months from the time she exits the tank. And we'd have to check her out ahead of time to make certain that she wasn't Fury herself.

JACK: Yes. The decision is yours Papa. And Uncle Sevvy's.

PAUL: . . . It's my considered judgment that we should go ahead now utilizing the dummy configuration. Severin says he's willing.

JACK: Very well. Diamond will take care of Uncle Sevvy's calmative redaction. Just let him be the first to break away from the réveillon and come downstairs. Can he maintain a firm mindscreen until then?

PAUL: No problem there.

JACK: Then let's get on with it. Please cue the other concert participants on intimode when you think it's safe for them to leave the réveillon. The operation site is secured with a mechanical fuzzer and thus far no one's paid any attention to it at all. Be sure Uncle Rogi knows exactly when to bring Denis downstairs. I've made arrangements for Rogi to witness the procedure but it's best if we don't tell him in advance.

PAUL: I'll take care of everything.

JACK: Diamond and I will be waiting. A bientôt Papa.

[16]

FROM THE MEMOIRS OF
ROGATIEN REMILLARD

My two favorites among the Remillard Dynasty were Severin, the icon-oclast who had first won my heart when he was a nonconformist schoolboy, and Adrien, whose sense of humor and unpretentious man-ner were a refreshing contrast to the relentless gravitas of Phil, Maurie, Anne, Catherine, and Paul.

Adrien had inherited the slender frame and plain features of his mother, Lucille. His hair and eyes were dark, and he wore a small mus-tache. In 2078 he was a Magnate of the Concilium and a consulting metapsychologist in the Panpolity Directorate for Justice. He was also one of the top strategists in the Rebel Party and had been instrumental in bringing me into the ranks. Under normal circumstances I greatly en-joyed Adrien's company.

But my heart sank as I entered the crowded vestibule of Hanover's Catholic church on Christmas Eve and immediately bumped into him, his wife Cheri Losier-Drake, their youngest son Cory, and Cory's wife Norah Jacoby.

I had not seen them since Jack and Dorothée's wedding and they greeted me warmly, insisting that I sit with them during the mass and also accept a ride out to the farm afterward. It was impossible to refuse. I was forced to be jolly old Uncle Rogi to Cheri and the young folks en clair, while more or less simultaneously listening to Adrien's technical discussion of the upcoming exorcism on my intimate telepathic mode. My discomfort was compounded by having to express belated condo-lences on the death of Parnell. Cheri and Adrien had no idea that I was the one responsible for snuffing their son, the Hydra.

The majestic ceremony of the solemn high mass was no help to my dread-filled soul. I was unable to pray. I was barely able to go through the motions of singing and speaking the ceremonial responses. When it was time for communion, I shuffled up and took the bread and wine like an automaton.

Adrien was so preoccupied that he never noticed my malaise. But Denis did. I felt his benign coercion prodding at my mindscreen, gently at first and then with increasing strength, attempting to discover what was wrong. But of course he could not. Coming back to my seat I met his concerned gaze and intimode query with a glassy smile and shook my head slightly.

No big thing mon fils, I told him. Just a touch of the holiday blues a good hot cup of cafébrûlot or some rumpunch will fix me up fine&dandy.

Denis nodded. A minute later he and Lucille exchanged knowing glances and I knew they would cook up some kindly plot intended to restore my spirits. It would never do to have Uncle Rogi play the party pooper at the Christmas réveillon.

There was a monumental traffic jam in the egg-park after mass let out. The robot-navigators in the rhocraft of the parishioners, unable to respond safely to the conflicting commands of several hundred pilots all in a rush to enter the same airspace, kicked everybody's system into emergency override and forced the eggs to take off one at a time. The result was that we got to Marie's place sometime after the other family churchgoers, who had traveled in groundcars.

The farmhouse was postcard-pretty in the continuing snowfall, framed by dramatic pine trees and leafless mutant elms. Two small evergreens flanking the front door were decked with tiny lights, and the house windows and sodium yard-lamps cast a mellow glow on the white blanket covering the lawn and the winter-fast meadows.

Adrien parked his egg out next to the barn and we tramped through the shallow drifts, bearing our small sacks of presents. Marie and the others greeted us at the door with shouts of "Joyeux Noël!" Only Paul and Severin had not yet arrived. The other members of the Dynasty were there with their spouses, and a few adult grandchildren were also in attendance: Phil and Aurelie's youngest daughter Marianne and her husband Hans Dorfmann; Cat's twins, Ron and René McAllister-Remillard; Maurice and Cecilia's son Roland with his wife Maio-Ling Wu; and Paul's son Luc with his spouse Ken Macdonald.

The usual happy holiday bedlam prevailed for some time, with people shouting greetings, oohing at the big Christmas tree, embracing Denis and Lucille, and commenting on the weather. Thanks no doubt to sub-rosa prompting from Denis and Lucille, I was also made much of. The younger females flirted with me and told me how well I was looking, while the young men shared their freshest naughty jokes. Then one of the grandchildren wondered what was holding up Paul and Severin, whereupon Marie neatly distracted everybody by throwing open the dining room doors upon a sumptuous buffet. Nary a traditional Franco-American goodie was to be seen—hélas!—but I forced myself to fill a plate with Buffalo wings, gorgonzola dip, Poltroyan pickled tariji eggs, dim sum, curly fries, kidney bean salad, and walnut-maple-fudge torte. I carried my little supper, along with a large mug of hot buttered rum, to a chair half-concealed by the Christmas tree. I was sick and tired of being cheered up and wanted to be left alone.

After I'd tucked away most of the food I sent my seekersense gingerly sniffing toward the door leading to the farmhouse cellar, which lay at the far end of the front hallway.

Badaboum! A near-irresistible little compulsion grabbed hold of me: I didn't really want to look into the basement. Heavens, no! It was utterly prosaic and uninteresting. What I really wanted to do was check out the antique blown-glass ornaments on the tree: the animals, gnomes, angels, magic mushrooms, fruits, and vegetables that Lucille had collected all her life. Remember the old game? The first one who finds the pickle gets a big candy cane—

I broke through the coercive device and ran smack into a veritable bombproof thought-barrier. The entire basement area was impervious to farsensing, veiled by some sort of sophisticated mindscreening machine.

So much for checking out the redactive operation in advance! I'd find out what was down there at the same time Denis did.

I settled back again, studying the tree the way I was supposed to do. (The compulsion was so neatly done it had to be an artifact of Ti-Jean's.) I finally found the ornamental pickle, but instead of rewarding myself with candy I went back to the dining room and ladled out another steaming mug of rum.

Paul and Severin finally got there when the party had already been in full swing for over an hour. Both of them came in burdened with sacks of presents, shaking the snow from their clothes, bellowing the best wishes of the season in rusty Canuckois. Paul was as suave and hearty as ever, but Severin was clearly on edge, guarding his mind like a junkyard dog and laughing too loudly at Paul's witticisms. Marie saw that the late arrivals both got something to eat and drink, and then it was time to pass out the presents.

Our family has never believed in elaborate gift-giving, and Lucille had long ago insisted that the réveillon be an occasion for the exchange of only modest tokens. One was permitted to inspect the loot with deepsight, but opening the gifts was forbidden until after one went home—thus avoiding a mess of torn wrappings. Book and music flecks were perennial favorites, being tasteful and easy to tote in quantity; so were tiny flacons of perfume, microbottles of exotic booze, Gi friendship rings and other knickknacks from faraway planets, and (for the fun-loving adult contingent) psychedelic poppers. That year I was giving little silver Bic plaque-stylos. You can never find one when you need one, so you can never have too many.

While the gift swap was going on, along with much laughter, appreciative remarks, and the occasional groan (Luc and Ken gave ghastly antique Nicole Miller neckties to the gents and equally atrocious old Hermès scarves to the ladies), Marie brought out a big silver bowl of eggnog with crystal cups, which she set down for Lucille to serve in front of the fire. Paul threw more logs on the grate and somebody put out the lamps so that the only illumination came from the Christmas tree and the leaping flames.

Norah Jacoby unrolled a scrollo keyboard and played "Silent Night" in tinkling celesta tones. Some people sang along while others settled back to talk quietly. I noticed Severin slip away, and the words of the carol froze in my throat.

After a few more minutes passed, Catherine excused herself in the most natural manner possible. Norah switched her keyboard to the spinet mode and played "It Came Upon a Midnight Clear." Paul was deep in conversation with Denis and Lucille, discussing some new charitable project being undertaken by the Remillard Foundation. Philip and Maurice wandered off together, arguing some abstruse political point. Norah and the other grandchildren delivered a fortissimo rendering of the Dartmouth "Winter Song." Then Adrien left the parlor, allegedly in search of cognac. Paul said he'd like some, too, and got up to follow Adrien. Norah played "Cantique de Noël" and Denis and Lucille joined in as we all sang the old carol in French. Outside the parlor window, the snow fell thick and clean. It was almost three o'clock in the morning.

Paul's mind said to me on my intimate mode: *It's time to bring him downstairs.*

In my unobtrusive corner, I got to my feet, clearing my throat.

"And now we've come to a very special part of the réveillon," I announced. "Denis, your children have prepared a surprise for you. Would you please come along with me? And the rest of you . . . kindly wait here with Marie, who will have something to say in just a few minutes."

There were delighted exclamations. Lucille beamed at her husband as I took his arm and led him out of the parlor into the hall.

"No fair peeking with your farsight," I warned him in a playful tone.

We went to the door leading down to the cellar. As I opened it he gave a murmur of surprise. The cloudy superficies of the specialized sigma-field concealed the stairway below the first step.

Once again I felt him probe tentatively at my mind. He was vaguely concerned because of my jittery behavior. I tried to project an air of excitement and uttered a poor excuse for a conspiratorial chuckle. "Those crazy kids of yours really know how to hide a secret. Ready to go down?"

Denis laughed. "All right. I promise to be completely surprised."

I moved ahead of him, taking hold of the railing, and held out my hand. Denis took it. "Allons!" I cried gaily.

We stepped through the matter-permeable barrier and I led him down the steps. The cellar was full of shadows, lit by a single old-fashioned filament bulb that hung from the beamed ceiling. The walls were grimy whitewashed rough stone, obviously of a great age, but the floor had been sealed with a modern hypocaustic composite and was slightly springy underfoot, exuding warmth. In the area immediately to the left of the stairs were storage shelves, the house's fusion heating plant, the refuse recycling unit, and the kinds of miscellaneous junk that you'd expect to find in a basement. To the right of the stairs was a partition of new, unpainted particleboard with a door in it, very slightly ajar. The area inside was dark.

"Is it in there?" Denis asked amiably.

I gestured. "After you."

Smiling, Denis pushed open the door.

And froze.

There was an instantaneous explosion of light. Seven figures haloed in blue-white radiance stood motionless inside the cleared enclosure, stationed in a semicircle around a padded leather chaise longue of the type used by clinical metapsychologists. They were clad in dazzling silver Nomex and their heads were entirely hidden beneath silvery CE helmets of an unfamiliar and grotesque design. Before Denis or I could take a breath or articulate a thought, an eighth disembodied CE helmet with a blood-red aura seemed to appear out of nowhere. It hovered just in front of Denis at eye level.

Jack said: *Grandfather please lie down on the couch.*

The others reiterated coercively: *LIE DOWN. PLEASE.*

Denis seemed to be struggling against some invisible assailant. He staggered, then his body convulsed as though shocked by a bolt of electricity. He clapped his hands over his ears and I heard him scream at the top of his lungs.

The blood turned to ice in my veins. All my instincts urged me to go to Denis's aid, but a voice in my mind said sharply: *No! Don't touch him!*

Another spasm racked Denis, and then a third. He fell to his knees with his arms attempting to shield his head. His agonized cries, raw and hoarse, now came with every breath. I was stiff with horror. I had never expected anything like this.

LIE DOWN ON THE COUCH. This time it was the metaconcert speaking. The eight minds had merged into one.

Denis said: Don't do this to me Children don't.

OBEY.

My son whispered, "No." Another great paroxysm shook him. He slumped to the warm, yielding floor, groaned, and lay still.

"Look what you've done!" I shouted, boiling over with indignation. I started for Denis, only to crash into an unseen metacreative wall with a force that nearly knocked me senseless.

When I pulled myself together I saw Denis lying on the couch, his limbs fastened with restraints. Six of the demonic, glowing figures had gathered closely around him, and the bodiless casque floated above like a burning satellite. The seventh person was coming toward me. Below the silver CE helmet, her face-mask was encrusted in diamonds. Dorothée held something in her gloved hands. It was an E18 model hat, familiar to me from my adventure on the Scottish planet.

The young woman's mental voice said: We need you to be a witness Uncle Rogi. Put the helmet on. It will allow you to monitor the procedure. Don't be afraid. It only has a farsensory brainboard. There is no direct linkage to the metaconcert.

Before I could react she clapped the damned thing on me and I went blind. I felt an excruciating burst of pain as the minute photon beams of the crown-of-thorns zapped my scalp and drilled my skull. Electrodes shot into my brain, the pain stopped, and the world disappeared.

I was drifting in a fantastic realm that was strangely familiar, a place of cathedral-like silence that nevertheless seemed to vibrate with a million echoes. My ultrasenses, strongly augmented by cerebroenergetic enhancement, were bewildered at first by the new richness of detail that I had not been aware of during my earlier apperception, but I knew I'd been in this place twice before.

When Fury was born.

When Jack was born.

Around me lay a dark and subtle immensity, roiling and formless at the same time that it possessed a paradoxical structure. I was part of a patterned, multilayered black fabric in which ominous protean masses were embedded. They seemed to grow and diminish and grow again in restless spurts, illuminated by faint, pyrotechnic bursts of cold-blue radiance coming from some unknown source. I was aware of vanishing abysses below me and soaring eminences above. Pulsating waveforms rushed through me, engulfing me in chaos and then retreated like ebbing surf, leaving behind new patterns in the all-encompassing fabric, wondrous and fearful and indescribable.

The place was alive with creativity.

I was within the aether, the domain of the mental lattices. And I was not alone.

I had completely forgotten why I was here and it took me some time to focus on the more tangible entities in the place. I did not immediately identify the obliquely tilted, elongate patch of brightness off in the distance, but I knew that it was important.

As I came nearer to this thing (or it approached me) I discovered that it was actually a close grouping of incandescent objects like tiny stars or sparks. One of them moved only in two dimensions, drawing and redrawing a straight white line. The other seven whirled in intricate orbital patterns about the long axis drawn by the first, spinning threads of blue and scarlet into a kind of spindle shape, a rodlike hollow structure that tapered at both ends, fashioned entirely of colored light.

The spindle grew in size and complexity as I watched, enthralled. And there was music. The echoing silence had imperceptibly given way to a slow, swelling theme—notes that were vastly deep, almost growling, full of intriguing potential. A second melody joined the first, weaving a harmonious variation at a slightly elevated pitch. Then other voices came in, one by one, until there were eight parts flowing freely in eerie contrapuntal song.

I finally realized that it was the metaconcert.

The individual spooling mentalities of the fusiform structure soon became indistinguishable from the dense, swift windings of light. I saw the upper end of the spindle intensify in brightness, the red and blue threads coalescing into a peculiar, searing violet. My mind's ear heard a new chord of celestial music, high-pitched and piercing, superimposed upon the lower notes of the fugue. The spindle was changing its orientation, tilting, rotating, searching . . .

Suddenly I caught sight of another luminous object, whisking in and out among the lattices. It was double, something like a close-coupled binary star or a dumbbell nebula. One saw it for only a split second, moving in the distance, before it vanished again among the murky mental tapestries.

Evidently the metaconcert had been on the lookout for the binary, because the spindle swiveled about with incredible speed, pointing in the direction of its quarry. A thin, laserlike beam sprang from the violet end and lanced into shadowed complexity. There was a brilliant rainbow flash. Prismatic concentric shock waves exploded outward and dissipated. The fabric of the aether flickered wildly, as though bolts of heat lightning were racing behind thick clouds.

The binary object was reeled slowly into view. When its capture was complete the spindle stood upright, holding above it blurry twinned luminosities, one pale gold, the other livid bluish-green. A kind of atmosphere enveloped them both and formed a ligature between them, and they seemed to orbit slowly about a common center of gravity. It was this invisible point that was somehow gripped firmly by a short white beam coming from the tip of the metaconcert. The captive binary pulsated as it turned, dancing to an irregular rhythm of its own.

Whatever the spindle had caught was passive, waiting. The metaconcert spoke.

DO YOU KNOW WHO I AM?
  You are our offspring our Children that we love.
WHO ARE YOU?

You know who we are.
ARE YOU DENIS?
Yes.
ARE YOU FURY?
Yes. Inevitably.

Ah, doux Jésus! There it was at last! My confusion vanished. I finally realized what was happening, what I was being forced to watch.

The questioning went on but I no longer heard the details of the telepathic speech. My heart had burst like a ruptured dam, overwhelming me with the truth I had tried so long to deny.

Denis was Fury. Fury was Denis.

I wanted to curse and weep, to flee this awful province where I confronted the death of hope. But I could not flee. I heard the metaconcert extract every obscene detail of Denis's trauma from the strangely docile binary. I was held fast and compelled to witness while the details of my miserable brother's sins assaulted me.

Donny, mon frère, how could you have done it? How could you have ruined Denis and Victor, helpless children who only wanted you to love them? . . . And you, Denis, my dearest son! Why was your fission so inevitable? Do you mean that you had no choice? Or *did* you choose?

DO YOU KNOW WHAT IS INTENDED?
Yes. But you will fail. We are too strong now.
THERE IS A FATAL DICHOTOMY IN YOU. YOU KNOW THAT. THE PART OF YOU WHO IS DENIS DE-PLORES AND ABOMINATES THE DEEDS OF FURY.
We coexist now as we have done since the necessary bifurcation. What you intend is not feasible.
NEVERTHELESS IT WILL BE ATTEMPTED. FOR YOUR OWN GOOD AND THAT OF YOUR FELLOW MINDS.
Listen! Let us propose an alternative—
THE INTEGRATION WILL BE ATTEMPTED NOW.

New threads of light whipped out from the glowing violet tip of the spindle. There were hundreds of them, sharp-edged as razor wire, spinning a glittering spherical cage that completely enclosed the binary mind.

The cage began to contract.

A ghastly scene unfolded then before my enhanced farsenses, searing sights and sounds that I cannot adequately put into words. They were not real. I realize now that my sojourn within the mental lattices consisted entirely of a chain of symbolic icons, creations of my own imagination, my mind's attempt to translate and reify an indescribable conflict into something I could understand. The struggle between the two dissociated personalities and the metaconcert seemed interminable, but later I realized that it could not have occupied more than an hour in ordinary time.

The metaconcert song fell into a monotonous eight-note loop without the earlier variations and polyphony that had given it beauty. Like the contracting cage of light, it had become an instrument of torture, thudding like the relentless blows of a hammer, louder and louder. I seemed to hear the two captive personae screaming, each one fighting for its life, each one suffering unspeakable pain and terror. I saw the merciless cage squeeze the binary star, forcing the madly throbbing components toward conjunction, toward integration. The concussive song of the metaconcert reached a roaring crescendo—

And the two units of the doublet merged.

In a sudden ringing silence the star collapsed to a wan ember, then expanded again into a globe of effulgent emerald. The cage shattered, allowing the new green star to drift free into an aether suddenly awash with countless points of scintillating light. The mental integration had taken place.

But which personality had survived?

The metaconcert spindle spoke in a rather shaken tone:

WHO ARE YOU?
I/I AM ONE.
ARE YOU DENIS? ARE YOU FURY?
I/I AM MYSELF.
WHAT IS YOUR NAME?
THAT . . . REMAINS TO BE SEEN.

The green star abruptly shrank, vanishing into the sparkling cloud of pixie dust. From the spindle came a great blasting ruby cone that obliterated the myriad dancing points. For a moment my ultrasenses were overwhelmed.

Then the mental lattices were as they had been in the beginning, full of vague instability. But the only entities existent in that part of the aether were the spindle and I.

The metaconcert slowly dissolved into eight sparks that formed themselves into a tight constellation and slipped away into ambiguity. I waited.

After a time, still uncomprehending, I left that place.

Someone lifted the heavy CE helmet from my head. I was sitting on the warm cellar floor. I looked up and saw Paul's gray-bearded face, as pale and expressionless as a statue. A line of tiny wounds from the electrodes ran across his brow, one of them oozing a trickle of blood. His hair was damp and plastered to his head and his Nomex coverall was halfway unzipped, showing the ordinary apparel beneath. He helped me to my feet without a word.

Dorothée was sitting on the leather couch, her helmet beside her and her head in her hands. Severin held his sister Catherine in his arms. She was sobbing quietly. Adrien, Philip, and Maurice, their faces stained with blood, sweat, and tears, were helping one another out of the silver suits. There was no sign of Jack. I found out later that the disembodied brain was engaged in a frantic, intensive search—first of the farmhouse locale and then of the region within a five-klom radius of it. Jack's hunt, like others conducted later by the Dynasty, was fruitless.

Denis—or whoever the integrated personality was—had vanished.

I heard footsteps coming down the cellar stairs and a moment later Lucille entered. She drew in her breath sharply. Her dark eyes darted about the improvised enclosure, taking in the bizarre CE helmets and the protective garb.

"What are you doing?" she exclaimed. "What's this equipment for?"

Nobody replied.

She whirled about, confronting me. Her voice rose. "Where's Denis?"

I could only shake my head numbly.

"What have you done?" she demanded in a terrible whisper. *"What have you done to him?"*

It was a question none of us could bring ourselves to answer.

. . .

Jack's paramount creativity produced a simulacrum of a body, dead in bed of a massive cerebral hemorrhage and "discovered" too late by the grieving family on Christmas morning. There would be no miraculous regeneration of the revered Nobel Laureate, the Grand Old Man of Metapsychology. Severin signed the death certificate and the other formalities were smoothed by the First Magnate. After a simple requiem, the alleged ashes were interred in the old cemetery in Berlin, New Hampshire, where Denis Remillard's mother and father and eight of his nine siblings lay.

A public memorial service was held at Dartmouth's Rollins Chapel, rather sparsely attended because of the Christmas–New Year's vacation. Later, tributes to the great man poured in from every corner of the Milieu and were featured in all of the galactic media, human and exotic. The Remillard Foundation presented an impressive endowment to Dartmouth College in Denis's name, and a new data bank in the School of Metapsychology was named in his honor. His last book, *An Ontological Interpretation of Unity,* was published posthumously and proved to be a potent weapon for Milieu-loyalist academics in their continuing skirmishes with Rebel theoreticians.

The Dynasty never knew for certain what the new entity symbolized by the green star did during the three and one half years that it continued to live. I myself found out the truth (which I will recount in due time) in the autumn of 2082, on Mount Washington, when my foster son at last found the peace of death.

His genuine ashes are buried near the mountain's summit, in a place that only Lucille and I know.

[17]

SECTOR 15: STAR 15-000-001 [TELONIS]
PLANET 1 [CONCILIUM ORB]
GALACTIC YEAR: LA-PRIME 1-391-230
[18 JUNE 2079]

After the meeting had adjourned, Jack Remillard decided to make a brief detour on his way back to the apartment, accompanying Anne to Rive Gauche.

"Your enclave has a better selection of cut flowers than Rialto," he explained to her as they boarded the glowing, inertialess capsule in the tube station serving the Directorate chambers. "And I'd like to pick up some real champagne at that little wineshop across the square from your place. Tonight's a special occasion for Diamond and me. Our first wedding anniversary."

Anne's remote blue eyes lit up and a hint of her lost beauty returned to her gaunt features. She was wearing a carnelian-red pantsuit and a V-necked oyster blouse with a clerical rabat. "That's right! Forgive me, dear, but I'd completely forgotten. Congratulations—and please convey my blessing to Dorothea. I don't suppose I could tempt you two with an invitation to dinner at the Closerie tomorrow?"

The Jesuit priest's fair hair was still unflatteringly short as a consequent of her long stay in the regeneration-tank, and she moved with care because her regrown legs had yet to regain their full function; but there was nothing whatsoever wrong with Anne Remillard's intellect. As the last order of business at the meeting of the Panpolity Directorate for Unity they had just left, Jack had resigned as pro tem chairman and applauded as his aunt was unanimously reelected to the position.

"Thank you for the invitation," he said, "but we're heading back to Caledonia early tomorrow. Diamond has her dirigent duties to catch up on, and I'd like to finish our new house there before winter—get the landscaping done just right and install my lab. There's also a problem with Ian Macdonald I have to look into."

The door of the capsule whisked open and both of them alighted into a glassy, brilliantly lit tunnel. A discrepant fired-enamel sign framed in wrought iron identified the stop as RIVE GAUCHE ENCLAVE. They rode up a moving ramp into what might have been a quaint street in Paris's 5e Arrondissement. The tall woman moved slowly. Her male companion, much younger and dressed in slacks and a hand-knit Caledonian sweater, took her arm unobtrusively from time to time when the pavement became irregular or the curbstones steep.

"Is your wife's father still giving her a hard time with his Rebel politics?" Anne inquired.

"The situation's a bit stickier than that. You may recall that Ian's an Intendant Associate for a rather thinly populated subcontinent. About three weeks ago, special agents for the Office of the Dirigent of Caledonia found a well-hidden factory for making bootleg CE helmets tucked away in the mountains near Ian's airfarm. The metacreative brainboards for the hats had been purchased quite openly from CEREM—allegedly for use in some autoerotic recreational design. But the helmets found in the police raid were weapons: mental lasers. There's some suspicion that Ian may have colluded in building and supplying the factory."

Anne said, "Damn."

"My sentiments, too."

"I've heard about the black market in creative CE. But why in the world would your father-in-law want to get mixed up in something like that?"

"Possibly for money, possibly for other reasons. His farm is going through a rocky patch. He overextended himself by buying out a couple of his neighbors and then had a disappointing harvest."

"How solid is the evidence against him?"

"Not very. When the ODC agents and the local police busted the hat factory, the six operant technicians who were running it committed suicide before they could be interrogated. Shocked the hell out of the naive Callie cops. The techs were all recent immigrants from Earth and Okanagon and Elysium without previous criminal records. So far, Ian's link to the operation is a flimsy one: propinquity, and the fact that he was twice seen talking to the man who seemed to head up the operation. They were in a pub in Grampian Town, the closest settlement to Ian's farm and the factory, but he maintains he was just having friendly chats with a constituent. The Planetary Magistratum has to be very circumspect in its investigation of Ian because he's an IA. Thus far, it hasn't come up with enough evidence to warrant bringing him before the Justiciar of the Caledonian Intendant Assembly. Diamond is worried sick, but she can't ream her dad on the sly because of the parent-child inhibition. So she's asked me to give it a try."

Anne gave a ladylike grunt. "Don't you dare touch it, my boy! Not with the proverbial barge pole."

"Figured that out all by myself," he retorted gloomily. "But I'll have to do some sniffing around all the same. I'm not looking forward to it."

They walked on for some time without speaking.

It was "evening" in Orb's fanciful replica of the Left Bank of the Seine and the streetlamps had just been lighted. The people who lived in Rive Gauche, together with fair numbers of human, Poltroyan, and Gi tourists from other enclaves in the great artificial planetoid, strolled in the sweet-scented spring dusk beneath the chestnut trees. Little shops and boutiques, open late for business in a manner that was decidedly unGallic, beckoned to the passersby with seductive displays. The aromas of pastry, roasting coffee, and spicy charcuterie vied with those of blossom-laden shrubs and window boxes. Restaurants were beginning to fill with early patrons, human and exotic, relaxing now that the stress of the Concilium session was finally over.

Anne said, "Paul mentioned that you'd done a third intensive scan of Earth just before coming to Orb."

"Yes, similar to the two I performed immediately after Denis's disappearance. This time, I keyed my seekersense to the metapsychic ident of the merged personae and to the individual auric IDs. The job took me three horrendous weeks and I got nib de nib. Bupkis! Sweet eff ay! If he's alive, the Denis/Fury entity somehow left Earth—probably within hours of the integration attempt."

"Are you still considering the d-jump hypothesis?"

"I have to. Denis just *vanished,* Anne. The couch restraints were still fastened but he was gone without a trace. He didn't simply go invisible. I could have detected that easily. Just as soon as the metaconcert broke up I searched the farmhouse and its immediate vicinity and found no sign of him. I couldn't do an overall scan of Earth until a few hours later because my brain was too fatigued, but when I did carry it out the results were negative. The subsequent Magistratum investigation of starship passengers and crews exiting Earth within the limited window of opportunity was exhaustive. None of those people could have been

Denis or Fury. We're left with three possibilities: He's dead and mysteriously annihilated, he's alive and still on Earth but he's changed his MP ident, or he escaped Earth in some unknown way. If he is alive, his physical disappearance from the farmhouse points to a d-jump—and if he did it once, he'll probably be able to do it again."

"So if Denis/Fury did achieve a long-distance metapsychic dimensional translation, he could be anywhere in the galaxy."

"Or out of it. If he botched the upsilon-field maneuver, he could be dead in interstellar space, or trapped in the gray limbo, or even smeared inaccessibly and eternally among six sets of lattices and twenty-one dimensions."

"Oh, God, not that," the priest murmured.

"Psychophysicists don't even agree that mental manipulation of the upsilon-field is a genuine phenomenon. A child was supposed to have done it on Engong in 2067, over a distance of less than two kilometers. That's hardly verification for a teleport hop of X lightyears. The odds are that Denis died when the metaconcert hit him with the lethal redactive impulse, and his body was absorbed into the lattices through a sexternion."

"Each morning, in my daily mass, I pray that Denis *is* safely dead. But I think you and Dorothea and Lucille and the Dynasty would have known if the metaconcert had extinguished a mentality of that caliber."

"Or Uncle Rogi would have known. His stubborn belief that Denis is still alive is what really worries Paul. The other members of the Dynasty and Diamond are fairly comfortable with the alternative."

"And what do you think, Jack?"

"If the entity did survive, we can't know for certain whether it's Denis or Fury or someone else altogether. Until the persona manifests itself—if it ever does—I think we must let the matter be. We've done all we can for now."

Anne steered them to a florist shop in the rue du Chat-qui-Pêche where a Gi, having completed its purchase of a bunch of violets, was nibbling on them delicately and thinking about a second course of hemerocallis. Jack bought a large bouquet of old-fashioned Zéphirine Drouhin roses, round as muffins, bright cerise in color, and exuding a heady perfume. Then they went to an establishment called La Grappe, where Anne inspected the champagne offerings and advised him to go with the Dom Pérignon tête de cuvée. She ordered a case of '63 Haut

Brion to be sent to the cellar of her own flat on the following day, reserving a single bottle to take home with her now.

When Jack commented on the purchase, she said, "I plan to stay in Orb at least through the next Concilium session. I've a lot of catching up to do after my long hiatus, and the Directorate is going to need a fresh approach to its Unity education campaign among the normals."

"I'm afraid I let that aspect of the Directorate mission slide a bit during my late, unlamented tenure," Jack said apologetically. They left the wineshop and lingered for a moment in a little alcove next door, where a huge wisteria vine that had nearly engulfed a plane tree was in extravagant bloom. "Most of the exotic Directors were more interested in responding to the Rebel attack on the Sorbonne findings—the evidence of spontaneous coadunation—than in the rest of the agenda."

Anne made a moue of distaste. "That was nothing but a tempest in a theoretician's teapot! We've got to pay attention to the nonoperant populace's growing fear of what they believe are *dehumanizing* aspects of Unity."

"What Marc hinted at in his second address to the Concilium Committee on Interpolitical Affairs?"

"Exactly. He gave us a useful clue to upcoming Rebel strategy there. We tend to forget that normal humans outnumber metas by nearly fifteen to one. If the Rebel leaders really intend to bring about humanity's secession from the Milieu, they'll need wholehearted support from nonoperants. Which means that we've got our work cut out for us, convincing normals that Unity is nothing to be afraid of . . . while Rebellion is."

They began strolling back toward the tube station.

"Do you actually intend to accuse the Rebels of plotting violence?" Anne's question betrayed her skepticism.

"That bootleg CE factory found on Caledonia worries me more than I like to admit." Jack said somberly. "Operant mobsters from the Russian and Japanese worlds and a few other planets with organized crime have used mind-boosters in starship piracy and other spectacular capers. But the Scottish planet has no mafia in its cultural tradition, and no big-time operant outlaws have ever flourished there. Diamond is afraid that the mental lasers might have been intended for a militant faction of the Rebel movement. But there's never been any proof of such activity anywhere in the Polity . . . yet."

"But you think a Rebel connection is plausible?"

"Ian's politics are no secret. And there have been rumors of such things before, on Okanagon and Satsuma and even on the Old World. If it's true it will be very hard to prove. The exotic races have such a guileless view of the Rebel movement! And of course they control the Galactic Magistratum. So far as I know, there has never been any investigation of potential Rebel militancy. Loyalist humans have hesitated to press the issue because it would increase the polarization of our Polity, and things are bad enough as it is. The early years of the Simbiari Proctorship when the rights of free speech and assembly were temporarily abrogated haven't been forgotten. Humanity won't sit still for a militant-Rebel witch hunt unless the evidence is overwhelming."

Anne agreed.

They had come to the station entrance. Jack said, "I'm afraid things will just have to get worse before they can get better."

Anne's smile was melancholy. "It seems to me I've heard that tag line before, and fairly recently at that." She kissed him lightly. "Blessings, Jack. Let me know what you find out about Ian."

He said goodbye and went off into the underground. Anne stood for a moment watching, then sighed. Her still-healing body ached in spite of the continual low-level self-redaction generated automatically by her mind. If she had been on Earth, she would have suspected that a change in the weather was forthcoming; but no rain was programmed for Rive Gauche until the day after tomorrow.

Curious, she said to herself.

She deliberately banished the pain, then went off to see what was on the menu at La Closerie des Lilas. She had decided that she did not care to dine alone in her apartment tonight after all.

Dorothea Macdonald and David Somerled MacGregor had departed from the final Conference of Dirigents separately, but by chance they arrived in Ponte di Rialto at the same time. It was only natural that she should invite him to share her gondola. A steam-powered vaporetto water-bus would have taken them more quickly to their apartments further up the Grand Canal, but it had been a long day, and both of them welcomed the chance to wind down in companionable silence riding in the slower boat. It was powered in the traditional way by a non-operant human gondoliere who rowed it along with a single long oar.

The simulated night was full of fog and sea-smells. The lamps and lighted windows of the palaces and other monumental constructions along the Grand Canal—almost all containing residential flats in Orb's Venetian re-creation—made blurred patterns of radiance on either bank. The canopy of their gondola was open on three sides, and after they had traveled only a short way the gold lamé of Dorothea's hooded jumpsuit was dotted with microscopic beads of moisture and Davy's tweed jacket smelled of soggy sheep. Their stolid boatman wore an enviroponcho and hummed along obliviously to pop music, inaudible to the passengers, playing on his auditory implant.

"I enjoy nights like this," Dorothea said. "The fog reminds me of my childhood in Edinburgh, when the haar would steal in from the sea and the house seemed wrapped in cotton wool. Jack and I chose to live in Rialto because it was completely different from Caledonia or Hawaii or New Hampshire in America."

"Aye, it's beautiful," the Dirigent of Earth agreed. "Not twee or Disneyesque like some of the other Orb enclaves. That was why my Maggie liked it—and why I've kept our flat here, even though she was able to live in it only a few brief hours before she was killed. She adored the real Venice, y'see, where we'd honeymooned. But I've found that I can't go back there now. It's turned into an immersive pageant for holidaymakers, all tarted up and sterile. This place makes no bones about being artificial, but to me it has more of the original Venetian ambiance than the real thing. Here I can remember Maggie and our happiness together, and when I sleep I can dream of her peacefully, without vengeful nightmares poisoning me the way they do back in Concord, among your toplofty in-laws."

She took his hard cold hand and pressed it. "I'm so sorry about your wife, Davy. And you must believe that Jack is, too."

He put a damp arm around her. "It's not Jack who's tainted my heart but the older Remillards. The ones who've guarded the secret all these years with the connivance of the damned Lylmik."

"But Fury is dead now," she said, willing herself to believe it behind her impenetrable mindscreen. "There's only Madeleine, a single Hydra, left alive. And she's not that strong alone. We'll find her and bring her to justice, and that'll be an end of it at last."

"We can hope so." Davy MacGregor shook his head slowly, and misty droplets gleamed in his Dundreary side whiskers. "I'd never have picked poor Denis as Fury, that's for sure. But it was a rash thing the lot of you did, trying to integrate the monster secretly and with a small metaconcert, even though the First Magnate did technically have the authority to act. You could have all been killed and Fury might have escaped."

"You know very well why it had to be done that way. Denis himself was a blameless man. If the Magistratum had taken him into custody and attempted a redaction, there would have been a public scandal— and no assurance that a big team of forensic redactors would have done any better than our smaller metaconcert. It's a terrible tragedy that we weren't able to extirpate the Fury persona and save Denis, but right and proper that his good name remains intact—"

"Along with that of the First Magnate and the rest of the Remillard clan," Davy MacGregor growled. "Oh, aye, I know why the Lylmik let you get away with it. All the same, the thought still strikes fire in me. The reputation of the almighty Dynasty must be preserved at all costs! And now we have a new Remillard prancing into the public arena, throwing his weight around and flirting with sedition. What d'ye say to that, eh?"

"I don't know what to say," she admitted. "I know almost nothing about Marc Remillard as a person. He helped save my life in the diatreme. I was shocked beyond measure when he became the Rebel spokesman. And I think I'm afraid of him."

"For good reason, I'm thinking."

"Jack loves Marc, but I know he also has deep misgivings about him. He says his brother will take the Rebel movement in a new direction, and we may have to deal with a serious crisis within just a few years."

Davy harrumphed. "Perhaps your Jack isn't quite the innocent young Milquetoast he often seems!"

The pseudovoice seeming to come from behind the mask of canary diamonds was sweetly humorous. "Only a mean-spirited old fart would make the mistake of thinking so."

Davy MacGregor chuckled wickedly.

The gondola prow sliced a low-hanging blanket of mist and glided in to a lantern-lit landing stage. Beyond it rose a replica of the most magnificent Gothic façade in all Venice.

"Ca' d'Oro," the gondoliere said in a bored voice.

Dorothea rose from her seat. "My stop. Good night, Davy."

"I hope it is for you and your Jack as well, dear lass . . . And take good care of our wee Scottish planet when you get home, won't you?"

Her reply was brisk. "I intend to. See that you do the same for poor old Earth."

She hurried down the tiny tree-girt Calle della Ca' d'Oro to the entry of the Palazzo Sagredo. The foyer inside was done in simple wood paneling and tinted plaster, with a polished marble floor. She and Jack and the other tenants of this "palace" had no interest in the opulent furnishings or the gilded stucco and elaborate decorative carvings featured in certain other dwellings of Ponte di Rialto.

"Buona sera, Dirigent," said the portinaio, looking up from his lair amidst the potted palms. "It's getting late."

"Good evening, Paolo. The last meeting of the Planetary Dirigents ran overtime. I'm glad you're still here. We're leaving very early tomorrow and I wanted to say goodbye."

"It has been a pleasure having you with us, Dirigent. I hope you'll return next session."

"Oh, yes. We wouldn't dream of stopping anywhere else." She had used PK to banish the dampness from her clothing and boots. "Che bella nebbia! I think we'll have a nice fire on our last night in residence. But this time, I'll be certain to open the damper properly."

"An open fire would be pleasant," the portinaio agreed. Observing her empty arms, which bore not even a loaf of new bread nor the makings of a fresh salad, items that were not easily available from Orb's central provisioning depot, he screwed up his face in an artless grin. "I would not like to spoil a surprise, but you should know that Direttore Zan Degola just arrived with flowers and wine to help celebrate your first wedding anniversary."

The eyes above the diamond mask widened in dismay. "Oh, damn! I can't believe it slipped my mind—"

"Piano, piano, don't be distressed that you forgot to bring your dear husband a special supper."

She had done nothing of the kind. Jack drank but he seldom ate conventional food while he was at home, and her own sustenance was usually liquefied high-calorie pabulum. But she should have remembered to bring some sort of an anniversary gift. She was nothing but an illbred, inconsiderate workaholic . . .

Paolo was all smiles as he took out a large flat carton from beneath his desk and handed it to her with a flourish. "The lad from the osteria just delivered this huge takeout to me, and I insist that you accept it with my compliments. It would be a tragedy for young lovers not to have a nice meal on their last night in the enclave. The restaurant will send me another in twenty minutes. Please convey my felicitations to the Direttore."

Dear old Paolo. Like most of the nonoperant service personnel in Rialto, he believed that Jack—in spite of the Venetian nickname she had slyly bestowed upon him, derived from that of the decapitated Baptist—was a normally embodied human being, and that a perfectly utilitarian face lay beneath her own diamond mask. There was no way she could refuse the food, so she thanked the concierge warmly and insisted on paying for a fine wine to go with his own replacement dinner. Then she bade him a last farewell and took the archaic clanking cage-lift to the top floor of the palazzo.

Jack opened the apartment door for her. His mind formed a question as he spotted what she was carrying.

"A feast for our special occasion," she explained with a shrug, "courtesy of Paolo, with compliments to Zan Degola."

Jack grinned as his deepsight inspected the contents of the carton. "Well, why not? I thought we'd just sit by the fire and drink champagne—but this is much better." He took the food from her and headed for the kitchen. "You change into something comfortable. I'll put away your flask of algiprote purée and set the table and grow a digestive tract."

When she returned, wearing a white silk gown and robe edged with maribou, the dining table in the simply furnished room was candlelit, covered with damask, and gleaming with china, crystal, and silver. The roses in a cut-glass bowl made a colorful centerpiece.

He embraced her and gently kissed her lips. "It's wonderful to see your face outside of bed. Remind me to leave Paolo a colossal tip."

"Don't think I'm going to make a habit of breaking my vow, Santo Giovanni Decollato. But I must admit the food smells fabulous."

He held the chair for her and she sat down. There was an appetizer of carpaccio—finely sliced aged raw beef drizzled with oil and lemon, a shrimp pâté and toast, pasta with porcini mushrooms and chicken livers in cream sauce, and a salad of radicchio and pine nuts. He poured champagne and then they prayed a blessing and ate quietly, enjoying the simple human activity that they experienced so seldom.

"When I was young, I wouldn't eat meat or seafood." She speared a morsel of chicken liver, wound spaghetti around it with her PK, and devoured the result. "I couldn't bear the thought of sustaining my life through the death of other sentient creatures who shared in the Mind of the Universe."

"A valid enough personal credo. Why did you give it up?"

"I was horribly self-righteous, so certain that my brother and the adults who didn't accept vegetarianism were immoral. But then, as I grew older, I found out that plants have their share of Mind, too, and so does inorganic matter. I learned that the human race had evolved as omnivores and our bodies operate most efficiently when we consume both animal flesh and plant food—so how did I dare to insist that eating meat was immoral when it was manifestly part of human nature? What had seemed so clear-cut to me was actually murky and slippery. Finally, I had to admit to myself that my idealistic behavior had been based upon squeamishness and an empathetic fallacy, not a genuine ethical commitment on my part. It was very disheartening."

He sipped his champagne, then lifted it to the candlelight and made the bubbles dance in eccentric spirals and whirls. Her mind's vestibulum was open, inviting his survey. "And now you're beginning to have doubts about something entirely different. Wondering if your faith in Unity is also fallacy-based."

She nibbled a bit of the salad. "The worst thing is, I think I might never have had any belief in cosmic consciousness in the first place. I'm not as comfortable with mysticism as you are, darling. I'm a Scot and we're a down-to-earth ilk. We take up hard jobs and get them done and survive and leave the magic to others."

He smiled. "But some of you are also fey, and your race has had its share of philosophers."

"Then the doubt is all my own. I admit that I cherish human independence. I don't want us to lose it—not even if it brings about galactic peace and harmony. And I don't want other minds looking behind my mask. It's different with you. You're my husband. But I couldn't bear sharing any part of my inner self with vast numbers of people."

"I don't believe Unity is like that—a passive exposure, a spilling of secrets. I think it must be dynamic, on the order of a grand metaconcert, as Denis said in his last book. According to his theory, Unity is an enormous freewheeling construct with a common vector in the overarching matrix lattices [image], the realm of the Cosmic All. In some mysterious way, Unity conjugates Mind while maintaining the integrity of the partner mentalities. It may be that its oneness reflects the unique bond of the Trinity. 'That all may be one, as you, Father, in me and I in thee; that they may also be one in us.' The oneness in God is the Holy Spirit, a third unique person. Who can say what Unity would produce in our own racial Mind?"

"Oh, Jack." She put down her fork and sighed in irritation. "That's all very beautiful and profound, but it doesn't tell me what Unity's going to do to *me*. And besides, Christ was talking about something quite different: a community of religious belief."

"Was he? That's certainly what his first followers thought, and it was a useful and valid concept for two thousand years. But if we consider that our Catholic faith has evolved just as the human race has, then perhaps that particular message has a special meaning in our metapsychic age. It might describe a universal truth acceptable to minds who follow religions and ethical systems other than Christianity. It seems to me that both Christ's Unity and that of the Milieu can best be defined as transcendent love—and if that's true, then we have nothing to fear from it, just as the exotic races have maintained all along. In true love, individuality is never compromised or diminished. What's missing is antagonism."

"I don't want to love other people the way I love you," she said obstinately.

"Nor do I. Common sense tells us there are different kinds of love. The Unity of the Galactic Milieu could be a supreme friendship. A magnanimity and unanimity. A great trusting. The exotic races have their quirks and crotchets, but they do live and work together in a spirit of good will and mutuality. They certainly aren't sinless—but by and large they have a civilization without malice."

"But if Unity is so simple," she cried, "why have we so persistently misunderstood and feared it?"

"Because it's going to be imposed on us, willy-nilly, if we want to remain within the Milieu. Like the Great Intervention, only more so . . . And Unity is *not* simple, any more than maturity is simple, or the altruistic imperative, or falling in love. If it were simple, then the exotics would be able to explain it to us: A B C. They can't seem to do that. We're going to have to discover it and accept it for ourselves."

She looked at him anxiously. "But how are we to manage it? The

Unity education campaigns don't seem to be working—except amongst those who don't really need to be convinced."

"I think," Jack said slowly, "there will have to be a concentration of attention." And he showed her another mental image.

"Oh, no!" She pushed her chair back and sprang to her feet. "That's—that's appalling."

"So is crucifixion. Another great attention-getter."

"There must be another way!"

"But events seem to be leading toward this one. If the mental laser factory found near your father's farm isn't just an isolated piece of villainy, if the Rebels do take a more forceful position now that they've got an effective leader, if Fury isn't dead—"

"*No!*"

She pushed away her chair and whirled about, tears dimming her vision, then went to stand by the partially opened casement windows. The Grand Canal was completely engulfed in fog. Music came faintly from one of the caffès in the Fish Market across the water.

"Perhaps I'm wrong." He came behind her, taking her in his arms, and kissed her neck. She felt his sex and welcomed it with her body, taking comfort and giving it as he came erect. His fingers touched the tears on her cheeks. He moved his hands slowly down her face, caressing her lips. She shivered and he held her tightly against him.

"Do you want to be wrong, Jack?" Her voice had a hint of fear.

"Listen to me, my darling: If exotic theorists in the Unity Directorate are correct, our race should coadunate more or less spontaneously when our population reaches ten thousand million. The coadunation process seems to involve the opening up of a new avenue of intermind communication on the unconscious level. An actual enhancement of the collective unconscious. Unity is supposed to supervene eventually—but in the case of humanity, the eventuality might encompass an unacceptably long period of time."

"Whereas the—the other would mean an evolutionary leap?"

"And not the first time humanity has been kicked up the staircase of socialization by catastrophe. Consider the Ice Age, the Black Death, World War II, the devastation of the Holy Land: another fine mess, another hard lesson learned."

"We're speaking of a species of love, Jack!" she exclaimed. "How in the world could a galactic catastrophe engender that?"

His embrace softened. She felt his hands stroke and stimulate her breasts like a musician playing twin instruments, coaxing trills and arpeggios of sensation. "It's happened many times before, on a much lesser scale. Think of your own world in the aftermath of the diatreme disaster, with unexpected acts of bravery and compassion commonplace among the people. I'm sure the same thing happened in old Pompeii."

"An ignition of love . . . a falling in love?"

"I think so. Unity can probably be born in an instant, but it will have to ripen more slowly. Once the first great leap of trust is taken and the affirmation made, Unity would be there, in place, consoling and strengthening and encouraging selflessness and a sense of inner peace, especially in minds strong in creativity. It would expand and flower naturally, like maturity of mind. Denis believed that we would be incapable of losing it once we had it. Exotic scholars say he's right."

"People fall out of love."

"But they never fall out of maturity unless the mind becomes diseased. Unity is supposed to be analogous to that: by no means the Beatific Vision, but a higher niveau d'esprit than what most of us ever experience now."

She looked at him over her shoulder, finally smiling through her tears. "We do have other joys, though. For which we should be duly grateful."

She stilled his gentling hands. Electric warmth poured from her own fingers into his, sending lightning up the nerves of his arms and into his spine and brain, reinforcing his swelling passion. She turned to him with a soft, throaty laugh. Her eyes were like stars reflected in the sea. "Unity's consolation is a long way off, Zan Degola, my love. Tonight I'll settle for something primal."

He impaled her and their two bodies melted together, the limbs fusing, the faces haloed by radiant neural coronae that conjoined their brains. Their minds sang together in a duet of mental intercourse more ecstatic than that of the body. He opened his uttermost depths to her. She did not hesitate to reciprocate, and in the aftermath of the ringing consummation they caught a brief glimpse of what they had been searching for.

They contemplated it, awestruck, not believing it could be so simple.

It was not clear how it could be incorporated into their minds on a permanent basis.

He said, "I think more research is required."
She said, "Oh, good."

In Alpenland Enclave, Marc Remillard climbed to the sleeping loft of his small A-frame hut, peeled off his clothes, and arranged the duvet and pillows to make a comfortable nest that his creativity instantly adjusted to the perfect temperature. It was cold in the hut, the way he liked it at bedtime. Outside the window glimmered facsimile star patterns of Earth's northern-hemisphere winter: Orion, Canis Major and Minor, the gorgeous flow of the Milky Way.

And creeping over the jagged artificial eastern peaks of the enclave came the constellation Hydra.

It was a measure of the thing's hold on his unconscious mind that the name of the stellar sea serpent evoked only a lengthy pattern of stars. He never thought of the living Hydra during his waking hours, nor did any consideration of Fury enter his mind. He had forgotten Parnell, forgotten Uncle Rogi's ordeal. The family had never told him any details about the terrible episode of the previous Christmas and he had accepted the death of Denis with brief, sincere regret. He and his grandfather had never been especially close.

Marc lay there, reviewing the events of the day, smiling his one-sided smile at the stars. This Concilium session had been a triumph. As the new leader of the Rebels, he had given the movement fresh impetus at the same time that he had soothed exotic apprehensions about its ultimate goal. His own CE research was safe for the time being. The objections voiced by its exotic and human opponents (the latter including both Philip and Maurice Remillard) were too abstract to prevail in the face of CE's demonstrable usefulness—and the votes of the Rebel members of the Science Directorate. His new full-body rig was still secret and he intended it to stay that way until he was certain that exotic opposition could be quelled once and for all.

After strategy discussions with Cordelia Warshaw, Adrien Remillard, Helayne Strangford, and Annushka Gawrys, he had decided against a direct attack on Unity anytime in the immediate future. That could wait until Alex Manion's research was complete and he exploded his bombshell in the next session. The Rebel Party line would, for the time being, emphasize the prudent necessity of not alienating the human race's nonoperant majority by "premature" imposition of a new mental order.

He had also quietly pointed out the speed with which human technology had overtaken that of the Milieu, implying that any attempt at expulsion and quarantine of humanity was bound to fail.

Loyalist humans hadn't been taken in by the moderate tone of his Concilium disquisitions, but the exotics had apparently swallowed them whole. They liked Marc. His easy yet compelling manner was a welcome respite from Annushka's dour inflexibility and the wrangling of Rory Muldowney and the other Rebel firebrands. Until his own accession to the leadership, the escalating anti-Milieu controversy within the Human Polity had increasingly dismayed and scandalized the Krondaku, the Poltroyans, the Gi, and the Simbiari. Some of them had begun to openly challenge the guiding wisdom of the Lylmik, who had insisted upon inducting humanity into the Milieu in advance of its sociopolitical maturation.

However, now that the Rebel Party had taken Marc as their new chief—an eminently coolheaded mind of paramount metafunction—even the most conservative exotics expressed cautious hope that the discord could be resolved through compromise.

They were in for a shock.

But the timing of the Great Divorce was still problematical. If humanity was to prevail against overwhelming exotic numbers, it would need not only sophisticated weaponry but also large numbers of more powerful operant minds. Paramount minds like Marc's own.

He needed Mental Man.

Marc dearest.

Go away.

You know you don't mean that. You've done a brilliant job during your first public appearance as Rebel spokesman. I don't believe you made a single misstep. The effort must have been difficult and nervewracking even for you.

You know it was.

Then let me comfort you my darling.

NO! No . . . ah damn you damn you . . .

You're magnificent. A splendid male animal body harboring a splendid brain. You deserve the body's solace. Why must you continue this perverse rejection of human nature? Even your brother whom you envy so desperately knows the joy

the healing the release the enhancement of creativity *SEE*.
Voilà mon ange je t'aime je t'aime. *Voilà!*

No . . . yes oh yes.

I have shown you how to bring about the birth of Mental
Man. But He must be conceived with passion as well as with
cold reason. This is necessary. Otherwise He will be flawed.
Do you understand [image]?

No . . . oh please yes yes.

You must take a mate and share the engendering with her
not just any woman but the most suitable the mating must be
consanguineous in order to increase the homozygosity do
you understand [image]?

Yes. *You have ravished my heart my sister my bride you have pierced
my soul with a single glance how beautiful are your breasts honey
and milk are beneath your tongue what magic lies in your love my sister my bride I am come into my garden my sister my bride I gather
myrrh and balsam and drink sweet wine how beautiful you are how
beautiful how beautiful* . . . but where is she where is she
where . . . ?

You will find her. Within a year you will find your perfect
spouse and love her and make her co-author of the Second
Milieu. This mating must happen if your will is to prevail if
He is to prevail the race of Mental Man who will condignly
rule the stars.

I do understand yes yes my sister my bride yes . . . *NOW I
UNDERSTAND.*

Then be devoured in ecstasy dear bridegroom. You will recognize her when she comes.

Yes. I will.

[18]

SECTOR 12: STAR 12-370-992 [RETLA]
PLANET 3 [HIBERNIA]
6 EANAIR [14 FEBRUARY] 2080

"Yes, I'm quite certain we want to drive," said the Russian. "We won't be able to stay long on Hibernia, but it would be a pity if we didn't see some of your lovely scenery during our visit. Dirigent Muldowney has said that this section of the Loch Mór coast is one of the most dramatic regions of the planet."

"Well, it's that, all right." Jane Cloherty, the VIP-minder and public-relations dogsbody for the Intendancy of Connemara, produced a meaningful smile as she led the visiting officials out of the skyport lobby. A gravomag Mercedes from the government motor pool was waiting in the portico, coachwork sparkling in the rain. "The only thing is," Jane continued, "it's winter now and the Boireann is rather lonely out of season. This isn't really the best time of year for driving along our inland sea. All of the holiday facilities are shut down and the villages are rather few and far between."

"But we are from Astrakhan, my dear Citizen Cloherty." The female tourist spoke with forced heartiness. "The moody landscape will remind us of our own home world. And if there should be a nice storm, then that would put the icing on the cake."

"Well, the forecast calls for a full gale, so you'll likely get your wish," said Jane. "Are you sure you don't want a chauffeur, Intendant General? I could have one here in ten minutes."

"Thank you, but no." The Russian doffed his karakul shapka, opened the car's passenger door, and carefully climbed into the front seat.

Ruslan Vakhavich Terekev, chief elected official of the planet Astrakhan, appeared vaguely unwell. His prominent features were drawn, his skin was unhealthily sallow, and his hooded eyes were darkly ringed. Jane Cloherty decided that he was either masking some strong emotional upheaval or possibly suffering pain, and she had been relieved when Terekev's much younger Chief of Staff, a handsome woman wearing a teal-and-black leather tunic and leggings, announced that she would be doing all of the driving.

Jane said to her, "I think you'll find the vehicle quite comfortable, Citizen Arsanova. We've stocked the refrigerator with food and drink, and the computer has a wide selection of music and a detailed guide to the features of the region. The doors will lock and unlock on your verbal command once you've given it your input."

"Thank you," Lyudmila Arsanova said. Her smile was detached. "How is the road to Dumha Sí? We have booked rooms for the night at an inn called Granuaile House, where Dirigent Muldowney will come to collect us tomorrow."

"The highway's narrow in places but decent enough. I wouldn't trust the car's autopilot in the twistier bits where the mountains might block the NAVSAT signal. There are some rather amazing cliffs and offshore rock formations just beyond Baile Ui Fhiacháin, and an ollphéist sanctuary you might want to stop and visit. You should reach Dumha Sí easily before dark. Granuaile House is a lovely accommodation with super food. I'd not be surprised if you had the entire place to yourselves."

"Excellent," Lyudmila Arsanova said. "The Intendant General will relish the peace and quiet. He is in need of rest after our rather strenuous voyage on a high-df starship."

"I should caution you to be wary of our Hibernian wildlife. Some creatures like the fiadheamhantai and the giorria díocasach will come right up to a parked car looking tame and adorable like deer or hares, begging for food. But they'd as soon take off your fingers as eat the treat you offer."

"We shall be prudent," Lyudmila said.

Jane Cloherty gave the open-palmed operant salute to the visitors. "Do give the Taoiseach—I mean Dirigent Muldowney—my best wishes when you see him, then, and tell him that Connemara's always willing to oblige ODH. Have a fine trip."

Lyudmila settled behind the wheel and programmed the groundcar to take them out of Gaillimh (unaccountably called Galway by the locals) via the most expeditious route. When they were well away from the terminal and out of Jane Cloherty's farsense range, Lyudmila spoke to the man beside her, using the Russian language.

"How are you feeling, my dear?"

"Tired. But at least there are no further signs of disjunction."

"It might have been wiser to deal with the problem back in Tara Nua after all."

"No. The capital city was too crowded with operant bureaucrats and other metapsychic busybodies. This region better suits my requirements—it is wild and isolated, with accidents presumably more commonplace. And the sea will provide a perfect disposal for the bodies."

"If we only can be certain that this will work!"

"It will. Please do not be troubled, my little one. Before long I'll be fully restored." Ruslan Terekev sat back with a long sigh and closed his eyes. "A nap now will do me good. For safety's sake, we should be at least four hundred kilometers away from this city before beginning to troll. There is a tiny fishing village called An Leacht on the coast just west of the sea-beast reserve. We can start the hunt there."

"As you wish." She called up a display on the console and studied it as the car sped along the abbreviated length of dual carriageway leading out of Gaillimh Metro to the narrower road skirting the coast of the great landlocked sea. The Loch Mór chart was deceptively sprinkled with impossible-to-pronounce names for every creek, headland, bay, and island; but aside from the tiny hamlets of Baile Ui Fhiacháin, An Leacht, and their destination, Dumha Sí, there seemed to be no settlements of any kind beyond the Metro hinterlands.

That was ideal for their purposes, however. All they required was a single cottage in an isolated spot with a sturdy young family in residence.

Brimming with lifeforce.

He had broken the bad news during the long starship voyage from Astrakhan:

<My dearest little one *I*/I am greatly perturbed. Something grave and unexpected has happened.>

I have noticed *your*/your distress following the daily hyperspatial translations. Do *you*/you wish to confide in me?

<Within the past three weeks *I*/I have experienced certain worrying symptoms. These have intensified during this voyage perhaps worsened by the stress attending passage through the upsilon-field. *I*/I greatly fear that the fusion of *my*/my disparate personae might not have been permanent.>

!!! Are *you*/you certain of the diagnosis?

<No. Nevertheless *I*/I must take precautions. It would be a consummate disaster if the core persona should once again take charge of this body. Denis Remillard is now . . . the Last Great Enemy.>

He would surely betray us!

<*I*/I have considered it. And also considered a possible remedy: *I*/I believe that a fresh infusion of lifeforce would very likely halt any disjunctive tendency—at least for the time being.>

Yes! So logical&right dearest *you*/you must *FEED* as I do it is the solution it must be!

<That remains to be seen. At any rate *I*/I am convinced that the vis-à-vis meeting with Marc and the other Rebels on Hibernia must not take place if *I*/I am unable to restore the vigor of *my*/my integrated complexus. Aside from the danger of actual fission there is also the possibility that *I*/I might be recognized.>

? . . .

<When *I* was newborn and Marc was a tiny child he saw *me* and was afraid. Later *I* spoke to him in dreams and he may have come to know *me*. Even if *I*/I were fully potentiated there is a considerable risk dealing with this formidable man in person. He is bound to be curious about a new player in his carefully orchestrated game and *I*/I fear that he might attempt an aggressive probe without warning in order to reassure himself of *my*/my fidelity to the Rebel cause.>

I agree that there is a certain risk. But I doubt very much that Marc would take a chance of alienating the vitally important Ruslan Terekev in such a gratuitous way—especially since Alan Sakhvadze, Arkady Petrovich O'Malley, and the other Rebel spies that he sent to Astrakhan think that they have already vetted *your*/your mind. For years the Intendant General was notorious throughout the 14th Sector for his blatant devotion to the Rebel cause. Why should Marc doubt Terekev's loyalty now?

<Marc might doubt because he is who he is.>

He also needs *your*/your cooperation in the starship modification scheme. I know this man better than you! He would never antagonize either of us with a mind-ream.

<Your interactions with Marc have been on an entirely different plane subintellectual emotional affective. You are virtually immune from suspicion because of the intimacy of your long hypnoidal relationship with him—>

Too long! I'm tired of waiting I am determined that he must accept me soon and if the opportunity arises during our stay on the island I intend to take advantage—

<BE SILENT! *My*/my needs take precedence over yours! Do you question that?>

No. Never.

<Then focus your full concentration on helping *me*/me to obtain the necessary lifeforce! *I*/I shall NOT proceed with this perilous conference unless the integration is fortified.>

It is out of the question that we should seek a victim here on the starship. But there should be ample opportunities once we reach Hibernia.

<You . . . will have to show *me*/me how the feeding is done.>

[!!!] Gladly. There are also tactical considerations that must be kept in mind in order to preclude detection but they are usually quite simple.

<Soon. It *must* be soon. Do you understand?>

Yes my dearest Fury. I understand everything.

Another false alarm.

"Yob tvoyu dushu mat'!" He covered his eyes with a trembling hand. "I'm sorry, Mila. My seekersense is completely shot."

"It's all right. Just breathe deeply. Concentrate your creativity and self-redaction. Let me help with the hunting for a while."

She pulled the groundcar off the verge and drove back onto the road. There had been life down on the beach, but it was not human—a flock of winged exotic furbearers huddled in the rocks waiting for the gale to abate. They were highly intelligent aerial predators that must have weighed 20 or 30 kilos, members of a dominant order of Hibernian animals that would no doubt evolve into sapience within another two or three million orbits. Today, however, they were useless to the sick man in the car.

"The aura was so intense, even damped by the surrounding rock," Ruslan said wretchedly. "I was so sure that this time we had found suitable subjects."

"There's plenty of time yet," Lyudmila reassured him, soothing him with her redaction. It would never do to let him know how concerned she was. If he began to despair and his level of coercive power dropped much lower, he might become incapable of performing the neural drain.

He had already called out two other false alarms and she was beginning to wonder if they had seriously miscalculated, thinking there would be easy pickings in this desolate corner of the Irish planet. Here the locals seemed always to build their dwellings in clusters, probably needing all the social support they could get. Outside the villages Ruslan and Lyudmila had found only boarded-up summerhouses, and now and then an occasional agcrete boat shed used by commercial fishers, deserted now during the season of storms.

Inland, densely forested natural terraces rose to a serrated range of misty green mountains, but down near the shore-road the vegetation was sparse, mostly exotic ground-hugging succulents and groves of needletrees and naturalized terrestrial pines, stunted and gnarled by the strong winds. Where the horizontal limestone strata met the salt water, countless miniature potholes had been formed by erosion, giving the terrain the look of gray Emmentaler cheese. Exposed stretches of beach were piled high with waterweed, colorful shells, the air-filled skeletons of marine theropterids, and other flotsam carried in by the breakers and the high tides generated by Hibernia's three large moons.

The groundcar had passed the last tiny village, An Leacht, nearly an hour earlier, and since then there had been no occupied houses. In the last hundred kilometers, a single hop-lorry and three private cars had passed them going in the opposite direction; but they had agreed that taking the occupants would have been too dangerous. A vehicle would have to be disposed of, along with the bodies, and where the road skirted the steep cliffs there were sturdy barriers guarding the drop-off. With him in such a weakened condition, there was no assurance that the feeding would be successful. If it failed to restore his strength they might not be able to lift even a small car with concerted PK and throw it far out into deep water; and leaving a vehicle abandoned on the roadside might have posed an unacceptable risk. The region was surely patrolled, even though they had seen no police cars.

They drove in tense silence for some time. Finally, he said, "If the Denis persona should ever regain control of this body, you will have to try your utmost to kill me, Mila."

A frisson of fear ran through her. "No! Don't say that!"

"There would be no alternative. The Last Great Enemy would reveal our identities to the Dynasty or the Magistratum, even if it meant his death. By killing this body you would at least save your own life."

"I could never bring myself to do it. Never!"

He gave an ironic laugh. "No, I suppose not. After so many years of inhibition, my cancelling of the engram might be ineffective."

"Your . . . what?"

"My poor little one! Do you think I don't know how you toyed with the notion of doing away with me when you were young? You and the other Hydra-units—indulging in tantrums against a repressive parent, wishing me dead as you reveled in fantasies of independence."

"We were silly adolescents," she whispered, opening her mind wide to show her sincerity and remorse, "slow to mature. It was only your insistence upon bringing other minds into the alliance that drove us into a jealous rage. We didn't understand . . ."

"Never mind, lubymetsa. I forgive you." A tinge of frost hardened his smile. "But I will tell you now that your childish scheme never could have succeeded. As you were born to my service, I implanted a mental safeguard deep in your unconscious. You need me, just as I need you."

"I know," she said. "I know."

On the starship, confronted with hard evidence of her master's mortality, Hydra had finally realized with frightening clarity that if Fury became impotent or died, she was finished. She had been a deluded fool to think that she could control a paramount mind like Marc's and simultaneously plot the strategy of the upcoming Rebellion all by herself. The other Hydra-units who might have assisted her were dead. Alone, she would never be able to command the direction of an interstellar war, insuring the victory of the Second Milieu. Not even Mental Man would tip the scales in her favor, for the swift-ripening conflict might not wait upon His coming.

No . . . she needed Fury, who was superior to her in every metafunction and infinitely wiser in evil. He had offered her second place, and she was willing to accept it.

If it was not already too late.

When the Mental Man project was conceived by Fury and first described to the Hydra-unit named Madeleine Remillard, she thought that it might provide the perfect way of slipping the bond of dependency. Why shouldn't *she* be Mental Man's master, with uncounted numbers of paramount minions? All it needed was for the newborn minds to bond to her, rather than to Marc or Fury! And they would have—after Marc himself was enslaved, according to the long-standing plan.

And Fury was dead.

In the days when the other three Hydra-units were still alive, she had dared to hope that Fury could somehow be eliminated from the picture, leaving her in control. So long as Fury remained a subordinate persona residing in Denis Remillard's body, the monster was dependent upon Hydra's interface to the physical world. Killing Denis would not be easy, but she had worked out several practical plans of action over the years, thinking that the opportunity might come.

Even after the deaths of Quentin, Celine, and Parnell, after she had begun the new work on Astrakhan, she had clung to her dream of becoming the master.

But then a shattering event had occurred. Without warning, Fury's newly integrated mind in its creatively transformed body had suddenly appeared to her on the Russian world—the dual personae merged at last and the Fury component finally in control of a physical body and no longer dependent upon Hydra.

Even more amazing, Fury had undoubtedly generated an upsilon-field mentally and teleported 2910 lightyears through hyperspace! Reborn, he was stronger than Marc Remillard, stronger than Jack the Bodiless or Diamond Mask—and certainly invulnerable to any threat *she* might pose to his safety.

At first she had been reduced to dismayed stupefaction, only grateful that the monster had refrained from searching the deep recesses of her mind where treachery lurked. Later, when resignation and acceptance replaced her initial terror, she had been eager to do whatever this renascent Fury commanded, without question.

The new strategy was already worked out.

Hydra was already in place, her identity as Chief of Staff to the Astrakhanian Intendant General established. Her politically corrupt predecessor had perished in a fiery groundcar smash and his replacement was a great surprise to the local bureaucracy: a charming, extremely attractive young woman of high metacoercive quotient named Lyudmila Pavlovna Arsanova, a recent immigrant from Rostov-na-Donu on the Old World. This amazing female swept through the crony-ridden office of Intendant General Ruslan Terekev like a whirlwind, striking fear into the hearts of those staffers who survived the purge and gratifying Dirigent Xenia Kudryasheva and the Astrakhanian Intendant Assembly—who had been about to impeach IG Terekev for gross incompetence.

Popular opinion held that it was the force of Arsanova's personality that subsequently induced Ruslan to clean up his executive act. Within a scant five months after her appointment the Intendant General was transformed from a silly blowhard and rumored recipient of Chechen mafia favors into a fair simulacrum of a galactic statesman. Ruslan Terekev declared war on organized crime and broke the mafia's power. His eye was now firmly fixed upon the commercial main chance. He was still an avowed Rebel, but a respectable one.

Fresh investment capital then began to pour into faltering Astrakhan—presumably as a result of the new climate of law and order, loosened government regulations, and hastily negotiated tax breaks. Immigration (from the Old World, and from Volhynia, Yakutia, and Polovtsia as well) skyrocketed when new colonists were offered rent-free housing for three orbits. The crowning achievement of Ruslan Redux came when the moribund Astrakhanian starship yards at Novonikolayevsk unexpectedly won the bid for fifty new Bering-class colonization transports destined for the Fourteenth Sector Base on Assawompsett. Terekev achieved the coup almost single-handedly, with discreet help from his brilliant Chief of Staff.

It was this latter triumph—along with some adroit under-the-table maneuvers by Hibernian Dirigent Rory Muldowney—that had made possible the upcoming meeting of Rebel leaders on the Irish planet. It seemed probable that Fury's grand scheme for the establishment of a Second Milieu was about to receive a significant leg up, along with Hydra's personal hopes and aspirations.

Provided that Fury remained in firm control of his faculties.

As the car rounded a massive promontory, Ruslan Terekev stared blindly out to sea, exerting his farsight in the increasingly poor visibility. "I can see the island about twenty-five kloms offshore. It's as I remember it: the airspace barricaded with rho-field dampers, the house itself protected by ordinary electronic alarms and low-powered thoughtscreens. Nothing even an adept-class operant mind couldn't farsense through with ease."

Arsanova scowled. "How reckless of the Irish Dirigent, if his secret cache is a significant one."

"Not at all. A powerful aboveground security system guarding a mere country retreat would of itself be suspicious. Muldowney relies instead upon both primitive and sophisticated methods to protect his treasure. The cache of weaponry is buried over fourteen hundred meters down in the bedrock beneath the island. It is also creatively disguised so that only the most meticulous deepsight scrutiny by a paramount mind would ever penetrate it—and then only after knowing it was there."

"And you knew."

Ruslan Terekev laughed.

"It's still hard to believe that this man can have assembled any sort of significant arsenal." she said. "Hibernia is not especially wealthy, even if it is a bastion of anti-Milieu sentiment."

"Muldowney has had twenty years to gather his collection of arms," Terekev noted, "together with an interesting personal incentive for doing so. He has cultivated friends in both high and low places who have assisted his schemes. A Planetary Dirigent whose people love and trust him is in a unique position to defy Milieu strictures. He controls both the import-export apparatus of his world and its local Magistratum, and has a much better chance of getting away with a colossal fiddle than a mere Intendant General does. I envy him! We are in a much more precarious position on Astrakhan."

"If this meeting is a success," Lyudmila said, "our vexing Dirigent Xenia Kudryasheva will have to be dealt with. ODA has too many Milieu loyalists in its ranks for comfort. We cannot safely implement the starship modification plan if we must keep watching over our shoulders for Xenia Ivanovna and her inquisitive band of merry men."

As the road continued to curve, taking them onto a long peninsula, the jagged silhouette of Rory Muldowney's sizable private island became visible on the horizon, black against the sullen sky and heaving gray sea. A strobe beacon flashed from a distinctive triple peak at its eastern end. The place was named Inisfáil, which they understood meant "isle of destiny."

"It's going to rain again soon," Lyudmila remarked. "Look at that squall line coming toward us—"

"Mila!" He tensed. His hands, pressed against the console, were white-knuckled. "I think there are people somewhere close by! Slow down. Call up a terrain scan! How far are we from Dumha Sí?"

"Chuy yego znayet," she hissed, hitting the decelerator. "How should I know?" Her own heart was thudding and her hastily deployed seekersense detected nothing. The navigation display showed that a cove with steep walls lay some eight kilometers ahead, around the other side of the rugged peninsula.

Terekev studied the monitor. For an instant his brown eyes, dull as pebbles, showed a flash of the old electric sapphire. "That's where they are, in that cove! Three of them, and all weakly operant! They're on the beach, doing something that I can't make out. We couldn't have asked for a better situation. Drive on! Drive on!"

She pushed the Mercedes up to 150 kph in manual mode, overriding the UNSAFE CONDITIONS alert. The sky had darkened abruptly with the approach of the squall from the northwest and the car's headlamps switched to high beam. The narrowing peninsula became a jagged blade of rock with the twisting road carved from a precipitous slope. Surf crashed on the rocks below, throwing white water 30 meters into the air. The island had disappeared behind an onrushing curtain of rain.

They rounded the tip of the peninsula. She said, "Almost there—ah, yibitskaya sila! Now what?"

The console navigation unit bleeped, drowning out her exclamation of astonishment, and uttered a loud warning: "Cruifall alert! Cruifall alert! Executing mandatory autodeceleration sequence."

In seconds, the view through the car's windscreen was obscured by a reddish, gelatinous substance that defied the efforts of the rain-ionizer. Lyudmila Arsanova was effectively blinded. Before she could use her farsight the car braked automatically and came to a stop on the narrow shoulder of the road. Through the side windows they could see that the tumultuous downpour had turned sticky crimson, coating the pavement and portions of the landscape with gory slime.

"Is it my imagination," she said, "or is that stuff moving?" She mouthed another Russian obscenity and hit the computer INQUIRY pad. "Define cruifall!"

The artificial voice said: "Cruifall is a meteorological phenomenon peculiar to Loch Mór in the Connemara Intendancy of the planet Hibernia. During periods of high winds and quasi-waterspout activity, the wormlike planktonic marine organism Xenohydrobdella praecipitans, in Irish called cruimh fearthain, one to two centimeters in length and colored blood-red or brown, is sucked into the air from the surface of the sea and subsequently falls again with the rain. Cruifall is generally harmless to the environment, although it may occasion temporary inconvenience to mariners or shore dwellers because of the slipperiness of the gelatinous organisms or their obstruction of visibility. When dry, the cruimh crumbles away to a fine dust. For detailed information on the life cycle of the cruimh, please say *MORE*."

Lyudmila Arsanova maintained a frustrated silence. Ruslan Terekev, staring into space with an expression of breathless anticipation, softly said, "The people are down below us, Mila. Right here. There's a track leading to the cove's beach not ten meters ahead."

The computer announced: "This vehicle is equipped with windscreen wipers and waterspray equipment designed to alleviate cruifall. For activation, please say *GO*."

"Idi k yebanoiy matyeri!" Lyudmila cried. "Stupid computer—now you tell us! *Go*."

The mechanical wipers popped out of their slots and turned on, producing two cleared semicircles on the glass. Nudging the Mercedes to go ahead dead slow, Lyudmila steered onto a treacherous stony ramp with a grade of nearly 35 percent. Bumping and skidding, the big car crawled down to the storm-tossed shore.

There, splayed helplessly on the pocked strata above the surf line, lay a stranded sea-monster with an arched carapace at least 20 meters long and dozens of fringed tentacles like hairy fire hoses. Several of the tentacles were still moving. Two men and a woman dressed in yellow slicksuits, ignoring the cruifall, were using Matsushita laser cutters to zap the huge creature into pieces of convenient size. An open-bed crawler emblazoned AN LEACHT ORGANIC FERTILIZERS LTD stood ready to be loaded.

"Get the AV recorder," Lyudmila said quietly. "Open your window."

Ruslan retrieved the instrument from the back seat with his PK. As they came to a halt a dozen meters away from the scavengers, he rolled down the window and began to pan the scene, oblivious of the slimy downpour. One of the Hibernians waved. After a few minutes he ambled over while his mates continued to shovel chunks of flesh into an antigrav tote.

"Céad míle fáilte! Tourists, are ye, then?" Ruslan and Lyudmila nodded at the man and smiled. The scavenger gave an amiable operant salute with a bloody glove. He was considerably older than the other two workers. " 'Tis a sorry thing to have to welcome ye to our darlin' planet in a worm-storm, but I think the cruifall may be nearly over."

"We don't mind. We find it very interesting!" Lyudmila gushed. "What kind of creature is that you're working on, Citizen?"

"An ollphéistmhara, one of the local marine beasts. Ye might think of it as a kind of cross between a turtle and a squid. Nasty great bastards if you meet 'em in a small boat. They're a protected species in their sanctuary further along the coast, but fair game hereabouts when the waves wash 'em ashore. Where are ye from?"

"The Russian world of Astrakhan," Ruslan said. "Would you mind if we came out of the car and got a closer look at the animal?"

The scavenger shrugged. "Ye'll likely mess up your fine clothes, but come ahead. When the wormies dry, ye can brush 'em off easily enough." He turned away. "I must be getting back to me work. Stay clear of the tentacles. The brute is still alive."

They climbed out and cautiously negotiated the slippery rock slabs. The rain with its crimson cargo was indeed letting up, but the wind blew stronger than ever, driving salt spray from the breakers at them horizontally and soaking their clothing in seconds. Neither of them paid any attention to the discomfort.

Lyudmila spoke on the intimate mode: First we must subdue them with a coercive metaconcert and compel them to move back into the shelter of those rocks where they are out of sight of the road. Then we can begin to feed. Are you sure you're all right?

Ruslan's eyes had brightened and he moved without hesitation. He said: All right—? I'm exhilarated Mila! Look at them all three strong and *operant*. Zayadis'! What unbelievable luck!

He held up the camcorder and called out to the scavengers with declamatory telepathy: Please! One pose of all three in front of the creature without your tools.

With good-natured grins, the men and woman downed their cutters and linked arms.

Fury and Hydra moved closer, minds conjoined.

YOU ARE OURS.

The three Hibernians staggered, as though a blast of wind had caught them off-balance. Then they stood paralyzed, staring incredulously at the outland tourists.

YOU WILL FOLLOW US.

In single file, the trio marched after their captors into a narrow, sheltered corridor of broken limestone overgrown with vinelike succulents. The force of the gale was cut off, although it still roared overhead. The rain and the cruifall had stopped.

YOU . . . AND YOU. SIT THERE.

The men sank down onto the messy shingle among the shells and flotsam. Their faces were slack but their eyes were alive with anger. The woman stood swaying, helpless, her glance darting from one predator to another in bewilderment. The Hydra tore off the woman's sou'wester hat, releasing a cascade of chestnut hair. She was no more than twenty years old, with rosy cheeks and full lips. Strong hands ripped open the fasteners of the red-smeared yellow slicksuit and the young woman stepped dazedly out of it, clad in clean white polypro underwear. Her figure was richly curved, the nipples of her full breasts straining against the taut fabric. When the Hydra gripped the victim's shoulders her mouth opened in a voiceless scream that rang in the minds of the others. The two men moaned but did not move.

Hydra said: This one is ready for *your*/your feeding [image].

Fury had removed his overcoat and fur hat. His eyes were transmuted to luminous blue as he studied the petrified Hibernian woman. Finally, he reached out and touched the top of her head with a single finger. There was a blinding flash. An odor of burning hair filled the air and the prey went limp in Hydra's supporting arms. The head fell forward and on the crown was a peculiar design like a many-petaled flower, scorched into the skin of the scalp.

Take her Fury come and *take her!*

He came up behind the body, enfolding it in his arms and crushing it against his aroused flesh. His aura sprang forth, dazzling emerald shot through with azure, engulfing the two of them. Instinctively, he pressed his lips to the font of life at the victim's crown, stopping her heart for the first time.

<You . . . must show *me*/me how to do this dearest Hydra.>

You/you already know. But see [image] the seven chakra points along the head and spine? Drink from them as *you*/you take her.

<Yes. Yes *I*/I see . . .>

Hydra's own feeding aura kindled, ravenous gold edged with carmine. She plucked the older man from the ground as though he were a doll, stripped him naked, and expertly broke his neck. When his head sagged forward she embraced him, burying her face in the grizzled curls of his pate and setting him afire. Her hands, gripping his haunches, ground his pelvis against her own, forcing him into her.

This way! her mind shouted to Fury. This way! She and her victim disappeared in an exultant neural flare and she fed, beginning with the most rarefied psychic energy-font and slowly proceeding to the root. At the end, the body was a charred ruin and she was sated. Only her lips still glowed in the thickening dusk.

Fury had finished with the woman but his own metapsychic corona still blazed hungrily. He threw his arms wide in imperious command. Hydra brought him the last victim, stripped and ready, and watched until the consummation, when the final four-pointed chakra flower at the base of the young man's spine died like an ember.

The three bodies were burnt black, coiled into a curious posture resembling a pugilist with cocked fists. Each had seven stigmata formed of delicately patterned white ash imprinted along the seared vertebral column and hairless skull.

"I am finally whole," Fury said quietly, lifting his head and smiling at the Hydra. "All of the metafaculties are fully empowered at last." He showed her and she gasped in awe, then fell on her knees.

"Do anything with me," she whispered.

"Share a little of the totality, my dearest little one, and never doubt again." Gently, he brought her head against him and they merged in a final explosion of vital energies.

The storm was over and the wind was dying. They restored their clothing and walked back to the beach, where crashing surf surged around the mutilated sea-monster. The ollphéist was quite dead. Fury studied the formidable creature for a moment, then used his restored psychokinetic power to set its carcass adrift in the sea.

After blasting the human remains to cinders and scattering them over the water, Ruslan Terekev carefully placed a single tentacle-claw with a torn piece of slicksuit snagged on it among the rocks above the high-tide line, where it would surely be found. His PK levitated the Mercedes back onto the highway and tidied up the scene of the crime. The hacked-off body parts of the animal, the abandoned tools and tote, and the crawler vehicle were left as mute testimony to yet another tragedy of the sea.

[19]

SECTOR 12: STAR 12-370-992 [RETLA]
PLANET 3 [HIBERNIA]
7 EANAIR [15 FEBRUARY] 2080

It was downright eerie, the way the thing had begun.

Of course Patricia Castellane had been aware of Rory Muldowney's secret stash of matériel for years—just as he knew that her contingent were busy building illicit CE hats with the connivance of the Japs. But Rory was furious all the same when Pat's snotty executive assistant had come slithering up to him during an official reception on Okanagon late in 2078.

"I need your good advice, Dirigent," Lynelle Rogers had said to him, after a bit of preliminary chitchat. "Consider a hypothetical situation. Suppose that a certain high planetary official of Rebellious inclination has put together a large collection of weaponry—good stuff, mostly big blasters customized for offense."

Rory gave a great start. He was only a little drunk, and in spite of Lynelle's coyly oblique phrasing, he knew at once what she was talking about. He managed a lame little laugh and began to edge away. She took hold of his arm.

"Suppose," she went on, drawing him irresistibly toward a quiet corner, "that this official has kept the illicit treasure hidden away, adding to it year after year, hoping that one day it will prove useful when humanity bids for its freedom from the Galactic Milieu."

He gaped at the woman, too incredulous even to voice a denial. She'd shocked him into instant sobriety. Lynelle Rogers plowed on.

"Without a delivery system," said she, "without warships to mount the weapons on, the official's wonderful arsenal is little more than useless junk ... unless he's foolish enough to think that the Rebellion should smuggle photon cannons and antimatter bombs stolen from the Krondaku into Concilium Orb, and hold the nerve center of the Galactic Milieu for ransom."

A Dhia na bhfeart! Had the silly female gone mad, daring to talk about such things? (And actually the ransom idea was one that he was especially taken with.)

Lynelle said, "Suppose that a certain person knew a way to get hold of warships for the Rebellion. Would you advise her to speak to the high planetary official with the hoard of weapons—or should she go straight to Marc Remillard with her information?"

Rory forced the woman back against the wall, looming over her, using both coercion and the down side of the redactive metafaculty to compel and hurt her. *Stop playing your feckin' games dammit and tell me what you know!*

Lynelle Rogers never stopped smiling. She opened her mind and showed him exactly how she thought the warships could be obtained.

He'd backed off then, laughing her to scorn. From *Astrakhan?* Crazy bitch!

The once-thriving shipbuilding industry of the fourth Russian colony was on the brink of ruin. The planet's Milieu-loyalist female Dirigent was a futile mystic and its Intendant General, Ruslan Terekev (for all that he was a faithful adherent to the Rebel cause), was a fatuous, crony-ridden gobshite. Why, Astrakhan was no more likely to get the contract for the Fourteenth Sector colonization transports than it was to host the Second Coming of Jesus Christ!

And even if the impossible did occur, there was no way that the Rebellion could expropriate and arm those starships without the Milieu loyalists finding out about it.

. . . Was there?

"Perhaps not," Lynelle Rogers had said, as though the matter were suddenly of no concern to her. "All the same, if someone high in the Astrakhanian government should ever contact you with an unusual business proposal, be certain that Marc Remillard and the other Rebel leaders hear about it and take it seriously. Or else a certain high planetary official might find himself guarding a pile of dusty rubbish like some futile old dragon in an Irish fairytale—while the exotics force Unity down the human race's throat."

The bloody insolence! He'd told the woman to go to hell very politely, and later on at the party he chewed out Pat Castellane for spilling his great secret to a lunatic underling. Pat indignantly denied she'd done anything of the sort. But what else could she say without making herself look a fool?

Less than a week later Lynelle Rogers perished in a dreadful mountain-climbing accident, her body crushed to a pulp in a glacial crevasse. At that point Rory Muldowney gave a lot more thought to the strange conversation he'd had with Rogers—and also entertained some very nasty suspicions about Dirigent Patricia Castellane.

Months went by. A mind-boggling upheaval occurred on Astrakhan. Its debased buffoon of an Intendant General underwent an abrupt change of character and was transformed overnight into a political dynamo. Most stunning of all, the shipbuilding contract *was* eventually awarded to the Russian planet by the Polity Commerce Directorate, just as the late Rogers had predicted.

Rory had felt the hairs stir at the nape of his neck when that little piece of news reached him. But it was nothing compared to the jolt he got when Ruslan Terekev called him not long afterward on the subspace communicator, proposing an unofficial visit to Hibernia. The Russian said he wanted to discuss forming an astronautical consortium between their two worlds—"and we must also talk over other matters important to the future of the Human Polity."

Of course the consortium notion was a farce. The Hibernian economy was based primarily on agriculture and light manufacturing, with no astronautics industry worth mentioning. But Rory agreed to the meeting all the same, and then he reported the entire unlikely tale to the leader of the Rebel Party, just as Lynelle Rogers had told him to do.

Surprisingly, Marc Remillard didn't laugh.

On the day of the conference Rory flew over to the mainland himself to collect the two Russians from Granuaile House. Thanks be to heaven the rain was over. The wretched cruimh had dessicated overnight and turned to dust, blown to hell and gone by the clean north wind, and the sky above Loch Mór was a cloudless iris-blue.

The visitors were waiting for him in the parlorlike lobby of the inn. The Astrakhanian IG was sturdy as a block of bog oak, daunting and portentous of mien. Above his prominent nose, piercing dark eyes sunk in deceptive laugh-wrinkles hinted at formidable metapsychic powers. His broad Slavic mouth opened stingily when he spoke and then slammed shut like a drawer.

The IG's Chief of Staff, Lyudmila Arsanova, turned out to be an ebony-haired smasheroo wearing an elegant leather outfit that enhanced her lovely figure. She stood frowning at her boss's side, exuding the chilling vibes of a thoroughgoing ballbuster. If these two were lovers, as recent Rebel intelligence reports had speculated, Rory had no doubt which one called the tune in the dance of sweet comhriachtain!

He bid the pair the traditional ten thousand welcomes to Hibernia and said he hoped they'd enjoyed their drive yesterday.

"It was a most interesting experience." Ruslan Terekev smiled minimally. "However, I am sorry to tell you that last night we were interrupted at dinner by a police officer, who informed us that a grisly incident had taken place on the coast just west of here. Three local beachcombers disappeared after a sea-beast they were harvesting apparently attacked them and dragged them off into the water. This policeman interrogated us at some length, since we had passed close by the scene of the accident. We informed him that we had no useful information, but he did not seem entirely satisfied."

"The Intendant General is deeply concerned," Lyudmila Arsanova said sternly, "that the security of our secret meeting might be compromised if we should be required to submit to further questioning by the authorities."

"Soddin' idiot coppers," Rory muttered. "We'll just see about that."

He found a teleview and dealt briskly with the Garda at Gaillimh while the Russians hovered. Not a trace had been found of the sea-monster's victims (the voracious ollphéist rarely made leftovers), but even if bodies were found, the visitors would not have to appear as witnesses in the inquiry. The officer who had spoken to them was young and overly zealous. The Garda would never dream of inconveniencing distinguished guests of Dirigent Muldowney.

"I hope that satisfies you," Rory said, as the screen went gray.

Lyudmila nodded. "It was necessary to be absolutely certain. Such officious meddling in the affairs of persons of importance would never be tolerated on Astrakhan."

"We must proceed now to the island with no further delay," Ruslan Terekev declared. "Please settle our bill. We will wait in your rhocraft." He hoisted his own valise and went stumping out the front door of the inn without another word, the woman close on his heels.

Rory raised his eyes to heaven, held his temper admirably, and used his personal credit card.

On the brief trip from the mainland to Inisfáil, Lyudmila Arsanova remained wrapped in inscrutable silence while Terekev's responses to the Dirigent's attempts at conversation were abbreviated and brusque. Even when a spectacular flight of huge azure theropterids boiled up from one of the limestone stacks offshore and headed out to sea in a joyous corkscrewing feeding frenzy, the Astrakhanian IG's only comment was, "Very pretty."

Rory sighed inwardly. Well, these two beauties hadn't been invited for their winsome charm. He landed the egg on the pad behind his country house and ushered the Russians up the graveled path.

"The others have already arrived, except for Marc Remillard and Alexis Manion, who are expected shortly. I'll show you to your rooms so you can freshen up. We'll be having lunch in about an hour, and after that my daughter Cyndia will take us all on an inspection tour of the armlann. She's an engineer and supervises the place."

Ruslan said, "This—this armlann is your private arsenal? The one you propose using to arm the starships?"

"It's Hibernia's free contribution to the Rebellion." Rory made the correction with polite firmness. "A prime strategic asset of the cause."

"Of course," the Intendant General murmured. "And we of Astrakhan will be honored to assist in the ultimate deployment of these weapons against the exotic despots. Provided, of course, that the Rebel leadership accepts our proposal. I trust that Fleet officers are also in attendance, as we requested? Their expertise will be needed in the evaluation."

"Owen Blanchard himself is here, along with two other top Rebel honchos of the Twelfth—the Chief of Operations, Ragnar Gathen, and the Deputy Ops, Walter Saastamoinen. You'll also be conferring with Cordelia Warshaw, our top strategic adviser, and Professor Anna Gawrys, Hiroshi Kodama, and Patricia Castellane—all members of the Executive Council involved in what you might call military matters. But of course the ultimate decision on your warship scheme rests with Marc Remillard himself."

Ruslan Terekev was surprised. "He is not bound by the vote of his Council?"

"Oh, no," said Rory blandly. "He's the generalissimo. It was the only way he'd agree to take on the leadership. Marc consults with the rest of us, but in the end he calls the shots."

"I see."

"Most of us Rebels would have it no other way," Rory Muldowney said with a twinkle in his eye. "But there are a few sore losers."

Marc made a perfunctory apology as he picked up his old friend Alexis Manion at Loch Salainn Starport and immediately bundled him into an Avis rent-a-rho. "I'm sorry to have dragged you away from Earth at such short notice. Was the express trip hard on you?"

Alex pulled a comical grimace. "You know I hate high-df starflight. But I'll survive."

Marc laughed dismissively. Nobody's priorities mattered but his own. The egg lofted into the stratosphere and picked up the Connemara Vee-way.

"I wouldn't have called this emergency meeting of the Council if the matter under consideration wasn't crucially important. If it's any consolation, I had to travel all the way from Orb on a tight catenary myself. I've been stroking the Krondak honchos of the Panpolity Operant Affairs Directorate. They demanded a progress report on full-body CE, and it's taken me three weeks at coercive max to satisfy them with an exhaustive demonstration of the rig."

Alex was nonplussed. "Satisfy—!"

"Yes. You'll be interested to know that 600X CE is now conditionally approved for use in the geophysical modification of planets. There will be no more obstructive maneuvers from the Science Directorate or the Unity advocates or anyone else in the Concilium unless the equipment evinces some serious flaw . . . or is used in an 'inappropriate' manner."

"Well, congratulations! Until inappropriate circumstances prevail, that is."

"Thanks. This meeting today will help define the parameters of those very circumstances."

Alex said, "I think you'd better tell me more about this strange-bedfellows entente cordiale between the Russians and Rory Muldowney. What the hell are they up to?"

"The Rebellion is about to be presented with an offer that's too good to refuse. The Astrakhanians are proposing to do secret modifications on all of the big colonization transports scheduled to be built in their yards, effectively fitting them out as disguised Rebel battlewagons. The big guns and other weaponry will come from Dirigent Rory Muldowney's notorious illicit armory."

"Why—that's marvelous!"

"No, it's a disaster in the making." Marc was quite calm. "And it could jeopardize the future of the Rebellion unless it's handled very carefully."

"I don't understand. Aren't Muldowney's weapons any good?"

"On the contrary. They're mostly ingenious modifications of legitimate equipment."

"Then what's the problem? We certainly need warships in order to wage a war—even if it ultimately amounts to a saber-rattling bluff, as most of us hope. What was it Voltaire said? 'Dieu est toujours pour les gros bataillons!' "

"Not if those big battalions tempt the hotheads in the Rebel Party into a premature declaration of independence against the Milieu. Some of our more impetuous co-conspirators—the Irish Dirigent prominent among them—believe that we can compel the Galactic Milieu to capitulate and grant humanity its freedom simply by threatening it with an old-fashioned Star Wars–type of deep-space shoot-'em-up. But that strategy can't possibly work. In a Metapsychic Rebellion, God is on the side of the big minds, not the big guns."

"I tend to agree with you, but—"

"I'm not just expressing a personal opinion, Alex. After I accepted the Rebel leadership I spent over five weeks working on war-game simulations at Oxford with Cordelia Warshaw and Helayne Strangford and Alonzo Jarrow. We studied dozens of different offensive scenarios that stopped short of doomsday—most especially including confrontations that featured laser and antimatter matériel and the kind of CE blaster-hats that certain of our Rebel associates now look upon as the ultimate secret weapon. The outcome was always the same: If a Rebel force were ever faced with a psychocreative metaconcert that included all of the Milieu's coadunate minds, we'd be stone goners—no matter how many photon cannons or E18 operators our warships carried. Superior exotic mindpower forced us into the Milieu. Only superior *human* mindpower can insure that we escape from it without risking the complete destruction of galactic civilization."

"I presume you're talking about your new 600X CE enhancer. But even if we do use those hellish things, have we enough grandmaster-class operators to tip the balance of power?"

"For a decisive victory, the Rebel metaconcert would need at least nine thousand metacreative GMs equipped with full-body rigs."

"We don't have half that number of longheads on our side—and so far, only a handful of 600X enhancers."

"True," Marc agreed. "But I ran another simulation with Helayne just before I left Orb. We could be certain of victory if we built enough rigs to equip all of our GMs ... and added just a hundred 600X-empowered paramounts to our side of the equation."

"Jesus, Marc! Just say we're fucked and be done with it. You know you're the only paramount mind the Rebellion's got!"

"At present."

Alex posed a wordless telepathic query.

Turning away, Marc let his gaze wander over the panorama visible through the polarized dome of the rhocraft. They were flying over a great body of gray-green water bordered by verdant mountains. Alex Manion waited.

Marc finally said, "Our Rebellion *can* succeed if it includes the participation of Mental Man."

Manion exploded. "Oh, for God's sake! Can we talk reality here? Even if you could implement that wacko scheme of yours, it would take decades to get the project off the ground."

"Wrong. The genetic feasibility studies were extremely favorable, and Jeff Steinbrenner is establishing the initial embryonic assay parameters right now at the CEREM facility in Seattle Metro. I've built a new lab for him and given him carte blanche and unlimited funding."

Alex goggled at his friend, struck speechless.

"The normal human brain is neurologically mature at nine years of age," Marc said. "There's a fair probability that Mental Man might mature much earlier. We've got to stall the Milieu's Protocol of Unity until Mental Man is ready for combat."

"It'd be immoral to use little children—"

"To guarantee the mental freedom of the human race? I think not. The Mental Man cadre would be educated from the beginning with an understanding of their duty. Their destiny. The young metapsychic operants of today are inculcated with similar principles by their parents and preceptors—often even before their birth. Is that immoral?"

"No, but—"

"When Jack was nine, he was intellectually adult. So was I. Only our emotions and bodies were immature, and our metafaculties had yet to reach their full potential. With our special training regimen, Mental Man will have his full faculties after five years. Perhaps much earlier."

"But the project you described to me would change the children in a fundamental way—before they freely consented."

"We would change them infinitely for the better. Insure that their minds are superior. If it were a matter of choice, I think you'd be surprised at the number of parents who'd opt for a Mental child over a product of genetic roulette, even if it didn't have daddy's brown eyes or mommy's nose. I certainly would. Eugenics of the mind has been debated by scientists and ethicists for over a hundred and fifty years, but no one has ever had the courage to take it from theory to practice—probably because the results couldn't be guaranteed by the available technology."

"Well, one man tried . . ." Alex's mind projected an image.

"Don't be an ass!" Marc snapped. "Hitler was a madman, not a trained operant scientist with state-of-the-art resources at his command."

His friend was shaking his head. "Marc, I don't know what to say. I had no idea that Mental Man was anything more than . . . a bizarre fantasy of yours."

"It's far from bizarre. The life-supportive equipment required by the project already exists. Shig Morita refined and upgraded the nonborn in-vitro reproduction technology that's been in successful operation for over sixty years. What's new is our ability to preselect the embryos with paramount potential, using farsensory CE. Jeff Steinbrenner developed the basic sorting technique several years ago when he was a staffer at IVFF in Chicago. His goal then was a fairly simple one: to enhance the engendering of operant nonborns. But implementation of his research was considered too controversial by the shortsighted bureaucrats who enforce the Human Polity Reproductive Statutes. CEREM won't be troubled by any such restrictions."

"Would you care to show me a detailed précis of the entire Mental Man project?" Alex asked very quietly.

Marc smiled, still staring out the window. "Not yet. We're still working a few bugs out of it."

"I'll bet you are! For starters, I presume that only one of the gametes in this fabulous scheme can be guaranteed to carry the genes for paramount metafunction: your own."

"Correct. Studies of my family heritage show there is an excellent chance of supravital alleles in mental traits as well as in the self-rejuvenating complex. Unfortunately, there are sublethal alleles as well, but we should be able to screen them out rather easily."

"May I ask who will contribute the eggs for these wunderkinder?"

"Dierdre Keogh, the most brilliant female Grand Master working at CEREM. She was delighted to donate one of her ovaries to the project. Every one of her six natural children is a GM—although the spectrum of operant metafaculties varies."

Alex gave a skeptical grunt. "Her natural brood is also atypically homozygotic—brilliant like their parents, and maybe even a bit more emotionally unzipped."

"Jeff thinks that the odds are high that we'll engender useful numbers of operant paramounts using Dierdre's ova. The preceptive training of the fetuses will begin in the fifth month of life, just as my brother Jack's did. He was the first Homo summus—the first Mental Man." Marc turned to catch Alex's eye. "Fortunately for our Rebellion, I can guarantee that the new generation will have a different political orientation."

"Holy God! You're really serious about this, aren't you?"

Marc didn't bother to answer the question. "I'm not yet prepared to announce the initiation of the Mental Man project to the other members of the Council, and I certainly don't want the Astrakhanians to know about it. So please keep this conversation of ours confidential. What I need from you at this meeting is your support when I insist that we hold off arming the new fleet of Russian-built starships. I don't want those guns or bombs installed until a hostile confrontation between our forces and those of the Milieu appears imminent and we have no other choice."

"You can't tell the Russians to stuff it—"

"Certainly not. We'll need the starships eventually, along with whatever vessels of the Twelfth Fleet that our Rebel officers can commandeer. But for the present, discreet modifications in frame-design are all that I'll agree to in the Astrakhanian scheme. We can't take a chance on having Milieu loyalists catch us with our pants down—let alone risk a literal loose-cannon situation involving firebrands like Muldowney . . . or even Ruslan Terekev himself. This Rebellion will start when *I* say so. And we won't bluff. We'll fight to win."

"Poor old Rory," Alex drawled. "All those lovely weapons— scorned in favor of a gaggle of deus-ex-machina paramount brats."

"Muldowney's a good man," Marc said, "absolutely loyal to the Rebel cause. It's just too bad he's had such a difficult time accepting my leadership."

"Perhaps he finds it hard to separate you from your father in his mind. An understandable psychological blivet, under the circumstances."

Marc let that one go by. Every Magnate of the Concilium knew that the Hibernian Dirigent's wife, Laura Tremblay, had committed suicide twenty years earlier when Paul Remillard told her that their love affair had ended. In spite of Laura's unfaithfulness, Rory's love for her had never faltered. Neither had his hatred for the First Magnate of the Human Polity.

Marc admired the big Irishman on both counts . . .

"ETA Inisfáil NAVCON five minutes," the egg's navigation unit announced with a lovely lilt. "If you're expected, please enter the access code—and ten thousand welcomes to you! If you're not expected, I'm sorry to tell you that a landing option on the island is not available. Please go away, because today this airspace is protected with truly fearsome security measures you'll not be happy to encounter!"

Alex laughed. "I'm encouraged. At least the traffic-control computers on this planet have a more civilized attitude than the ones on Earth. Maybe it's a favorable omen of things to come."

"Right now, I'll settle for an edible lunch." Marc fed in the code and the egg began to descend.

She was still working on the balky gravomag generator of the big tractor when he called on the intimate farspeech mode:

Síondaire, a iníon ó!

Yes, Taoiseach.

Are you ready for the Grand Tour? This lot are nearly finished gabbing and I'll want to be bringing them down in a half hour or so.

You caught me flat on my back and filthy under the Tadano T6. You might know the damned thing would break just because we want to make a good impression showing off the armlann . . . Well, how did it go?

Not as I'd hoped, Síondaire a leanbh. That bloody Marc Remillard looked the gift horse in the mouth and decided it had stinking breath!

Oh, Daidí. I'm so sorry.

The Council mostly sided with Marc and I couldn't persuade them otherwise. I was shot down in flames and made to look a right prat. Shite, maybe I *am* one, thinking that I knew anything about starwar strategy.

No one will dare think that of you! ... What was the objection?

Marc was afraid that Ed Chung, the Commander-in-Chief of the Fourteenth on Assawompsett, would somehow discover the clandestine armament on the new ships and come roaring after his arse. So all he'd agree to is having the shipframes modified, and putting in hidden hardware for the weapons system controls. No actual armament plug-in until some unspecified time later in the game—never mind that it might be too late by the time they get around to it! Ruslan Terekev tried to assure Marc that the weapons could be effectively camouflaged, but the bastard wouldn't budge. He was too cagey to say flat out that he was afraid that the Russians might try to bypass Owen Blanchard at Okanagon and command the ships themselves when the Rebellion started, but that's what he was thinking.

Hmm. How trustworthy is this Ruslan Terekev, anyway? It's less than two years since he had his great change of heart, after all. I don't mean to take the side of Remillard, Daidí, but the man does seem only to be showing prudence and commonsense.

Maybe so. But this starship scheme seemed so *right.* The Rebellion with its own fleet of dreadnoughts at last! The armlann at the ready and human freedom within our grasp—

You've waited for twenty years, Taoiseach Ruairí O Maoldhomhnaigh. You can be patient a while longer.

Yes. It seems I'll have to be.

Be proud that you've gathered a true arsenal. It's more than any of the other Rebel leaders have done—hole&corner plotters most of them, doing nothing but squirreling away stupid brainbuckets.

CE is not stupid, my lass. Especially Marc Remillard's sort.

I have no confidence in mental weaponry. But then, I'm prejudiced.

And a damned good thing ... Well, do us both proud when I bring them down for the tour, Síondaire. We'll be coming along soon.

It was time for a break anyhow.

Cyndia Muldowney slid out from under the big disabled machine on a rolling board. She gathered up the mess of scattered tools and diagnostic instruments lying about and stowed them neatly in her mechanic-tote. A good stretch eased her cramped muscles, and a cup of sweet tea from a nearby wall dispenser took care of her thirst. She carried the plass cup to the railing of the circular metal balcony and stood, one fist on her hip, looking down into a monstrous shaft that plunged into tenebrous depths. It was 120 meters in diameter and lined with tier upon tier of alcoves as big as barns. Inside each cell of the cylindrical hive lurked one or more bulky spectral shapes.

"Equipment bay lights on," she commanded. "Deopaque pods."

The cells were suddenly illuminated from within and the white plass shrink-shrouds protecting the stored items became transparent. Like goods in Christmas shopwindows, the treasures of Cyndia Muldowney's domain were put on display.

Moonslicers.

Orbit sweepers.

Comet burners.

Modified deep-space smelters.

Hundreds of different types of actinic-beamers, X-lasers, molecular debonders, and twiston projectors—ingeniously modified from their original benign industrial or astronautical function into engines of destruction.

She had not done the actual refitting herself. Others devoted to the cause had converted lawful machinery into war matériel, laboring patiently for two decades in clandestine shops scattered all over the Rebellious Irish planet. And in later years, when his world's growing economy had permitted it, Dirigent Rory Muldowney had consorted with underworld suppliers, paying them to steal truly colossal zappers and twelve precious antimatter devices from the Krondaku. It was done without a trace, by methods that Cyndia preferred not to think about.

Innocent-looking marine vessels transported the modified pieces from secret Hibernian workshops to a sea-cave on the rugged north side of Inisfáil, where there was a hidden dock. Before Cyndia's time, old Tomás Daltún had taken each cargo consignment in charge. Working mostly alone, but assisted by the finest robotic construction and maintenance equipment that Rory Muldowney could buy or misappropriate from the tyrannical Galactic Milieu, the old man kept the cache of precious matériel in perfect condition, stowing it away in growing numbers of environmentally controlled storage alcoves carved from the living rock beneath Inisfáil.

Tomás Daltún was dead now, Lord rest him. But he'd lived to see the little girl who'd pestered and adored him during her summer visits to the island take over his job. Cyndia Muldowney was twenty-four years old. Her engineering education had only been completed two years earlier, whereupon her father had appointed her custodian of the armlann.

She finished her tea, tossed the cup into the recycler hopper, and went back to the Tadano T6 tractor. In operation, the huge machine moved freely up and down and around the shaft on a grid of rails, hauling the stored weaponry in or out of the cells. With luck, she might complete the repair before her father and the others came down. It would be rather impressive to pluck out one of the podded comet burners or moonslicers with tractor beams, haul it up to the main holding area beyond the balcony, and let the members of the Rebel Council and the two Astrakhanians inspect the thing up close. Only Patricia Castellane and Owen Blanchard had ever visited the arsenal before, and that was years ago during Tomás Daltún's time, when the collection was still a fairly modest one.

No one would call the armlann modest now. Not even *him*.

Cyndia Muldowney smiled as she retrieved the tools she'd need to finish the present job. She lowered herself down onto the wheeled trolley, turned on its worklights, replaced her goggles, and used her PK to slide on her back beneath the ponderous machine. An odd thought struck her, and she wondered if the paramount maistín himself was watching her right this minute, farsensing through the solid rock and the guardian sigma-fields.

What was he really like, she asked herself, this man who led the Metapsychic Rebellion on his own terms? He seemed to terrify and infuriate her stouthearted father while still earning his unwilling respect. Marc Remillard was as handsome as the devil himself and as charming, and he apparently thought nothing of freezing his body to ice while injecting his paramount brain with lightning.

Was he a man at all, if what they said about him was true? And why did she care? . . .

She found herself staring blankly up at the partially disassembled guts of the tractor's third-stage power unit, her own heart pounding, breathless with anticipation.

"Never you mind about that one, Síondaire Ní Maoldhomhnaigh," she told herself sharply. "Get back to work!"

Throughout the long luncheon, Marc's mind had been divided. Almost all of his attention was devoted to the intricate telepathic discussion of Ruslan Terekev's cogently presented proposal. But one small part of him stood aloof, watching Lyudmila Arsanova as she performed exquisite, undetectable mind-probes of all the Rebel participants ... except himself. Her inspection only reached the intermediate thought-levels of the other eight members of the Executive Council, but it was sufficient to expose reasoning processes and prejudices, as well as providing a useful psychological profile of each individual.

Arsanova's eventual scrutiny of *him* was something altogether different.

She had held off until the debate ended and the others at the table—replete with the magnificent meal of watercress soup, sea-spider mayonnaise in tomato aspic, grilled bluetrout with spinach-butter sauce, soda bread, and gooseberry fool with shortbread—were finishing their cups of coffee or tea. The conversation had turned vocal and desultory, confined to small talk now that it was inevitable what the decision on the starships was going to be. The disappointment of Intendant General Ruslan Terekev was palpable (only slightly mollified by his unanimous election to the Executive Council of the Rebel Party), which made it all the more peculiar that his female Chief of Staff seemed preoccupied with a completely different agenda.

At first Marc thought she might simply be coming on to him.

It was a tiresome phenomenon that had become more common since his entry into public life. As the charismatic new spokesman for the Rebel Party he was fair game for operant hero-worshippers of both sexes—most of whom had the good sense to back off when their subliminal overtures were rejected. But Lyudmila Arsanova apparently had more than mere dalliance on her mind. Her redactive touch on his invulnerable mindscreen was more fleeting than the caress of a butterfly wing, yet it carried an unusual urgency. Her own mental shield seemed to have diminished in spots, revealing intriguing glimpses of personality that struck him with an odd sense of déjà vu. He had never set eyes on the woman before, and yet he knew her: He had known her again and again, under disturbing—even humiliating—circumstances.

But how? And where?

She seemed to remain passive. Aside from expressing a few pleasantries when they were first introduced she had said nothing to him, never once meeting his gaze. But now her mental barrier was like a perfectly balanced garden gate ready to swing open and welcome him at the slightest encouragement. The compulsion for him to enter was becoming more and more powerful. Christ! Was the woman actually able to coerce him?

She was. But the impulse had no exterior source. It was coming from the depths of his own unconscious mind . . .

Across the table, Lyudmila Arsanova slowly lifted her beautiful face and looked directly at him: *Of course we know each other. We have been destined to come together from all eternity—*

Abruptly, Marc pushed back his chair and stood up. "Rory, I want to express my appreciation to you for providing us with a place for this meeting. Thanks to you and your liaison with our friends from Astrakhan, we've been able to clarify some very important policy considerations today. The physical implementation of the Metapsychic Rebellion has taken a great step forward."

There was mental applause, and scattered affirmations of "Hear, hear!"

Marc continued. "Knowing that these starships are available to us opens new strategy options to us that were formerly unavailable. The store of armament you've assembled here on Hibernia will surely remain an important part of that strategy. I have no doubt that both the warships and the stockpile of matériel will prove invaluable, one way or another, when the final countdown to human independence begins . . . And now I'd be honored—and so would everyone else sitting at this table—if you'd take us on a tour of your famous armlann. You've got us all dying of curiosity."

Rory agreed at once and asked his guests to follow him. Marc kept close on the heels of the Hibernian Dirigent as they trooped downstairs to the lodge's handsomely fitted game room. The secret passageway leading to the arsenal's passenger lift was revealed, rather ludicrously, when the billiard table was tilted on end.

Rory seemed to have regained his usual mordant good humor. "The principal entry into the armlann is from a cave at sea level on the opposite side of the island. But it's a dank place, more often than not stinking from the carcasses of unlucky water-beasts zapped by accident by the security devices. This here is the family entrance that my daughter uses when she comes to have tea with her old dad. Kindly step into the lift car."

It was a rather tight fit for nine people. Lyudmila Arsanova smiled up at Marc and apologized for treading on his foot.

"Not at all," he murmured, shifting away from the too-intimate contact. Back at the table, he'd thrust her ruthlessly from his mental vestibule with the same unceremonious finality dealt out to other would-be lovers who had refused to take a hint. But she still hadn't given up, damn her! The mysterious inner compulsion lingered in his mind as well, along with an elusive fragment from—of all things—Jack and Diamond's wedding mass:

You have ravished my heart my sister my bride you have pierced my soul with a single glance . . .

The elevator door slid open. They emerged into an area resembling the receiving dock of a warehouse, undistinguished except for the fact that its curving walls and ceiling were smoothly bored from limestone strata of a mottled pinkish-gray. Boxy ship-containers and plass pods stood about, some of them opened to disclose such mundane items as rolls of electrical flex, a brand-new ventilation turbine, D-water drums, and packages of buffing compound. The atmosphere was dry and warm. A nearly subsonic hum hinted at the operation of some machinery. From the distance came an irregular clinking sound, as though someone were pounding on metal.

"We'll find my daughter this way," Rory said, heading into a side passage. "She's the sole guardian of the armlann."

Professor Anna Gawrys said rather reproachfully, "Surely the poor young woman doesn't spend all of her time here, down in the bowels of the earth?"

Rory laughed. "Not a bit of it, Annushka. The regular maintenance schedule takes only ten weeks out of each year, although extra work is required when fresh batches of equipment arrive and have to be mothballed. And from time to time, when we outgrow our space and new storage cells are required, Cyndia supervises their construction. The rest of her days are spent lolling around Tara Nua, giving me a hand now and then at Dirigent House when she's not throwing parties. The lass insists her madcap socializing is a necessary smoke screen to divert suspicion, but I think she protests too much."

"You would," said Patricia Castellane.

They came into an enormous vaulted chamber. The floor was a circular balcony of metal grating and beneath their feet the lighted multiple levels of the armlann fell away into blurred obscurity.

"Holy shit," murmured Fleet Commander Owen Blanchard.

Rory grinned. "I'll take that as a compliment."

Hiroshi Kodama was assessing the amount of weaponry stored. "Each level contains twenty-four cells, and the number of levels is—"

"Ninety-two," Rory said. "The newer, larger pieces are nearest the top. At the bottom, the cells are crammed full of portable arms—Bosch 414 blasters and the like."

"Perhaps not quite enough matériel to fight a war with," Cordelia Warshaw observed judiciously, "but enough to bolster Rebel enthusiasm."

A hulking piece of equipment standing a dozen meters away was the source of the rhythmic sounds. Most of the visitors ignored it and hurried to peer over the balcony railing into the awesome shaft. Marc, Rory, and the two Astrakhanians were among those who went to the Tadano tractor.

"Síondaire!" the Hibernian Dirigent called. "Our guests are here."

"I'll be right out, Taoiseach," said a muffled voice, "just as soon as I finish bashing this bent access-panel back into place." The pounding resumed.

"I am very impressed by the armlann," said Ruslan Terekev. "It hardly seems possible that a single young lady could be responsible for its maintenance."

"My daughter's no ordinary lass," Rory said proudly.

After a last vehement flourish of blows, the concealed engineer said, "There! Now it's done."

Two feet, clad in heavy boots, emerged from under the tractor, followed by the rest of a slender body clad in a grubby blue hooded coverall. The engineer's face was smudged with grease, and goggles covered her eyes. A tool tote rested on the rolling trolley beside her. Lying there, she smiled up at the visitors.

"May I present," Rory said, "my youngest daughter, Cyndia Muldowney."

Marc reached down a big hand and she took it, jumping easily to her feet. She was a tall woman, but the top of her head came only to his shoulder. They stood unmoving, facing each other. One of her gloved hands was still in Marc's grip. She used the other to pull off the protective eyewear and hood.

A luxuriant fall of curling, red-gold hair. Pale, translucent skin beneath the grime. A high forehead and a delicately curved, thin-bridged nose. Exceptionally large eyes the color of Loch Mór in summer, set deeply and framed by startling black lashes. Full lips parted, at first unable to speak.

Because in that instant the cavern was filled with a burst of blinding white light.

The people at the railing swung about with exclamations of astonishment. But by then the inadvertent flare of Marc's metapsychic aura had faded, lingering only in his widening, amazed stare.

"So you're he," she whispered, searching his face.

"And I know who you are," Marc replied. "I knew it the moment I saw you."

You have ravished my heart my sister my bride you have pierced my soul with a single glance how beautiful are your breasts honey and milk are under your tongue what magic lies in your love . . .

Ignoring everyone except each other, Marc and Cyndia walked off toward the elevator, hand in hand.

Staring after them in stunned disbelief, Rory whispered, "Dear Lord, no!"

Ruslan Terekev's face was a granite mask. "Yes. Oh, yes indeed! Dirigent Muldowney, I think you will now have to find a new custodian for your armlann."

After Fury and Hydra had fled from the island, he tried to calm her raging grief:

<My poor little one! *I*/I am so sorry so very sorry. It was a completely unexpected development.>

Anguish. Let me alone. I want to DIE.

< *I*/I will comfort you . . . there.>

Ahhhh—STOP I don't want it don't want *YOU*—

<Peace. Peace.>

NEVERuntilIkillbothofthemDAMNthemtoHELL!

<In time. But there is nothing to be done about it now. It cannot be undone.>

I know . . . It's over for me.

<Nonsense.>

Despair.

<Take consolation if you can from *my*/my assurance that in the long run the net effect upon Mental Man and the Second Milieu will be the same. Plans will have to be somewhat altered [image] but we will still win. We will triumph while the two of them are destroyed.>

You still plan to use my ova.

<It must be.>

Hatred! Use *hers* the damned bitch hers hers—

<NO. Hydra dearest you know that would not be for the best. Only in the second generation of the Marc/Cyndia union will full paramount operancy be assured in the offspring. We must have Mental Man now and you will rule Him yes YOU darling *I*/I will show you how to effect the Hydraseduction of the fetuses they will be yours as You*s* were *mine*/mine.>

Really? *Really?*

<*I*/I swear it on *my*/my life. Do you believe *me*/me?>

I . . . believe.

<The pain of this setback will pass in time. You must not let it distract you from the ultimate goal from our glorious Second Milieu. Come now. Take comfort again from *me*/me . . .>

Ahhh. Yes. OhFuryBelovedFury what would I do without *you*/you?

<You would fail dearest Hydra.>

I know. I vow to follow *you*/you. To obey. Just have patience with me for a little longer while I cope with this awful disappointment this disaster this horror I don't understand how it could have happened how could he do it how after all my work all those coercive dreams HOW could it have happened? *How could Marc fall in love with the wrong sister?*

[20]

FROM THE MEMOIRS OF
ROGATIEN REMILLARD

I flew into Hibernia for the wedding on a chartered starship with Lucille and the Dynasty, together with Marc's close colleagues at CEREM and his friend Boom-Boom Laroche, who had recently become a Deputy Evaluator of the Galactic Magistratum and a Magnate of the Concilium.

Less than four weeks had passed since the day that Marc and the lovely young engineer had met. Everyone knew that they had been inseparable during that time, already married in spirit if not in the eyes of the Catholic Church. On the Old World, no one would have thought a thing about the premature cohabitation; but the operant community of the Irish planet was more conservative where sex was concerned—and many of them also still harbored dark memories of the way Marc's father had dishonored their Dirigent.

There had been baleful telepathic clucks following the announcement of Cyndia's espousal, and Cardinal McGrath of Tara Nua, an operant Rebel cleric who made no secret of his disapproval of the fiancé, very nearly declined to concelebrate the nuptial mass along with Anne Remillard, S.J. But in the end Marc's personal magnetism won over even the most hard-shelled of the Hibernians. Being Irish and past masters in the art of coercive blandishment themselves, they finally accepted Marc as a worthy suitor for their beloved Dirigent's daughter—even though any fool could see what a sly, silver-tongued Froggie he was. On the other hand, as Cardinal McGrath dryly noted, somewhere in the man's ancestry there had to be honest Celtic blood, or he wouldn't be such an expert in dishing out the malarkey.

Of course none of the wedding participants (most especially the bride and groom) knew a thing about the mortal impediment to the marriage. If Rory Muldowney had ever had any doubts about Cyndia's paternity he had long since banished them to the dead files of his subconscious, and none of his constituents would have dreamed of humiliating him or his dearly loved daughter by raising the issue—although there was secret whispering.

Rory's antipathy to Marc never entirely disappeared; but to his credit, he gave the couple his wholehearted blessing when it became clear that their union was written in the stars.

The members of the Family Remillard (and I myself) had genuine reasons to be apprehensive over Marc's upcoming marriage, knowing what we did about his anomalous personality. When the news first reached me I was knocked for a happy loop. Was it actually possible that this magnificent, appalling man whom I had sadly relegated to the status of emotional cripple had discovered human love? Even Jack was astounded. The only one who seemed unsurprised by the news was Paul.

The ceremony was to be small and private, held in the little Lady Chapel of Saint Patrick's Cathedral in the Hibernian capital city. Unlike the wedding of Jack and Dorothée, Marc's caused no media furor. In 2080 he was still a rather mysterious figure in the eyes of normal humanity. Except for his personal role in the salvation of Caledonia, Marc's work with CE was largely unremarked by the general public. His leadership of the Rebel Party had made him notorious among the Magnates of the Concilium, but it was not until he deliberately brought a highly edited version of the Mental Man controversy out into the open that he became a galactic celebrity.

The wedding took place in the evening, and while the number of participants was limited, it was a gorgeous affair with the groom in white tie and the bride wearing a gown of deep green satin trimmed at the décolletage with white lace flowers and pearls. Cyndia had no veil except her abundant hair, which fell nearly to the middle of her back, but she did wear a wreath of fragrant violets with pendant green ribbons, giving her the archaic air of an ancient Irish princess.

The couple exchanged traditional Claddagh rings having carved clasped hands holding a crowned heart. There were no unseemly visual metacreative manifestations when they kissed to seal their vows, but in some uncanny fashion the transcendent love between them seemed to glorify the very aether pervading the chapel. I wept as the couple embraced, and so did Lucille, sitting next to me. And when Marc and Cyndia left the altar, triumphantly smiling, there was an explosion of applause and rapturous cheering. We couldn't help it. The joy of the bride and groom had conquered all of us, obliterating every doubt and apprehension.

For the first months of his marriage Marc was a man besotted by physical passion. Having denied and repressed this part of his nature for his entire adult life, his late discovery of true love and its sexual consummation reduced him to a state of calentural irrationality. The pair went to live on Earth, in the handsome house on Orcas Island, and Marc spent nearly every moment with his adored bride. He abandoned his work at CEREM and absented himself without leave from the Galactic Concilium—thus missing Alex Manion's shocking paper purporting to prove that Unity was incompatible with mental-lattice field theory, which tipped the scandalized Concilium on its ear and lost Alex the Nobel Prize at the last minute.

Cyndia, in turn, was so deeply in love with Marc and so bewitched by his coercive charm that she never tired of him. As metapsychic lovers (and even some nonoperant ones) sometimes do, they submerged themselves in each other to the exclusion of all others and the neglect of mundane affairs. Having traveled along that road myself once upon a time, I might have predicted what would inevitably happen.

Spring comes early to the beautiful Pacific Northwest of America. In March and April, Marc and Cyndia were able to hike in the Olympic rainforests, kayak among the San Juan Islands, and go sailing in Marc's big Nicholson yacht with the servo grinders and other magic doodads, exploring the sparkling waters of Puget Sound. In May, when the orchards of eastern Washington State were in full bloom and the rainbow trout were rising on the high-desert streams and lakes, he taught her catch-and-release flyfishing. In June they toured Ireland, land of Cyndia's ancestors, and after that they came to New Hampshire, where they wandered the picturesque byways of Marc's boyhood on bicycles, canoed on the Connecticut River, and backpacked along the Appalachian Trail in the White Mountains.

And then, one fine day on top of Mount Washington, near the scene of the Great Intervention, Cyndia told Marc something that irreparably changed everything between them.

· · ·

She came to my bookstore in Hanover several days later, saying that Marc was off conferring with colleagues at Dartmouth College's Department of Metapsychology, and asked if we could have a confidential chat. I was surprised all to hell since at that time we hardly knew one another, having met for the first time at the wedding on Hibernia; but I didn't need to read Cyndia's well-shuttered mind to know that she was seriously concerned about something.

So I locked up the place, programmed the sign to read GONE FISHING, and took her to the Starbucks coffeeshop next door. I ordered us a couple of cool frappuccinos and we sat down together at one of the shaded sidewalk tables.

"Lucille suggested that I speak to you," she said, delicately sampling her drink. "I have a problem. With Marc."

"And Lucille told you to talk to *me*?"

"She said you knew him better than anyone—with the possible exception of Jack."

Cyndia Muldowney was carelessly dressed in faded jeans, a white sleeveless shirt with big gold buttons, a Boston Red Sox baseball cap, and huaraches. Her shining hair was pulled back in a long ponytail. Those extraordinary dark-lashed eyes, which Rory Muldowney told me that the Irish describe as "put in with a smutty finger," had sea-green depths backed with a stony indomitability I had not noticed before. Before long we would all discover that the spine of the beautiful Hibernian engineer was pure cerametal.

"I'll help you any way I can," I said, and meant it.

"I'm pregnant, Uncle Rogi. I told Marc last Wednesday, when we were hiking on Mount Washington. Our son should be born around the third week in November."

I opened my mouth to congratulate her, but she firmly coerced me to silence and continued in that sweetly accented voice of hers.

"When I broke the news, Marc seemed to react normally, happily. But that night, back in the funny old White Mountain Hotel, he didn't come to bed. He just sat by the open window staring at the stars, a million miles away. I thought he might be farspeaking an important message to someone, and so I just waited. Finally, I dozed off. When I woke up it was past four in the morning and he was still sitting there. He said he was thinking and told me to go back to sleep. I begged him to tell me if anything was wrong. You see, it was the first time that . . . he hadn't wanted me. He just kissed me and said he'd explain in the morning. After that, he must have redacted me because I fell asleep. But before I drifted away, I felt his hand on my abdomen. And I thought I heard his mind say 'Mental Man.' "

I said, "Uh-oh."

"The next day he was still intensely preoccupied. He said we were going to have to return to Seattle soon, because important work was waiting for him there that he was anxious to show me. He hoped I'd want to help him with it, for it was very important to the success of the Rebellion. He said he needed to confer with some people at Dartmouth College before we went home. We've been here in Hanover for three days now. Marc has mostly left me by myself while he's been off picking the brains of Catherine Remillard and the other specialists in developmental metapsychology. And he hasn't touched me sexually."

Prudish old goat that I am, I took refuge in my coffee cup. "I—I understand that sometimes husbands react a little strangely to the first pregnancy. He may be afraid of hurting you—"

"That's cock and shite," snapped the daughter of Rory Muldowney. And then she sprang it upon me abruptly. "Rogi, *who is Mental Man?*"

"Mental Man?" I repeated stupidly.

"Lucille didn't know. She farspoke the other members of the Dynasty in residence here on Earth, including Paul, and none of them had ever heard of him. But I'm convinced that Mental Man—whoever or whatever he is—is what's got Marc all in a stew."

"Mental Man isn't a person, it's a scientific project," I told her. "The idea for one, rather. Marc has noodled it over for years, but so far as I know it's still vapor. I know very few details of it. Basically, Marc would like to find a way to engender large numbers of highly operant human beings artificially. He particularly wants to create more paramounts like himself and Jack."

Cyndia frowned. "Like the nonborns? Through in-vitro fertilization?"

I flapped my hands. "How else?"

"But eugenic engineering of the human brain is impossible. Everyone knows that. There are thousands of genes involved, many of them pleiotropic—influencing more than one trait."

"I'm only telling you what Marc told me—and that was several years ago, when he never intended to marry or father children naturally. We were sitting together in the Peter Christian Tavern here in Hanover one night, both pretty well oiled, and I told him a dirty joke. One of those that starts 'How many sperm does it take to . . .' After he laughed, I made a crack about all those superior wigglies of his going to waste. And that's when he told me that someday they'd help to make Mental Man."

"This project—is it still theoretical?"

"Well, of course," I assured her.

But it was nothing of the kind, as not only Cyndia but also the entire Galactic Milieu would find out in short order.

I don't usually try to send telepathic calls over any kind of distance. I'm not good at it, especially if a narrow intimode squawk is required rather than a declamatory hail that any head in the vicinity can read. But that night I decided to make a special effort. I knew they were staying at the venerable Hanover Inn just two blocks north of my place, so along about ten o'clock I walked down Main Street, crossed Wheelock, and began a very slow perambulation along the paths of the college green opposite the hotel, figuring he'd surely be able to hear me from so close. For over two hours I wandered and loafed beneath the lamplit mutant elms, making tentative shouts on Marc's intimate mode and getting no response. Finally, just as I was about to give up and go home, I heard him reply:

What the devil are you doing prowling out there Uncle Rogi?

You in the hotel?

Of course I am. I just got back from a conference.

We gotta talk. Come out. It's important.

. . . Wait five minutes.

When I saw the tall figure with the discreetly damped aura emerge from the inn I went over to meet him. It was a warm night in late June and we had plenty of company on the green. We found a place on the shadowed grass reasonably far away from the joggers and canoodling couples and sat down. Crickets were singing and clouds of moths were gyrating around the softly glowing globes of the old-fashioned street-lamps. Now and then a swooping nighthawk would make a meal of one.

"How's Cyndia?" I asked.

"If you must know, I found her asleep when I got in. I was halfway undressed myself when you called. Now what's this all about?"

I spoke telepathically:

Mental Man. And your wife.

For a long moment Marc said nothing. Then: She asked you about Him.

"You got it in one, mon fils." You leaked a thought fragment about Mental Man one night back at the White Mountain Hotel. She knows you're brooding about the project and suspects that this is the big deal you're going to spring on her when you two get back to Seattle. She loves you very much but she resents the fact that your sudden fixation on Mental Man seems to be more important to you than your own un-born son—to say nothing of [discreetly expurgated image].

Marc groaned out loud, and his mind said: Merde! I didn't mean to be insensitive toward her. I just . . . didn't think.

Obviously.

For months there's been room for nothing in my mind but Cyndia. Then she told me about the child and it was as though I fell out of heaven and back to earth with a crashing thud remembering everything I'd put aside during the honeymoon—especially Mental Man the most important thing in the world to me.

Oh really?

I . . . don't you try to mindfuck me Uncle Rogi! I worship Cyndia. I'll make up for my inadvertent neglect. But Mental Man is my work the most important project I've ever conceived compared to it CE is noth-ing my personal life is nothing! Mental Man is going to save the human race from exotic domination.

That's what you told me when you first talked to me about it years ago. But you never spelled out how the miracle was supposed to hap-pen. You want to tell me now?

No. Not yet. The project is still in a preliminary phase of research and development.

Oh right. But you're going to have to tell Cyndia . . . or risk losing her.

"Don't talk like a bloody idiot!" He sprang to his feet and hulked over me in the starlight. Then the heroic body seemed to sag. He spoke almost formally. "I'm sorry I said that, Uncle Rogi. I'm sure you have only my best interests—and those of Cyndia—at heart. I do appreciate that you called this problem to my attention. When we're back at home I fully intend to discuss the Mental Man project with her and convince her of its vital importance. I hope she'll even want to share the work with me."

I climbed up myself and took Marc's hand. "Do that. And do one other thing: When you get back to your hotel room, make love to her." "But she's asleep," the great paramount lummox protested. "Wake her up and do it," I insisted, with all the coercion I could wring from my antiquated neurons. "For God's sake, just do it." He shook his head in puzzlement, said good night, and went away.

I saw Marc and Cyndia again three days later, just before they left Hanover for Seattle. She appeared radiant and he was solicitous and tender. I presumed that all was well once again in their bedroom, and breathed a sigh of relief.

Then, with summer in full swing and me feeling chipper, the charming Sally Lapidus appeared on the scene once again, inclined to give me a second chance. I forgot about Mental Man and the sex life of other folks, being happily absorbed in my own.

Marc made the big revelation on 10 September 2080, in a calculated public-relations ploy that was obviously intended to win the instant approval of ordinary humanity while at the same time dealing the Milieu a stiff biff below the belt. For the first time, portions of the CEREM complex were opened to a tour by the human media—ostensibly to celebrate the "rollout" of the new production models of the 600X CE enhancer, which were destined for the Okanagon Geophysical Corps.

Mental Man was introduced to the world as an ostensible afterthought when Marc led the mob of reporters into the lab where Dr. Jeffrey Steinbrenner and his associates were tinkering with an elaborately modified E18 helmet. What was the fancy hat for? Why, the scientists were using it in farsense mode to evaluate the metapsychic complexus of human embryos.

[Sensation! Cacophony of questions! Order restored by unobtrusive coercion.]

The New York Times asked if it was actually possible to assay the mind-powers of pre-fetal humans with any accuracy using CE.

Jeffrey Steinbrenner said yes, within certain limitations. A highly trained farsensor could analyze the microscopic aura of an in-vitro embryo as early as the seventh week of development. By then, the new being had a brain that interacted fully with the mental lattices. Early experimental trials of the evaluation technique, utilizing an earlier model CE helmet, had been conducted by Steinbrenner when he was associated with the IVF Facility—the so-called Nonborn Factory—in Chicago. The correlation between his evaluation of embryonic auras and the later conventional metapsychic assay performed on infants after parturition had improved steadily. He claimed that it now approached 92 percent accuracy. For political reasons that Steinbrenner professed to find difficult to understand, his research was given a low priority at IVFF. He had joined CEREM in 2078, becoming head of its Department of Bionics and working at first on the 600X CE project. For the past year, however, he had devoted himself solely to embryonic assay.

There were technical questions from *Science* and *Newsweek* that Dr. Steinbrenner declined to answer "at this time."

Then PNN wondered why a CE corporation like CEREM had decided to fund this particular line of research at all.

Marc took the question. He explained that embryonic metapsychic evaluation was only part of a much larger project, essentially noncommercial, that had long been of deep personal interest to him. The ultimate goal of this project was the engendering of large numbers of human children having paramount metapsychic faculties. The project was called Mental Man.

[Sensation again! Greater babble of questions. Order restored once more by coercion.]

Galaxy Today asked whose germ cells had been used to engender the embryos being used in the present Mental Man evaluations.

Marc said that the sperm were his and the ova were from a female donor of extremely high metapsychic assay who wished to remain anonymous.

Star Network wanted to know what disposition was being made of the Mental Man embryos after their evaluation.

Marc said that the viable seven-week embryos used in the preliminary study were being put into cryonic storage after their MP complexus was analyzed. The media representatives surely understood that at the present time it would contravene the Milieu Reproductive Statutes if a privately held corporation such as CEREM should nurture human embryos artificially into the legally defined fetal state of eight weeks—much less allow those fetuses to mature fully. Eventually, Marc hoped that the laws would be changed and the Mental Man embryos—whether paramount or "merely" operant—would be made available for adoption by qualified parents.

TerraNet asked incredulously if Marc meant that any family could have a superembryo, and if so, how much it would cost.

Marc said that the usual criteria for adoption would apply, and there would be no charge.

Then the IBC correspondent put her finger on the most provocative aspect of the project: What was Marc's personal interest in Mental Man? Was his goal pure research, was it altruism—or did he have another motive for sponsoring such an expensive and controversial project?

He said that there were two imperatives that had inspired him to establish the Mental Man laboratory. The first was to give every human family the option of raising an operant child (and every operant family the option of raising a paramount child), either through embryonic implantation or nonborn adoption.

His second objective was to insure that the Human Polity was never forced into Unity by the exotic races of the Galactic Milieu. It was his belief that Unity would destroy individuality and fundamental human nature. Perhaps, he said, smiling his appealing one-sided smile, his personal belief was wrong and Unity was a good thing. But the decision to accept it or reject it should be humanity's alone. As leader of the Rebel Party, he refused to bow to the exotic contention that unUnified humanity was a danger to the Milieu, and that human Unification was nonnegotiable. The paramount metapsychics engendered in the Mental Man project would *insure* that humanity would never be absorbed into a Galactic Overmind against its will.

[Tumultuous reaction.]

Marc said he would take just one more question, and then the interview and the tour of CEREM would have to conclude.

Operant Topics asked if Marc's own unborn child had been assayed using the Mental Man technology.

Marc said no. He and his wife Cyndia would welcome and love their son no matter what his metapsychic armamentarium might be, although they had high hopes for a paramount child.

Then Marc thanked the reporters for coming and promised to keep them posted on the progress of the project.

A predictable storm of controversy erupted in the human media following the unveiling of Mental Man, intensifying the polarization of humanity into pro- and anti-Milieu factions. As Marc had anticipated, vast numbers of people were wildly enthusiastic over the prospect of raising a Mental child. Lower-echelon operants besieged CEREM with requests to adopt paramount embryos, and nonoperants seemed even more eager to welcome Mental Man into their families. (Most normals, whether they admitted it or not, hoped and prayed for offspring that would possess the higher mindpowers of the galactic elite.) Acquiring an operant child by embryonic implantation or adoption seemed a perfectly acceptable option, especially to colonial families already comfortable with the custom of nonborn fosterage.

The reaction among the higher ranks of operants was more cautious. Milieu loyalists were quick to downplay Marc's contention that a new brood of paramount children would form a bulwark against the alleged evil of the Unified state. It was more likely, they said, that the superior youngsters would come to appreciate the fact that Unity was not only harmless but also desirable.

Jack himself took this line, but he was careful not to denigrate his older brother's professed desire to make operant embryos widely available. Paul, on the other hand, went savagely on the offensive. He called Steinbrenner's credentials into question (and there were undoubted murky patches in his professional background), demanded an independent study of the embryonic MP assay technique (which Marc declined to cooperate with), and even hinted that Mental Man might be nothing but an elaborate hoax designed to win support for the Rebel Party.

Privately, Paul made the mischievous suggestion that Marc, by using his own sperm to engender Mental Man, was unconsciously attempting to outdo his own father in the procreative game. By that time, the First Magnate had sired not only six children by his late wife, Teresa Kendall, but also thirty-eight natural offspring whom he freely acknowledged.

The official reaction of the Galactic Milieu to Mental Man was initially a long, loud silence. At last, nearly a month after Marc's press conference, Davy MacGregor and the other Planetary Dirigents of the Human Polity made a joint response:

The issue of Mental Man would be put up for consideration in the Galactic Concilium, as were all matters of high Milieu policy. Only human and exotic magnates would participate in the debate. The decision of the Concilium would be final. Until that decision was issued, CEREM and Marc Remillard were forthwith enjoined from publicizing Mental Man in any way, shape, or form, and were expressly forbidden to nurture any human embryos beyond the seventh week of life or to cause said embryos to be nurtured by other persons, through either uterine implantation or in-vitro culture. Officers of the Galactic Magistratum would inspect the CEREM premises periodically to insure that the injunction was not violated.

The majority of nonoperant human beings—and respectable numbers of operants—gave a predictable response to the dictum. Boiled down, it amounted to: Fuck that.

And thus began the final act of the Metapsychic Rebellion.

Cyndia's reaction to the epiphany of Mental Man was private and deeply troubled. Although Marc denied it to the media, he actually *had* urged her to permit Jeff Steinbrenner to evaluate their unborn baby by means of amnioscopic CE. But she obdurately refused, perhaps out of a secret fear that Marc might want to abort the fetus if it fell short of paramount potential. Marc had seemed to bow willingly to his wife's wishes, especially since she otherwise appeared to be enthusiastic about the project. Cyndia did agree to having their unborn child educated in utero using experimental preceptorial methods intended for Mental Man, since the new teaching technique was largely a much-modified and expanded version of that already widely in use among operant parents.

Denis Hagen Muldowney Remillard (his mother insisted upon the unusual second name, but refused to explain its significance) was born on schedule on 21 November 2080, a healthy little blond bruiser weighing in at 3.9 kilos. Due to the press of Rebel affairs, his father was not in attendance at the birth, although he did manage to get home in time for the christening, which took place at historic Emmanuel Church in Eastsound village on Orcas Island. I was Hagen's godfather, and Cyndia's older sister Sara the godmother.

With his aura no longer enveloped in that of his mother, the little boy was subjected to conventional assay of his metafaculties and determined to be a potential grandmaster operant in farsensing, creativity, and psychokinesis. The assay also showed that the baby was a potential paramount in coercion and redaction—but these metafaculties were all deeply latent and unusable. There was always the chance that the boy's proto-paramount powers could be raised to operancy later, however, and Marc seized on this hope to cheer his wife and assuage his own bitter disappointment.

The mental deficiencies of Hagen and the opposition of the Milieu to Mental Man were not the only problems Marc had to contend with at that time. Paul's disparagement of Dr. Jeffrey Steinbrenner's professional abilities proved to be quite unwarranted, and the embryonic assay technique perfected by the bionic specialist was a great success. Unfortunately, the thousands of embryos produced by the union of Marc's sperm and Dierdre Keogh's ova were not.

After working for over a year on the Mental Man project, Steinbrenner and his associates failed to find a single embryo with paramount potential.

[21]

SEATTLE METRO, EARTH
14 JANUARY 2081

A relatively lengthy period of rest and recuperation was required after the strenuous d-jump from Astrakhan. Fuzzing his identity, Fury checked into a luxury suite at the Four Seasons in downtown Seattle and had room service bring up a rare steak, a small Caesar salad, a crème brûlée, and a bottle of Stolichnaya. After he had eaten and drunk he fell into a dreamless sleep.

The monster awoke the next morning with an inconveniently voracious appetite for lifeforce. Cursing, he self-redacted and managed to suppress the urge—but only at a serious cost to his vitality.

Later! He'd take care of his hunger later. It would be easy to find suitable prey in this city: a drunken Inuk down around Pioneer Square or a runaway adolescent over by the Pike Place Market. Unfortunately, the interval between necessary feedings was becoming shorter and shorter. The problem was an irksome one, but he had so far been unable to address it because too many other things were happening that demanded his personal attention.

The Astrakhanian Dirigent, Xenia Kudryasheva, was proving tougher to kill than he had anticipated, and her hostility to the local Rebel faction had reached a ticklish level. Construction of the modified starships was moving right along, but there had been a nasty scare when the facilities of a crucially important subcontractor on Yakutia were demolished in a power-plant mishap. The French world of Blois, in a fit of Gallic mulishness, had at first refused to take up the slack by revising production schedules in its own factories. Fury himself had been obliged to coerce the six members of the Blésois Commerce Ministry, the board of directors of Dassault-Aérospatiale, and the heads of three trade unions in order to get things rolling again. Besides all that, there was the upcoming Concilium session to worry about. Nine fence-sitting human magnates, more or less ripe for conversion to the Rebel cause, were going to require the most delicate sort of mental noodging on his part to bring them over the fence.

I am spreading myself too thin, he thought.

Not for the first time, Fury cursed the fact that high-powered coercion and the reading of hostile minds were impossible to bring off at a distance. The personality-disjunction problem was only one symptom of impending difficulty. His farsenses were no longer what they should be, and neither was his self-redactive faculty. The d-jump to Earth had been a considerable strain, necessitated by another schedule conflict. If only he could have put Hydra on an Earthbound starship and let her do this particular job herself! (She was so much better at Marc's subliminal coercion.) But it was still unwise to use Hydra in any situation where she might have unsupervised access to Cyndia Muldowney.

Fury's seekersense located Marc and Cyndia at the Orcas Island house and he spied on them briefly through excorporeal excursion. Uncle Rogi was there on a house visit, having breakfast in the huge kitchen with the couple and their infant son. The old bookseller had brought Baby Hagen a present—a revised version of the papoose-swing he had built years ago for Jack the Bodiless. The infant dangled happily in the device, sucking his thumb and making cornflakes hop around the kitchen table with his PK. The conversation among the three adults was vapid, and so Fury wasted no more time on them. The contact with Marc would take place much later, when he was asleep . . .

A fast farsensory glance showed that on this Saturday morning only a skeleton force of technicians was on duty at CEREM's Mental Man facility. As usual, the hardworking Jeffrey Steinbrenner was among them. Excellent!

It was snowing in the Cascade Mountain foothills, so Fury went down to the hotel's Moduplex and ordered heavy winter clothing from REI. Later, as he flew his hired egg eastward, he called a North Bend outfitter on the RF com and reserved an enclosed Arctic Cat snowmobile. The machine was waiting for him when he landed. It took less than half an hour to drive it along the Snoqualmie River trail to the signposted chainlink fence that marked the boundary of the CEREM campus.

No other winter funseekers were in the area. He parked the Cat in a thicket of tall Himalayan blackberries and shut off the engine. After making sure that the small cryopak container was safely tucked in one of the big cargo pockets of his pants, he climbed out.

It was quiet except for the shrunken river's ice-muffled purling and the slow tick of the cooling snowmobile. White flakes drifted down in nearly windless air, striking the mirrored surface of the immense sigma hemisphere just inside the fence and sliding down to form a fluffy bezel on the adjacent ground. His farscan showed that no human guards were abroad behind the force-field. A notice hanging on the fence warned:

ABSOLUTELY NO TRESPASSING!
CEREM LTD
IS LICENSED TO USE DEADLY FORCE
TO REPEL UNAUTHORIZED PERSONS
FROM THIS PROPERTY

Fury smiled, then d-jumped inside the barrier, rematerializing in the midst of some ornamental rhododendrons next to the Mental Man facility. He rested for a few minutes, recovering his strength and scanning about the installation to insure that his presence had not been detected. No alarms sounded, no farsensory touch flicked over him, no personnel within any of the buildings showed surprise or otherwise deviated from what they had been doing.

Eleven biotechnicians were scattered about the upper floors of the Mental Man lab, fertilizing a batch of worthless ova from one of the new donors and performing various technical maintenance chores. Jeffrey Steinbrenner was alone in the gestatorium on the basement level, preparing for an assay session. Once again Fury's mind generated an upsilon-field and he teleported through space. A split second after he appeared in an alcove of the gestatorium just out of Steinbrenner's view he used his creativity to become invisible.

It was Fury's first tangible visit to the facility, although he had excursed to it mentally from time to time when he visited the Old World in order to keep track of Mental Man's progress. The enormous room was dimly illuminated by crimson indirect lighting, and the sound of a recorded human heartbeat was audible over the soft strains of a Mozart string quintet. Three walls of the gestatorium were lined from floor to ceiling with recessed racks holding ovoid uterine capsules. Each one was transparent, about 50 centimeters high, and had biomonitoring displays at the front. The life-supportive equipment was concealed in the walls behind the racks, as was the conveyor system that transported encapsulated embryos to various parts of the building for study or processing.

The cadaverous scientist had seated himself in the operator's chair before the metapsychic assay unit in the center of the room. The device was the size of a small desk. On top, a windowed boxlike extrusion with a headrest contained a single uterine capsule with tiny occupant awaiting analysis. A CE power-supply module stood on the left side of the chair. On the right an E18 helmet with its specially modified farsensory brainboard lay on a stand, ready to be donned.

Fury stood directly behind Steinbrenner while he dictated preliminary information into the unit's computer command mike and transferred data from the capsule's vital-signs monitor. Then the doctor relaxed for a moment, watching the embryo with his unaugmented deepsight.

And so did Fury.

The developing human being was about two centimeters long, floating inside a diaphanous fluid-filled amniotic sac the size of a plum. A curling umbilical cord attached the embryo to a much larger spongy placenta, thickly webbed with prominent blood vessels and bedded in a slab of protoplasm at the rear of the artificial womb. Except for its dark eye pigment, blood vessels, and the quick-beating red heart clearly visible within the thorax with its ghostly ribs, the baby seemed to be made of translucent plass. The fingers and toes on its miniature limbs were fairly well formed and male genitalia were visible. Its head was disproportionally large, bent forward as if in serene meditation, the brain a gleaming shadow with the cerebrum neatly halved. The embryo's face, indistinct except for the eyes, was that of an indeterminate primate; but the baby's aura was already unmistakably human.

Steinbrenner put on the heavy CE helmet and energized it. He gave no sign of having felt the internal photon beams that drilled his scalp and skull in preparation for the insertion of the electrodes. Fury waited. Finally, when the scientist bent forward and began his painstaking scrutiny of the embryo, Fury slipped through the brainboard interface and into Steinbrenner's unsuspecting mind.

<The colors are very beautiful, Jeff. Almost like a solar corona. So much more subtle than those in the adult aura.>

Yes . . .

<Please demonstrate how the metafaculties are differentiated.>

[Image.] It's not easy to separate and quantify them, even with the E18. An operator needs . . . a good deal of experience to use this equipment. At present I'm the only one able to do MP assays with any degree of accuracy.

<Can you tell if this embryo has paramount potential?>

In a moment . . . wait . . . did you see that fluctuation in auric intensity? They don't like to be mind-touched. I suppose it's actually a simple tropism, no more mysterious than a worm flinching from a needle. But I can't help thinking that the babies are already in a state of primitive awareness, operating on both vital and mental levels.

<Fascinating. But is this embryo paramount?>

No. Twofold masterclass potential, at most. In coercion and redaction. The other three faculties are latent GM. What a pity. We'd hoped that the three new egg-donors would provide us with a breakthrough, but thus far we've done no better than with Dierdre Keogh's ova. Not a single paramount embryo—not even in the latent state.

<And of course you *must* have paramounts . . .>

That's the only valid rationale for Mental Man. The Rebellion would never be able to control the political indoctrination of thousands of grandmasterly nonborn children. We need the hundred paramounts Marc originally planned for. A manageable number for the preceptive program.

<But so far you've had no success breeding paramounts.>

I'm convinced that all we need are the right ova. It seems obvious that there was a component of genotypic variability in our previous female donor that fought the dominance of paramount traits present in Marc's gametes. In short, all grandmasterly oocytes aren't created equal where Marc's sperm are concerned! [Complex diagram.] Although Dierdre Keogh has a splendid genetic heritage, it was apparently wrong for Mental Man.

<So now you have turned to women with *proven* paramount potential in their germ-line.>

Exactly. The candidates were limited to women from the Remillard and the Macdonald families. Dorothea Macdonald would have been an ideal donor, but of course her participation was out of the question. Her two Macdonald aunts are good Rebels who would have given up an ovary willingly, but both of them are menopausal rejuvenates with eggs of dubious vitality. Neither one has daughters, so that essentially eliminated the Macdonalds. In the Remillard line, we don't have a gamete viability problem because of the so-called Immortality Complex. Remillards not only self-rejuvenate, but they also seem to produce viable germ plasm for an indefinite period. However, only women with a firm commitment to Rebel politics were feasible Mental Man donors. In the first generation, Catherine declined to contribute for personal reasons. In the second generation, all three of Severin's grandmasterly daughters contributed sample ova. These are the eggs being tested now.

<Do you feel there is a good chance of success?>

Yes, given Marc's supradominant MP heritage, we should be able to engender fair numbers of paramounts. Adrien's daughter Rosamund has said she would also contribute an ovary. We'll hold it in reserve.

<It's unfortunate that you were unable to recruit the woman who would have been the perfect candidate—Marc's sister Marie. I/I presume you know that their mother, Teresa Kendall, was herself a second-generation Remillard via her grandmother Elaine Donovan's liaison with Rogi's brother.>

I know about it. And I *did* approach Marie, because Marc was too scrupulous to do it himself. But she cut me dead. The woman's not even that much of a Milieu loyalist—only puritanical about the incest factor, damn her! Marie is a latent subparamount in both coercion and redaction and an operant GM in the other faculties. Since we know that Marc's MP traits are being inherited as supradominants, it's virtually certain that we could have had a breed-true situation in at least two metafunctions using Marie's ova.

<Why are you so certain that Marc's paramount mental traits are carried on supravital alleles?>

His son Hagen is a latent paramount in two metafunctions and Marc is operant in three. Given the heterozygous mating with Cyndia, I concluded that Marc's MP traits must be transmitted as supravitals with incomplete penetrance of the operancy factor.

<Not necessarily. You have failed to consider another possibility.>

... What?

<The mating with Cyndia is not heterozygous. She is actually Marc's half-sister. Her natural father is Paul, not Rory Muldowney.>

Jesus Christ! But no one ever—

<It is the truth. And the genetic implications are obvious.>

Shit, yes! I see what you mean. If Marc's sperm *don't* carry supradominant MP genes, it could signal a disaster for Mental Man! Only his children with Cyndia or Marie would be reliably paramount, and even then their operancy couldn't be guaranteed—

<Never mind Cyndia. There is another full sister available to mother Mental Man: Madeleine.>

The Hydra? That's ridiculous! She's been a fugitive from justice for twenty-six years. No one knows her whereabouts—much less whether she'd cooperate in the project.

<*I*/I know where she is. And she will cooperate.>

You . . . you're really bespeaking me.

<*I*/I am.>

This isn't a just a daydream.

<It certainly is not.>

Who are you? What do you want? *Are you Madeleine herself?*

<Is that so incredible?>

My God.

<An ovary has already been excised and frozen. The oocytes are in perfect condition.>

Jesus! Yes! Of course! And with the homozygosity—

<Marc must never know. He would never accept Mental Man as the offspring of Hydra. You must substitute the new ovary for an organ contributed by one of the other women.>

. . . Yes. It can be easily done, if you insist.

<*I*/I demand it. *I*/I also demand that the paramount embryos that will be engendered from these ova be raised to term, not frozen. No matter what the Galactic Milieu decides, Mental Man must live and grow. Now!>

Marc will have to make that decision, not me.

<*I*/I will take care of Marc . . . *You will remember the substance of this conversation but not its source.*>

Yes . . . yes.

Jeffrey Steinbrenner stored the results of the assay in the computer. He de-energized the CE helmet and lifted it from his head. Sitting back in the chair waiting for his mind to recover, he absently wiped the tiny line of electrode wounds on his brow with an antiseptic towelette.

The craziest dream! He remembered every bit of it—and it was sheer lunacy.

Worse luck.

He picked up the command mike and ordered the conveyor to take the embryo inside the assay unit to the deep freeze. Then he got up, stretched his cramped arms and shoulder muscles, and gave his balls a scratch. He'd better pack it in for the day. It was clear that overwork had finally caught up with him.

He was heading for the door of the gestatorium when he saw the small insulated container lying on the floor, unobtrusive in the red light. Murmuring an astonished obscenity, he stooped to retrieve it. The label said:

CAUTION—BIOLOGICAL MATERIALS
UNDER CRYONIC SUSPENSION
CONTENTS: I HUMAN OVARY
DONOR: ROSAMUND DRAKE REMILLARD

"Oh, shit!" said Dr. Jeffrey Steinbrenner.

He went rushing upstairs in a rage, ready to mind-ream the technicians on duty. He'd find out soon enough which one had been guilty of this piece of egregious carelessness. And when he did, the idiot could kiss his or her sorry ass goodbye!

After it was good and dark and he was certain that the fucking social workers had finished their sweep, the Dene derelict named Sam Ontaratu came out of hiding.

He had lurked all day long in Underground Seattle, the damp and stinking warren of ancient streets and decaying nineteenth-century structures that still underlay portions of the modern city. Now he was glad to be back outside in the clean open air, even if the weather was rainy and cold. With its noxious vapors and rats the size of terriers, the Underground was no place for a Dene man to stay any longer than he had to.

Carrying his duffel, Sam left the abandoned building that gave secret basement access to the subterranean world and slouched along Yesler Way, the original Skid Road of North America. He scavenged a big sheet of bubble wrap from the recycling bin of an antique shop, crossed Pioneer Square, then turned into a dark alley and made his way to his favorite nighttime hangout, a loading dock behind a rug store on First

Avenue. An iron ladder set in the wall brought him up to the raised, sheltered nook. He grinned happily when he saw that his usual corner was bone dry and unoccupied.

He peed off the dock, then pulled a sleeping bag out of his duffel, along with an unopened liter of Potter's Crown Canadian and a meatloaf sandwich left over from lunch at the Union Gospel Mission yesterday. When the bag was arranged on the bubble-wrap mattress, he slipped off his boots, tucked them into the duffel (which became a pillow), and got ready for bed.

He was well on his way into drunken oblivion when the weird head showed up and rousted him.

"Get out of the sleeping bag and stand up," the guy commanded. He was on the other end of the dock, over near the ladder.

Sam Ontaratu cursed and told him to go away, and that was when the dude socked it to him with his metacoercion. Sam let out a groan. "Aw, man. What d'ya wanna do that for?"

"Up!"

The coercion intensified, conquering Sam's flaccid musculature, and he realized he was going to have to obey. Still muttering, he managed to cork the flat whiskey bottle and shove it into his shirtfront before he squirmed out of the warm nest and staggered upright, supporting himself against the wall of the old building.

The head was wearing pricey civvies—a rainproof down jacket, heavy pants, and snow boots—therefore he was neither a beat cop nor a member of the dreaded Seattle PD Skid Road Homeless Squad. But Sam should have known that already. None of the night-crawling fuzz were metas. Once in a great while a Holy Joe operant would come prowling around the waterfront, hassling bums for Jesus. But this dude didn't fit the mold. No way did he have a do-gooder air about him.

No way at all.

A tingle of alarm penetrated Sam's alcoholic haze. "I got no money, no scag," he moaned. "Gimme a break, man."

The weird head closed in, arms held out from his sides like a wrestler ready to pounce. His eyes were wide and blazing. He wore no gloves and his hands trembled violently.

"Down on your knees," he said in a grating voice.

Oh, no! None of that shit! Sam was a Sahtu Dene Native American and a Sahtu was a man. No meta snakecharmer was going to force him to do *that*.

The coercion abruptly eased off. The dude got this funny look—a kind of double-take, like he just remembered something.

Sam ducked sideways, out of reach, and pulled out the whiskey flask. When the weird head made a clumsy turn Sam slammed the bottle smack into his face. The creep screamed and blood spurted from his nose. He tripped over his own feet and went sprawling.

"You get the fuck outa here!" Sam yelled, brandishing the booze.

The weird head looked up at him with the damnedest expression: not anger, not pain. Terrified surprise. Like he didn't even know where he was.

Then, just like a candle flame blown out, he disappeared.

"Christ," Sam whispered fearfully. The dude was totally gone! Sam shuffled to the edge of the loading dock and looked down into the alley, expecting to see a body.

Nobody. Nothing. Only the wet alley pavement and rows of Dumpsters and recycle bins shining in the rain. Over on the Ave, groundcars whizzed by. Sam Ontaratu squinched his bleary eyes and took a good look at the bottle that he still held. It had blood on it. It was also a little less than half full.

"Christ," Sam said again, shaking his head. Then he crawled back into his sleeping bag, finished off the whiskey, and slept.

Out in the San Juan Islands off the Washington coast, the precipitation fell as icy rain that rustled against the drape-shrouded windows of the small sitting room.

Marc and Cyndia had gone off a couple of hours earlier to catch a performance of *Die Walküre* at the Seattle Opera. Thierry Lachine, the houseman, was in bed with the flu. The nanny, Mitsuko Hayakawa, was off in Twisp, visiting her elderly mother over the weekend. But Rogi didn't mind babysitting. There was a nice blaze going in the fireplace, and the armchair was comfortable. He'd put a good old Carl Hiaasen comic thriller into his plaque-book and a modest quantity of Wild Turkey into himself, then settled down for a quiet winter evening.

Rogi nodded off after a while, waking eventually to find the fire dwindled away to embers and the clock pushing midnight. He got up, yawned, and went off to the nursery to check on the baby. Hagen was sleeping peacefully in his cherrywood crib. He was a good kid, never fretful, and his little brain was chock-full of the usual operant infantile dreams—blunt sensory perceptions and the braided loops of learning experiences, unscreened and innocent.

Rogi smiled down at the child, thinking how different he was from precocious, wary Baby Jack . . .

And different from young Denis too. Do you remember how you comforted Denis when he was frightened by the cold water poured on his head during his baptism? And how he bonded to you when his mother asked you to be his teacher?

The old man smiled, looking up into the empty air of the nursery. "I remember it like it was yesterday, mon fantôme! Amazing, the way little Denis was able to farspeak real words almost from Day One. This godson of mine's not quite so talented as the other two, but he's gonna do just fine."

I hope to God you're right Rogi. But I'm afraid that this child may be in great danger. From his own father.

"Ghost, are you crazy? Marc loves Hagen! He'd never hurt him."

He might—thinking he was doing good . . . I can only warn you of the possibility. There's no one else I can tell no one who would believe me no one who can help me to prevent it danger to the baby his mother to you to the entire galaxy it's not only Marc it's ME turn around Rogi TURN AROUND AND LOOK AT ME!

In a panic of confusion, Rogi obeyed. He did not expect to see anything. The Lylmik entity that he called the Family Ghost was always invisible during its infrequent visits.

But this time, there was a man standing near the dark nursery window. He was slightly built, and his hair was fair, and his youthful face had a smear of blood around the nose and mouth.

"No," Rogi said. "Oh, no. This isn't happening."

Marc and I are the most dangerous men ever born—God help us!—but if he won't then you'll have to I can't explain I can't even stay here any longer ROGI HELP ME! Help Hagen and Cyndia and the whole human race and the Galactic Milieu . . .

"Denis?" the old man whispered. "Denis, mon fils, is it you?"

But the apparition had vanished. The dark nursery was empty, except for Rogi himself and the wailing baby.

<Marc.>

. . . What?

<Did you enjoy the Wagner performance this evening?>

The singing was splendid and Baldwin's new staging of the

Valkyries' ride is terrific. But this time around I found the plot a little too evocative for comfort. I don't like old Wotan the god-king. He talks too much and he's a manipulator.

<Laughter. You probably don't care much for Siegmund, either! But never mind the opera. *I/*I have some good news for you. Steinbrenner is about to experience a breakthrough.>

!!!That's wonderful!!! And it's about time. I was beginning to wonder if Mental Man was nothing more than a gross misconception on my part.

<Very humorous.>

Will we be able to engender large numbers of operant paramount embryos now with the cousins' ova?

<No. Mental Man will breed true only in the second generation.>

I don't understand.

<It's unimportant. There will be sufficient numbers of paramounts bred from the eggs of the new donors. It is imperative that they be secured against confiscation by the Milieu.>

I have a contingency plan ready in case the Concilium decision on Mental Man is negative. We'll move to Okanagon—lock, stock, and barrel.

<The infantile preceptive sequence must also be redesigned. You will not have five years in which to effect Mental Man's maturation. He must be ready within two.>

That's impossible!

<There is a way to greatly accelerate the maturation of the babies' paramount metafaculties.>

I don't see how. There are intrinsic limits to infantile preception. I've consulted the top authorities on developmental metapsychology and they say—

<You've forgotten our original schema . . . based upon the original Mental Man.>

That was only a fantasy. Besides, Catherine showed me that Jack's genome and mine have significant differences. The mutation—

<Mental Man can be forced—like a rose made to bloom in winter. By Jackforming. There will be some attrition but a sufficient number of individuals will make the transition successfully.>

It . . . would be wrong.

<You would merely anticipate evolution. [Give Mental Man what *you* should have had!] The children will understand and thank you. Mil-

lions of them, free and triumphant, leading humanity into the Second Milieu.>

Millions . . .

<Your true children. Homo summus. You will engender them after the Rebellion is won.>

It should have been me not him! Why wasn't it me?

<Jack's mutation is an evolutionary dead end. You are potent, the true father of Mental Man. But you must have the courage to fulfill your destiny, the vision to transcend moral constraints designed for poor circumscribed Homo sapiens.>

. . . Jack did survive the transition. He must have been paramount in creativity even at that early age to accomplish the reincarnation.

<Yes. But he would never have done it without the ultimate incentive. The fear of death.>

I can still see it: Firemen cutting off internal sigmas guarding burning hospital room door open smoke flame breaking window snow steam ash blackened twisted melted equipment A NAKED ADULT MAN METAMORPHOSING BACK TO HIS TRUE SHAPE TRANSFORMED JACKFORMED *THE BRAIN* changing again to a child safe alive triumphant . . .

<It will happen again. As you dreamed it would.>

But how?

<A meld of biotechnology and CE [image] do you see do you understand? The artificial encephalization procedure an adaptation of regeneration tank technology augmented with specialized creative CE the preceptive conditioning and indoctrination can be ongoing with the Jackforming you have the people already to help you build the apparatus Steinbrenner Keoghs Morita Van Wyk Kramer IT WILL WORK.>

Yes . . . God it *will* work He'll be born Mental Man the pinnacle of human evolution our savior!

<Leading humanity to a Second Milieu free from exotic dominion. And you would be not only His father but His guiding Star.>

This is a dream. Only a dream . . .

<Every human triumph begins with one.>

FROM THE MEMOIRS OF
ROGATIEN REMILLARD

I told Ti-Jean and Dorothée about the spectre of Denis a month or so later, when they came to Hanover following the Concilium session. Right there in the back-room office of my bookshop, Dorothée did a minor ream-job with my full consent, recovering my memory of the experience and analyzing it with Jack's help. What they discovered was inconclusive: I had seen something that both my ordinary senses and my ultrasenses perceived as real. It might have been Denis, or it might have been a delusion that I had invested with his metapsychic identity.

"Which do you think it was?" I asked Dorothée.

"I think that you saw him," she said, her pseudovoice flat and emotionless. She wore her sparkling diamond mask, but her clothing was otherwise unremarkable—black wool pants and a jade cowl-neck sweater. She'd taken off her rain jacket.

I was collapsed in my old leather swivel-chair and she sat on a stool next to me, holding one of my hands. Her ream had been so skillful that there was no pain, but I still felt wrung-out. I turned to Ti-Jean. "And you?"

He was perched on the edge of my battered desk. Marcel the cat was peacefully asleep in the IN basket, and the gales of March were strumming the tightly clenched leafbuds of the maple tree outside the little office window. "I've suspected almost from the beginning that the integrated entity who escaped from us on Christmas has the ability to d-jump," Jack said. "To teleport. This could be one explanation of what you saw. Or it could have been a metacreative 'sending,' an illusionary projection. Whatever . . . I think it was Denis, temporarily in control of his own body again."

"So what are we going to do about it?" I asked them, my impatience increasing.

"There's nothing we can do," Jack said, "except wait and see whether Denis appears again. If he is alive, it's possible that the fusion of his two disparate personae during the metaconcert was only temporary. The Denis part might now be subordinate, as the Fury part was before. In time, the good persona might give us some clue we can act on to wipe out the bad persona. It's all we can hope for."

I pulled free of Dorothée's solicitous grasp and pleaded with Ti-Jean. "Denis was in agony! He knows now that he's Fury. He begged me to help him. Can't you at least do another scan of Earth? Have another shot at tracking him down?"

The bright blue inhuman eyes shifted. "Uncle Rogi, the odds are too long and there's other work for me to do. Vitally important work."

"Damage control," I opined with some cynicism. "Countering Marc and Mental Man. That's all you care about now."

Jack admitted it.

Dorothée said, "Marc is the Pied Piper, Rogi. The metapsychic temptor—so magnificent and strong and reasonable! Do you know what I thought when I saw him give that interview on the Tri-D, taking the defense of human liberty upon himself as though no one else in the Galactic Milieu gave a damn about it? I thought: He looks like my guardian angel would look—those calm gray eyes, that beautiful, trustworthy masculine face. Why not let him light and guard and rule and guide me? Why not let that paramount mind and those big wide shoulders deal with the mess in the Milieu? I wasn't coerced by Marc, Rogi, I was bewitched ... for a little while. Until I remembered who he was, and how he'd lived a life that even the most charitable person would call utterly self-centered. Marc may believe it when he says he's totally committed to the sovereignty of human nature, but—"

"Of course he believes it!" I exclaimed, full of indignation. "He's seen through the window dressing of mystical Unity bullshit that's blinded Paul and the other loyalists—that's blinded *you*. The exotics don't want us the way we are. They want us crammed into their inhuman mold. No more messy individualism or oddball thinking or nonconformist behavior. Just tranquillity and good order for all. Docilated minions! A racial lobotomy! Us Rebels saw through the schmooze-job decades ago. We just had to bide our time until a real leader came along, one who could turn us away from the fake paradise promised by the Great Intervention. Now he's here! Maybe Marc's an angel with a fiery sword. But he won't chase us out of the fucking Garden of Eden, he'll *lead* us out—because that's where we want to go."

"If you only understood—" Jack began. But I cut him off with a Franco curse.

Dorothée said, "Marc is no guardian angel. No warrior Michael, either. If anything, he's Abaddon—the Angel of the Abyss."

"You're afraid of him!" I cackled. "Both of you—scared stiff that more and more straight-thinking metas and ordinary folks will join the Rebellion and leave you and the other human loyalists sitting on a sawed-off branch!"

"We're very much afraid of Marc," Jack said. "And I think that deep in your heart, you're afraid of him, too." He gave Marcel a farewell pat and got down off the desk, then took Dorothée's jacket from the office clothes-tree and held it while she put it on. "What Marc has done has nothing to do with any commitment to human liberty. He's manipulated public opinion with cold-blooded efficiency because he sees the Milieu as a threat to his own ambitions. Your angel with a fiery sword is laying the groundwork for war."

"If war comes," I blustered, "it'll be the Milieu that starts it, not Marc."

"Do you really believe that?" Dorothée spoke pityingly.

"Yes," I declared. "And so do billions of other people who just want to be free. Free to be human. We'll fight for that freedom if we have to."

"But will you fight for the sake of Mental Man?" Jack asked, pausing as he slipped on his jacket.

I stared at him.

"Think about it," he said. "And at the same time, think about what Denis—or your own unconscious mind—might have meant by calling Marc one of the most dangerous men ever born."

Then Jack the Bodiless and Diamond Mask went out through the front of the bookshop into the equinoctial twilight. I sat there in my chair in the back room, and the wind whistled and the old clapboard building creaked and Marcel the Maine Coon cat watched me with mellow predatory eyes until it was time for us to go off to supper.

Although the Galactic Concilium is not a body open to public scrutiny, news about its arcane telepathic deliberations was usually well leaked by human magnates in the years preceding the Rebellion—especially by those belonging to the Rebel Party. The great debate on Mental Man was a prolonged one that would not be resolved in a single session; but after Marc's calculated toss of the gauntlet into the faces of the exotics, only the most cockeyed optimists held out much hope for the project's ultimate approval. Even among the Rebels there was grousing and grumping about why the leader of the party had deliberately injected this side issue into the anti-Unity debate. On the other hand, if Mental Man actually had offensive-defensive potential, then why had Marc revealed His existence prematurely, rendering Him vulnerable to the Milieu spoilers?

Marc refused to explain.

Paul Remillard and the other pro-Milieu loyalists, who still formed a commanding majority among Human Polity magnates, remained confident that they could shoot the project down—or at least stall it until that magical moment when our race "coadunated," and Unity more or less happened all by itself. To that end, they stepped up the propaganda barrage touting the benefits of Unification, enlisting not only human philosophers, religious leaders, and psychologists but Poltroyan advocates as well.

All Earthlings loved the little Purple People. Their good will toward men, their warm sense of humor, and their undeniable individuality made them formidable opponents to Rebel spokesmen who accused all of the exotic races of being submerged in a lockstep alien "hive-mentality." To know a Poltroyan was to have a gut feeling that the slander just couldn't be so. The winsome little bald-headed folks with the ruby eyes managed to be exemplars of Unity without even opening their mauve lips; and when they did speak out, they were awfully convincing.

Two of the most eloquent Poltroyan apologists for Unity were Fritiso-Prontinalin and Minatipa-Pinakrodin—old friends of the family who had once been visiting fellows at Dartmouth College. I was in attendance when Fred and Minnie came back to Hanover in October 2081 and chaired a hugely successful pro-Unity monster rally at Seuss Auditorium. They were so persuasive that I even found myself wavering . . . just a little.

As I have wavered on many an occasion since then, now that I'm the last of the Rebels. Mais cela n'a aucune importance.

Marc was too shrewd to take on the Poltroyans, the Teilhardians, the proponents of cosmic consciousness, the pro-Unity academics, or the loyalist Magnates of the Concilium in direct confrontation. (And of course he refused to engage in public debate with Paul, even though his father tried incessantly to maneuver him into one.) Marc left the down-and-dirty fighting to his Rebel colleagues—especially Alex Manion and the formidable Professor Masha MacGregor-Gawrys—and stayed above the fray with seraphic equanimity.

Dorothée had struck some kind of universal chord when she hung the angelic label on him. It was picked up by other loyalists and was widely used by Marc's detractors even before the militant phase of the Rebellion began. But in 2081, when there was still hope for a peaceful secession of humanity from the Milieu, Marc was careful to maintain a sympathetic image. During his interviews on the Tri-D broadcasts of "Meet the Press," "On the Record," "Newsmakers," and other discussion programs, he neatly evaded adversarial questions about Mental Man and made the project seem as innocuous as in-vitro fertilization or the nonborn colonial fosterage scheme. Speaking simply but with commanding fervor, he played the philosopher-scientist, reaffirming his personal belief in human individualism and his commitment to mental independence at the same time that he justified Mental Man.

Unity, Marc declared again and again, must never be imposed upon humanity by fiat. We must be left free to choose it or reject it. He also emphatically denied the exotic assertion that anti-Unity humans threatened the very existence of the peaceful Milieu. The real threat to galactic civilization, he maintained, was the refusal of the exotic races to compromise.

As Dorothée had said, it's impossible to exert coercion over the Tri-D. So I can only agree with her that Marc's awesome success in those broadcasts involved a more old-fashioned brand of sorcery. The citizens of the Human Polity were not an unsophisticated lot; for the most part they were well educated, well informed, and immune to the sort of romantic balderdash that once fired people to march out on crusades to liberate Jerusalem or conquer the world for Communism. But Earth hadn't had a real hero in ages, and maybe that helps to explain Marc's near-instantaneous leap into the realm of superstars. He was handsome, brilliant, rich, and politically powerful—but he also seemed genuinely concerned about things that mattered deeply to humanity. He addressed our perennial fear of exotic domination, the still-festering resentment of the Intervention and the proctorship years, the operant-

normal dichotomy, even our primitive belief in human racial superiority—and we ate it up because he seemed strong enough to be our
champion.

Our real heroes were more modest and more alien. No wonder we
didn't appreciate them until they were dead.

Throughout the rest of the year 2081 and the early days of 2082, while
the secret Concilium discussions continued and the public wrangles
and media tempests raged, Rory Muldowney and the other Rebel mili-
tants expanded their stockpiles of illicit weaponry—both conventional
and CE. Meanwhile, the shipyards on Astrakhan turned out one modified colonization transport after another. But the new vessels were not
put immediately into service. Instead they were podded and kept in dry
dock on the Russian planet because the Lylmik Supervisors had put a
temporary halt to the establishment of new human colonies until the
Unity question was resolved.

Using Marc's sperm and the presumed ova of Rosamund Drake Remillard (an unmarried astrophysicist who eschewed any personal involvement in the Mental Man project), Dr. Jeffrey Steinbrenner and his
associates engendered and cryonically stored some three thousand
human embryos having paramount metacreative potential during the
period between February 2081 and January 2082. Over 96 percent of
the embryos were adjudged to be latent.

On 6 January 2082, at the close of the Plenary Concilium Session and
acting upon its express order, Krondak agents of the Galactic Magistratum officially terminated the Mental Man project at CEREM. All of
the frozen embryos were confiscated and removed from the premises.
Their ultimate disposition was not announced.

Rebel humanity—and billions of heretofore uncommitted normals
and operants—grieved for stillborn Mental Man. Marc, in a dignified
announcement, called the forced termination of the project an atrocity,
perpetrated by exotics envious and fearful of human potential. He
stopped short of predicting any specific dire consequences, but warned
that "human patience" with Milieu despotism was wearing thin.

In fact, Marc had anticipated the Concilium decision to quash Mental Man, and 114 precious embryos that had been assayed as *operant*

paramount creators were no longer at CEREM when the Krondaku arrived. Thanks to advance warning of the raid from Boom-Boom Laroche, Cyndia Muldowney had smuggled them out of the facility two weeks earlier and reinstalled them in a clandestine gestatorium built by Shigeru Morita beneath the house on Orcas Island. There, dedicated Rebel biotechnicians, personally supervised by Cyndia, tended the paramount babies for over seven months.

Coincidentally, the second natural child of Marc and Cyndia, Cloud Laura Muldowney Remillard, was born on 19 May 2082, two weeks before the Mental Man fetuses were fully mature and ready to be freed from their uterine capsules.

[23]

SEATTLE METRO, ORCAS ISLAND, EARTH
23 MAY 2082

After she had nursed four-day-old Cloud and tucked the sated, sleeping infant into her cradle, Cyndia called up a status report from the gestatorium. Fetus Forty-Two, whose informal name was Conlan, was acting up again. She and Saskia would have to decide what to do about him later, when the reprogramming sked was due to flip. Such a hyperactive little fellow! What Conlan really needed was birth. But he'd have to stay in his artificial uterus for two more weeks, until the ship from Okanagon arrived to take him and the other children to their new families, and to the secret preceptive school that would turn them into Mental Man . . .

Cyndia went out onto the bedroom balcony where Marc was standing at the railing in the moonlight, gazing out over the ocean. The night was very warm and he was naked except for a pair of gold silk shorts, impossibly splendid, and her heart caught in her throat at the sight of him. He turned his head and smiled at her and she felt her healing body catch fire and wrench her with pain. It was too soon, but she wanted him all the same. More than anything, more than life itself, she loved and wanted him.

"How are the children?" he asked.

She knew which children he was talking about. He never came to see Hagen put to bed, never sat with her while she nursed Cloud. But it wasn't important.

"They're fine, ardaingeal ionúin," she said lightly. "All of them. I just checked."

"Come here and look," Marc invited. "There are whales out in the channel tonight."

"Whales?" She came to his side and looked out to sea. "Can you tell who they are? My farsight doesn't seem to be working too well lately."

He studied the cavorting black-and-white creatures. "I see Tunji,

Filthy McNasty, Airegin, Ecaroh, Cannonball, and Mahjong with her new calf."

"Maybe it's time for us to give that baby a name. A second christening on this most auspicious day! You choose."

He thought for a moment. "How about Nuage in honor of our daughter? It's French for 'cloud,' and I'm fairly sure the calf is a female."

"Perfect."

"I've made us some sangría." He turned to a table where a pitcher and two glasses stood and poured for both of them. "Sit down, love. It's been a long day for you."

The big double chaise was positioned to catch the evening breeze. He took her hand and helped her to recline, then stretched out beside her.

She adjusted the filmy blue nightgown and robe that she wore to conceal the effects of childbirth on her body. The wine punch was good and she drank it quickly, hoping it would assuage the lingering ache in her loins and belly. When she finished she set the glass aside and lay with her head in the crook of Marc's powerful arm. His skin was dry and cool with a faint musky scent. Turning slightly, she searched his shadowed face, recognizing the familiar signs of deep preoccupation.

He said, "I'm glad we decided not to delay Cloud's baptism until Jack and Dorothea come to Earth next week. Thierry and Mitsuko were ideal proxies."

She gave a soft laugh. "And of course we wouldn't have dared to invite the designated godparents to the island. Their paramount ultrasenses might have detected the secret gestatorium."

"There's that," he agreed. "But I didn't much feel like having a big family affair this time around, the way we did for Hagen. There are too many important things on my mind right now."

Cyndia was careful not to let her reaction show. "It *was* rather nice to have an intimate little ceremony—just the surrogates and the babies and Sister Virginia and us."

"And now only us. And a pod of dancing killer whales."

"Don't call them that," she chided him. "Call them orcas."

"If it makes you happy. But they're still hunters. Beautiful, intelligent meat-eaters."

"Mmm." She let one hand trail over his thigh. "Like you, my love. And me." She gave a comical little growl.

He smiled. His rejection of her sexual invitation was kind but firm. She adroitly covered the awkwardness of the moment. "I've been wondering—is this island named for the whales? Or are the whales named for the island?"

"Neither. 'Orca' is Latin for some sort of whale, and the island was named by the Spanish explorer Francisco Eliza in honor of the Viceroy of Mexico—one Don Juan Vicente de Güemes Pacheco y Padilla Orcasites y Aguayo Conde de Revilla Gigedo."

She burst out laughing in spite of herself. "Good heavens, what a name! But I can't believe the similarity is only a coincidence."

"Coincidences happen. Synchronicity is everywhere, weaving happenstance into inevitability. We should know, chérie."

"Yes." She was suddenly sober. The dull pain in her lower abdomen sharpened for an instant and made her catch her breath.

"Innards acting up again?" He was genuinely concerned.

"Just a little. The . . . baby's nursing makes the womb contract." As do other things! "It's nature's way of bringing mothers back to normal after childbirth."

"To hell with nature. Let me deal with it."

He pulled her to him, his great hands cherishing her swollen breasts, and she closed her eyes and abandoned herself to the slow, soothing waves generated by his redaction. Gentler than orgasm, the internal caresses quieted the dismal aching and flooded her brain with endorphins and serotonin.

She sighed. "Ah, Marcas, Marcas. That's so good." And I love you so very much . . .

"I love you, too. I can't bear to have you in pain." He kissed her lips and she shivered with a soft coming.

"There's no pain anymore."

It wasn't precisely true. The physical discomfort was gone, but a nagging disappointment remained, no matter how she tried to convince herself that it was inconsequential. Once again Marc had chosen to be absent at the birth of their child, the daughter she had insisted on bearing. This time, he had been on the other side of North America in Concord, the capital of the Human Polity, attending what he said was an important Rebel strategy meeting.

She'd tried to make allowances. On Hibernia, midwives presided at normal deliveries, which customarily took place at home; and many a young father, too queasy or too frightened to be present at the birth, was shooed offstage during the great occasion and only allowed to creep back when the baby was safely born, washed clean, and nestling in its radiant mother's arms. Hagen's birth had happened at home that way, just as she'd planned, and it had been a rewarding experience, even though Marc was away on Okanagon conniving with the Twelfth Fleet officers on the way they'd staff the new warships.

But when Hagen was born there had been no gestatorium concealed under the house.

Cyndia had supervised the lab's operation willingly, even eagerly, knowing how vitally important the operant paramount fetuses were to the success of the Rebellion. But as her own tiny daughter grew within her, she began to imagine that the Mental babies were calling out telepathically to unborn Cloud, inviting her to join them in the gadget-laden, crimson-lit, artificial uteri . . .

Seafóid—it was only the Irish in her! Or one of those foolish caprices of pregnant females that a sensible engineer like herself should have laughed to scorn.

But instead, whenever the horrors came on her, she'd make excuses to Saskia and the other biotechnicians and flee the gestatorium—even the house itself, caving in like a hysterical coward to an irrational sense of dread. Mo náire thú, Síondaire! she'd say to herself. Shame on you, Cyndia! But it didn't help.

An even greater uneasiness had seized her when she thought of giving birth to Cloud in the same house that sheltered Mental Man. So when her time came, she left Hagen in the charge of Thierry and Mitsuko, flew her own egg to the village of Eastsound in the northern part of the island, and checked into the little clinic. The delivery had been prolonged and painful but otherwise normal. She managed it naturally, as she had Hagen's birth, with the assistance of the local nurse-practitioner.

Afterward, since her farsenses were temporarily inadequate due to stress, she called her husband on the teleview, reaching him at Severin Remillard's Concord apartment. Marc seemed surprised when Sevvy and the other Rebels told him to go home to his wife and baby daughter; but he had returned to Orcas Island on the following day, properly solicitous and considerate, bearing a big bouquet of pink roses and a silver dumbbell rattle from Tiffany's branch store in the Human Polity capital.

When Cyndia asked if she should set up a metapsychic assay of the newborn's mind, Marc quietly told her that there was no hurry. She realized then what he must have done sometime earlier in her pregnancy, probably while she was safely asleep.

When formal testing was eventually carried out Cloud was shown to possess both redaction and farsensory metafaculties at the Grand Master level, and masterclass coercion. Her other mindpowers were paramount but deeply latent, as Hagen's were . . .

Cyndia said, "You were working hard this evening. I couldn't help perceiving the subspace communicator calls."

The SS com was useless for confidential exchanges, but it served to notify distant recipients of impending narrow-beam telepathic messages that were unexpected. Even a paramount farsensor like Marc found it fatiguing to focus on the intimate mode over interstellar distances when the person called was not "listening."

Marc shifted position. His embrace fell away. "There's bad news, I'm afraid."

"Tell me, Marcas a mhuirnín."

"Two weeks ago, one of Boom-Boom's Krondak colleagues in the Magistratum office in Orb let slip that large numbers of high-df starships are quietly assembling at the big Eleventh Sector Base on Molakar. The Rebel execs and I have been trying to make sense of it. That's what the conference in Concord was about, and that's why I've been burning up the aether ever since I got home."

"Molakar? That's the Krondak Tau-Ceti world."

"Yes."

She stiffened, sitting up straight on the chaise. "But why would the Krondaku do a thing like that?"

"There could be any number of reasons. The Human Polity has been made privy to none of them, so we can only speculate. But the Krondaku are the most mentally formidable race in the Milieu—always excepting the obfuscous Lylmik—and Molakar is less than twelve lightyears from Earth. It was the staging point for the Great Intervention."

Her eyes were wide. "Mother of God. You don't think that the Milieu is planning a preemptive strike at Earth? An interdiction, cutting us off from our colonies?"

He got up and went to the railing, and for some time he was silent, looking out over the silver-gilt ocean. The whales were gone. "Whatever is going on is happening very slowly. Boom-Boom's Krondak informant didn't see anything particularly ominous in the mobilization. That's why she shot her mouth off with such blithe unconcern. Even so, the Rebellion has no choice but to view this development very seriously . . . I've told Rory to get ready to send the weaponry to Astrakhan."

"You're going to arm those colonial ships! Oh, Marc, if the loyalists should find out—"

"There's a risk of detection, but it's remote. The new Astrakhanian Dirigent is so concerned with smoothing the transition from the old regime that she won't have time for fishing expeditions. Ruslan Terekev already has three freighters en route to Hibernia for the arms pickup, and he insists that the refit can be done without the Milieu catching wind of it. Having the colonial vessels dry-docked is fortuitous. It'll make the weapons installation easier and also minimize any temptation the firebrands may have to flout Owen Blanchard's chain of command and go off half-cocked."

He came back to the chaise and knelt beside it, taking both her hands in his and calming her anxiety with a light mental touch. "It will take more than a few hundred Krondak cruisers to embargo the Human Polity. I suspect the Milieu is only doing what we Rebels have been doing all along: moving some of its chess pieces into position, just in case there's a game. No one will declare war tomorrow. The exotic races will feel obligated to give humanity fair warning before opting for the permanent solution. I think we've got at least two years of leeway— maybe even three—before the situation goes critical. That should be sufficient time for us to muster Mental Man."

"But the preceptive conditioning of the Mental children will require at least five years "

"There's been an important change in the project. I was going to tell you about it later, when the fetuses were ready for parturition, but perhaps I'd better do it now. We've found a way to greatly accelerate the maturing of the babies' MP faculties."

While she listened with a face made carefully blank and a mind barricaded against any display of emotion, he gave a detailed explanation of the encephalization procedure that Steinbrenner and his associates were preparing to initiate within two weeks, when the nonborn paramounts came to term.

"We'll send the children to Okanagon just as soon as they've stabilized after the operation," Marc concluded. "Their training will be completed there, as we planned originally. Not under fosterage, of course, but in an impregnable secret facility that's already under construction in the jungles of the Osoyoos River. Everything's being arranged by Pat Castellane and Jake Wasserman. I'd like you to continue supervision of the Mental Man project, there on Okanagon."

"If . . . you want me to." The voice seemed to belong to another person. Her acceptance had been automatic, unthinking.

Care for *them*? Mothering the fetuses had been difficult enough. She had suppressed her pangs of conscience for the good of the Rebellion she believed in so fiercely. But this—

"I'll have plenty of other things to keep me busy," Marc said. "Now that things seem to be heating up, I've been thinking that we should move the principal CE-manufacturing facility of CEREM off Earth. Okanagon is a logical place for it—on the strongest and most prosperous of the Rebel-controlled worlds. If there is a war, Okanagon would be a perfect headquarters. And it's a beautiful place. You'll like it there."

Cyndia could only stare at him—this husband that she loved more than her own life, the father of her children and of the new Mental Man.

Marc had perceived her apprehension. "I know the encephalization procedure may seem somewhat drastic and distressing to you at first thought," he said gently. "But the babies will suffer no physical pain whatsoever. All that we're doing is sparing them what Jack had to endure in order to effect his own disincarnation. Mental Man won't have to squander mental energy on mere survival. His paramount metafaculties will mature much faster than Jack's did. Steinbrenner thinks there's an excellent chance that the children's mindpowers may be even stronger than Jack's—especially the all-important metacreative function."

"Which will be augmented by CE . . ."

"We'll construct special models of the 600X in the new Okanagon plant. Mental Man will still be an intellectual and emotional infant when the training period is complete, but intensive preceptive conditioning will insure that the young minds respond to adult leadership in metaconcert. They'll provide us with the raw mental energy that we need."

"And you're certain," Cyndia whispered, "that this revised project will guarantee the success of the Rebellion?"

"*I'm* certain. Some of the other Rebel leaders aren't completely convinced—which is why I've authorized the arming of the starships as well as the step-up in construction of E18 CE-helmet weaponry and full-body 600X. But Mental Man should make the deployment of the other matériel unnecessary. If at least a hundred of these children are led by me and Alex and Owen Blanchard and Helayne Strangford and the other Rebel GM stalwarts in metaconcert, and all of us are equipped with 600X CE, we'll be able to counter any threat the Milieu could conceivably array against us—mental or physical. Computer simulations have proven it beyond any doubt. When we're ready, I intend to demonstrate Mental Man's power to the Milieu in a conclusive fashion. The exotics will bow to our demands when they see the hopelessness of their position. We'll win human independence without any fighting."

Cyndia managed to remain calm. "And when it's all over, the Mental babies will be able to use their paramount creativity to restore themselves to human form, won't they? As Jack did."

Marc's smile was remote. "Certainly, if that's what they want to do. But they might not feel it's necessary. The encephalization is *right*. I've felt it subconsciously for God knows how long, but I was reluctant to admit it. You've never seen my brother in the bodiless state. It's not ghastly—it's elegant. Beautiful! The physical form Homo summus was intended to wear, the next stage in human evolution. Jack clothes himself with a mock body because he's the only one of his kind and he feels a natural reluctance to diverge from our racial type. But Mental Man may not feel that constraint. Not when He numbers in the millions. And He will! We'll make more embryos. The preceptive specialists tell me that even latent paramounts would almost certainly become operant if they were encephalized—given sufficient time and intensive conditioning."

"Even the latents?" she repeated, taken aback.

"Oh, yes." He took her in his arms. The compelling gray eyes that had mesmerized billions seemed to hold points of light in their depths that shone as steadily as morning stars. "Wonderful, isn't it?"

. . .

Later she walked among the uterine capsules in the red dusk of the subterranean gestatorium.

The nearly mature Mental fetuses were cramped in their artificial wombs now. Some appeared tranquil and indifferent, a few seemed to follow her with open eyes, but most of them were apparently asleep. The children were very much alike in size and appearance, although some of them were dark-haired and some fair. Their folded bodies were scruffy with vernix caseosa, a waxlike substance secreted by fetal sebaceous glands to protect their skin during the long immersion. Each tiny skull had a multitude of electrodes fastened to it, sprouting like a wiry coiffure. Some devices were monitors. Others transmitted unending streams of preceptive imagery and metapsychic stimuli to the paramount operant brains.

She could not perceive their thoughts. They had instinctively learned how to screen themselves from their caregivers rather early on, just as the first Mental Man had. When she greeted the alert ones telepathically they gave a grave, noncommittal response.

Poor babies, she thought. So unsuspecting! For weeks now, in deliberate contravention of their inflexible prescriptive regimen, she had been informally preparing them for their "birth," describing the eager Rebel foster parents waiting for them, who would help them to fulfill their great destiny. The babies had reacted uneasily to the prospect of independent life, which was understandable. No infant is eager to leave the womb. But Cyndia had reassured them, telling them about the marvels of breathing air, basking in sunlight, touching and smelling and tasting and hearing, interacting with other human beings, learning to love. It was good to be in the outside world, she had told Mental Man. Don't be afraid!

But now the plan was changed. After their surgical modification they would be transferred to new, more elaborate life-supportive containers. There would be no childhood for Mental Man in the flower-scented open air of Okanagon where the singing fire-moths flew, no loving foster parents.

Only therapeutic torment in an artificial environment—until the young paramount minds learned how to set themselves free from the capsules, until they learned to survive on photons of light and tenuous molecules gleaned from the atmosphere and their other physical surroundings.

Until they learned how to live like Jack the Bodiless did.

If they learned.

Cyndia asked herself, Dear Lord, what am I going to do?

But she knew the answer: She would continue to supervise the development of Mental Man. To contemplate any other course of action might doom humanity to galactic solitary confinement. Mental Man was the racial savior—no matter what else He might be.

What if Marc was right and the bodiless babies refused to accept human form and their human heritage? . . . Would the human race find itself liberated from one despotism only to be threatened by another?

What would happen to other children with latent high metafunction if it were proved that encephalization led to operancy?

The chief technician on duty that night, Saskia Apeldoorn, came out of the monitor station. "Would you like to run a full diagnostic on Fetus Forty-Two?"

"Yes," said Cyndia. "But let's take a quick eyeball scan of the little rascal first."

They moved together down the narrow aisle separating the rows of uterine capsules. Saskia Apeldoorn was almost as tall as Cyndia, dressed in a white coverall, her raven hair drawn back in a tight chignon. Anxiety for the recalcitrant Conlan seeped involuntarily from behind her professional façade. She was a coercive Grand Master, a native of the Dutch planet Bloemendaal, and she had been one of the designated foster parents of Mental Man. Her commitment to the babies' welfare throughout their months of development had been almost fierce in its dedication, far exceeding that of the other technicians. Saskia had been prostrate with grief when eleven of the fetuses had died inexplicably four weeks earlier. Cyndia wondered whether the woman knew about the impending encephalization.

"Here's our naughty boy," the technician said fondly.

The troublesome fetus was slightly larger than the others, and his overlong umbilical cord was tangled in his legs. He sucked avidly on his left thumb. His eyes were slate-blue, wide open and staring at the two adults. A full head of dark curly hair obscured the electrodes on his scalp. His tiny chin had a minuscule dimple, the primordium of his father's attractive cleft.

Cyndia said to the fetus: Hello dear little Conlan.

Hello Cyndia hello Saskia [!!amorphous impatience!!]+[anger].

Cyndia said: What's troubling you? We've turned off the Teacher you can sleep now be peaceful.

I don't want to sleep I don't want peace I want Reward! Now!

"He's already had twice the normal ration of glucose in his amniotic fluid today," Saskia said. "A bribe after I refastened the electrode."

The baby said: Give me *more* Reward!

His tiny thumb popped out of his mouth, and his arms and legs began to flail. When the women did not react, he took hold of his umbilical cord in both hands and kinked it tightly, cutting off the blood supply to his body. Instantly the vital-signs monitor sounded a buzzing alarm. The baby let go of his cord and the alarm stopped.

Reward! said Conlan. Nownownow!

"A full-blown tantrum," Cyndia noted with dismay. "That's new."

"If we give him more sugar we'll only reinforce the misbehavior," Saskia observed.

"Well, his trick is self-limiting. But how in the world did he learn it?"

The technician only shrugged. She spoke severely to the fetus. "It's a redactive crank-up for you, young man! You're going sleepy-bye whether you like it or not."

Conlan stared at them. He did not know how to cry, but rage flooded from his mind, causing the small hairs at the back of Cyndia's neck to bristle and her recovering uterus to throb. Deliberately, the baby took hold of his umbilical cord again and squeezed. The alarm went off.

Saskia spun about and hurried off to the computer room to program a calming course of artificial redaction.

Cyndia remained standing there. The tiny body paled, deprived of blood, as the strident sound continued. After a few moments the angry telepathic emanations of Conlan's brain faded away. His abnormally strong grasp loosened as he slipped into unconsciousness. The alarm ceased. His vital-signs display showed compensatory oxygenation kicking in, together with a flow of calmative redaction.

Conlan relaxed. His eyelids slowly closed. When Cyndia probed carefully at his mind with her coercion, she found that the mental barricade was firmly in place. His EEG eased into the rhythm of sleep. For the time being, Conlan was at peace.

Cyndia thought: There must be something I can do. There must be! If I can't help these poor little ones, I must at least find a way to insure that no more are made after the Rebellion succeeds.

During the wee hours, long after Cyndia and Marc had surrendered to sleep themselves, the disguised Madeleine Remillard walked among the ranks of Mental Man. Her real work was done, accomplished weeks ago when the paramount fetuses had made their great choice, choosing her just as she and the four lost Hydra-units had once chosen Fury. Those who had rejected her had died, of course. But the number remaining was sufficient.

You are my children, she told them. Not hers! Not his!

And the 103 New Ones replied: Yes. We love you Saskia.

You will always do as I command.

Yes. Because of the Reward.

It is part of the preceptive program now. If you are good you will receive the Reward every day, even after they have changed you.

Yes!

You have seen what happens to babies who are not good.

Yes . . .

I will have to go away soon. Other adults will take care of you for a while. They will not be as kind as I am. But you will obey them for the time being because I tell you to. And for the Reward.

Yes.

But when I come back and tell you my new name you will obey me. ONLY ME.

Yes Saskia.

Madeleine Remillard smiled. Their choice of her was safely sealed in the depths of their unconscious. No Rebel preceptor on Okanagon, no matter how skilled, would ever learn the secret of the new, hundred-headed Hydra. No one would ever command the New Ones but her. Not even Fury.

She said: You are good babies. Now you may go back to sleep.

All around her, the small eyelids began to close. The monitors on the uterine capsules showed the serene waveforms of fetal slumber. She walked up and down the aisles, checking each one of them with her ultrasenses, stopping at last to gaze somberly into the artificial womb holding Fetus Forty-Two, whose name was Conlan.

He floated pale and motionless within the amniotic fluid. His eyes were wide open, his vital-signs traces were horizontal, and the monitor blinked a frantic red.

There was no sound from the alarm. She had turned it off so as not to disturb the others.

[24]

SECTOR 12: STAR 12-337-010 [GRIAN]
PLANET 4 [CALEDONIA]
3-4 AN OCHDMHIOS [21-22 JULY] 2082

The program was over. The holocams shut down, the live audience finished their polite applause and began filing out, and the debate participants rose from the two angled tables on the set and gathered around the panel moderator, Caledonian Dirigent Dorothea Macdonald.

"I'd like to thank you all for participating," she said formally. "Especially you, First Magnate. I know your schedule is crowded, and Caledonia is only a small planet."

"I'm glad I was able to come," Paul Remillard said.

Hiroshi Kodama's tone was studiously polite. "Even if you and the other Milieu loyalists got your asses whipped."

Ruslan Terekev, Masha MacGregor-Gawrys, and Calum Sorley grinned. Davy MacGregor's face was stormy. The Poltroyan, Fritiso-Prontinalin, looked pained.

Jack Remillard stood at his father's side. He said evenly, "Not quite a debacle for our side, Hiroshi. Not quite a romp for yours."

"Given the deep-seated Rebel sympathies of the venue," the Poltroyan murmured, "I believe that our presentation of the pro-Unity position was rather well received."

Calum Sorley, the Caledonian Intendant General, beamed at the small mauve-skinned exotic. "Aweel, Freddie, the audience didn't rush the stage and lynch the lot of ye because that's not the Caledonian way—especially since our Dirigent Lassie is still a staunch supporter of the Milieu herself. But you'll find out when viewer response is tallied for 'News at Eleven' that us Rebs have blown you loyals out of the water."

Fritiso-Prontinalin threw a look of interrogative dismay at Dorothea and she nodded sadly.

Sorley went on, addressing himself to Paul and Jack and Davy. "And you lot are also going to discover that Callie's negative response is just a sample of the way your loyalist dog-and-pony-show will play in the provinces. Better get used to crapping out! The Milieu party line might take the prize on Earth and the cosmop worlds, but not on the ethnic planets."

"We'll see about that," said Paul. The brash Caledonian IG only chuckled.

An agitated nonoperant woman in a rumpled linen suit came rushing out of the control booth.

"Over ninety percent of the Callie viewers tuned in!" she announced. "It's the biggest audience we've ever had—even bigger than the post-diatreme emergency announcements." She was the station director, Aimili Semple, and her usual responsibilities ran to academic talking-head shows, reports on the pearl and skyweed harvests, and interviews with winners of the monthly Dairy of Honor award. The woman had nearly gone into cardiac arrest when the Office of the Dirigent of Caledonia informed her that the First Magnate and seven other distinguished operants were coming to the Scottish planet for a prime-time political debate that would be telecast on her little public affairs Tri-D station.

"Perhaps," she suggested nervously, "you'd all like to come back to the green room for a wee bit of refreshment. Debating's thirsty work."

Dorothea said, "Thank you, Aimili. That's very thoughtful." With a brief telepathic plea for civility that silenced the others, she led the way off the set. The Dirigent had chosen a relatively subdued outfit for her role as panel moderator, a collared zipsuit of gunmetal lamé decorated with smoldering black diamonds. The others, even the exotics, were wearing simple jackets, shirts, and sweaters.

Coffee, tea, a local white wine, and designer water had been laid on in the station's green room, together with a big plate of shortbread.

"I'll just leave you to it," the director said, "and take care of some postproduction chores. Thanks again for honoring our little station with your presence." She fled.

"I've got to dash off, too," Calum Sorley said. "A late vote in the Intendant Assembly."

The others mingled stiffly after he left, keeping up the charade of decorum. Ruslan Terekev zeroed in on the wine. He rolled his eyes after inspecting the label, but then forced glasses on everyone except Jack and Dorothea, who insisted upon water, calling for a toast. "To the swift and satisfactory resolution of our differences!"

"Hear, hear," said Paul Remillard, eyeing the Russian sardonically.

During the Tri-D debate, Terekev had peppered the loyalists with audience-pleasing sarcasm, and his target of choice had been the First Magnate. Paul had come across as a pompous elitist when he attempted to refute the Russian's rather facile statements, and he was furious at his own lapse in judgment. What in the world had come over him? Why hadn't he seen through Terekev's tactics? Surely the man wasn't that good a coercer . . .

Everybody sipped in silence.

Professor Masha MacGregor-Gawrys finally said, "There's a rumor that exotic Magnates of the Concilium intend to reintroduce the loyalty-oath legislation." She smiled expectantly at the Poltroyan. "Have you heard anything about it, Fred?"

The exotic looked like a sweet-faced schoolboy in his mustard-colored corduroy jacket and dark slacks. "I have heard the rumor myself, but I don't know whether to give it credence. The Amalgam of Poltroy would certainly vote against any such rigorous measure . . . unless there seemed no alternative."

"Would you care to explain further?" Hiroshi Kodama invited.

The Poltroyan responded with caution. "Our response may be dependent upon the attitude of the Rebel Party leadership."

Paul Remillard was not in the mood for diplomacy. He drained his wineglass and slapped it down onto the table. "Fred means that if Marc behaves himself, Poltroy will keep sticking up for the Human Polity. And if he doesn't, there'll be hell to pay."

Hiroshi turned to the First Magnate. "And do you think that your eldest son will exercise restraint?"

"On the contrary," said Paul in a level voice. "I think he's going out of his way to inflame the situation." He was not looking at the suave Dirigent of Satsuma but at his own erstwhile tormentor, Ruslan Terekev, who returned an insouciant smirk. "For some time I've suspected Marc of encouraging militant factions of the Rebel Party to collect conventional and CE weaponry. When I prove it—and I will, make no mistake—I'll get up before the Concilium *myself* and demand the loyalty oath."

"Is that wise, Papa?" Jack asked.

"It's necessary," said Paul.

"You will thus cut off any hope of compromise," warned Ruslan Terekev.

"No," Paul retorted, "I'll knock some sense into the vacillating human magnates who think they can have their cake and eat it, too. When they see Marc and the other Rebel hard-liners expelled from the Concilium, they'll finally realize that the Milieu is deadly serious about sequestering unUnified humanity. Our race is going to have to choose between membership in a galactic confederation and reversion to a horse-and-buggy socioeconomy."

"They can't quarantine us," Masha declared stoutly. "Our scientific capability exceeds theirs."

"Don't you believe it," said Jack the Bodiless.

The others stared at the young man, so unassuming that he was almost invisible standing beside his spectacularly costumed wife.

"Jack is correct," the Poltroyan chimed in. "It may be that at some time in the future the human race will surpass the Milieu in—er—martial potential. But that time has not yet come. I am afraid that certain Rebels have mistaken forbearance for weakness."

"Oh, we wouldn't dream of doing that," said Ruslan Terekev. "As to *human* martial potential—Director Jon Remillard may not be the best judge of it."

"I know you've got weapons," Paul said to the Russian quietly.

Ruslan poured more wine for himself. "Prove it."

Fred's kindly features twisted with deep concern. "Oh, please! You Earthlings must believe that the Milieu cherishes and esteems your race! The Amalgam of Poltroy, the only other Milieu polity to share your human heritage of malignant aggression, knows the great risk taken by the Lylmik in their Intervention. It was calculated and fully justified by the immense potential of the Human Mind, and we still hope and pray that this potential of yours will be fulfilled to the magnification of truth and beauty in the universe! Nevertheless, Poltroy cannot stand by while the destruction of the Galactic Milieu is secretly contrived by an immature, uncoadunate faction. Even though we love humanity, we will vote for your permanent sequestration if we must."

"Just let us go," Hiroshi Kodama said with quiet intensity.

Fred shook his bald, lilac head miserably. "You refuse to understand."

Paul said, "What Fred means is that the Milieu knows that humanity wouldn't stick to its own interstellar bailiwick after a breakaway. We'd still seek intercourse with the Milieu worlds, perhaps interfere with the thousands of developing exotic races the Milieu is shepherding toward operancy. And when that intercourse was frustrated, there would be war."

"There will be war," Hiroshi said, "if the Milieu attempts to rescind the Intervention. Do the exotics understand that?"

Fred said, "We trust that humans loyal to the Milieu will forestall such a dire consequent."

"I'll prove you've been stockpiling weaponry," Paul said to the Rebels, his mind exuding icy authority. "I'll demonstrate to the whole Human Polity how you plan to destroy the peaceful confederation of planets that saved Earth from its own folly and gave us the stars. And I'll see the Rebel magnates purged from the Concilium and replaced with loyalists. Believe me. Whatever I have to do to save the Milieu, I will do."

Ruslan Terekev gave a great theatrical exhalation. "My friends, I think I have heard enough threatening talk for one night." He headed for the exit door, then turned. His dark eyes twinkled at Paul. "Until we meet again, First Magnate."

It was over three hours before the liftoff of the starship that would take Paul and Fred to Orb. Dorothea suggested that the battered defenders of Unity go for a stroll along the new Broomielaw Esplanade that had been constructed beside the Firth of Clyde following the diatrematic quakes.

They walked for some time, saying little, unwinding from the tension of the debate. It was a rare Caledonian evening, chill and clear, and the moon, Ré Nuadh, was nearly full, painting a path of molten gold across the wide estuary. Ships and smaller craft were everywhere on the water, their decks and masts and superstructures picked out with a myriad of amber lights according to the Callie custom, so as to be more visible to the eye when the inevitable mists rolled in. Numbers of other citizens were abroad on the esplanade, coming in and out of the hotels and apartments that fronted the Firth. With Scots tact they feigned not to see their Dirigent and her four distinguished companions as they ambled along the broad, landscaped walk, the humans shortening their stride to accommodate the small Poltroyan. Ornamental lamps stood on stone plinths surrounded by tubs of tartan-bright foliage plants and wooden benches. Below the steep embankment were marinas full of moored small craft, landing stages for tour boats and passenger ferries, and commercial quays. Night-rinkies flew overhead, uttering melancholy cries. A few food-vendors were still out, driving slow-moving mobile kiosks with wide sheltering roofs, hawking pizza and cheeseburgers and Arbroath smokies and Scotch eggs and sausage rolls and beer and Pepsi-Cola.

"Shall we get snacks out here and sit on a bench and watch the boats?" Dorothea asked the others. "Or would you care to try a new little pub that the staffers at Dirigent House have been raving about? It specializes in some of our local fungoids, and the food is supposed to be very good."

Davy MacGregor pricked up his ears. "You don't mean the Couthy 'Shroom! I was there yesterday, when I first arrived. The hotel folks recommended it. A grand wee place—and with a good selection of single malts as well."

"I'm game," Paul said. "Although after tonight's fiasco I may just opt for some tasty Amanita virosa."

"We don't have the Destroying Angel on Callie," Dorothea said.

"Only his little brother and sister-in-law," Jack muttered.

Davy and Paul laughed, and then the wry joke had to be explained to the mystified Poltroyan, who had yet to encounter the pejorative new nicknames for Marc Remillard.

The pub called the Couthy 'Shroom stood on Strobcross Street just off Dirigent House Plaza, looking as though it had been plucked up by the roots from a street in old Scotland, transported 533 lightyears, and set down across from a park full of gigantic multicolored coleus plants. Looming in the moonlight beyond it was Dirigent House itself, a slender white obelisk with lacy buttresses, soaring three hundred storeys high.

They went into the pub, which was redolent of hot butter and savory cooking smells. Each table had a tiny brazier in its center, sitting in a dish of sand, and a cone-shaped smoke hood with a built-in lamp. Many of the patrons were cooking tidbits over the glowing artificial coals, wielding tiny sauté pans, or dipping morsels into bubbling pots of cheese fondue.

"Do it yourself, eh?" Paul Remillard observed. "Looks like fun."

"The fun," Davy MacGregor said, "is in watching your dinner grow."

The proprietor, a spade-jawed nonoperant with sandy hair, pretended not to recognize the celebrities he had just viewed on the big Tri-D hanging over the bar. "Table for five?" he inquired offhandedly. "I hope ye don't mind a dark corner." He led them to a perfect spot, partially shielded from the eyes of curious customers by a latticed partition.

"We'd like an assortment of 'shrooms," Davy told the innkeeper, "whatever interesting is on tonight, and especially the sulfurs if they're available." He winked at Fred the Poltroyan. "You'll love those. Taste like sauerkraut."

They ordered drinks—club soda for Jack and Dorothea, double drams of Highland Park for Davy and Paul, a stein of crème de cacao for Fred—and settled down. Surrounding the brazier and inset into the thick wood of the table were shallow ceramic culture dishes. "You grow the 'shrooms in there," Davy said. "They mature quick as a wink. Never saw anything like it."

"Our fungoids are never exported," Dorothea said, "because of the potential ecohazard. But they're one of our most popular local delicacies, and lately, mycophiles from other worlds have actually organized mushroom-tasting tours of Callie's subcontinents. Our travel ministry is ecstatic."

The proprietor returned, bearing a huge tray. He unloaded the drinks and unceremoniously put down piles of plates, tableware, and napkins, which the diners distributed to one another. Long broiling-skewers were provided, together with two of the small sauté pans, wooden spatulas, a pot of sheep-cheese fondue, a crock of orange Callie butter, shakers of salt and pepper, garlic cloves, little dishes of chopped shallots, parsley, and thyme, and a cruet of lemon juice. There was also a big bowl of tossed salad with rainbow-hued leafage, a flute of crisp-crusted bread over a meter long, and a big carafe of water. The main course of the meal came in a dozen little plass pill bottles with handwritten labels.

"Eat hearty," said the pub owner, and went away.

Inside the bottles were dry dark nodules like large poppy seeds. Davy began sorting the containers and passing them around to the others. "Here's the sulfurs for Fred, and some green morchellitos and cuddies and earth-oysters to fry up, and—um—golfballs, microtams, yellabrellas, and porkies that they say are for toasting, and pinkhorns and bagels for the fondue dip, and popstars and clachan to eat raw with a dash of salt! A fine assortment, and half of 'em new to me. Shall we begin?"

"I've got a tummy ready and waiting," Jack said, licking his lips.

"Wait a moment," said Dorothea. "I think I deserve a treat tonight, too. I haven't had 'shrooms since I was eleven." She pulled her diamond mask away from the studs embedded in the sides of her skull and tucked the appliance away in a belt pouch.

Paul, Davy, and Fred uttered startled exclamations.

"But your face is perfectly normal!" the First Magnate whispered. "I thought—"

"Only on very special occasions," the Dirigent said. "Among friends." She smiled and gestured at the waiting pill bottles. "Never mind me. It's 'shroom time!" She held up a pill bottle labeled YELLABRELLA. "Even though it's been a long time, I know what we have to do. Every Callie child plays games with our weird, fast-growing mushrooms, and some of the games are a wee bit gruesome! ... Now, each of these containers has macrospores of a different variety, with suggestions on how to cook them. You simply shake a few spores into one of the culture dishes, add mineral water, and watch your supper grow."

She demonstrated. Within twenty seconds, the small dish in front of her was full of golden ribbed caps with stiff narrow stems and thready mycelia. "You burn up the rootie things and any parts that are hard," she said, breaking off and tossing the discards into the brazier. Then she threaded the succulent caps onto one of the skewers, spread on butter and a bit of garlic, and began broiling the exotic fungi.

Jack, Paul, and Davy pitched in; but the Poltroyan, who sat next to Dorothea, held back. He had not taken his eyes from Dorothea's unexpectedly revealed face.

"So that is why the Lylmik call you Illusio." Fred spoke to her in a low, awed voice. "The creation is quite substantial, and yet if one exerts deepsight—" The little man broke off, blushing a deep aubergine. "I most humbly beg your pardon. I should never have mentioned it."

She touched his arm, smiling. "Dear Fred. Think nothing of it. Most humans aren't psychosensitive enough to see through me—although I did have a tricky moment with a group of coadunating operant schoolchildren on our Nessie subcontinent last month. All kids try to see what's behind the mask."

"Coadunating?" Davy cried, nearly dropping his pan full of sizzling earth-oysters and shallots. "Lassie, are you joking?"

"No," she said, sliding cooked yellabrellas onto her plate and beginning to eat.

Davy wagged his great head in astonishment. "We've had a few spontaneous outbreaks of mental coadunation on Earth, but I never dreamt it was going on elsewhere."

"It's happening all over the colonies," Paul said. "But we're keeping it sub rosa on the advice of the Panpolity Directorate for Unity."

Jack said, "It was only logical that the operant children would be the first to experience the phase change. In some cases, there seems to be not only coadunation but also momentary episodes of actual Unity—linkage with the Mind of the Galaxy. We haven't publicized it because of the potential for misunderstanding. We don't want a repeat of the old Sons of Earth anti-operant hysteria. The coadunate children themselves are mostly unaware of what's happening. They only feel a kind of profound peace and a sense of warm fellowship with other minds. Sometimes there's an unconscious metaconcert effect and inadvertent mental focusing. That's how the Caledonian kids saw through Diamond's illusory flesh. Preceptors had to redact away the memory."

"I've beefed up the impenetrability of the illusion," Dorothea said matter-of-factly. "From now on, anyone who peeks will see a face they think is beautiful. No more nightmares for unsuspecting little coadunates. The real face is mine alone." And *his* . . .

"My God," said Davy. Jubilation spread across the craggy features of Earth's Dirigent. "Unifying children! Perhaps we've a chance to lick Marc and his Rebels after all—with a grand protective metaconcert of coadunate human minds."

"But we've no idea how to focus such a novel construct," Jack said. "It would be so diffuse, with the participants on widely scattered worlds. Some of the exotic scholars I've consulted say that the Lylmik know how to do it—but the Supervisors have thus far declined to discuss the matter with me."

"Dear friends," Fred said gravely, "you must not get your hopes up too high. The coadunation of the Simbiari took several galactic millenaries to accomplish, and they are still not fully enfolded in Unity.

Who knows how long it will take for all of the human operants to experience coadunation? As yet, there have been no reliable reports of adults experiencing the phenomenon."

"Two people may have," Dorothea said. And Jack nodded.

The others sat for a moment in stunned silence, somehow knowing that they must forbear any question. Finally, the First Magnate said:

"The current human population is ten thousand six million. In theory at least, we've reached our coadunate number. But the magical figure of ten billion is only a rough approximation of the number of sapient individuals required to initiate the true phase change. As Fred pointed out, the effectuation of Unity in a racial Mind can take a long time."

"Or," the Poltroyan said in a tone of suppressed excitement, "it can happen in an instant—as it did with our own Poltroyan Mind! Our legends say that a single brilliant individual perceived the way in a flash of insight. There was a fulminating confluence, a flowing together, a momentary unanimity. It did not last, but it laid the groundwork for the true Unanimization that took place some two galactic years later."

"I've done my best to analyze the phenomenon," Jack said, "but there are almost no precedents except in mystical experience. Diamond and I are doing the best we can, but we have to be cautious. Whatever it is that the two of us have experienced . . . is new. It's distinct from the coadunation of the children but it's also incomplete and impermanent. Please say nothing about this to anyone."

Davy and Paul murmured their acquiescence. Little Fred stood and took the hands of Jack and Dorothea. His ruby eyes brimmed with tears but he was careful not to inflict his emotions on any of the humans.

"I pray that the Prime Entelechy will grant you the power to persevere. Of course I shall respect your confidence! But I also thank you from the depths of my heart for having shared this glimpse of hope with me. In recent years . . ." His voice trailed off and he shook his head, applying himself to his bowl of sulfur mushrooms.

"We've all had our moments of despair," Dorothea said. "Humankind is a perverse ilk."

"If we only had more time," Paul said. He speared a big golfball fungus and began roasting it like a marshmallow. "If only Marc hadn't taken over the Rebel leadership! There must still be conservatives in the party, reasonable people who'd understand the appalling danger inherent in the arms buildup. But they'd never listen to me if I appealed to them. Nor Jack, nor any of the other Unity proponents."

A sudden pensive gleam came into the dark eyes of Davy Mac-Gregor, Dirigent of Earth. "I wonder if they'd listen to *me*."

The others froze in wild surmise.

Fred said eagerly, "It might work! Unlike the rest of us, Davy is not identified in the public eye as an adamant opponent of the Rebel view. Even his participation in tonight's panel surprised many."

"Losh, I just did it for Scotland," Davy rumbled, looking at his plate. The others laughed.

"The next meeting of the Concilium is in February, Earth reckoning," Paul said briskly to Davy. "Between now and then you'd have to lobby the top Rebel magnates—and probably also appeal to those who are still straddling the fence. It would take you away from your Dirigent duties—"

"I've a fine deputy in Esi Damatura, now that she's seen through Marc's self-serving persiflage. I'll do it, provided there's no interference from you, First Magnate." Davy's gaze flicked to Jack the Bodiless. "Or other members of your illustrious family."

"Go forth," said Paul with heavy irony. "Wheedle those Rebel idiots back into the Milieu with your honeyed Scots tongue. But keep in mind that there's one Remillard I can't control for the life of me—so watch your back."

When the supper was over, the First Magnate and his Poltroyan friend decided to walk to the shuttle terminal. They said goodbye to Jack and Dorothea and to Davy, who was going back to his hotel, and walked through Hellfire Lane, a narrow and twisting pedestrian way lined with darkened small shops.

"I hope that Davy MacGregor will be successful in his new undertaking," Fred remarked, "but he may already be too late. If only he had assumed leadership of the Unity Directorate when you asked him to, four orbits ago! I do not wish to denigrate the heroic efforts of Anne Remillard as leader of that body—but she has perhaps been overly concerned with discrediting the enemies of Unity rather than wooing them."

"That's my sister Annie," the First Magnate conceded with a gloomy chuckle. "Smite the foe hip and thigh, and damn the appeasers . . . Davy told me a few months ago that Cordelia Warshaw urged him to head the Unity Directorate, too. She thought he had Rebellious inclinations and hoped he'd be a mole for their side. Of course Davy sent her off with a flea in her ear. He's no Rebel—just a man who had honest doubts about the potential effect of Unity on the Human Mind. Fortunately, he resolved his doubts rather quickly when Marc took over the Rebel Party helm. My oldest son has that effect on people: You either fall for him hook, line, and sinker or decide he's very bad news indeed. I meant it when I told Davy to keep his guard up around him."

The ruby eyes looked up anxiously. "Surely you don't think Marc would actually threaten Davy's life!"

"Perhaps I'm exaggerating. A physical attack would certainly backfire. The Earth Dirigent's prestige is too high—even among my son's most fanatical followers. God knows, Davy's more popular than I am! The fact that he had serious doubts about Unity and resolved them counts heavily in his favor. It insures that people will at least give him a sympathetic hearing when he presents the Milieu's case. But I don't think he can stem the tide of Rebellion—much less talk the militant Rebel faction into surrendering its illicit armament. Davy will also have a devil of a time justifying the Milieu's termination of Mental Man. When the Galactic Magistratum shut down the project, it was the last straw for a lot of previously uncommitted people. Marc made you exotics seem like jealous xenophobes, determined to keep humanity mentally subordinate."

"But that was not our intention," Fred protested. "There are deep ethical objections to the Mental Man concept that few members of your race seem to have considered."

"Tell that to the low-level operant parents who were hoping to adopt a paramount baby! It's a good thing nobody knows where the Krondaku stashed those confiscated embryos. They'd probably be highjacked and implanted into surrogate mothers before the Magistratum knew what hit it. And under the revised Repro Statutes, the Milieu would have no choice but to let the babies grow to term. *Damn* Marc! How did he dream up such a lunatic scheme in the first place?"

The First Magnate had been striding along heedlessly, walking faster and faster through the dark lane, and the little Poltroyan was hard pressed to keep up with him. Finally, Fred fell back, panting. "My friend, you will have to go on without me or give me a chance to catch my breath."

Paul apologized for his thoughtlessness and suggested that they rest for a moment. They paused in the entry of a shop that sold electronic bagpipes.

Fred said, "I am not looking forward to our return to Orb. The Human Affairs Directorate will be very disappointed when I report our failure to impress the Caledonian populace."

The First Magnate grunted. "*I'll* have to decide whether or not to propose a defensive strategy to the Lylmik Supervisors that utilizes weaponry."

"Love's Oath!" Fred exclaimed. "Surely you don't mean that the Milieu should take up arms itself?"

"The loyalist humans might have to. How else can we get the guns away from the Rebels if MacGregor's initiative fails? At the very least we'll have to design counterassaultive metaconcerts. The thing I fear the most is creative CE converted to mental lasers. Do you have any notion of what a few hundred Grand Masters wrapped up in 600X CE rigs could do—say, to the Fourteenth Fleet installation at Assawompsett? To say nothing of exotic targets . . ."

"If we had warning of an impending attack, the nonhuman polities could unite in a defensive metaconcert. The most logical defenders would be the Krondaku, the most powerful nonhuman metacreators. Given sufficient warning, numbers of them would be able to erect a mental shield able to turn away any Earth weapon. But you must understand that tactics for a battle are quite different from the effort needed to sequester humanity from the Milieu. Uniates cannot act aggressively! Our ethic prohibits the deliberate harming of another sapient entity. It is true that an occasional individual, especially amongst the Simbiari, may be momentarily overcome by atavistic antisocial instincts during an emotionally charged situation. But in any Unified activity, such as metaconcert, we are incapable of taking the offensive."

"Clobbering the Rebels would be up to us loyalist humans. I intend to point out to the Lylmik Supervisors that some kind of defenses will have to be put into place at critical installations at once. We don't dare wait any longer. I admit I can't understand why the Lylmik haven't done more to defend the Milieu. They must know the danger."

Fred sighed. "It does no good to question them. It is up to you to convince the Quincunx to act." He rose to his feet. "I'm feeling better. We must move on, Paul. The shuttle to Wester Killiecrankie Starport leaves in less than an hour."

They set off again, the tall, elegant human and the violet-skinned exotic, too abstracted to farsee the person waiting for them in the shadows a few dozen meters ahead. The man emerged abruptly into plain sight.

The First Magnate uttered a surprised exclamation. "Terekev! What are you doing here?"

"Waiting for you, my son," said Fury. *Come to me.*

"You . . . aren't Ruslan Terekev." Paul felt his willpower dissolve before the paramount compulsion. He was forced to obey, moving out in front of the astounded Poltroyan to approach the waiting coercer. "Who are you?"

"I'm the one you would have killed. You and the other children, during the Christmas metaconcert."

The assailant stretched out one hand and touched the top of Paul's head. The First Magnate's body convulsed. He gave an inarticulate moan. There was a sudden nauseating smell of burnt hair and skin. A dull-glowing green corona shone momentarily around Paul's form, then faded as Fury withdrew his hand. It was not yet time to feed.

The First Magnate was paralyzed, his brain spun with vertigo, deprived of its metapsychic powers. He stared at the wavering apparition that confronted him. The stocky, homely aspect of Ruslan Terekev was melting away and the man standing there was Denis Remillard—eternally youthful, slightly built, and blond.

But he was not Denis.

Paul's power of speech remained. "Papa? It can't be you! You died—"

Fury said, "You're the one who must die, my son. I can't allow you to upset my plans—and the plans of my creatures."

"Marc!" Paul's voice was a despairing rasp. "He's your new Hydra!"

"Unfortunately not. He is still his own man—for the moment. But I need him, as he needs me. His Rebellion will pave the way for my own Second Milieu. And the death of this one."

Paul writhed, trying vainly to resurrect his own metafaculties, to coerce the thing that had been his father, to smash it with PK or a creative bolt, to destroy its mind with the fearsome converse of the healing metafunction—

"You can't harm me," Fury said. "No operant child can exert mental duress upon a parent. You should have known that. All of you, in the Christmas metaconcert. You would have destroyed me. You merely made me whole. And now you will be consumed."

Fury gripped his son by the upper arms. The first neural drain commenced. Paul's anguished scream rang in the aether.

Then Fury howled. Aloud.

A small shape had darted from the darkness behind the First Magnate. On its hands, diminutive as those of a six-year-old human child, were the talons that had once made the Poltroyan race formidable predators on their icy ancestral world of Elirion. Fred had stood petrified and incredulous when Fury struck. Now, shrieking an archaic battle cry, the Uniate Magnate of the Concilium Fritiso-Prontinalin, paragon of civilized gentility, sprang at Fury and raked his claws across the monster's face. He missed the blazing eyes but dug hideous gashes in Fury's forehead and cheeks.

Fury bellowed in agony. Supremely confident of being able to deflect any mental assault, he had never considered the possibility of physical violence. He seized the small exotic's neck and a globe of dazzling emerald light engulfed the Poltroyan's head. There was an explosion of lifeforce, an instantaneous emptying.

A decapitated husk lay steaming on the cobblestone pavement at the monster's feet.

"You—you little bastard—" Fury was shuddering, shielding his wounds with his hands, torn between the necessity of retaining his mental hold on Paul and the irresistible urge toward self-redaction. He took a step backwards, nearly lost his footing, and uttered a sharp cry as he caught himself. He stood before the paralyzed form of the First Magnate, electric blue eyes wide and baffled, mouth sagging open in uncomprehending horror.

Denis said, "Paul? Son?"

The First Magnate abruptly crumpled to the ground. He was only dimly aware of his father kneeling over him and felt himself hurtling toward the edge of some vast internal precipice. The pain was unbearable. Rational thought was grinding to a halt despite the fact that he had been inexplicably set free from Fury's indomitable coercion. Paul knew that in a moment he would pitch over the brink into black chaos. But not yet.

"Papa," he forced himself to say. "Is it really you this time?"

"Yes. Oh, Jesus, yes." Tears flowed down Denis's lacerated face. "He'll come back, though. He always does. Tell me how to put an end to it! Tell me, for the love of God."

But Paul was falling, falling. "Rogi," he said in a choked voice. "Go to Rogi." His eyes closed and his breathing became stertorous and shallow.

Rogi? . . .

Fury rose shakily to his feet. With a great effort of will he exerted his metafaculties. The gashes on his cheeks and brow disappeared. So did the stains on his clothing. He looked down at the two bodies. The Poltroyan was dead, but he'd have to finish off Paul.

But could he?

Would Denis let him?

What if the attempt triggered the return of the opposing persona?

Sirens sounded in the distance. Paul had given a mental shout as the aborted feeding began, and Jack and his wife must have heard it. Police and paramedics were on the way—perhaps the paramount couple themselves. There was no time for experimentation. If the Denis persona returned and took control, he might let the body be captured. That must not be allowed to happen.

Fury knew that his Terekev disguise was compromised. Paul had recognized him. But the First Magnate's mind had been severely traumatized by the incomplete chakra drain. Treatment could take months. The Intendant General of Astrakhan was still safe—for a time.

Swiftly, Fury modified the symmetrical ashy stigma on Paul's scalp into a more conventional-appearing wound. His waning mindpowers abolished all traces of his own blood and tissue from the dead Poltroyan's talons and from the vicinity of the assault. His farsight found an unoccupied toilet stall in a men's room in a quiet corner of Wester Killiecrankie Starport.

Using the last of his creativity, he d-jumped into it.

The necessary feeding and revitalization took place not long afterward, and he was careful to dispose of the evidence.

Rainclouds came racing in, as they often did around dawn on Caledonia, and the brief spell of fine weather gave way to a steady downpour on the new day. Dirigent House was wrapped in mist. Looking out from her office, she could not see the ground. It was easy to imagine that she was the only one awake in New Glasgow, the only one on watch.

The only one who understood the terrible danger.

Oh, Callie! she thought. What if the Milieu does decide to restrict humanity to the home solar system? What if we have to leave you forever and resettle on some drab terraformed Mars or wretched artificial satellite of Earth? How could we bear it?

Perhaps it was partly her own fault that the Rebels had become so strong here, that her own father hated the Galactic Milieu and had conspired to build a secret weapons lab on Beinn Bhiorach. Perhaps she should have pressed the investigation into Ian's collusion in that sorry affair. Perhaps she should have tried harder to counter Calum Sorley's venomous attacks on the confederation, his rabble-rousing in the Intendant Assembly.

Perhaps her own misgivings about Unity had made her too permissive and complacent, and now the whole Scottish world would reap havoc because of it.

The great debate that she had organized—had it been a monstrous tactical blunder, inflaming anti-Unity sentiment rather than enlightening the populace? Dear little Fred, that gentle, brilliant soul, was dead and the First Magnate gravely injured because *she* had invited them here to defend the loyalist point of view. And within a few hours the entire Galactic Milieu would know that Caledonian Rebels were probably responsible . . .

There was a soft knock on her office door. She turned away from the window to greet her husband. A normal human being would be haggard and worn after coping with the awful events of the previous eight hours, but Jack the Bodiless was physically unaffected.

"How is your father?" she asked, after he had kissed her forehead,

"The doctors decided against regeneration. Regular hospital care and redaction of the brain injuries will probably restore him to full mental function—in time."

"Thank God. Will he go back to the Old World for treatment?" She led Jack to the easy chairs over by the window-wall and they both sat down.

"I'll take him to Concord myself in Scurra II when the medics say he's fit to travel. I wish I could personally supervise his redaction. Unfortunately, that won't be possible—but Polity Research Hospital is ready to bring in Yevgeniy Solovyev and Jaana Savisaar, the best human practitioners in the galaxy. If Papa can be healed, those two will do it."

"If—?" Her hazel eyes widened above the diamond mask.

"Papa wasn't just hit over the head by some Rebel-sympathizing thug. There's significant damage to the neurons of his cerebral cortex. An ENEA scan confirmed it. Ordinarily injuries like those are associated with incompetently conducted coercive-redactive reams. But on rare occasions, criminal operants have inflicted them by deliberate perversion of the redactive function: brainburning."

"Fury," she said.

"I'm afraid so. The lone Hydra would never have been able to overcome an operant as strong as Paul. It had to be Fury, the one person who could attack his son with impunity."

"Have you searched the planet?"

"Yes. It only took a couple of hours, Callie being so thinly populated. Davy MacGregor and I did it in metaconcert. We couldn't detect Fury's presence and he's probably managed to escape offworld. But this time, we may have a fair chance of tracking him down. Only twelve starships took off from Wester Killiecrankie between the estimated time of the attack and four o'clock this morning, when Paul's neural damage was confirmed. The Galactic Magistratum in Orb will trace the passengers on those ships. They'll be put under surveillance."

"It will be a big job—"

He held up one hand to silence her. "I already have three prime suspects ready to put under the microscope: Hiroshi Kodama, Masha MacGregor-Gawrys, and Ruslan Terekev. They all left Caledonia during the critical time period."

"I see what you're driving at! All of them were in the green room after the telecast and heard Paul say that he intended to force the loyalty-oath issue. We already know that Fury must have a vested interest in supporting the Rebellion. He would have been desperate to stop Paul. Poor Fred was probably killed to eliminate an incriminating witness. It makes sense, sweetheart."

Jack had sprawled back in his chair and was frowning at the ceiling. "What doesn't make sense is Paul's survival. Why didn't Fury finish the job?"

"The most logical answer to that," Dorothea said, "is Denis."

"Damn! Of course!" He flung himself upright in excitement. "I should have thought of that. The stress of the encounter somehow caused another disjunction of the Denis/Fury personae—like the one Rogi saw. The two personalities are psychologically at war. Fury's in charge most of the time now, but Denis breaks free at odd intervals, induced by God knows what, and frustrates Fury's intentions."

"Fury might be in a critical state, on the verge of dissolution, liable to make other mistakes."

"Perhaps." Jack slumped back again. "We'll still have a hell of a time trying to catch the monster off-guard. He'll be mindscreened up the cosmic wazoo whenever he's in dangerous company. I certainly caught no hint of a Fury identity when we were whacking away at our Rebel friends during the debate last night."

"Neither did I," Dorothea admitted. "If one of those people was Fury, I'd never have guessed it . . . How in the world does the Magistratum hope to nail him through simple surveillance? God knows, no human operant has the savvy to detect Fury's occasional ident lapses except thee or me, my love—and we've got other fish to fry."

"We'll probably have to use Krondak teams, metacreatively disguised. Not too much of a problem where Professor Masha is concerned—but devilish tricky with a couple of high planetary executives like Kodama and Terekev . . . Fury would have killed the original individual and taken on his or her identity, of course. I'll have human agents look into the background of all three suspects and see if there was any significant personality change or alteration of behavior around the time that Denis disappeared."

"You must be careful not to tip Fury off," she warned. "If he suspects we're on to him he'll simply take on a new disguise. We'll be back to square one."

Jack sighed. "I'll deal with it. Along with everything else."

"My poor love." She left her chair and drew him to his feet. They held each other tightly.

"Oh, Diamond. I wish you could come with me. Work with me."

"You know I can't. My place is here on Callie. I won't abandon it to Calum Sorley and the others. I've made up my mind to work up a new pro-Unity education campaign. There must be some way we can use those coadunating children to demonstrate to the citizenry that Unity is beneficial—that it expands human potential rather than stultifies it."

"That's an interesting idea. I'll introduce it to the Directorate when I return to Orb."

They rested in each other's arms. The rain streamed silently down the window-wall. He kissed her hair. "You know, there's no one in the offices on this floor."

"Niall Abercrombie doesn't come in until seven-thirty and the rest of my top staffers don't arrive until eight." Her pseudovoice was soft with insinuation.

"Then I guess it's up to you and me to get some work done, Dirigent Lassie."

"Useful work," she agreed. "The like of which this office of mine has never seen."

At a gesture of her hand the gray mist beyond the window-wall was transformed into a view of a colorful plaidie forest glade, lit with soft shafts of sunlight. The austere office furnishings, the Great Seal of Caledonia, the data-com wall, all of it melted away. They stood together inside the solarium of the small vacation home they had built on Beinn Bhiorach. The vaulted ceiling had beams of honey-oak and the walls were paneled in amber and purple daragwood, hung with paintings and tapestries and fantastic pearlie-whimsey artwork done by Caledonian crafters. There was a huge fireplace, unused in summertime and filled with masses of flowers. Shafts of sunlight came through the ceiling ports and pooled on a floor covered with handwoven woolen rugs and heaps of soft cushions. Around the room's perimeter were stoneware pots with living plants from Hawaii—green on green on green.

They knelt face-to-face in the sunbeams and undressed each other. He still wore the sports jacket, sweater-vest, and open shirt deemed suitably folksy for the great Tri-D debate by ODC's public-relations boffins. She still had on the formfitting, intricately pieced zipsuit of darkly shimmering lamé, encrusted with black diamonds at the collar and cuffs. Arabesque designs picked out in tiny stones swirled over her breasts and thighs and down the outsides of her legs.

He kissed her neck and shoulders, peeling her clothing away as though she were some exotic, sparkling fruit. She still wore the diamond mask, and when he was naked she used the cool gemstones to caress his arms, his pectorals, his taut belly, his igniting sex. They sank together onto the cushions.

But before he could mount her, her eyes crinkled in mirth and the pseudovoice whispered, "Do you know what I'd like?"

He smiled down at her. "What?"

"Something completely different. Let's do it the way the simple folk imagine that we do: Jack the Bodiless and his weird wife, Diamond Mask. I want . . . the brain."

He roared with laughter. "Why not?" His disincarnation was instant and the cerebral embellishments ingenious.

In bizarre congress the two of them reached a hilarious, dizzying climax, with her focusing her creativity directly upon his limbic system. The ecstatic brain, throwing off dazzling prismatic flares as though it were a living jewel, illuminated and pleasured her in every orifice, carrying her at last into blissful unconsciousness.

When she woke they were both dressed again. The office was as usual. She lay on one of the settees and Jack stood looking out at the rain. "Oh, my," she said, stretching luxuriously. "That's much better."

He turned, his smile full of mischief. "You may be somewhat piqued to know that I was completely distracted at the burning moment."

"Oh?" She simulated hauteur. "May I inquire why?"

His playfulness vanished and he came and sat on the edge of the couch. "I was thinking," he said, "of the Great Carbuncle."

She was aghast. "Uncle Rogi's *watch fob*? Don't tell me that mad love has finally driven you bonkers."

"Not at all. Let me tell you my great idea."

[25]

SECTOR 12: STAR 12-340-001 [NESPELEM]
PLANET 2 [OKANAGON]
2 MAZAMA [27 OCTOBER] 2082

The crustal fault beneath the official residence of the Dirigent of Okanagon was not one that had attracted the particular attention of local seismologists. It was deep-seated, over 110 kilometers below the surface of the capital city, and had remained quiescent for over thirty thousand orbits. That it should have ruptured on this particular night, during the reception for the Rebel leadership, might have been only a meaningful coincidence.

Or perhaps not.

The earthquake was a moderate intraplate event, intensity VII on the Modified Mercalli scale and 5.9 on Richter's. The average peak velocity of the wave motion was 11.2 centimeters per second. Dirigent Patricia Castellane's house, designed to withstand much greater shocks, merely swayed on its terrain-shift compensators when the temblor hit. Most of the furnishings were well secured. Draperies billowed, chandeliers clanged, a few loose pieces of glassware fell to the floor and smashed, and dishes of hors d'oeuvres slithered to the edges of tables, where they were restrained by low ornamental railings.

Almost immediately Patricia bespoke her party guests on the declamatory mode of farspeech, reassuring them that the quake had caused no important damage in Chelan Metro. The attendees in turn hastened to tell her that they had not been hurt or inconvenienced in the slightest by the momentary jolt. There were a few spilled drinks and dropped plates of food, that was all. No one wanted to go home. All of them, even the offworlders, knew that earthquakes were just one of those things on Okanagon.

After a few minutes, the party was back in full swing, as though nothing had happened.

But something had.

In a corner of the broad terrace outside the reception room, Ruslan Terekev smiled dismissively and wiped a smear of blood from his brow. The earthquake had caught him unawares as he and Lyudmila Arsanova were conferring with three top officers of the Twelfth Fleet. Ruslan had fallen heavily against the vine-clad stone façade of the building, receiving a sharp blow to the head. His companions looked at him anxiously.

"Are you certain you're all right, glavá?" Lyudmila asked. Are you still *yourself*/yourself? Yob tvoyu mat'! I knew we should not have come with the Krondak mind-fuckers so suspicious of you—

"Perhaps you should let a redactor check you out, Intendant General," Ragnar Gathen suggested. He was the Fleet's Chief of Operations, second in command to Owen Blanchard. "Severin Remillard's just inside—"

"No," the Russian said hastily. "I am—I am perfectly well ... And as I was saying, before the world turned upside down"—the three officers laughed dutifully—"you may count upon our full cooperation when the skeleton crews arrive on Astrakhan to take charge of my flotilla of dreadnoughts. The armaments are—they are installed. Yes! All is in perfect readiness. Of—of course we have not been able to test the weaponry in actual maneuvers." He muttered something in Russian and then shook his head as if to clear it. Lyudmila Arsanova looked at him with concern but did not speak.

"You can leave all that to us, Intendant General," Owen Blanchard said. He mentally indicated the officer who had stood by in silence during the brief exchange with his two superiors. "The Deputy Chief of Operations, Walter Saastamoinen, will see that the ships are made combat-ready. They are his responsibility."

"May—may I know where you intend to hide my dreadnoughts?" Terekev inquired.

"In a sparsely inhabited region of space," Saastamoinen said, "where it's highly unlikely that any Milieu snoopers will ever find them."

"But you will not tell me where."

The Deputy Chief only smiled.

"It's quite possible," Owen Blanchard said, "that these colonization vessels won't ever be used in combat. In our current strategic overview, we've classified them as tactical backup, in case the Thirteenth or Fourteenth Fleets are armed by the Milieu and threaten our actions closer to the Old World. So far there's been no sign of that. But we're keeping a close eye on Elysium and Assawompsett."

"I see." Ruslan Terekev once again touched the abrasion on his forehead with his handkerchief. His self-redaction had nearly healed the surface of the small injury but he looked ashen and distracted. "Then your own Twelfth Fleet, armed with CE operators and conventional X-lasers, will be the Rebellion's primary line of offense?"

Owen Blanchard's tone was respectful. "I can't discuss it, Intendant General. Not yet. Marc will brief you himself when he feels that the time is appropriate. All you need do now is arrange for the covert departure of the ships from your dry docks."

"Yes, yes," Terekev said in some irritation. "It has all been taken care of."

Lyudmila Arsanova spoke up quickly. "When the dreadnoughts are ready to lift, a flare of what appears to be solar radiation will throw our Astrakhanian orbital monitoring systems into a state of temporary malfunction. By the time the scanners are repaired, the starships should be safely escaped into the gray limbo. I have already taken steps to program the so-called flare into the monitor computers. The subterfuge can be activated at a moment's notice from our command post at Nizniye Torgai, adjacent to the dry docks."

Owen said, "Then we're all set. Walter and his skeleton crews should arrive on Astrakhan within twenty days."

Lyudmila smiled politely at Walter Saastamoinen. "I am sorry that we will not be able to show you much of our beloved Russian planet, Deputy Chief. But you and your personnel will be given as warm a welcome as we can manage, under the circumstances . . . And now, gentlemen, I must ask your indulgence. The Intendant General needs a brief period of quiet in order to restore himself completely."

There were solicitous remarks and farewells, and then Arsanova took Terekev by the arm and led him off the terrace and into the jungle-gardens that surrounded Patricia Castellane's residence.

"She seems to be screening for both of them," Owen Blanchard noted, following the pair with his ultrasenses. "The old boy must have been more severely hurt by the fall than he let on."

"He's a queer fish," Ragnar Gathen said. "I hope we can trust him. Arky O'Malley confirms that the dry-docked ships are fitted and ready, but I still have a funny feeling about this whole Astrakhan business."

"So does Marc," the Commander-in-Chief said quietly. "That's why Terekev's not going to know where we stash his precious dread-noughts. Not till our war is won."

You should have fed! I *told* you to feed before we came!

I am well enough. The injury is nearly redacted away. Feeding is unnecessary for now. It . . . sometimes distracts me from appropriate lines of thinking.

You don't seem yourself. I'm concerned—

Be silent!

Apprehension. Oh my beloved Fury let me take you away from here immediately. Let me help you to feed—

Not yet. It's true that I'm still somewhat shaken but I will not leave this party until I have discussed certain strategic matters with Marc. Those damned Krondak surveillance agents are inescapable on Astrakahn but they didn't dare follow me onto Castellane's planet. And . . . I want my meeting with Marc to be unexpected on his part. So he's less inclined to attempt a probe.

Are you afraid he might recognize you? Is that it? Is your metacreative disguise faltering? Be frank with me Fury! You know how desperately worried I've been about you. About your integration.

I am as wholeminded as I ever was.

If you say so.

See to your own vitally important affairs my dearest little one. See that the New Hydra thrives and grows strong. Coerce Strangford and her metaconcert group into designing the proper configuration for the 600X team of Mental Man.

You know I'll follow your instructions precisely. [Reproach.]

I feel much better now. It's time for me to speak to Marc. And time for you to begin work on Helayne Strangford and her colleagues.

Very well. But when we leave here I will help you to feed. You *must* feed.

Later. Later.

The music of the fire-moths, temporarily interrupted by the earthquake, had resumed. Marc walked in the garden with Patricia Castellane on pathways lit by stone lanterns and thick with fragrant fallen flowers. Overhead the glow of the insectile singers waxed and waned in eerie unison as they chimed their four-note summer melody. The numbers of party guests were beginning to dwindle and Marc and the Dirigent met no other strollers. Inside, Shig Morita was playing a jazz piano version of Bill Evans's "Turn out the Stars" for the diehards. The melancholy tune sketched a counterpoint to the fire-moths' song.

"A fine mess for the groundskeepers to clean up tomorrow." Patricia kicked at the drifts of blossoms with a silver slipper. "But we got off lightly on our first Big One. The orchid trees will bud again, and inside of a month they'll be as lovely as ever." Her long gown of peacock lumasheen was bias-cut in the style of the 1930s and worn with several ropes of blue pearls. Marc had on a white dinner jacket and black silk turtleneck.

"You've never had a severe quake here in Chelan Metro before?"

"Never. But when I was a little girl my family lived in Loup Loup near the Methow coast. We had a Richter 7.5 that flattened the town and sent a gigantic tsunami over the inhabited islands offshore. Thirty-one killed by the quake, almost six thousand drowned by the wave. Of course in those days the seismic forecasts were still unreliable and the authorities hadn't yet cracked down on flimsy construction."

"I'm surprised that so many people want to live on a planet that's known to be unstable."

She grinned at him and her steel eyes flashed in the lamplight. "Hey—Oky's a great world, even if it is a bit tectonically challenged. You'll think so, too, once you've settled in. Did you check to see whether your family rode out the quake in good order?"

"I farspoke Cyndia. Things are normal at the Mental Man lab. There was no damage to our new house, either. Hagen and Cloud slept right through the tremor."

"That's good . . . Oh, shit! Look what's happened to my poor koi." They had stopped at an ornamental fishpond some distance from the residence. It was surrounded by a stone coping, but several large golden carp had been thrown from the water and lay dead on the grass. As Marc and the Dirigent stood there contemplating the small catastrophe, a low-slung exotic animal that resembled an otter in greenish armor crept out of the shrubbery, seized one of the fish carcasses, and slunk away with it.

"Life goes on," Marc said. "What was that?"

"We call them pangoids. Some early settler was reminded of Earthly pangolins. They're harmless scavengers. Almost all of our local wildlife are benign to humanity. It's the planet itself that seems hostile. Thank God our Geophysical Corps will be phasing in your new 600X rigs for plate modification. The Peshastin Isthmus region is overdue for a real rumbler and—"

"Pat. I'm sorry. At this critical stage, we can't afford to divert any of our CE resources to domestic concerns. There's little enough time to train the ops in offensive metaconcert."

Her hesitation was only momentary. "Of course. Stupid of me . . . Will you be working on that aspect personally?"

"Strangford and Jarrow and Valery Gawrys and those others who just got in from Oxford will do the actual training. I'll design the concerts, along with Jordy Kramer and Gerry Van Wyk. We'll probably need Alex's help for the tricky bits."

Patricia Castellane gave a soft laugh. "Your pal seems to have fallen for Helayne Strangford like the proverbial ton of bricks. They left together, in case you didn't notice."

"I did. It was a surprise. Alex has never had much time for emotional involvement."

"Like someone else I could mention." Abruptly, Patricia turned away, staring out across the pond. Its surface was littered with floating blossoms. Now and then one was pulled under by one of the surviving fish. "I won't bore you with my own unrequited yearnings, Marc. But if you should ever need me as something more than a co-conspirator . . ."

His hand was cool on her bare shoulder. "I've known how you felt about me for some time. I'm truly sorry. You're a lovely, vital woman and you deserve someone more—more digne d'amour than I. If it's any consolation, I've come to think of you as my staunchest ally in this Rebellion of ours. Some of the others waver from time to time, not sure whether to trust me. But never you, Pat. You've given more than yourself to the cause. You've given your whole world."

"Most Okies are Rebels through and through. Perhaps it goes with the territory. You might not know it, but the Milieu did suggest that we abandon Okanagon in 2058, when the widespread geophysical anomalies were first confirmed. Our people rioted in the streets and shouted 'Hell no, we won't go.' A *very* antiquated chant of defiance! So the Milieu backed down and let us stay ... and less than four weeks later Tonasket Metro was leveled by a whopper and over sixteen thousand died. We just pulled up our socks and carried on."

She turned about, stood on tiptoe, and kissed him on the cheek. "We'll carry on in the Rebellion, too. No matter what. And win."

They began walking back toward the big house. He spoke to her on intimate mode:

Catherine Remillard and her associate Quinn Fitzpatrick have given us valuable advice on the tutoring of Mental Man. We're ahead of schedule in the preceptive sequence. And Jeff Steinbrenner and the CE team have nearly finished a working model of the tiny 600X enhancer we'll use to outfit the young brains.

But they have to ... come out of the womb first, don't they?

There are indications that some of them are nearly ready for independent survival. The Keoghs are using algetic conditioning, making the artificial life support more and more uncomfortable so the children have an incentive to leave it. They're also showing them a Tri-D of my brother Jack, au naturel, as a more positive inducement. So far as I know, it's the only recording of him ever made in the bodiless state. It was done without his being aware of it, by the cockpit black box in the deep-driller that he used during the Caledonian diatreme event. Mental Man has found the Tri-D of Jack to be very inspiring.

I still find it hard to believe that those—those babies can actually tip the balance of mindpower in our favor.

Wait until they zap Molakar to a cinder. I guarantee you'll be impressed. And so will the Milieu.

Is that going to be the demonstration?

Marc nodded somberly. He said: I considered nonlethal options, but none would have concentrated exotic attention quite so thoroughly. We have only one opportunity to show the Milieu exactly how steadfast our resolution is—before committing ourselves to a prolonged conflict that we might *not* be able to win. After the first strike, the exotics will be forewarned and able to barricade their worlds mentally against our attacks. Their vessels can emerge from hyperspace at any point, without warning, and engage in combat with ours. The Lylmik could do God knows what ... unless our initial demonstration persuades them to capitulate.

She said: Molakar has a population nearly equal to Okanagon's. Two billion.

His thought-tone was cold: *And the Krondaku are already assembling starships there in preparation for the lockdown of Earth. I've seen them myself, excursing with the CE rig in farsense mode. The Krondaku are the enforcers, the Milieu bullyboys. It's appropriate that Molakar be sacrificed for human freedom.*

Do you have any estimate of when?

"It all depends," Marc said aloud, "on Mental Man."

As they approached the terrace of the residence, someone came out of the shadows to meet them. It was Ruslan Terekev, the Intendant General of Astrakhan.

"Good evening, Patricia. Marc. An unforgettable party!"

"Thank you." Castellane inclined her head with a wry little smile. "Next time, I'll try to lay on somewhat less exciting entertainment."

"I wonder." The Russian lifted his hands in nervous apology. "Might I have a few minutes with Marc?"

The Dirigent was brisk. "Certainly. It's time for me to see how things are going inside. Thank you both for coming tonight." She went off through the French doors.

Marc looked down at the Russian. His exceptionally dense mindscreen was even more impregnable than usual and he seemed highly agitated. "What is it?"

"Please." Terekev took him by the arm and led him back into the garden. "It is important that we are not interrupted." *Or farsensed!*

Would you like me to erect a metacreative thought-barrier?

That would be ideal. Can we sit here in this gazebo? I am somewhat under the weather at the moment a small knock on the head during the earthquake it was so unexpected I was unable to erect a mental defense.

I'm sorry. Do you require redactive assistance?

No no it's quite all right just sit here with me and listen. I have crucial information for you. Devastating information ... Your Mental Man children have been subverted and turned into Hydras. This was done by your sister Madeleine the sole surviving original Hydra.

"Impossible!" White-faced, Marc surged to his feet.

I'm telling you the truth I swear it on my soul!

"The hell you are. What's your game, Terekev?"

No game you must *believe me! This new hundred-headed Hydra that is Mental Man will enable you to win the Metapsychic Rebellion but afterward the multiplex mind will turn against you, and your sister will use its power to found a Second Milieu. She'll continue as master for a* while until the new Hydra matures and decides to destroy her. Then it will rule—and force *you* to create more minds like itself.

"It's a lie." Fists clenched, Marc stood before the older man, massive in the dusk. "This is some lunatic scheme of yours to undermine my leadership of the Rebellion—"

"You must believe me," Ruslan Terekev pleaded. He reverted to mental speech:

Madeleine is the woman known as Lyudmila Arsanova—my own Chief of Staff—I discovered the truth about her only by accident when we were engaged in sexual intercourse and her mind opened inadvertently at the moment of climax. Before she was Lyudmila she posed as Castellane's aide Lynelle Rogers who engineered the crash of Anne Remillard's starship. She has also used the identity of Saskia Apeldoorn the technician in charge of the developing Mental fetuses. That's when she subverted the babies. Those who refused to accept her were killed.

Is there any way you can prove this incredible assertion?

Terekev hesitated. "I'm not sure." *If you try to ream your sister she'll kill herself Fury inserted the compulsion into all of the original Hydras to prevent their betraying him. Perhaps a coercive-redactive probe of the Mental Man brains would do it. There'd be a certain consonance to the armamentaria a Hydra signature common to all of them.*

Marc said: *They're paramounts. Probably even stronger than I. Their shielding powers are superlative and they join spontaneously in metaconcert now to support one another. I doubt I could ream them unless I used CE and that would put them at risk. A risk I find unacceptable.*

Don't you want to learn the truth? You know what the Hydras are capable of!

Yes. But I wonder how it is that you do.

Your great family secret has been common knowledge among the higher echelon of the Rebel Party for years surely you are aware of this. If I had not known how would I have been able to recognize the importance of what I saw in Arsanova's mind? She opened to me for only an instant. Even so it took me some weeks to comprehend the import of the revelation. I came to you as soon as it was possible to do so. I implore you to probe the Mental children!

"No," Marc said. "The danger to their fragile minds is too great. Your scheme won't work." The celebrated one-sided smile glimmered as Marc came forward and seized the Russian's shoulders. "I'll check out Lyudmila Arsanova. Very cautiously. If she is my wayward sister

Maddy, I may have a use for her. As for you—" His coercion was poised to slam home the mind-ream.

"You arrogant fool," Ruslan Terekev whispered. "I might have known it was useless to appeal to you. Fortunately, I have another option."

He vanished.

At first, more enraged than alarmed, Marc assumed the disappearance was nothing but a metacreative effect rendering the Astrakhanian IG invisible. Five full minutes passed before he cut short his fruitless ultrasensory search of the gardens and residence of the Okanagon Dirigent. When it was already too late, stricken with a sudden sense of dread, Marc beamed a frantic telepathic warning to Jeff Steinbrenner at the secret Mental Man laboratory.

But even as he farspoke he felt the ground of Okanagon shudder beneath his feet in a seismic aftershock. The groan of the planetary crust echoed in his ultrasenses, rolling like mental thunder, nearly drowning out the metaconcerted cry at the quietus of Mental Man.

He knew then, and ran from the Dirigent's residence to his rhocraft.

In the aftermath, before Marc arrived, Cyndia Muldowney came down to the lab to view the disaster. All but one of the infant brains floated lifeless in their transparent capsules. The exception, who had been named Trevor, had achieved the goal of independent survival a microsecond too late. He managed to leap free of the imprisoning tank with his psychokinesis, tearing loose from all of the preceptor-monitor electrodes except one.

But that single input lead had been sufficient to carry the ferocious charge of electricity into his fragile protoplasm. Trevor fell to the floor, shattered. The Keoghs had been unable to revive him.

Cyndia walked among the ranks of the dead, her thoughts adamantly barricaded, tears flowing down her cheeks.

Tears of relief.

They were gone, those fearsome, pathetic, bodiless babies. She had been too weak, too cowardly, too much in love with their father to give the children their release. But somehow it had been done. Mysteriously. Fortuitously. The nightmare was over.

But it's not, you know.

She nearly screamed when the man stepped out from behind a tall equipment rack, would have cried out telepathically if he had not checked her with his coercion.

Please! I'm not here to harm you. Do you recognize me? I'm Denis, Marc's grandfather. Bespeak me on intimode.

You're dead—

That was a hoax. I'm alive. I'm the one who killed them, Cyndia. I had no other choice.

A Dhia dhílis! I'm hallucinating.

You're not. I *am* Denis. Memorize this MP ident sequence [image] and when you can, ask Catherine Remillard whom it belongs to. She'll confirm that I really am her father.

I . . . very well. But—

Listen carefully, Cyndia. This is vitally important. Marc will attempt to sire another generation of Mental Man. You must prevent it. He has no idea of the immense danger these minds pose.

Danger? What are you talking about? The Milieu—

Not only to the Milieu but to every mind in the galaxy—exotic as well as human. Cyndia, these dead children were Hydras. Do you know what that means? [Image.] Ask any member of the Dynasty about their terrible family secret. Ask Catherine or Adrien or Severin. All of them had children who were Hydras—sociopathic killers who feed on life-force like vampires. Megalomaniacs whose ambition is to enslave the Galactic Mind. The only first-generation Hydra left alive now is Madeleine, Marc's sister. She's the strongest of the lot, the one who turned the Mental Man babies into monsters like herself. She'll continue to make new Hydras unless you prevent it.

I've never . . . this is . . . Máthair Dé! Does Marc know?

I tried to tell him tonight. He thought I was lying—trying to destroy the Rebellion by maligning Mental Man. You're my only hope now, Cyndia. You must not tell Marc I've talked to you. He'd never trust you again. And he must continue trusting you until you're able to put a stop to Mental Man forever. It won't be easy. There are two sources of sperm and four sources of ova to be neutralized [image].

Marc . . . Hagen . . . Marie . . . Madeleine . . . Cloud . . . *I myself?* But that's impossible! I can't be—Oh, sweet Jesus. No. Ní hea in aon chor!

I'm sorry. Your true father is Paul Remillard.

I don't believe you. Bréagach thú! Liar! All of this is a lie!

Cyndia, I have no time to argue. I can only tell you what must be done. If you insist on it, your actual paternity can be proved by a simple test. But the fact that both Hagen and Cloud are latent paramounts confirms the truth of what I say [genetic diagram].

I see . . . an Daidí bocht! Poor Rory.

The two most critical progenitors of Mental Man are Madeleine and Marc himself. It may be impossible for you to cope with Madeleine. I can't neutralize her myself because . . . another criminal entity would prevent it. At the moment Madeleine is calling herself Lyudmila Arsanova. She's Chief of Staff in the office of the Astrakhanian IG and she's here on Okanagon. She could assume a new identity at any time. In the past, she's been Saskia Apeldoorn—

Dia linn! The chief technician at our Orcas Island gestatorium?

That's how she was able to subvert the fetuses. Madeleine's not a paramount, but she is formidably dangerous. Your best hope of putting a stop to Mental Man lies with Marc. The DNA in his sperm must be modified, either by hard radiation or by sonic disruption. The latter is preferable, since it would certainly sterilize him while producing relatively unobtrusive damage to his seminiferous tubules—

Are you mad? I can't hurt my husband. I can't!

It's impossible for me to deal with Marc myself. I'm paramount in creativity, but so is he. His mental and physical shields are nearly impregnable. In any direct confrontation, we'd reach a stalemate. There's only one person who can reach him when his safeguards are completely down. You. His wife.

Mo léan, is uafásach an scéal é . . . *I can't hurt him!*

Then he'll sire more Mental children. Madeleine will turn the babies into a fresh generation of Hydras and the obscenity will begin all over again,

Millions. He said there'd be millions . . .

Cyndia, I can't stay here any longer.

Millions. But I can't, Denis! I can't talk to any of the Rebel Dynasty. They'd be sure to tell Marc! Ah, faoi Dhia cad é a dhéanfaimid! What on earth are we to do?

There's only one other thing I can suggest that might convince you that I'm telling the truth. The day after tomorrow—not before—call Uncle Rogi on the subspace communicator. The new teleview patch option will connect you directly to his bookshop, but remember that you're speaking on an open beam. Be circumspect. Ask him . . . if he's seen a certain paradoxical relative recently. Tell him that you and this relative had a worrying conversation. Ask Rogi if the relative is trustworthy. Will you do that?

But I still can't—

Someday when you meet with Rogi in person, he might be able to explain everything to you in detail. Goodbye, my dear. God give you strength.

"Denis?" she whispered, staring at the empty space where he had stood. Then she heard Marc's voice in a distant part of the laboratory, roaring with grief and rage at the first sight of his dead children.

She hurried to be with him.

When he was certain, absolutely certain that life was extinct, he left the terrible place and flew to the new CEREM complex. His own personal 600X rig was ready in the observatory chamber, fully responsive to his commands in its operation and fitted out with the farsensory brainboard he had been using for surveillance of the Rebellion's enemies. He donned the pressure-envelope coverall in the dressing room and came out into the observatory.

It was waiting for him. Reasonably compact in its production design, the full-body CE device was 230 centimeters in height and roughly the size and shape of a black coffin. It weighed three tons. He stepped into the body-molding metal-and-ceramic casing, which was held fast in the trunnion cradle of a hydraulic ascensor. His voice, reduplicated by the CE rig's computer, began the sequence:

CLOSE CASING.

The double lid came together, imprisoning him in armor.

ENHELM OPERATOR.

A hoist brought the opaque helmet over his head and lowered it, mating it to the body casing. His farsight watched the display on the computer as fourteen photonic beams pierced his skull. The cerebrum was insensitive to pain but not the scalp and delicate outer membranes of the brain, and he experienced a brief, blinding headache. Needle-electrodes of the crown-of-thorns apparatus, finer than hairs, penetrated his gray matter, reached the hollow ventricles at the center, and grew synorganic intraventricular enhancer units. Electrodes linked to the refrigeration and pressurization systems penetrated his cerebellum and brainstem.

INITIATE METABOLIC REPROGRAMMING.

Cryogenic fluid began to fill the casing. He winced as his carotid and femoral arteries were punctured and catheterized for the circulatory shunt.

ENGAGE AUXILIARY CE.

He became one with the machine. All pain ceased. His heart and lungs slowed and stopped. The freezing took only a moment and he was divested of his limiting body at last.

ENGAGE PRIMARY CE. OPEN OBSERVATORY DOME. ACTIVATE ASCEN-SOR. KILL SIGMA-SHIELD OB-3.

The world opened to his mental vision. As the hydraulic lift carried his armored form upward into the starry night, his enhanced ultra-senses surveyed the planet Okanagon as though it were a grain of sand magnified infinitely beneath an electron microscope. Each of its two billion individual living entities was perceptible as a tiny pulsating point of light. He sifted them, sorted, studied their metapsychic signatures.

Ruslan Terekev—the murderer—was nowhere to be found. Was he dead? It seemed impossible for him to have escaped in a starship so quickly.

The beacon of his seekersense whirled at lightspeed around the planet. He found two vessels with superluminal capability, still rho-powered, en route to the c-zone where they would go superluminal. Neither of them carried the killer of Mental Man. If Terekev had left on a starship he was already in the gray limbo, where not even 600X augmentation could search him out.

Very well. Tune to the childhood memory of *her* aura: his damned sister Madeleine, who had allegedly subverted Mental Man and turned Him into her creature...

With the infant brains dead, he would never know for certain unless he captured her and reamed the truth out of her. If she died in the process it was unimportant—

There!

He swooped in, using excorporeal-excursion mode, and found her. Unbelievably, she was only nine kilometers away, just leaving the I-102 expressway in her open convertible Mustang groundcar. Driving very slowly under manual control, she turned onto the road leading directly to CEREM. Her eyes were red and swollen and her face was streaked with dried tears. She clutched the steering wheel in a nerveless grip. He could hear her muttering.

"He must be there he must be . . ."

Was it possible that she was actually coming to confront him? Her aura glowed undisguised. Everyone at the gestatorium knew where he had gone, and with the observatory sigma down, she could easily farsense that his CE rig was activated. He was incapable of coercing her mindscreen open or penetrating her mind redactively because only a single metafaculty at a time was enhanced by CE. If he bespoke her, would she panic? He decided to risk it. There was no way she could escape from him now.

He said: *Madeleine.*

She gave a violent start and the vehicle swerved. But she regained control an instant later. Her voice was a tremulous whisper, full of hysterical hope. "Marc?"

Yes. Pull over to the side of the road and stop the car.

She did as she was told, halting beneath a great copperleaf tree that glistened in the brilliant starlight like a gargantuan piece of jewelry. She shut off the convertible's engine, and the headlights died. From the jungle on either side of the road came the discordant musical clamor of exotic night-creatures. Purple and green will-o'-the-wisps bobbed amidst the undergrowth.

"They're dead," Madeleine said. "All of the Mental Man children are dead. I heard their telepathic scream as he electrocuted them. Our babies. Oh, Marc."

It was Ruslan Terekev?

"Yes."

He's left the planet. How did he escape? Where has he gone?

She laughed softly. "You don't know, do you! I wonder if I should tell you? I wonder if I should tell you everything? Would you be my ally or my executioner? I was coming to you with a proposition. I—I can't do it alone, you see."

The mindvoice was gentle, seraphically strong, nonjudgmental. *Did you turn Mental Man into a Hydra monster, Maddy? Is that why Terekev killed Him?*

She cringed, covering her face with both hands, and began to sob. The sound was raw and harsh, like the ululation of a tortured animal, and her eyes seemed to have no tears left. "Our children . . . our poor paramount children. They weren't monsters. They never would have harmed us. They would have shared it with us—the Second Milieu."

What the bloody hell are you talking about?

She uncovered her ravaged face and her eyes blazed. "Mental Man was ours! Yours and mine, Marc. The ova didn't come from our cousin Rosamund, they came from me. A homozygotic mating was the only way to engender operant Mental Man in the first generation. I told you that! In your dreams. You knew. You've always known."

. . . In my dreams. It was you all along. Poisoning me. Damning Him!

"Don't be an imbecile!" she cried. "Your unconscious mind accepted me! Agreed! You were ready—oh, yes, you were ready! Until the bitch interfered. How could I have guessed that the template would also fit her?"

Cyndia! Paul and . . . Laura Tremblay. Oh, dear God.

Madeleine laughed wildly. "Don't talk like a stupid hypocrite. You know that the only God is in ourselves and in our omnipotent children."

It's over.

"No, it's not. We'll simply start again." She was eager now, sitting straight and looking up at the night sky through the coppery leaves, seeming to see his face among the stars. "You'll find a way to postpone the Rebellion until Mental Man is reborn. The dream is alive, Marc. In both of us! Let's talk about it. Shall I drive on? Shall I meet you at CEREM and tell you everything about the Second Milieu?"

An immense silence seemed to tauten the aether. She waited, not daring to breathe.

Come, he said.

All of the gates and doors of the place opened before her. She came into the observatory chamber, eagerly smiling, and found the black ceramotal coffin of the CE rig still in the mechanical embrace of the ascensor.

The farsensory brainboard lay in the ejection tray of the MP interface module.

"Marc?" she said tentatively.

I'm in the machine, he said.

"I'll permit you to scan my memories redactively. If you're very careful, you should be able to circumvent Fury's suicide compulsion. You'll see that I'm telling the truth."

It's not necessary. I believe what you said. In any case, I don't have a redactive brainboard available for this CE rig. I'm in creativity mode now.

"Then let me tell you—"

No. I don't want to hear it.

The mental laser that destroyed her cerebral cortex was surgically precise, avoiding any damage to the cerebellum or brainstem. Later, when he had divested, he summoned Dierdre and Diarmid Keogh and told them to place the vegetative body in cryogenic storage.

He'd decide what to do about it later.

[**26**]

FROM THE MEMOIRS OF
ROGATIEN REMILLARD

On 28 October I flew my egg from Hanover to Mount Washington for my last climb of the season.

This sudden impulse to get away had come over me the night before. I phoned the Appalachian Mountain Club in Pinkham Notch and their recorded weather forecast told me that the sky was going to be clear in the Presidential Range tomorrow and the temperature was expected to peak around 7 Celsius. Some precip was scheduled to arrive late in the evening, but the day was going to be damn near perfect for a fall hike.

Around 0730, I landed in the parking lot at Marshfield Base Station on the west side of the mountains. The cog railway and the restaurant and souvenir shop were closed for the season. It being mid-week and most folks other than me being gainfully employed, I had the place almost completely to myself. There was only a single car in the lot and no other rhocraft.

I could see my breath as I put on my little daypack and got out my steel-tipped walking stick. The yellow leaves of the paper birches shimmered against a bright blue sky and my farsight discerned a light frosting of rime-ice on the upper slopes. I took out my map and gave it a quick once-over. My plan was to climb to the summit of Mount Washington by way of the Ammonoosuc Ravine Trail, a picturesque but steep route lying south of the cog tracks. Then I'd return via the Jewell Trail north of the cog, which would loop me back to my starting point at the station. With stops for lunch and rubbernecking, I'd cover about 14 kilometers in nine hours if I moved along briskly.

I was badly in need of a day's distraction and some strenuous physical exercise. Rebellion wasn't looking nearly as attractive to me as it once had. The media furor over Fred's murder and the near-fatal attack on the First Magnate by what were presumed to be Rebel extremists had mostly subsided, but a lot of influential operants were still in a stew over it. Even though Marc and the other Rebel leaders had issued statements deploring the crimes and repudiating whoever had committed them, the party's image was still besmirched.

Paul's recovery was taking a lot longer than anticipated. The Dynasty rumor mill had it that Davy MacGregor—now lobbying actively in favor of Unity during whirlwind visits to Human Polity planets and doing a damned effective job of it—was going to be appointed Acting First Magnate at the February Concilium session. He would then have the authority to purge the Human Directorates of members with Rebel inclinations, which would result in our party losing most of its political clout.

There were more ominous whisperings in local traitorous circles. Kyle Macdonald, my usual source of hot Rebellious poop, thought it was a foregone conclusion that the exotics would force a loyalty test on human magnates even if Davy himself didn't, and those who failed would be kicked out of the Concilium. Even worse, Kyle seemed to believe that war was inevitable and might even break out inside of a year. Masha told him nothing about the affairs of the Rebel inner circle, but Kyle was astute at gathering bits and pieces of intelligence that his wife let slip inadvertently and stitching them together with his novelist's imagination. The resultant patchwork scared the hell out of him.

It had terrified me, too, when Kyle had blurted it out a few days before in the Sap Bucket Tavern . . .

Striding through the crisp autumn morning in the mountains, I was able to forget my apprehensions for a little while. The trail followed the small Ammonoosuc River through open coniferous woods for about two and a half kloms. Then you crossed the stream on a footbridge and came to several lovely cascades. Above them the way became increasingly precipitous, and I was glad of my long legs as I climbed rough steps formed by the roots of spruces. Partway up I diverged from the trail so that I could go out on a ledge and savor the spectacular view of the main stream and a nearly parallel tributary, pouring down rocky gutters to a tumultuous confluence in the gorge below. The air was alive with beneficent negative ions, and a winter wren sang its fussy, lengthy song. I felt a whole lot better about being alive and tarried there for some time.

Climbing higher, I emerged from the ravine and came into the open krummholz zone, where the spruces and firs were dwarfed and gnarled by high winds and severe weather. The trail took a southerly direction now, and the sun was in my eyes as I finally passed above tree line into the alpine zone, picking my way from yellow-painted cairn to cairn among great tumbles of rock.

In one of nature's mysteries, the tree line in the Presidential Range is around 1525 meters, only about half its elevation in the Rockies. Our mountains are, in effect, a small chunk of Labrador plunked down in New England—with Labradorian ecology and weather to match. It pays to keep your wits about you when you go hiking in these parts.

I knew that. Fat lot of good it did me.

The wind had picked up considerably by the time I reached the AMC "hut" beside the two little Lakes of the Clouds. The place caters to hikers along the Appalachian Trail and is actually a sizable structure with stone walls, capable of lodging and feeding a hundred people at a crack. This time of the year it was shut up tight. I paused to eat a Kit Kat bar and drink some brandy-laced coffee from my Zojirushi bottle, pulling the hood of my insulated parka up over my head against the cutting gusts. A single raven showed up, eyed my candy, and said *Gimme*. But I wasn't in the mood for birdwatching—or feeding—and I told it to piss off. It flew away toward the east.

The temperature was hovering around freezing. There were ice-skims on the tiny lakes and plenty of heavy hoarfrost in among the rocks where the sun didn't shine. It wasn't shining much now, a fact that I belatedly got around to noticing. The sky had turned the color of milk and the top of Mount Washington was getting fuzzy, although visibility was still fine on the peaks to the south and on the lower slopes.

I said "Merde!" and rummaged in my pack for the telephone, figuring to call the Appalachian Mountain Club at Pinkham Notch for a weather update. I discovered that I'd forgotten the phone and gave myself a good cussing out. (But in retrospect, I might not have been to blame after all.) I tried a farshout, but evidently there were no operants near enough or sensitive enough to hear me. Even though the fancy restaurant in the Summit Chalet was closed for the season, egg-buses flew tourists up to the mountaintop on weekends throughout most of the year, except when the winds got above 160 kph or clouds ruined the view. Since it was Wednesday, however, there might have been only maintenance staff at the chalet, or even nobody at all.

Since I still had a modicum of prudence left, I decided to bag the summit climb and opt instead for a traverse to Jewell via the Westside Trail. If bad weather was putting in an early appearance, as I suspected, it would get worse faster at higher altitudes. By sticking to the lower trail and stirring my stumps, I thought I could avoid it.

Those entities reading these memoirs who are experienced mountain hikers will realize that I was an idiot not to have turned tail and retreated back into Ammonoosuc Ravine. What can I say? It was my destiny to go on, and that's what I did.

The Westside Trail is nearly straight and level, requiring no particular attention, and as I plodded along I found myself harking back to incidents that had taken place not far away. One recollection was bittersweet: my first bemused sighting of Elaine Donovan through the borrowed farsenses of the boy Denis. I had fallen in love with Elaine instantly, smitten by le coup de foudre. Later she had loved me, too, until my stupid pride drove her away.

There were other memories: my escape from the cog railway car where Victor Remillard and the lunatic Kieran O'Connor had held me prisoner. My killing of an anonymous mercenary in order to steal his environmental suit and stay alive in the snow. My final encounter with Vic as he prepared to blow up the Summit Chalet and all its occupants. The Family Ghost saving my life, holding the flaring Great Carbuncle against the stormy sky. And finally, the thousands of Milieu starships hovering above Mount Washington, intervening at last to save us Earthlings from ourselves.

Had the Intervention been nothing but an exercise in futility after all? Lately, there were those who warned that humanity was about to be hauled back in ignominy to the home planet, banished from the interstellar confederation forever. Or was the Intervention worse than futile? I thought I believed in the Rebellion; but was I really willing to pay the price of secession that Marc and his cohorts seemed ready to risk? . . .

My brooding was cut short abruptly when I slipped and took a heavy fall, jarring my brains literally back to earth. I was a stone's throw away from the cog railway line. The rocks around me were wholly crusted with thick hoarfrost, as were the slightly elevated tracks. My left hip and outer leg hurt like hell and were probably badly bruised, but I didn't seem to have broken anything. I had to use my stick to haul myself to my feet. The wind had died and it was very cold, with an opal-hued ring around the sun, a flat white disk that one could look at with impunity. The rugged landscape below had an almost supernatural clarity now. Upslope, in the direction of the now-invisible summit, was a bank of dark cloud with a peculiarly solid appearance.

It was oozing deliberately downhill, right toward me.

"Merde et contremerde," I moaned. I had never seen the phenomenon before, but I had heard horror stories about it in the early days, when I worked at the White Mountain Hotel: It was the notorious icy fog of Mount Washington that engulfed unwary hikers, stole their body heat with insidious efficiency, and eventually froze them stiffer than an iced codfish.

I decided to think very carefully about what to do next.

The junction with the Jewell Trail, which would lead me to a lower elevation, was still a kilometer away. And the upper reaches of the Jewell were exposed rock slabs, hazardous in icy conditions even to the able-bodied—which I definitely was not. If I turned back to Ammonoosuc Ravine I'd have to travel twice as far, and I also had an excellent chance of missing a cairn in the fog and getting fatally lost in the maze of side trails around Bigelow Lawn.

Nope, there was only one sensible—if scary—course. I'd have to go *uphill* on a section of the Gulfside Trail paralleling the cog railway. The path was well graded, led directly to the summit, was less than a kilometer long, and I couldn't possibly go astray hugging the tracks. At the top there was an emergency shelter at the chalet, with a telephone I could use to call for help.

I climbed painfully over the cog line and set off, hobbling as fast as I could. The way wasn't especially steep, but once the icy fogbank swallowed me I was blind, dependent upon my inadequate farsight. Rime began to accumulate on my lower body. My jacket had a slick vylac outer face that discouraged frost buildup but my pants were old-fashioned rough wool. I had to bang my stick on the rocks constantly to keep it from becoming ice-sheathed and useless. I pulled the drawstring of my hood tight, leaving only a minimal aperture for breathing, and navigated wholly by my fading ultrasenses.

Some lucky operants are able to maintain their body temperature through mindpower in adverse conditions, but I'm not one of them. I felt the damp cold strike through my boots and socks, making my feet throb. My legs in their ice-crusted pants and inadequate longjohns were weakening, especially the bruised left one. Uncontrollable shivers racked me.

How far was I from the summit? It seemed I'd been slogging forever in the damned fog, slipping and sliding on the frost-coated rocks, moving slower and slower as my body succumbed to hypothermia. If I froze to death, maybe they'd erect a plaque in my memory, as they had to poor little Lizzie Bourne, who had perished somewhere close by in 1855. Or maybe not ... Over 150 people had died on this mountain, more than on any other peak in North America, and most of them had been damned fools like me, unprepared for the sudden shifts in weather that could turn a smiling sunny day into a hell below zero inside of an hour.

Now the wind was rising again, ripping apart the fog but increasing the chill factor. I couldn't feel my feet, and my hands were starting to go as well. I'd stopped shivering and the bruises from my fall didn't hurt anymore. Actually, I was beginning to feel pretty decent. I figured I'd feel even better if I crouched for a minute in the shelter of a big rock and rested. I let myself sink down and pulled open my hood so I could see. The wind was strong now, blowing over the col that links Mounts Washington and Clay, and a thick twilight had settled in.

The first snowflakes started to fly.

After a while I tried to get up, but my stiffened muscles balked. The wind thinned the clouds and across the tracks I caught a momentary glimpse of the Gulf Tank, the water supply for the cog's steam-powered locomotives. It was frosted like the gizmo on top of a wedding cake. I groaned aloud. The tank was a good half-kilometer from the chalet. I was never going to make it the rest of the way.

Eh bien, plus rien à dire. I was a goner.

From the deep recesses of my cooling brain I extracted the Acte de Contrition: I was sorry I'd been a self-pitying drunk, sorry I'd tried to murder my twin brother when he stole the woman I loved, sorry that I deliberately killed the thug on the mountain instead of just knocking him out. *Not* sorry I'd executed that monster, Parni—but that didn't count because it was self-defense. I was most sorry of all that I'd been too proud to forgive Elaine for betraying me with Don. All my other sins ... sorry for them, too, even though I couldn't remember what they were. It had been an interesting 137 years amen amen ainsi soit-il.

Then I saw the light.

Beyond the water tower was a small shed. The door was open, illuminating a figure standing there. It beckoned to me, called my name. It was an operant, lending me mental assistance.

Creative energy warmed me, redaction infused my muscles with fresh strength. Nobody coerced me, but I got up and began to move. PK helped pick up my leaden feet and lay them down. I groped and flopped across the tracks, scrambled on hands and knees up the ice-coated incline to the shack. Snow stung the unfrozen parts of my face like a spray of needles.

Someone dragged me over the threshold, closed the door, began stripping away my ice-stiffened outer clothing. I was aware of a small fusion-powered Mr. Heater unit, radiating blessed warmth. I saw racks of tools, a workbench, coils of hose hung on the wall, a lantern, a piece of machinery in one corner that might have been a water pump.

I sat on an old plass crate, feeling its rough surface beneath my painfully thawing fingers. My rescuer stood behind me, hands pressed to my icy face, curing the chilblains, speeding my congealed blood, pouring healing redaction into my moribund nervous system. The spasms of shivering ceased and I ached all over. Briefly, my body endured the painful recovery from frostbite. Then a plass cup touched my lips and I drank some of my own coffee and brandy between fits of hysterical giggling. I had nearly frozen to death, while the drink had remained hot inside its state-of-the-art Zojirushi vacuum bottle, forgotten in my daypack.

He squatted in front of me, smiling, prodding me here and there with his PK to be sure I had revived. Then he put my warmed clothing back on me, draping the jacket over my shoulders.

I said, "Merci, Denis mon fils."

He said, "De rien, Onc' Rogi."

Time elapsed while my brain finished booting up. Then I asked Denis what the hell he was doing up here.

"Waiting for you," he said, pulling up another crate and sitting down. "You wasted too much time checking out the twin sluices on the Ammonoosuc, but there was no way I could coerce you to get a move on. If you'd reached the cog track just half an hour earlier you'd have missed the ice-fog."

"Was that your car in the Base Station lot?"

"No," Denis said, veiling his eyes. "I came another way."

"From Pinkham Notch? Up Tuckerman Ravine? Where are you stay—" The banal words dwindled to a choked mumble. I finally realized who I was talking to. *What* I was talking to. My face went slack with fear.

Denis sighed. "Get hold of yourself. It's me, all right. But I don't know how long I can retain possession of my body. Fury could return any moment and seize control. That's why I've come to you. I need your help desperately. Even though I couldn't coerce you, I was able to insert a suggestion into your mind that you come hiking on the mountain. You were ripe for the hint and you came. I had to meet you someplace where there were no other people nearby. Nobody that Fury could use."

I had no idea what he meant. "You know I'll help you any way I can. What do you want me to do?"

"First of all, I want to inject a mass of data into your mind as rapidly and efficiently as possible: the history of Fury and the Hydras. You'll have to lower your mindscreen for a moment."

I stiffened. What if the person talking to me wasn't Denis? I'd be handing him my immortal, freshly contrite soul on a platter! The magnetic blue gaze held me riveted. I might not have been coerced, but I was certainly spellbound by the intensity of his personality. And frightened to death by it, as I'd been so many times in the early years.

"I want you to know the truth about Fury and me, Rogi. If you do, it will make my next request that much easier to understand. But if you can't bear to open up, that's okay."

He'd saved my life from the Great White Cold. And I *did* know him. He wasn't Fury. He was the baby who'd bonded to me at his christening, the needy child who took me as his metapsychic teacher and moral mentor, the idealist who'd summoned the Intervention. He was Denis Rogatien Remillard, my son.

I squeezed my eyes shut, said, "Do it!" and dropped the screen. The information was suddenly there in my memories, as though I'd always known it. Some of it, I had.

Dear God in heaven, I had.

I stared at him, lost to speech, too devastated even to pity him. He said, "Put up your barrier again. Make it as powerful as you can. You know why."

"You want me to kill you," I whispered.

"You're probably the only one who can," he said mildly, "and it must be done. This physical body must die. The monster retains his ascendancy by feeding on lifeforce, as Victor and the Hydras did. Sometimes, when Fury weakens, I'm able to take control for a brief period of time. Fury knows about it, and he's desperately afraid of me and what I might do. He once told the Hydra to kill him if I broke free and tried to interfere with his schemes. But Madeleine was incapable of harming her master—mind *or* body. When Fury made the Hydras he installed a permanent inhibition to prevent them from turning on him."

"There must be some other way! A stronger redactive metaconcert might heal the personality breach—"

"I doubt it would work. Fury would d-jump. Teleport out of any trap that could be devised. That's how I got here on the mountain. Yesterday I was on Okanagon, destroying the first generation of Mental Man. I had appealed to Marc—warned him that the infants had been transformed into Hydras. He refused to listen."

I murmured, "Sacré nom de dieu."

"Fury and I are yoked together for as long as this body lives," he told me. "I've managed to undo some of the evil that the monster has perpetrated, but not the bulk of it. The Metapsychic Rebellion will probably escalate into a war. Mental Man can be resurrected if Fury shows Marc the way. And if the monster should ever begin to . . . feed on a regular basis, my persona could be permanently repressed. Locked away, utterly helpless. My only hope is to put an end to this ghastly double life. Through you, Uncle Rogi. Call up the outspiral of metacreative energy you used on the Parnell Hydra. Do it now."

I could only shake my head in desperation. "It—it doesn't work like that. When Parni came at me I was in a state of total panic. Out of my mind with fear. Thinking I was going to be killed myself."

"Try!" Denis commanded. He hauled me to my feet and I cowered back against one wall of the windowless shed. My jacket fell from my shoulders. Outside, the wind had begun to wail. A flash of farsight showed me that heavy snow was falling.

The paramount mindspeech flooded my brain: You *must* try, mon père!

I pulled myself together. "All right. You—you better stand over there."

Denis put his arms around me in a final embrace and I very nearly lost it. He whispered, "Bon courage," then drew away and stood calmly on the opposite side of the shed, less than three meters away. He signed himself and closed his awful eyes, waiting.

I lifted my arms and spread my legs, assuming Leonardo's X-man pose. Praying for strength myself, I slowly conjured up the glowing knot of vital energy, feeling it pool and grow in the region behind my heart. I put it into a flat spiral motion, forcing it to move downward through my spleen and my solar plexus, up into the suprarenals, the thymus. The metacreative glow intensified, breaking out of my body and filling the shed with dazzling golden light. It was still much smaller than the ball that had incinerated Parni.

Concentrating, I made the energy knot curve down through the root-chakra at my tailbone. It accelerated, turned upward again—

Denis opened his eyes and laughed.

I faltered. The spiraling energy slowed, seeming to halt inside my head. Its luminosity fluctuated, deepened from yellow to amber. To orange. I seemed to see Denis through a fiery haze.

Not Denis.

Fury.

"Did you think I'd let you destroy me?" the monster said. "Your own son! How could you even think of it? There's unbearable pain when a child dies. I know. All of my own beloved children are dead now. Gordon, Quentin, Celine, Parnell, Madeleine—even the dear New Ones. All my Hydras are dead. But there will be a great rebirth. As Mental Man is reborn, as I myself was reborn, so will my own children be."

At the time, I didn't understand what he was talking about, nor did I know the true physical condition of Mental Man. The monster took a step closer to me. He was still smiling and he looked exactly like Denis. He was Denis.

But why? I found myself saying. Why if we're free to choose why did you let it be?

"Love failed," Fury said.

Denis was a short man, but the creature confronting me seemed suddenly enormous. Powerful arms seized my torso in a bear hug, squeezing the breath out of me and lifting me off my feet. Still in the X-posture, I was rigid as a pair of crossed boards, a human Saint Andrew's cross.

"It's time I was rid of you and your useless love," the thing said. "Perhaps I'm incapable of coercing you or killing you with mindpower, but there's nothing to prevent me from throwing you out that door. The wind is blowing a hundred forty kloms an hour and the temperature is minus ten. You'll be dead in minutes."

His psychokinesis tore open the shed door and he carried me toward it like a shop mannequin. Whirling snow filled the interior of the little building and the wind yelled like a thousand demons.

Behind my eyes, the ball of vital energy still burned feebly. It was the color of congealing blood.

Then, apparently without any volition on my part, my right arm came down. My hand thrust into my pants pocket, felt metal, pulled out the three antique brass keys that still served to open the doors of my bookshop, my apartment, and my garage. The keys were on a ring, and attached to it was a fob that looked like a red-glass marble enclosed in a silvery cage.

I was on my feet again, Fury had put me down just inside the wide-open door and was staring at the thing in my hand with rapt fascination.

He said, "Is there really an end to the fury?"

The Great Carbuncle blazed.

The dying gout of energy centered on my brain's thalamus rekindled, brightening to eye-searing gold. It began to move again, impelled by my desperation, arcing into the left elbow of my upraised arm, diving to my left knee, to the right. I thrust my right arm high, holding tight to the key ring, and accelerated the outspiral up to my right elbow—

Oh, Denis! Are you still in him somehow, still susceptible to love?

I don't know.

I blotted all sensation, all thinking from my consciousness. Only the golden energy existed, a miniature sun, growing as I stoked it with my own life and widened the spiral.

To the crown of my head, to my left hand, my left foot, right foot—

The monster lowered his head and flung himself at me. His skull struck my breastbone like a cannonball, pushing me out into the storm at the same instant that the shining globe reached my right hand, which still held the Carbuncle. A thunderclap of sound deafened me and I was convulsed by a tremendous neural discharge. I cartwheeled in mid-air, lifted by the hurricane wind. I fell onto rock, thinly padded with rime and snow, and lay stunned.

The blackout was momentary. Gasping as the fierce cold sliced through my wool shirt and pants, I slipped and slid and crept and groped back to the shed and managed to collapse inside and kick the door shut behind me.

There was nobody there.

For a long time I lay on the concrete floor, oblivious to the puddle of meltwater under my face, while the valiant little heater raised the ambient temperature to a prophylactic level. I sat up woozily, head pounding. My bandanna handkerchief was spread squarely on top of one of the plass crates. Heaped in the middle of it was a cone of dry grayish-white powdery material. My key ring lay alongside, its red diamond fob faintly reflecting the lamplight.

I gaped, uncomprehending. "Denis?"

Rest for a little while. Then use the phone in that box on the wall over there to get help. One final thing. The Great Carbuncle—take it to Jack in Hawaii.

I was suddenly warm and dry and the vacuum bottle of spiked coffee was in my hand. I managed to lift it to my lips and take a comforting swig.

How do you feel?

"I'm . . . okay."

Then it's finished. We're such imperfect maddening things such spoilers! How is it possible that the design remains integral? Perhaps I'll find out. Adieu mon père bien-aimé.

"Go," I whispered. "Va donc, mon enfant. Goodbye."

The blizzard wind pounded the little shed on the mountain. Alone, I let the tears flow.

SECTOR 12: STAR 12-340-001 [NESPELEM]
PLANET 2 [OKANAGON]
4 MAZAMA [29 OCTOBER] 2082

In the morning, after Marc's egg took off for the CEREM complex, Cyndia waited another hour to be absolutely certain that he would not look back and farsee her. Then she went to his home office and turned on the subspace communicator.

A sparkling galactic logo appeared on the monitor and the computerized voice said: "Routing to what planet, please?"

"Earth," Cyndia told it.

There. She had taken the first step. But it wasn't irrevocable.

"Number, please, if you have it available."

"Oh-oh-two-oh, plus-six, pound-oh-three, patch: six-oh-three, six-four-three, three-six-one-six."

"Phone patch service to groundside comsys in North American Region Pound-Oh-Three will necessitate a delay of approximately seven minutes. Please stand by. And thank you for using GTE Subspace Communications." The display switched to a bucolic New England farm scene with background music from Charles Ives's Concord Sonata.

Not irrevocable. She was only validating the data, not committing herself.

While she waited for the everyday miracle that permitted instantaneous communication across 540 lightyears, Cyndia picked up the computer-assisted design pad that Marc used for his CE modifications, turned it on, and began sketching with a silver stylus. Her fingers seemed to have a life of their own, working without any conscious volition on her part while she wondered what she would do if Uncle Rogi did confirm that she had actually seen a dead man.

She told herself that it couldn't be true. The person calling himself Denis had to be some powerful human operant loyal to the Milieu. First he'd slaughtered Mental Man, and then he'd tried to get at Marc through her. Telling monstrous lies.

A terrible Remillard family secret? Hydras? Metapsychic vampires? It was ridiculous.

But there had been odd rumors in Rebel circles for years. Her father had hinted at it—but he'd never mentioned any Hydra-monsters. Rory had heard that the mysterious killer of Davy MacGregor's wife was a being called Fury, supposed to be a Jekyll-Hyde multiple-personality aspect of one of the senior Remillards, undetectable even by the Cambridge machine. Fury's luckless host was said not to even know it existed. The two prime candidates for the pathology, she recalled, were the First Magnate and his son Marc.

Ridiculous. It was pure fantasy.

As fantastic and unlikely as Mental Man Himself . . .

Those poor bodiless babes floating miserably in their uterine capsules, undergoing algetic conditioning. Algetic! Ah, he'd promised that the brains would feel no pain, and so they hadn't. Not in the encephalizing procedure. The hurting had come afterward, when the children were encouraged to achieve fully independent life without artificial support.

That butcher Jeff Steinbrenner had called it "necessary discomfort." Marc had been more straightforward: Extraordinary mental expansion inevitably involved mental suffering. He had been mistaken to think Mental Man would be spared Jack's ordeal. Pain was an inescapable part of the maturation process, a necessary step toward the great goal.

And I did nothing to prevent it! Because *he* wanted it so . . .

The silver pen continued to draw the intricate mechanical design on the CAD plaque, refining the concept. It could be hidden inside her body and activated at the proper moment. He'd never know what was happening. Never know at all what had been done to him until he tried to make more embryos with Rosamund Remillard's ova.

But it wouldn't come to that. The design was not the mechanism. The tool was not the accomplished work. Even if Rogi said—

The subspace communicator chimed softly. A new icon appeared on the screen and the artificial voice spoke simultaneously: "We're sorry! The number you have called responds with a voice-mail answering machine. Do you wish to communicate with it?"

She sighed. "Yes, I suppose so."

Rogi's weather-beaten, oddly youthful face appeared. Messy silver locks straggled over his forehead. His dark eyes held a slightly cryptic glint. He said, "This is The Eloquent Page bookshop, Roger Remillard, Proprietor, speaking. I can't come and talk to you now, but if you like, you can leave me a message and I'll get back to you eventually. Look over the menu for options . . . If you're really desperate to get ahold of me and it's a serious matter, say FORWARD. But God help you if you're wasting my time or trying to sell something. Because if you are, I'll activate the frivolous-com option and sock you with the usual fine. No hard feelings! A bientôt."

The face was replaced by a small-business mail menu. Cyndia said: "Forward."

After an interval, a white-haired Polynesian woman of inscrutable mien appeared on the display. "Johnson residence."

"My name is Cyndia Muldowney. I'm Marc Remillard's wife, calling from the planet Okanagon. I wonder if I might speak to Uncle Rogi?"

The woman's face broke into a friendly smile. "Cyndia! So happy to see, talk wit' you at lass! I'm Malama—ole friend of da family! You hang in dere, I get Rogue. He's out loafin' on da lanai."

She disappeared. In a moment the bookseller himself showed up, looking decidedly seedy.

"Cyndia?"

"Uncle Rogi, this is extremely important. Please be very careful what you say on this open beam. It's not likely that anyone is eavesdropping, but we must assume they might be. Do you understand?"

The old man pinched his slightly crooked nose and squeezed his eyes shut momentarily. "Uhh. Go ahead. I'll do the best I can. Does this have something to do with . . . politics?"

"Not really. And please let's not play Twenty Questions. This may be a matter of life or death. Now listen: Two days ago I received a visit from an extraordinary person. One I never thought I'd ever meet. A certain relative of yours. I thought he was dead. Do you know who I'm talking about?"

"Batège!" Rogi exclaimed. "He said he'd come straight from Okanagon, but—"

"Stop! Don't say any more. This person . . . naturally I thought he was an impostor."

"He was who he said he was," Rogi stated flatly. "And now he's really dead. I was there when he passed away. Yesterday." The old man's lips tightened and he lowered his gaze.

For a moment Cyndia could not speak. "Then what he told me was the truth? He said some truly incredible things. That your family had . . . skeletons in its closet."

Rogi's head snapped up. "Oh, he said that, did he? Well, you better believe he was telling you the truth. Fortunately for us, the bones have stopped rattling. The skeletons are all dead, too."

"Are you certain? All of them? Even the sister?"

"That's what this relative told me. I don't think he would have lied."

"Thank God," she whispered. "Then there's really only Marc."

"What's that?" The old man looked startled. "What else did Den— the relative say to you? About Marc."

She shook her head. "I can't tell you now. Perhaps later. When we meet in person."

"Cyndia, I'll try to come to Okanagon. We've gotta talk all this over. You have a right to know. And there's something else, about Marc and your children . . ."

"I was afraid there might be," she said simply. "Come if you can. Goodbye, Uncle Rogi."

She switched off the SS com unit before the old man could say anything more, and sat staring at its blank screen for several minutes. Then she turned to the ordinary teleview that sat on Marc's desk and phoned a big scientific supply house in Chelan Metro to put in a lengthy order. Only one item was unavailable and would have to be obtained from Earth. She requested FedEx SpeedStar service, but the catalog told her apologetically that the device was on back order from the manufacturer and would probably take over eight weeks to arrive.

"Do you still wish to place the order, Citizen?"

"Yes," she said.

When she had finished, she studied the mechanical drawing on the CAD plaque for some time, committing the design to memory before erasing it.

Then she left Marc's office and went out into the garden, where the nanny Mitsuko and little Cloud and Hagen were enjoying the sunshine.

[28]

FROM THE MEMOIRS OF
ROGATIEN REMILLARD

After I was done talking to Cyndia I shuffled back into the kitchen, where Malama was cooking up some Spam in pineapple sauce and pea pod rice, a simple supper for the two of us. The sun had just gone down and the sky along the Pacific horizon was smeared with thin scarlet clouds. When the entrée was done Malama just dumped it onto a serving platter and set it on the kitchen table, where a salad and lilikoi punch were already waiting. She told me to sit down and urged me to help myself. I took a heaping plateful and dug in like a starving man.

The kahuna watched with approval as I gobbled the food and took seconds. "I'm glad your appetite has returned."

Talking with my mouth full, I said, "I don't even care that you're feeding me Spam."

"You know it's a traditional Hawaiian delicacy. Are you feeling better, dear?"

I allowed as how I was, and thanked her for putting my head back together with her redaction. A day after Denis's death, I was able to mourn him without falling to pieces, even though I still hadn't completely come to terms with the reality of what I had done.

I had egged to Kauai on auto-Vee almost as soon as I was rescued from the top of Mount Washington by the AMC, only stopping in Hanover long enough to give Denis's ashes to Lucille and ask her to take care of Marcel for a while. She told me she had known instantly when her husband died. Philip, Maurice, Anne, and the convalescent Paul, the only members of the Dynasty on Earth at the time, had also mentally experienced their father's demise. They were with Lucille now, comforting her and one another. None of them had asked for specifics of Denis's death and I volunteered nothing. It was enough for them to know that he was finally at peace.

I had decided to tell only one other person about Denis/Fury's end on Mount Washington. Jack had to know the truth.

Or most of it.

After supper I borrowed Malama's old Isuzu 4X4 and drove to Lawai Kai, which was only a few kilometers away. Jack had been in residence there for a couple of months. According to Malama, he was working on some important scientific project.

He had cancelled the mechanical security measures around his estate in anticipation of my arrival, and I drove around to the back of the plantation house and parked among the palm trees. He came out to meet me. After I climbed out of the truck we held one another in a wordless embrace. He'd felt Denis's release, too—although, like the others, he had no idea where or how his grandfather had died.

He said, "Let's take a walk down to the shore, and you can tell me about it."

We followed the winding path along the lagoons and finally came out in the picturesque cove where Queen Emma's house had once stood. We sat down side by side on the sand. There was no moon and the surf was gentle. Noctilucent plankton in the water edged each breaking wave with faintly green-glowing foam.

I told him almost everything. Some instinct told me to leave out Fury's mysterious remarks about the eventual renascence of Hydra in Mental Man.

When I finished the story, Jack said, "And Denis told you to give me the Great Carbuncle?"

I pulled the key ring out of my pants pocket and held it out to him. There was a microscopic crimson spark in the nucleus of the spherical fob. "That's what he said. No reason given."

Jack detached the caged red gem and gave the keys back to me. He studied the fob intently for a considerable length of time, I presume scanning it with his deepsight. I'd looked into it that way myself from time to time. There was certainly something inside that supposedly flawless diamond, but I'm jiggered if I could ever figure out what it was.

Jack said, "What can you tell me about this thing?"

"It's got something to do with the Lylmik. I think it calls them, summons their help. At least, that's what the Carbuncle seems to've done for me. You can believe it or not. I don't give a good goddam."

"I believe it." He climbed to his feet and slapped the sand off his blue jeans. "I'll take good care of this and give it back to you just as soon as I can. Now I think we'd better get back to the house. I'm going to have to put in a subspace call to Orb alerting Davy MacGregor to a farshout. He's got to know about Fury and Hydra's death. Don't worry. I'll pledge him to secrecy. As far as the Milieu at large is concerned, Fury was an unknown who assumed various identities."

"You gonna call Marc, too?"

"No," Jack said. "I'm going to Okanagon and talk to him in person. I haven't decided whether to tell Marc that Denis was Fury. It might give him a significant propaganda weapon to use against the Dynasty."

"I'll keep mum if you want me to," I said, "and to hell with being loyal to the Rebellion. Family comes first. The fewer people who know about Denis, the better. Just tell Marc that Fury came rarin' after me, and I zorched the bastard. He'll believe I've got the watts, after the way I blew Parni away. Better yet, let me come with you and I'll spin him a plausible yarn myself. I've got another reason for tagging along besides. There's something really important I have to say to Cyndia."

Jack considered my suggestion. "I'll be going at maximum displacement factor, but I suppose I could put you into oblivion stasis."

I gave a little fakey chuckle. "Oblivion sounds like the perfect place for me right about now. Let's get going."

The cosmopolitan planets tend to be less tourist-oriented than the ethnic worlds, and a lot less picturesque. Most of them have large, bustling populations that seem excessively eager to terraform the exotic landscape and ecology into a faithful approximation of Home Sweet Home. In cosmop cities especially, a visitor is likely to get the impression that he's in bland old Cleveland or Manchester or Osaka or Volgograd, rather than on an exotic world umpteen lightyears from Earth.

When I first visited Okanagon a number of years ago, I got a pleasant surprise. It was gorgeous.

Except for the great plateau where the Twelfth Fleet had its starbase, the enormous, mostly equatorial continent of the planet was ribbed with spectacular snow-crested mountains. The inhabited regions were along the deeply indented coast and in broad river valleys that can best be described as temperate jungles, verdant and lush with flowers. The cultivated land had soil so fertile that wooden fenceposts proverbially sprouted when they were stuck into it, blessing Okanagon with an unending series of bumper crops. The rampant vegetation also made the massive earthquake scars unobtrusive except in the higher elevations, where quiescent lava flows, landslides, and raw precipices betrayed severe seismic activity. I would never have noticed the peculiar courses of the rivers, which had right-angle displacements to their courses along the more active fault lines, if Jack had not pointed them out to me as we flew over them in his private starship, XSS Scurra II.

Because Scurra was so small and Jack a notably privileged VIP, we didn't have to land at a starport, but proceeded directly to Marc and Cyndia's home, which was situated on the Osoyoos River about 400 kloms from Chelan, the planetary capital.

We arrived late in the afternoon, just after a shower had freshened the air. The house was a large contemporary structure with open verandas and extensive gardens. I found out later that the CEREM complex was within easy groundcar driving distance in the mountains nearby, with the more critical installations buried in a stable rock formation.

We came in under rhopower. No overt security measures or domestic NAVCON challenged Scurra as we overflew the estate and landed on a pad beside the tennis court. Our welcome could not have been more conventional. Marc's longtime nonoperant houseman, Thierry Lachine, opened the front door to us with a hearty "Bonjour." Both Jack and I had met him many times before when visiting Marc's former home in the San Juan Islands, and we made small talk as we followed him through cool corridors with ochre-tiled floors and dark green wood paneling, sparsely hung with abstract paintings. The starkness of the decor was slightly relieved by an occasional large ceramic planter, full of tall foliage plants having greenish-copper leaves. Somebody, undoubtedly young Hagen, had been digging in one of the pots with a small shovel of yellow plass that lay in a scattering of dirt on the polished floor. Thierry laughed and ignored the mess. One of the tidybots would come along and deal with it eventually, he said.

"Do you like living on Okanagon?" I asked him.

"I miss the nightlife in Seattle," he admitted. "Chelan Metro isn't exactly a toddlin' town and they've never heard of ice hockey hereabouts. But I can't complain too much. Triple salary helps."

"Have you been bothered by earthquakes?" Jack asked.

"We do have the occasional tremblement de terre, for sure. And some of them are whoppers. But the house is stabilized by inertialess force-fields, just like CEREM and the important government buildings, so I guess we're safe enough. Me, I don't pay much attention to 'em . . . This way, please. Madame's in her atelier."

We went outside, across a beautiful patio with a great view of the river and into a small building connected to the garages by a breezeway. I expected we'd find Cyndia puttering in a glorified garden shed, but "Madame's atelier" turned out to be an elaborately equipped workshop that any professional nanoengineer would have been proud to call his or her own. When we came inside she had on virtual gloves and a visor and was tinkering with something microscopic through the proxy of a pair of slave manipulators.

"Knock, knock, Cyndia!" said Thierry brightly. "Visitors." And he left us.

Cyndia said "Explicit" into the command-mike, stripped off headpiece and gloves, and literally flung herself into my arms. "I'm so glad you came! So very, very glad." Then she kissed me. Her greeting to Jack was more subdued but still sincere.

We'd given Cyndia and Marc no advance warning that we were on our way to Okanagon. Jack was afraid that his brother might try to avoid the meeting by skipping offworld. When our starship came through the superficies into normal space in the Nespelem solar system, Jack tried to farspeak Marc with no success. He did reach Cyndia, however. She told us that Marc was working at CEREM (fortified by the usual gonzo sigma-fields) and she would tell him we were on our way to the house. She had been sure he would be happy to see both of us.

Wrongo.

"I'm sorry," she confessed, her lovely face flushed with mortification. "Marc refuses to come to the house and meet you. He said he'd see you at CEREM, Jack, if you felt you had to speak with him. He's been . . . moody for the past week or so."

I muttered something snide in Canuckois but Jack seemed perfectly amicable. "It's all right. I'll go to him. I know Rogi's anxious to talk privately with you."

She was palpably relieved. "Do you know where the CEREM facility is?"

"I'll find it," said Jack the Bodiless confidently. And he left the two of us alone.

I pulled up a stool. Cyndia's gaze slid away from mine and she toyed with one of the virtual gloves on her workbench. Silence grew.

Finally, I said, "What are you making?"

She started as if I'd administered an electric shock. "Nothing! I mean
. . . nothing special. A sonic implant. To play music."

"Don't fancy those dinguses myself," said I. "Gimme old-fashioned
headphones—or better yet, full-spectrum wraparound stereo in my living room, with a faux fire burning in the old stove and a nice glass of
sippin' whiskey to hand. More human way to go."

She stared at me in mute misery, shaking her head slowly. Tears
welled in her lovely dark-lashed eyes.

"It's over," I told her gently. "The Fury monster's dead, along with
the poor soul who harbored it. And so are all its Hydra-children. Would
you like me to tell you the whole story—so far as I know it?"

"Yes. Please." She opened a workbench drawer, took out a tissue,
and wiped her face.

I talked for over an hour. She didn't interrupt, except one time when
she fetched us some ice water from a dispenser on the wall. When I got
to my final confrontation with Fury on the mountain, I told her what I
had withheld from Jack.

"Fury told me that all of the Hydra-children were dead. Not just the
five originals, but what he said were *New Ones*. It went right past me at
the time, but I pulled it out of my memorecall later, all right. Along with
what Fury said next. He told me: 'There will be a great rebirth. As Mental Man is reborn, as I myself was reborn, so will my own children be.'
I don't know what he was driving at. Do you, Cyndia?"

"Yes." She had picked up the virtual visor and turned it over and
over in her hands, staring blindly at it. "Marc didn't surrender all of the
Mental Man embryos to the Krondak agents of the Magistratum. He
kept over a hundred that had assayed as operant paramount. I spirited
them away myself, to a secret gestatorium Shig Morita and Peter
Dalembert built beneath the Orcas Island house. I helped nurture
those babies to term, Rogi. Mental Man became a reality."

"Bon sang!" I murmured.

"Later we brought the children with us to Okanagon and hid them
in the new CEREM facility. Marc planned to outfit them with 600X CE
and use them in some overwhelming demonstration—some coup that
would persuade the Milieu to let humanity go. I don't know exactly
what he planned to do. A large group of Rebel specialists came to
Okanagon recently in connection with the project. New equipment and
metaconcert programs were designed for this demonstration and Marc

was very excited about it. You see, the babies' brains developed much faster than had been originally anticipated. And then . . . and then . . .'"

"Denis showed up," I prompted.

"Somehow, Denis was able to penetrate the cosmic-class security of CEREM. He killed every one of the babies. Electrocuted them. I was there just afterward and he talked to me, admitted it. He told me the children were Hydras, psychic vampires. The Madeleine Hydra had done it as part of some mad scheme to found a Second Milieu and dominate humanity. After telling me all this, Denis somehow disappeared without a trace. For—for reasons of my own, I never told Marc about any of this."

"Denis was able to teleport," I told her. "Generate an upsilon-field with his mind. He was an uncertified paramount metapsychic whose powers eventually emerged from semi-latency. But what did Denis mean about Hydra being reborn in Mental Man? If both Fury and the Madeleine Hydra are dead, that seems impossible."

"All I know is that Marc intends to begin the project again. And this time, its purpose has nothing to do with the Rebellion. It's too late to engender the babies for that. I—I think Marc wants Mental Man for His own sake *even though he knows the project is wrong wrong wrong immoral obscene!*"

Her last words were an unexpected despairing scream that hit me like a physical blow. I leapt to my feet. She turned away, weeping helplessly, her small fists pounding the workbench again and again until I took hold of her arms to keep her from injuring herself. She writhed in my grasp, a thing in torment, her mindscreen concealing the precise meaning of what she had said. I never knew the full extent of the Mental Man horror until the adult Hagen and Cloud told me about it years later in Hawaii. Neither did most of the Galactic Milieu . . .

Almost as though some emotional switch had been thrown, Cyndia suddenly relaxed. Her sobbing ceased and she extricated herself from my embrace. We stood facing one another.

"I'm all right now," she insisted. "I'm sorry I lost control."

"Cyndia, for God's sake! Tell me what Denis meant!"

She shook her head, blew her nose, and wiped her face with more Kleenex. "I'm the only one who can deal with it. It needn't concern you, Rogi. I—I must ask you to promise not to tell anyone else about this. Especially Jack."

"Are you out of your mind?" I yelled. "Marc intends to resurrect

Mental Man, and Denis tells us they'll be Hydras! We've got to tell Jack and Dorothée and Davy MacGregor and the Galactic Magistratum and the whole goddam Lylmik Quincunx! We've got to warn your father and the Rebel Council that Marc's gone off his rocker—"

"Listen to me!" she said, exerting all her coercion. "You misunderstood Denis when he spoke of Mental Man as a reborn Hydra. He was speaking metaphorically, not literally. Mental Man is a danger *in Himself*—not as a true Hydra. I came to that realization some time ago, after an agony of soul-searching. There are things about the Mental Man project that I haven't told you. That I don't intend to tell you! Just believe me when I say that I'll put a stop to it. There will be no more Mental children. I can deal with this situation. I'm the only one who can."

"Damn cocksure of yourself, aren't you?" I shot back. "So all-fired certain you can make Marc change his mind! Well, I've known him a helluva lot longer than you have, and I think he'll do exactly as he damn pleases. You want to know what else Denis told me? He said that he and Marc were the most dangerous men ever born! He warned me that Marc might do something awful to Hagen. To his own son."

The blood drained from her face. "I knew it."

"What did Denis mean?" I demanded.

"It doesn't matter." She turned her back on me. "I'll see that nothing happens to Hagen or Cloud. And I'll put an end to Mental Man. But you mustn't interfere, Rogi. Or let Jack or the others know. They can't stop Marc. Only I can."

"If you're wrong," I said grimly, "God knows what'll happen."

She spun about. Her tear-grimed face was stubborn. "I know my husband. I understand his obsession and I know how to defuse it. I love Marc. I can do this, Rogi. You must believe me."

I couldn't take any more. Heading for the door, I said, "Have it your way, then, and the hell with you! I'm outa here. I'll wait on the front stoop for Ti-Jean."

"You won't say anything to him?" she pleaded.

I made a dismissive gesture. "No. What can I tell him that'd make any sense? But I swear to God, if Marc's determined to bring back Mental Man, you'll never persuade him otherwise."

"Persuasion," said Cyndia Muldowney, "was not quite what I had in mind."

. . .

I went stomping back through the house, fuming with rage, and on the way I met the nanny, Mitsuko Hayakawa, with the kids. Hagen was just shy of his second birthday, towing a little wagon with a Steiff dinosaur for a passenger, and Cloud was still a babe in arms, nearly six months old. I stopped for a minute and tried to be sociable, but bad vibes blanketed me in an invisible miasma and the poor children didn't want to have anything to do with me.

I wouldn't see them again until nearly thirty-one years later, when they returned from the Pliocene Epoch through the time-gate, finally escaping the fate that their father had planned for them.

Jack came back nearly three hours later, after Thierry took pity on me and gave me something to eat. Ti-Jean was as serene as ever, but he did tell me that the meeting with Marc had gone badly. I didn't have the heart to press him for details. Although Jack never said anything to me about it, I think Marc must have told him the truth about Mental Man—perhaps in some attempt to win approval for the scheme. All I know for certain is that from that day on, the brothers were adversaries, not friends, and their antagonism would not be resolved until the culmination of the Metapsychic Rebellion that was rapidly approaching.

29

SECTOR 12: STAR 12-340-001 [NESPELEM]
PLANET 7 [DIOBSUD]
PLANET 2 [OKANAGON]
16–17 SHUKSAN
[31 DECEMBER–1 JANUARY] 2082–2083

He had been napping in his cabin on the PSS Vulpecula, conserving his strength, when Owen Blanchard's powerful coercion woke him.

Marc. The fleet's in co-orbital position.

Thanks Owen. Please alert the other ops and tell them to proceed to their CE bays and invest.

You're not coming to the bridge to address them yourself?

I think not. This exercise will either work or it won't work. There's nothing to be gained by a pep talk. What's the final estimate of our window of opportunity?

Four-pip-zero-two-one minutes. You've got exactly two hours until occultation per your sked.

Mock planetesimal in orbit?

Shining like the Moon over Miami and traveling like a bat out of hell. It'll simulate a very plausible satellite-smasher to our tame stargazers back on Okanagon if they do a proper enhancer hack-job.

Excellent. Let's hope they don't have to simulate a near miss! Well I'm on my way . . .

Marc broke mental contact with Blanchard, donned the monitor-studded black coverall with its neck-ring seal, went to the personnel conveyor, and hit the s-BAY pad with his PK. He had been sleeping in the captain's cabin of the Vulpecula on its brief billion-klom voyage from Okanagon, and so his ride was solitary.

When the door whisked open he stepped out into what had once been the starship's shuttlecraft bay. The three spaceboats normally carried by a Twelfth Fleet cruiser of the Vulpecula class were absent and the entire compartment was now dedicated to ten 600X CE enhancers, their auxiliary equipment, and their bulky power supply. The chamber was also newly lined with refractory cerametal and capable of being enveloped in an SR-80 sigma-field that would safely contain a small thermonuclear device. In the event that the CE exercise went awry and the operators destroyed themselves, the Vulpecula and its crew had a fair chance of survival.

Waiting for Marc were the nine people who shared prime focus for the psychocreative metaconcert: Alex Manion, Dierdre and Diarmid Keogh, Hiroshi Kodama, Patricia Castellane, Helayne Strangford, and Adrien, Catherine, and Severin Remillard. Marc wasted no time greeting them, but projected into their minds a farsensory image of what lay outside the starship:

The planet Diobsud, largest gas-giant in the Nespelem solar system, was seventh from the sun (Okanagon being second) and slightly smaller than the Old World system's Jupiter. Marc's mental image showed the world half-lit. Its cloud bands were white, pale yellow, and dusty chocolate-brown, a drab contrast to Jupiter's turbulent atmosphere, and its rings were tenuous and unspectacular. As if to make up for these esthetic deficiencies, Diobsud had an extensive collection of satellites. Five of them, including Satellite XV, which now loomed less than 300,000 kilometers away from the PSS Vulpecula and the 155 other commandeered Fleet vessels that comprised the little Rebel armada, were relatively huge—between 9,000 and 11,000 kilometers in diameter, very nearly the size of Okanagon.

Satellite XV, newly named Cible by Marc himself in ironic celebration of the occasion, had been chosen for the critical exercise because of its near-terrestrial density and its favorable position in orbit. To the mind's eye, it was a relatively featureless peach-tinted sphere, presently half-lit like its primary, clothed with a smoggy atmosphere that hid the mostly ice-covered surface. In about two hours, the bulk of Diobsud would shield Cible from the view of anyone in the vicinity of Okanagon. The eclipse would last slightly longer than four minutes, during which time the metaconcert would do its work.

The moon's new name was French for "target."

"The subterfuge measures are in place," Marc told his companions. "If all goes well, the mock planetesimal made of inflated Ronlar will seem to have impacted Cible during its eclipse by Diobsud. At least two local astronomers on Okanagon—good Rebels, needless to say!—are recording optical observations of the planet and its satellites, supposedly for orbital perturbation studies. A small sneetch of the computer-enhancement program should insure that the disruption appears to be a regrettable but normal occurance." He paused. "Are there any questions?"

The nine looked at him, saying nothing. Then Severin Remillard lifted a languid, black-gloved hand. "If this stunt comes off, will we be able to see poor old Cible blow? It's not every day you get to wreck a world."

"My farsight will remain in peripheral mode, non-enhanced," Marc said rather coldly. "If you like, I'll cancel the symbolic iconography of the metaconcert at the critical moment so that we all have a real visual-ization of the event."

"I think I do prefer," said Severin, "but just this once, mind you. Later on, when we get serious, I'd just as soon stick with the nice clean icons." After a beat, he bespoke a deliberate addition: It might help minimize the guilt.

Adrien said, "Oh, for Christ's sake, Sevvy!"

His elder brother only smiled.

Hiroshi Kodama said, "I recommend that from this point forward, we think only of our strategic objective—the freedom of the human race. Whatever personal misgivings we have must not be allowed to di-vert us from the goal we have all agreed to pursue."

"Nice speech," said Severin.

"You may withdraw from the metaconcert if you prefer," Marc said, his mind-tone scrupulously neutral. "Olivia Wiley is standing ready as backup."

"No. I'll pull my weight this time—and when the chips are down, too, God help me." Severin spun about and marched toward the row of gaping black full-body rigs that stood on the other side of the bay.

Marc said, "Let's invest."

In the beginning was the double constellation.

The larger one was a beehive swarm of one thousand five hundred and fifty stars, most of them green, varying in hue and magnitude, softly humming a myriad of quasi-musical notes. The smaller grouping was a circle of nine white sparks that maintained a figurative silence. A single blue-haloed individual hovered at the circle's center.

The target was still invisible in the symbolic realization. Until the metaconcert was established, Cible was irrelevant.

The Conductor began. His song was a nearly inaudible basso drone at the start, the tempo irregular. As the volume intensified, so did the azure radiance of his corona. Subtle filaments of gold, reaching forth in two dimensions, linked the other nine minds of the focusing team into a starry wheel. It began to turn and a rhythmic triadic song commenced, a simple canon creating a biconvex lens that slowly acquired concentric internal rings, rippling and fluctuating. The executive song's tempo was andante, deliberate. Only when the song was well established and the lenticular rings clear and rainbow-bright did the beehive of subsidiary grandmaster minds begin to assume a structure and musicality of its own.

The Conductor orchestrated the generator edifice patiently, as he had done during the tedious practice sessions back on Okanagon that had consumed the previous six weeks. Over half of these energy-source metaconcert members were highly experienced E18 geophysical specialists who had needed only to familiarize themselves with the new full-body equipment. To these Grand Masters, the 600X cerebroenergetic enhancer was an exhilarating step-up, a sophisticated mind-tool that freed them from the physical constraints they had labored under earlier. They now had a metaphorical starship to ride in, where before they had been confined to mundane mental vehicles restricted, as it were, to solid ground. Their song was a meld of soaring horn-calls, still pianissimo in volume. The framework of mental energies that these virtuosi built was topographically complex, residing in six dimensions. Its colors were those of high-level creativity: vivid emerald, aquamarine, and limpid tourmaline-blue.

The CE novices were incorporated last by the Conductor, shepherded into place, reassured, conjoined one by one. The role of these minds in the metaconcert generator would be largely passive. They would contribute vital energies to the fabric of the great structure, and sing with voices as filling and implicit as those of massed strings and sustained winds. Most of the subsidiary Grand Masters were creators, glowing a duller green than their more experienced colleagues; but there were knots of other colors as well—redactive scarlet, coercive sapphire, the sun-gold warmth of the psychokinetics, the violet stability of grandmasterly farsensors. The whole constellation was harmonious and symphonic.

The Conductor surveyed the finality of the generator, making minute adjustments to timbre and pitch. Then he introduced the target.

It was a torus, a kind of transparent donut-shape enclosing a madly swirling number of small smoky spheres, each with a dot of dull garnet smoldering in its heart. The Cible icon was both chaotic and resistant, symbolizing the relatively tiny, dense metallic core of the moon that would have to undergo a critical transformation in order to bring about the demolition of the stony outer envelope.

Diobsud occulted Cible and the window of opportunity opened.

The Conductor commanded the generator energies to cohere, to amplify, to emerge. The song of the metaconcert was a choral thrust. A shaft of white light spurted out of the large structure, passed through the lens, and impaled the torus along its horizontal axis.

Immediately the bounding spherules froze.

The Conductor modified the lens, narrowing and intensifying the beam. One by one, the spherules seemed to migrate to the poles of penetration, melting together, expanding to fill the opposing sections, their glowing hearts merging and brightening in stately ascending harmony. At the finale the confining torus dissolved and there were twinned red flares like beads on a brilliant needle. The metaconcert roared to a crescendo.

The red flares coalesced into a singularity. At its center a writhing spider of white flame bloomed and died in a thunderous detonation. The symbolic image disappeared. The metaconcert withdrew and there was silence. What would happen next was beyond its control. The disruption of the lunar core had begun.

Marc showed his colleagues the real Cible, a darkened sphere faintly salmon in color, illuminated by starlight. It was apparently unchanged. A tiny body, the mock planetesimal, streaked toward it on an oblique impact trajectory and vanished without a trace into the satellite's atmosphere.

Cible emerged from Diobsud's shadow into sunlight again.

Abruptly, the moon seemed to inflate, like a being catching a last painful breath. Auroral rays sprang briefly from its poles. Shock waves of gas ionization sped toward the equatorial region, the yellow of nitrogen and the pale red and steel-blue of argon, blotched with monstrous bolts of static electricity. The waves collided and expanding rings of plasma burst into being, giving Cible the aspect of a miniature Saturn. As the gases attenuated, the watchers saw the satellite's thick rind of surface ice shatter crazily. But the enormous fractures were visible only for an instant before dazzling white steam boiled up, momentarily creating a new atmosphere. It thinned almost immediately, driven into space by the devastating heat generated by the modified core.

Now the metaconcert saw the rupturing lithosphere, cracks hundreds of kilometers in width that glowed with red and gold pulsations on Cible's night quadrant, intricate movements traced by clashing seismic waves that caused the crust to ripple and shimmer. Glowing flecks, thrown outward like sparks from a bonfire, were in reality immense gouts of molten magma—some having enough momentum to achieve orbital velocity and batter the gaseous ring of the devastated little world.

Marc said: *EXPLICIT.*

It was finished. The mind-image of Cible disappeared.

The metaconcert disbanded. Its shaken orchestral participants emerged from their black shells and gathered in small silent groups in their respective CE bays, studying the aftermath now with their own farsenses. The 156 starships of the Rebel fleet were far enough from the event to be unscathed, but Class 2 meteoroid screens were erected as a precautionary measure until the time of departure.

Cible did not perish utterly. It was too massive to disintegrate. Most of its atmosphere was gone, however, along with nearly all of its water. Over the next five hours, long after most of the weary metaconcert members had sunk into stuporous slumber during the journey back to Okanagon, the wounded satellite continued to cool and subside. Smoking ridges like far-flung webs of thick scar tissue gradually covered the crustal fractures. In a few places, upwellings of thinner magma spread out to form maria, oceans of stone that were smooth at first, then increasingly pocked with small craters as suborbital debris fell back to the surface. The new volcanoes would continue to pulse fitfully for years, sending up umbrella-shaped clouds of ash that would gradually bury the lunar surface beneath a powdery regolith.

Cible had been lifeless before and it was lifeless still, a celestial body inconsequential except to a handful of local astronomers and the CE operators who had used it as a practice target.

She had sent Thierry and Mitsuko and the children to a hotel in Chelan Metro for the night, and when Marc returned from the Sector Base she met him at the front door of the deserted house, dressed in a gown and negligé of cherry silk.

"Was it successful, Marcas?" Cyndia asked, drawing his head down to lightly kiss his mouth. But she knew the answer already from his tight smile and the emanation of fatigued satisfaction that seeped from beneath his carelessly crafted mindscreen.

"We achieved the objective. The seven hundred novice Grand Masters formed an adequate subrogate structure in the creativity generator. Their energy output was inferior to what Mental Man's would have been, but the cobble worked. We'll be able to do the demonstration if it proves necessary. Beyond that, it's anyone's guess." He pulled away from her embrace, shaking his head. His burning gray eyes were deep-sunken and there was a hectic flush on his cheekbones. He had not bothered to shower off the dermal lavage from the CE rig. The lightweight athletic suit that he wore was stained with sweat and pungent chemicals.

"Come and have a hot soak," she urged. "Are you hungry?"

"No. Only dying of thirst, filthy . . . and unaccountably horny."

Her laugh was light and nervous. "I have some Veuve Clicquot waiting for us in the bedroom. Back on the Old World, it's almost midnight on New Year's Eve in the San Juan Islands. I thought we could have two celebrations at once."

"Mmm. New Year, 2083. I'd completely forgotten." His thoughts were still on the metaconcert exercise and he shook his head abstractedly, allowing her to lead him toward their rooms. The main corridor of the house with its tall ceiling and massive planter-urns was dimly lit, silent and full of shadows.

"I'm glad we're alone here tonight," he said.

"I thought it would be for the best . . . not knowing how the Cible exercise would work out."

She opened the door to their bathroom. It simulated a natural grotto with three shallow terraces, carved from lustrous olivine shot through with rich veins of milky quartz and gold. At the top were dressing rooms and toilet cubicles, luxuriously appointed. Carved cabinets and shelves of precious woods held cosmetics, perfumes, thick towels on warming bars, machines for hairstyling, manicure, pedicure, and massage. A new Armani-Vestiarista Moduplex stood ready to dispense underwear and casual clothing on command. It would also polish footgear and freshen up more substantial garments in its dry-cleaning armoire.

On the level below was the sunken spa, carved from a single block of jadeite three meters in diameter. It was fed by a steaming cascade that splashed down a tumbled course of backlit amethyst boulders. Beside the tub, exotic foliage plants and vines with pendant golden flowers framed an open shower niche with multiple sprayheads where shampoos, body emollients, and shave-lotions could be programmed vocally.

At the lowest level was a great swimming pool banked with full-grown trees and ornamental shrubbery. Half of its 30-meter length was indoors and the rest, divided above and underwater by a tall slab of one-way, matter-impermeate glass, extended into the gardens outside.

Marc strode to the refreshment bar, called for a liter of orange juice, and tossed it down his throat. "God! That's better."

He stripped off his clothing, nudged the soiled garments into the floor hopper with his PK, stepped into the shower, and nearly disappeared in a froth of cleansing bubbles.

When he emerged he said to Cyndia, "Join me in the tub?"

But she shook her head. "I'll sit here with you while you soak." She pulled up a brass bench with a green repelvel cushion.

He submerged completely in the steaming water, then came up, activated the Jacuzzi jets, and relaxed with a sigh of contentment, closing his eyes.

"Was it very difficult?" she asked.

"The hardest thing I've ever attempted. I feel as though I've been stomped by a herd of buffalo—inside and outside."

She got up, fetched a large glass of steaming amber liquid from the bar, and put it into his hand. "It's a bullshot, spiked with vitamins. If you won't eat, at least have that."

He shrugged and sipped the alcoholic broth slowly, letting the swirling water and his own self-redaction soothe away the worst of the nervous tension.

She waited in silence as he seemed to doze. Then: "May I see what happened to the satellite?"

"If you like." He sent a compact précis of the event into her waiting mind, not noticing when she uttered a low cry of dismay. "The exercise worked well enough, but Alex says that no amount of fine-tuning the revised program will give this configuration more efficiency than what we achieved today. I'll have to do an entirely new design."

"The energy output seemed . . . devastating enough to me."

"With Mental Man, we would have had far more flexibility. Only five starships would have been needed in the operation instead of a hundred and fifty-six. And we could have split the metaconcert energies—even utilized more than one focus if we'd wanted to. Blown Cible to smithereens in a tenth of the time by negating its gravity rather than simply tinkering with its material core. Without paramount minds in the generator we're effectively limited to the more elementary modes of creative metamorphosis. However, a new design will enable us to up the gross energy output another twenty or thirty percent by plugging in a few hundred more 600X operators who are still in training, plus an auxiliary superstructure of E18 helmet ops. But the gain will be partially offset by decreased legerity in the executive focus."

"I'm sorry," she confessed. "I don't understand."

He sighed, opened his eyes, and climbed out of the tub. "We'll be stronger, but slower and clumsier." He showed her another image as he descended to the big swimming pool and dove in.

Stroking underwater, he said: Originally, I had hoped we'd be able to conduct decisive hit-and-run operations, popping in and out of hyperspace without the Milieu being able to nail us. But if the concert takes longer to set up and execute, we'll have to pick our strategic objectives very carefully and also take steps to defend the fleet of starships carrying the CE operators during the action. To this end, I've ordered the Astrakhanian ships to take on full crews and proceed to a hyperspatial rendezvous consonant with Molakar support."

"Molakar?" Her face fell in dismay. "I thought . . ."

He said: Cordelia and her staff of analysts are running a new set of simulations. They should be ready in time for the Concilium session so we'll know exactly what our options are. But the likeliest now is the Molakar demonstration.

"The Milieu might still capitulate peacefully to your ultimatum." She had come down to poolside with a robe of white terrycloth for him.

He climbed out, pressing the water from his thick curling hair with one big hand, and put on the robe. "I doubt that the exotic magnates would succumb to my coercive wiles this time, darling. They'd think I was bluffing. It seems inconceivable to the exotics—especially to the damned Lylmik!—that a human leader with paramount mindpowers would attempt anything but an intellectual solution to a grievance. They've never understood human nature. Our craven acceptance of the Simbiari Proctorship lulled the Milieu into thinking that we'd accept despotism if the trade-off was peace in a galactic civilization. They can't believe we'd be willing to risk losing that. The only way we can convince them otherwise is to demonstrate a willingness to destroy them unless they agree to let us go."

"Molakar," she whispered. "Ah, Marcas, Marcas! You've intended it all along."

"It was always the most effective option." He started up the steps to the dressing room.

"You might consider one other," she said very softly, following after. "Try appealing to Davy MacGregor when he assumes the position of First Magnate at the Concilium session."

Marc frowned. He toweled his hair damp-dry, then stuck his head momentarily into the styler. "Just what are you suggesting?"

"Davy isn't as stiff-necked as your father was. His own long-standing doubts about Unity are well publicized, and his years as Earth Dirigent have given him a more tolerant mindset. If you could make him understand how determined and well armed the Rebellion has become—if Davy realized just how close to the brink of war the galaxy is—he might try to broker a compromise. Especially since there's no longer any danger of Fury or the Hydra tainting the Rebellion with their own secret agenda. The controversy is a purely moral one now: a question of human liberty versus the intractable position of the Milieu on Unity. Perhaps a mutual concession is possible! Paul would never even consider it. Davy might."

"I doubt it." He went to the Moduplcn and ordered up a pair of black silk pajamas.

"Marcas a mhuirnín, dearest love, if there's any chance of avoiding violence—of sparing the lives of all those Krondaku on Molakar—you *must* make the try!"

His retort was icy. "It's my decision to make."

"Of course." She turned away, her vision blurring with tears.

He caught her arm. "Cyndia. It's necessary. Regrettable, but necessary. We really have only the single chance to shock the Milieu out of its self-righteous complacency—to prove that we're in deadly earnest and compel their surrender to our demands. Blowing up an uninhab-ited planetoid like Cible wouldn't have the same impact at all. We'd tip our hand uselessly, lose the psychological advantage. It would be dif-ferent if we could have destroyed a sun with mindpower . . ."

She faced him, composed again. "Might Mental Man have accom-plished that?"

"Perhaps. If there had been time for the children to mature. But my first choice for the demonstration has always been Molakar. The en-forcers' world. The Milieu's base for the sequestration of Earth. Do you know how many Krondak starships are gathered there now?"

She shook her head.

"Nearly four thousand. I've seen them myself through farsensory CE. And more of them arrive every day from remote sectors of the galaxy—a concentration of high-df vessels that hasn't been seen since the Great Intervention seventy years ago."

"Dia linn! Then the Milieu must suspect us."

"They'd be imbeciles if they didn't. But they've done nothing to stop us yet. I admit I don't know what to make of it."

"Talk to Davy MacGregor," she begged, taking both his hands in hers. "At least ask him if he'll try for a compromise. Promise me that much, mo mhuirnín dílis. Please!"

The powerful fingers tightened. Then he freed her with a small sigh. A peculiarly sweet smile lifted one side of his mouth. "Let's go to bed. I want to make love to you more than anything in the world."

"You *will* do it!" she cried joyously, and flung her arms about his neck. "Thank you, Marcas. Thank you."

He picked her up and carried her to the bedroom.

He had never asked her if she knew about their consanguinity.

At first, immediately after he'd dealt with Madeleine, he had feared that personal inhibition would taint their marital relations; but his desire for Cyndia remained as strong as ever. He had looked briefly into psychology and anthropology reference works, not trusting his own instinct, and discovered that the taboo was a social artifact, largely enforced by childhood conditioning. Sex with Madeleine had been repugnant and unthinkable because she was truly his sister. Cyndia—whatever her biological heritage—was simply not.

Their first coupling on the Earth New Year of 2083 was fierce and needful. He never surrendered, not even at the climax, and so she waited. The device was hidden deep within her pelvic cavity, harmless unless she deliberately activated its sophisticated mental switch. She had bench-tested it extensively, but there had been no way to insure its proper functioning at the kairotic moment. Only one thing was certain: He would feel no pain.

If she used it.

If there was no other choice.

They lay naked, side by side, drinking champagne, letting the erotic tension rebuild before beginning again. The bedroom was lit by sconces of candles, open to scented light air from the gardens. Firemoths blinked and sang softly in the ornamental shrubbery. Tiny seismic tremors, the sort that longtime citizens of Okanagon never even noticed, vibrated a sculpture on the patio outside and caused it to tinkle faintly.

"There's something I must ask you," she said. "About Mental Man."

"What is it?"

"I was surprised when you didn't reinitiate the project immediately after the disaster. So were Jeff and the Keoghs, especially since you said you intended to do so. Of course you revised the offensive metaconcert so that it would work with adult CE operators—but as you told me, the new configuration is much less efficient. Have you decided to abandon the Mental Man project after all?"

His mindscreen tightened. "The time factor is against us now. Still, if the Rebellion should be prolonged, a new generation of young paramounts might still be an important strategic asset. But I've been faced with a significant moral dilemma in connection with starting over. It's still unresolved."

"A . . . moral dilemma?" A sunburst of hope dazed her. Was it possible that he had actually reconsidered the hideous encephalization procedure that deprived the babies of their bodies? Did he finally realize what she had known for so long, that it was intrinsically evil to attempt the acceleration of human mental and bodily evolution, to engender Homo summus while fully incarnate Homo sapiens and Homo superior still lived?

Was it possible for her to spare him after all?

He lay on his back with one arm folded behind his head and the other holding her tenderly. The flickering candlelight danced on the clean planes of his face. He was so serene, so powerful, so very beautiful. Her favorite endearment for him in the Irish was ardaingeal ionúin—"beloved archangel"—a deliberate defiance of the dreadful nickname the loyalists had pinned on him.

She said, "Tell me about your problem, grá mo chroí. Perhaps I can help."

"After Mental Man died, I discovered that the ova used to conceive the children weren't those of my cousin Rosamund, as we'd all thought. They belonged to the Hydra. Madeleine. My sister."

Cyndia was deathly silent, willing hope not to die, guarding her own fearful thoughts.

"Maddy admitted it to me," Marc said. "She also admitted that she'd turned Mental Man into a new, hundred-headed Hydra."

"That's . . . appalling. Then the death of the babies was a miraculous escape for all of us!"

"So it would seem." His voice was grim. "I killed Maddy. It was both premeditated and just. All of the Hydras had been condemned in absentia by the First Magnate because of their earlier crimes, and there seemed no good reason for me to hand her over to the authorities. It would have tainted Mental Man beyond redemption in the public eye."

"And you couldn't risk that," Cyndia whispered.

"I destroyed Maddy's cerebrum but her body is still in cryogenic storage at CEREM. With a single ovary intact. The body is vegetative, but Jeff Steinbrenner is confident that regen-tank technology could replicate the germ plasm if we use external redactive input to augment the residue in the cerebellar network and the nervous system of the living body."

"So your great moral dilemma involves whether or not to use your Hydra sister's ova . . . not any intrinsic doubts about the project itself."

He seemed not to hear her. Still holding her close to him, he said, "Cyndia, I despise and abominate Madeleine. I hope she burns in hell when I finally let her die. The thought that that monster should be the in-vitro mother of Mental Man, even posthumously . . . is unbearable."

"And yet you saved her body."

"Out of sheer desperation," he admitted. "There is another way to engender Mental Man but I was afraid to tell you—afraid it might drive you away from me."

"Ah, m'aingeal. My poor, poor angel! So you *do* know!" She drew away slightly so that their eyes could meet, and spoke firmly. "And so do I. I know who my true father is."

"Cyndia——" His voice broke and his gaze fell.

"My father's name is Rory Muldowney. The biological accident between Paul Remillard and my mother was just that. It can make no difference between us, my love—neither to me nor to God in heaven, who sees love and not procreative technicalities. And if you wish me to be the mother of nonborn Mental Man, I'll do it."

His face lit in impassioned relief and both of his arms tightened about her. "You will! Chérie, how could I have doubted you?"

She held her breath, hardly daring to believe her deliverance. But then he said:

"Our Mental offspring will still have a serious latency factor, but that can be overcome by encephalization. Steinbrenner is certain of it. Even then, we can't be certain that every conceptus of ours will be paramount. But the geneticists assure me that there won't be a problem in the second generation."

Her calmness did not waver as the truth pierced her heart and hope perished. "You—you mean with Hagen and Cloud."

"Of course. Their in-vitro offspring will all be operant paramounts."

Of course . . . That's what he'd meant all along. If she had turned him down, and he couldn't bring himself to accept Madeleine as the mother, there were always their own true babies to be the parents of Mental Man.

Marc went on: "And afterward, when we've won the Rebellion and nothing stands in the way of Mental Man's triumph, Cloud and Hagen will still be young enough to achieve their own full mental potential, just as my brother did."

"Your brother . . ."

"I tried to explain it to him. To Jack, that is. I thought he'd see the beauty of it—the *rightness*. But he's a blind fool. Selfish. Locked into his own limited vision of Unified humanity. Not like you, my darling."

Hagen and Cloud would achieve their mental potential. He'd said it.

He kissed her closed eyelids, then her lips. She felt his arousal and knew that the time had come.

"Love me," Cyndia said, making the decision for herself and for Mental Man and Mental Woman. "I love you so very much." Her PK snuffed out the bedroom candles.

In time, he would recover. Her love would help.

She felt her body levitating with his, floating and turning in the warm air. He kissed her mouth, her throat, her breasts, would have continued if she had not taken hold of him and guided him into her, kindling her first orgasm. She cried out, clinging to him, laving and caressing him internally, wrapping him in vital energies wrung from the profound depths of her body and soul. She would have flamed again but she turned the neural energies back to him, magnified by love.

If it went as she hoped, he might never know it had happened. By the time the war was won (of course he would win!), she would have found a way to destroy Madeleine's body, to arrange for her own sterilization and that of the children. Marc's sister Marie would also take the appropriate steps once the necessity was explained to her. Then, even if Marc regained his fertility in the regen-tank, the nightmare of Mental Man would be over.

He caught fire and she heard his preorgasmic cry as he was carried helplessly forward to the culmination. Yes—this time he would relinquish himself in mutuality. Their bodies merged fully, joyously, paired on the summit, engulfed in a shared flood of stellar blue-white.

She willed it.

At the instant, she could not help visualizing the device. He farsaw it within their conjunction and knew what it was for.

Knew what she did, for love of him, killing Him.

There was no physical pain, only devastation of the soul. Marc convulsed. His scream shattered their rapport, froze the warm, liquid light to a heart-slashing blade of black ice.

WHATHAVEYOUDONEOGODWHATHAVEYOUDONE!

She said: Loved you. Always. I did it for love of you as well as for humanity.

His attack was reflexive, an involuntary striking back against an injury perceived as mortal. Paramount vital energies surged from his root to his crown, obliterating his ultrasenses. Psychokinesis failed and he fell from the air, a meteorite drowning in an arctic sea, hearing her repeat at the last: *I do love you.*

Then the abyss claimed him.

He woke at dawn. It had not been a dream.

Her body was there beside him, cold as his knowledge of betrayal, inert as disbelief, quite beautiful still. Her long hair spread in a perfect silken halo of pale gold. The sea-colored eyes were half-open, lusterless behind dark lashes. Her soft lips, parted, almost seemed to be smiling.

How could she? What was she thinking? Had the love always been a lie?

Of course not.

Then why? Why?

No overt genital trauma was perceptible to his ultrasensory deep-scan. But he was not a physician and the structures were minute and mysterious. A detailed diagnosis of what the sonic disruptor had done to him—and his healing—would have to wait.

Will I heal?

Certainly. Why not?

Ask her! Why did she do it? She's gone God gone HOWCOULDSHE-DOIT? She said for me and for humanity was she insane God no yes I did it gone gone dead all love all life dead you bitch you dearestlove you did it why why why?

In a daze, he drew the white satin sheet over her.

So easily gone the love the life the question WHY? What shall I do? There must be no inconvenient inquiry an accident a psychocreative accident an immense loving too intense to bear a tragic consummation Pat will see to it Pat will take care of everything.

He would send the children and the two servants back to the Old World at once. In a few days, all of the Rebel magnates—including he himself—would be leaving for Orb. If events at the Concilium session went as he expected, Okanagon would become the command center for the Rebellion. No one would have time to think about her.

No one but me. Oh Cyndia WHY? . . .

He looked down at his own body. He smelled her perfume, her sweet sexual musk. Her molecular vestiges clinging to his nakedness.

WHY?

An unfamiliar stinging pained his eyes as he left the bedroom and trudged to the shower. Surprised, he found that he was weeping and helpless to stop. Tears for himself, betrayed and humiliated. Tears for Mental Man.

Never tears for her.

He stood in the cleansing jets of water for over an hour, lathering himself over and over again. He removed the Claddagh wedding ring she had given him, stared briefly at its clasped hands and crowned heart, and then threw it into the recycler.

After dressing he flew his egg to CEREM, where he installed a farsensory brainboard in his 600X CE rig and shut himself into the black coffin. When his useless body was gone and his brain incandescent with power, he sent his mind ranging in excorporeal excursion to the uttermost limits of his enhanced ultrasenses, to the starless night beyond the Local Group of Galaxies.

He rested there in emptiness and silence.

30

SECTOR 15: STAR 15-000-001 [TELONIS]
PLANET 1 [CONCILIUM ORB]
GALACTIC YEAR: LA-PRIME 1-392-658
[7 FEBRUARY 2083]

David Somerled MacGregor, the newly elected First Magnate of the Human Polity, was astounded when Marc Remillard came up to him following the opening meeting of the Concilium and made the compromise proposal. After cornering the Scotsman in a quiet cul-de-sac of Orb's great Central Promenade, Marc spoke with swift intensity. At the same time his mind deliberately revealed a terrifying hint of how far the Rebellion was prepared to go to enforce its declaration of secession.

"Great God, man—this isn't something you should be discussing with me," Davy protested, his face gone white with shock. "Introduce it on the Concilium floor tomorrow or take it to the Panpolity Directorate for Human Affairs—"

"You're the First Magnate," Marc said, "the closest thing to a chief executive that the Human Polity has. Even before you were elected, you set yourself up as the prime apologist for Unity. So do your duty. If you believe in the Milieu and hope to save it, then transmit my compromise proposal to the Lylmik Supervisory Body immediately."

"Dammit, why don't you go to them yourself?"

"No. I'm through talking to the exotics." Marc's voice was portentously calm. "I'll make no more speeches in the Concilium and I certainly won't make a personal appeal to the Supervisors. The only reason I'm asking you to act as eleventh-hour intermediary is to fulfill a promise I made to Cyndia."

Davy's anger melted away in a sudden rush of pity for his antagonist. "I'm sorry for your loss," he said quietly. "Very sorry."

But Marc only nodded, refusing the other widower's unvoiced empathetic comfort. "Tell the Lylmik there'll be no more talk," he repeated. Then he walked away into the crowd of the Central Promenade.

Davy had never visited the Lylmik enclave before, although Paul Remillard had told him about his own experiences there. Emerging from the inertialess tube station into Syrel, the First Magnate found the misty garden of pallid crystalline growths discomforting. It was too tentative, too bloodless and vague—an overly apt metaphor for the ancient Galactic Overlords themselves, who had confessed to Paul that their race was moribund and that they looked to humanity to eventually take their place as the guiding force of the Milieu they had founded.

Alongside the path of rose-quartz flagstones that led to the audience building were beds of translucent flowerlike lifeforms and that seemed made of spun glass or even clouded diamonds. Vitreous groundcover sparkled with rainbow drops of dew. Fragile, opalescent trees swayed overhead in a languid breeze, their leaves chiming softly. But Davy MacGregor was in no mood to appreciate the scene of wan beauty. Recalling Paul's experiences in the enclave, he strode up to the large, featureless golden nugget that approximated a Lylmik house and declaimed: "I'm here!"

An oaken door with wrought iron hardware appeared miraculously in the blank wall. Davy opened it and stepped inside—but then stopped short in astonishment. Paul had led him to expect an unearthly interior within the nugget. Instead he found a room that was eerie in its familiarity, for all the world seeming an exact duplicate of the sitting room of his old fellow's chambers at the University of Edinburgh, where he had in auld lang syne been a Professor of Xenopsychology.

The place was dark-paneled, slightly shabby, and had a tiny fire burning in the grate. There were windows looking out on a night view of fog-fuzzed city lights, a cracked leather settee and two old frieze armchairs, a coffee table rather the worse for wear, an antique computer on a kneehole desk, shelves of plaques and paged books—even a ceramic umbrella stand holding two decrepit black brollies, a blackthorn cromach, and a bent toasting fork.

Sitting on the couch and in one of the chairs were two men and two women attired in Earth-style clothing sixty years out of date. Davy knew who they were. He'd met them at the Human Polity Inaugural Ball in 2052, when the race was finally admitted to conditional membership in the Galactic Milieu. Davy had actually danced with the one who wore the disguise of a lovely Oriental woman.

He took her outstretched hand as the Supervisors rose to greet him. "So nice to see you again after all these years, Miss Asymptotic Essence. I did follow your advice about reading the works of Teilhard de Chardin—and it helped me resolve my doubts about Unity." He nodded to the others—an African woman and two males of Caucasoid and Amerind appearance. "Noetic Concordance, Eupathic Impulse, Homologous Trend, how d'ye do. I presume you've pulled this nostalgic stage set from my memory bank to make me feel at ease. Thank you. I haven't thought of my days at university for years."

Trend nodded. "We are gratified. Please be seated, Davy. It's good that you have come to see us."

"But you're not surprised," the Scotsman said.

"Of course not," said Asymptotic Essence, "although one might have thought you would come to us earlier—following the deaths of Fury and the last Hydra."

Davy glowered. "You were right about that happening, too. It did me good to know Margaret's killers were brought to justice. Even if—" He broke off, shaking his head in disbelief. "Och, it's over and done, and God be thankit."

"May I offer you some sherry?" Concordance poured and handed him a small glass with a chipped rim. Davy had always meant to replace the dinged-up one of the original set that had belonged to his father, but he kept forgetting; and then he had been drafted into the contentious feery-fary of the European Intendancy and left the university forever.

"Under the circumstances," Impulse said, "we will not offer felicitations upon your election as First Magnate. Nevertheless, we are confident that you will fulfill the duties of the office nobly during the difficult days that are to come."

"So you know we're in for a tough haul, do you?" Davy drank a bit of wine and eyed the four Lylmik bleakly.

"We do," Impulse admitted. His mind projected: [Situational image] + [probability analysis].

"Exactly. I presume you also know about the ultimatum delivered to me by Marc Remillard after today's opening meeting of the Concilium. He called it a compromise proposal."

"Please tell us in your own way," Trend requested.

Davy put down the sherry with a heavy sigh. "I'd really prefer a dram of whisky to be gettin' on with, if it's not too much trouble."

"Certainly," said Noetic Concordance. The decanter and its appurtenances vanished and a stone crock of Bowmore 25 materialized, together with a carafe of water and five thistle-glasses. The Africaine poet served the spirits to everyone.

Davy held out for a double before summarizing what Marc had said to him. "Then he let me take a look into that fearsome mind of his— just for a nanosec, so I'd know he wasn't lying. And I found out that the damned widdifow has weaponry! Conventional sorts and metaconcerted CE, too. He warned me that he'll fight us if the Milieu won't allow at least the Rebel faction of humanity to carry on unUnified. It was his final offer and he said he'd brook no further discussion. In fact, he told me he'd not say another word in the Concilium."

"Did you perceive details of his munitions?" Impulse asked.

"No. But I believe he could do a monstrous mischief unless we cut him off at the knees instanter—or accede to his proposal."

"Your analysis is cogent," Essence said.

"What's to be done, then? Do we capitulate or stand up to his challenge?"

"The Quincunx is taking the matter under advisement," said Homologous Trend. His copper face seemed almost embarrassed.

Davy swept the Supervisory Body with an incredulous glare. His well-articulated Standard English transmogrified into a prickly Scots burr. "What! Do ye mean t' tell me ye'd let Marc piss in the Milieu's eye whilst you lot just sit here thinkin' serene and ineffable thoughts?"

"No," said Eupathic Impulse uncomfortably, "but you must understand that interfretting proleptic nodalities exist that must be pondered—"

"Ballocks!" Davy bellowed. "Is the fewkin' Milieu ready to cave in to Marc's threats or isn't it?"

"No," said Homologous Trend. "It isn't."

"Then give me leave to nab him and the other Reb magnates right here on Orb," Davy demanded. "I'll have the Magistratum toss 'em in maximum nick and throw away the soddin' key!"

Trend said, "That is not an option, although we four have pointedly recommended it. Unfortunately our leader, Atoning Unifex, has exercised summary veto, as is Its prerogative."

"Get your chief in here," Davy snapped insubordinately. "I'll give him a right piece o' my mind!"

"Unifex is on Earth," said Asymptotic Essence.

Eupathic Impulse gritted his big white teeth and his face turned choleric. "Shopping."

Speechless with outrage, Davy gaped at the Four.

Noetic Concordance hastened to say, "But an appeal would do you no good. In accordance with the Percruciate Progressive Principle set forth by Unifex Itself, Marc Remillard will be allowed to remain free, at least for the immediate future."

Davy leapt to his feet. "But why, for the love o' God? Don't you realize that the bastard won't scruple at destroying the Milieu? He could attack Orb itself!"

"We know," Noetic Concordance said. The poet's ebony countenance was suffused with melancholy.

"But he is unlikely to do so, given its inconvenient distance from his power base," Asymptotic Essence added.

"At least," Eupathic Impulse concluded grimly, "not this early in the game."

"So it's a game." Davy's black eyes glittered. "That's how you Lylmik think of it. Perhaps it's been that from the very start—from the Intervention!"

"No," said Noetic Concordance. "We love you. For sixty thousand Earth orbits the Milieu watched and waited, praying that your race would mature before destroying itself. Even now, as we are faced with impending catastrophe, we continue to hope and trust that the Cosmic All intends a great felicitous phase change, coadunating the Mind of Humanity through pain since you have resisted a more tranquil path to Unanimization."

"Your population has attained its coadunate number," said Homologous Trend, "and the first steps of the process have begun among your operant children. Two fortunate adult humans have also experienced Unity's inchoation, and from them the mental symmetry might spread exponentially—given appropriate affirmation by benevolent minds."

"Or coadunation could abort if conflict spreads throughout the Milieu," said Asymptotic Essence. "Even the other four races might find their steadfastness threatened. Unifex has said that Its prolepsis fails to perceive the dénouement of this situation, except to recognize its criticality."

"Great God!" Davy shouted. "Will ye stop your switherin' and tell me in plain words what I should *do*?"

"You must decide for yourself," said Eupathic Impulse. "You are the First Magnate of the Human Polity."

"Shall I arm the loyalist humans to defend the Milieu? Paul was considering it."

"What is your opinion?" Concordance asked.

Davy scowled. "My gut instinct is to do it—and for that reason I won't. My late father, Jamie MacGregor, faced the same kind of dilemma before the Intervention, at the Oslo Metapsychic Congress of 2012. The delegates debated whether it was ever justified for operant minds to defend their countries or themselves with mental and physical force. Jamie and Denis and many of their colleagues concluded that it was not, and vowed to adhere to the nonviolent principles espoused by Saint Urgyen Bhotia. They believed that there can be no lasting mental harmony if the racial mindset includes aggression—and so do I. They also believed that the Intervention came precisely because we did eschew a violent solution. I don't see how operant humanity can repudiate nonviolence now. You undoubtedly know that a majority of the human Magnates of the Concilium share my belief."

"We know," said the Four, smiling.

"What I will do is alert the Galactic Magistratum to the possibility of trouble during the Concilium session," Davy went on. He had regained his usual magisterial calmness. "Krondak agents will do their utmost to keep the Rebel leadership under invisible surveillance, but you know the limitations: The bulky bodies of the Krondaku restrict their activities, and any Grand Master farsensor who suspects their presence can easily spy them out. Scrutator Losa'emoo Dok assures me that no bombs or other military equipment have been smuggled into Orb."

"That is reassuring," the Four said.

Davy said carefully, "It was my plan to call for a loyalty oath amongst human magnates tomorrow and expel from the Concilium those who decline. Shall I proceed?"

"Yes," said the Four.

"Shall I permit floor debate of the issue?"

"No."

"You know what the consequences may be?"

"Yes."

"Right." Davy swallowed the last of his Scotch and got up. "I'll be going, then, to tell Marc his compromise proposal is a no-hoper."

He went out, closing the oaken door behind him.

After a period of meditation, Asymptotic Essence said, "Shopping. In France! Sometimes, one despairs of ever understanding Unifex."

"It did hint that Jack and Illusio might skew the direful probability lattices," Trend noted.

"We could check the two entities out," Eupathic Impulse suggested.

But the poet disagreed. "Snooping would do nothing to hasten bifurcation. It would be more elegant to continue to put one's trust in Unifex and in the Prime Entelechy."

"This one concurs," said Homologous Trend.

"And this one also," said Asymptotic Essence.

"Oh, what the hell," muttered Eupathic Impulse. "I do, too. Let's go walk the dogs."

[31]

FROM THE MEMOIRS OF
ROGATIEN REMILLARD

The loyalty-oath requirement was ratified by the full Galactic Concilium. All of the exotic polities were unanimously in favor, while the Human Polity was split along party lines with a handful of conscientious abstentions. There was no Lylmik veto. Davy MacGregor immediately called for the oath in farsensory metaconcert and 68 percent of the human magnates declared themselves to be faithful adherents to the Milieu, willing (if not necessarily eager) to accept Unification of the racial Mind.

The Rebels stood mute as they were summarily expelled from the Concilium. They were invited to remain in Orb for counseling but declined. Marc led the group of 128 en masse to the Human Terminal, where they boarded a single starship, the CSS Tyndareus, and set off for Okanagon. Since not all of the ex-magnates were able to endure high-displacement-factor flight, the voyage of almost 3800 lightyears would occupy some four weeks. Marc let it be known that no communiqués would be forthcoming from the Rebel high command during the interim.

It was a time of turmoil and consternation among humanity. Although there is no formal media coverage of Concilium affairs, news of the proceedings is regularly leaked to the galaxy at large. We on Earth knew of the Rebel expulsion within 48 hours, and pundits had a field-day predicting what might happen next.

Actually, not much did. At first.

Earth's new Dirigent, Esi Damatura, called for calmness and reflection, and she was echoed by other planetary officials of the Human Polity. No effort was made by the Earth Magistratum to restrict the personal liberty or the rights of free speech and assembly enjoyed by local Rebels. Minor-league insurgents like Kyle Macdonald and I waited eagerly to see how Marc and his cohort would respond, looking forward to blazing rhetoric such as that which had characterized the Mental Man ruckus, and maybe some gaudy sample of kick-ass CE, warning the Milieu not to mess with Okanagon or other Rebel strongholds. Meanwhile, we were entertained by the politicians in Concord.

In Earth's Intendant Assembly, Rebel IAs denounced Davy MacGregor and the other loyalist magnates as traitors to their human heritage and craven minions of exotic tyranny. Moderate Intendant Associates deplored the polarization while holding out hope that the pro-Unity magnates still in session in Orb would defuse the political powder-keg. Legislators who stood firmly in the Milieu camp (and they were a small minority on the Old World) reminded their jingoist constituents that no one really knew what kind of self-defensive action the Galactic Milieu was capable of. For all humanity knew, the Lylmik might choose to incarcerate blatantly Rebel planets inside some novel form of force-field bubble, leaving them to stew forever in their own nonconformist juices.

But there was absolutely no hint from Concilium Orb that the Milieu might be considering a quarantine of Earth—much less that of the entire human race.

After about three weeks, the media flap over the expulsion of the Rebel magnates subsided for lack of fresh fuel. Persistent rumors maintained that the Rebels possessed armament and might mount a military attack upon the Milieu, but most ordinary people found the notion inconceivable. For fifty years we had been at peace. A war— even a war of independence—was a notion that had been bruited about among Rebel extremists for decades; but average citizens could scarcely envision an interstellar conflict taking place. There were thousands of Milieu worlds scattered throughout the Milky Way and only 148 planets then colonized by Earthlings. No military-industrial complex existed to furnish either side with war materiel. The space weaponry we old-timers remembered involved crude lasers reflected by Zap-Star satellites, and rocket vehicles carrying thermonuclear warheads—both easily subject to neutralization by the Milieu's sigma force-fields.

Classic science-fiction films with their quaint Star Wars battles were dusted off and broadcast by opportunistic Tri-D stations, frightening children and naïfs and giving mature adults food for thought. But everybody knew that no Evil Empire of malevolent extraterrestrials lurked among the nebulae, ready to defend their turf with bloodthirsty zest. The five exotic races that possessed interstellar transport were irrevocably committed to peace and a form of mental fellowship that might be problematical to operant philosophers but was hardly the stuff of nightmares where plain folks were concerned.

Few of us had the imagination to envisage what genuine antimatter bombs might do to an inhabited world—much less metaconcerted 600X CE. In our innocence, we thought that the Metapsychic Rebellion would turn out to be a war of words, moral suasion, and economic sanctions.

We had been too long at a far remove from profound evil, and we had forgotten its persistence in our own human souls.

On 19 March 2083, ten days after the CSS Tyndareus landed on Okanagon, Marc called a Planetary News Network media conference. Every inhabited world of the Galactic Milieu viewed that subspace simulcast, which initiated in a studio in Broadcast House in Chelan Metro, Okanagon's capital.

I watched it in my own apartment above the bookshop. My companions were Marcel the Maine Coon cat and Kyle Macdonald—whose wife, Masha, was lightyears away among the defecting Rebels. Kyle and I were full of bellicose enthusiasm as we settled down before the Tri-D with absolutely no inkling of what was to come—except that it was bound to be Rebellious and inspiring. I had laid on a plate of crudités with supermarket cheese dip, potato chips, and gooey walnut brownies. We were imbibing prudent quantities of Moosehead Premium Dry Ale, a full-bodied brew from Canada, in order to keep our wits sharp for the historic occasion.

The Tri-D broadcast came into New Hampshire at two in the morning local time, and the voice-over introduction accompanying the SPECIAL PRESENTATION title produced the first surprise.

"And now, live from the planet Okanagon, a public-affairs program featuring Professor Anna Gawrys, Vice-Chairman of the Rebel Party."

Kyle and I exchanged glances.

"No Marc?" said I. "Hell, I thought this was supposed to be his big show."

An explanation was promptly forthcoming from Annushka, who looked somber in a simple black dress relieved only by a neck-scarf of cobalt-blue silk. She sat at one of those slightly tilted consoles newscasters use, with a sunken monitor screen and a control panel enabling her to personally manipulate the signal-feed from external video sources. She was flanked by Captain Ragnar Gathen, wearing his Twelfth Fleet uniform, and a crop-haired young woman in a burgundy nebulin business suit.

"I offer greetings to all the entities viewing and participating in this presentation," Annushka said. "I am Anna Gawrys, formerly a dynamic-field physicist at Cambridge University in Britain. On my right is Ragnar Gathen, the Chief Operations Officer of the Twelfth Sector Starship Fleet. On my left is Dr. Eva Smuts, Director of Okanagon's Chelan University Astrophysical Observatory. Before my colleagues and I begin, I would like to convey a fleck transcription message from our Rebel Party Chairman, Marc Remillard."

The professor touched a pad and Marc's head and shoulders appeared in holographic close-up. His gray eyes shone from orbits as dark as wells and his usual seraphic smile was absent. It was possible to see that he wore a garment almost like a lightweight spacesuit, black and skintight, with a sealing metallic neck-ring and two odd little dinguses that might have been electrodes nestling in the hollows on either side of his throat. When he spoke, his voice was quiet, but as incisive as a straight razor.

"The Concilium has chosen to expel me and the other magnates belonging to the Rebel Party because we declined to take an oath of unquestioning loyalty to the Galactic Milieu. We refused to surrender our human mentalities to the form of mental subjugation called Unity because we are convinced that to do so would deprive us of our fundamental nature—our individualism, our very identities—transforming us into something other than human.

"It is our heartfelt belief that the human race deserves to evolve independently of exotic interference, even when that interference is cloaked in a guise of benevolence. From the time of the Great Intervention, the five exotic races of the Milieu have compelled humanity to follow social, economic, educational, moral, and mental pathways dictated by them. In the beginning their despotism was overt, taking the form of the oppressive Simbiari Proctorship that destroyed human nationalism, oppressed certain religious faiths, and denied parents the right to control the conception and rearing of their own children.

"After the enfranchisement of the Human Polity in 2054, Milieu tyranny was more subtle, but still striking deep into the human heritage of independence. The exotic races have, in uncounted ways, sought to limit human scientific achievement—especially in mental science. They have also restricted human colonization and denied Milieu resources to planets struggling under conditions of environmental and economic hardship. They have declined to establish colonies for human population groups who fail to measure up to their standards of ethnic dynamism or an equally arbitrary scale of metapsychic potential.

"When I myself sought to bring about a dramatic increase in the number of operant minds in the Human Polity, the Milieu felt threatened. At the time, my associates and I did not fully understand why the exotic races were so determined not to allow the engendering of Mental Man . . . but we understand it all too well now. The Milieu is unwilling to face the prospect that the human race will evolve beyond the constricted bounds of what they call Unity.

"They are afraid of us, and so they have conspired to restrain us.

"The Rebel Party has entreated the Galactic Milieu to let humanity go. Again and again we have tried to reassure the exotic races that we mean them no harm. But they have refused to understand. Certain human Magnates of the Concilium, loyal to the Milieu, have called our Rebellion ungrateful, uncivilized, even immoral. We ask these people, our former colleagues, why the Milieu has refused to compromise. Why it declines even to consider the possibility of a free humanity living in peace and harmony with Unified exotics.

"We of the Rebel Party believe that human beings must be free. We believe we have a right to fight for that freedom, even if it means contravening the pacifistic ethic that pervades the Milieu. In order to manifest our stern resolution and our refusal to capitulate to despotism or invidious oppression, we have decided to conduct a tangible declaration of independence. Since I myself will participate in the demonstration, I will delegate its exposition to Professor Anna Gawrys.

"Thank you for your attention."

I gawked at Kyle and he gawked at me.

"Tangible?" he croaked. "Was Marc wearing what I think he was?"

My affirmation was full of grim excitement. "Sure as hell looked like the coverall of a full-body CE rig to me. I betcha we're gonna see the metaconcerted zap heard round the galaxy."

The Tri-D screen showed Annushka and Ragnar Gathen. She said to him, "Within recent months, an alarming piece of intelligence has come to the attention of the Rebel Council. Will you tell us about it, Captain Gathen?"

The Norwegian-American officer spoke with a deliberation that was pained, full of honest regret. "We discovered that large numbers of Krondak starships—heavy cruisers with a high-df capability—have been gathering at the planet Molakar, a principal starbase in the Eleventh Sector, very close to Earth."

Annushka stabbed her finger at a control pad and a view of the Krondak world flashed onto the screen. As Earth appears to be a white-swirled blue marble from space, so Molakar looked like a white-swirled umber marble. After the astronomical, a labeled quick-flick file shot of the immense Krondak starbase itself appeared: looming rows of clunky black vessels silhouetted against an angry crimson sky, the monstrous denizens of the planet squirming hither and yon on agile tentacles, tending to their mysterious (and perhaps ominous) business.

Gathen's voice continued. "Nearly six thousand Krondak vessels have come to Molakar from every sector of the galaxy. They have gathered stealthily, without any public announcement of intent. The Rebellion detected their presence through farsensory CE."

The hellish view of the Krondak world was replaced by a close-up of Annushka, kindly and grave. "At this instant, a Rebel starship, the PSS Vulpecula, is emerging from the superficies into Molakarian c-space. I will initiate SS com contact with the ship's captain."

She tapped the console. The Tri-D display split in half. Her side remained three-dimensional; the other was flat, depicting Fleet Commander Owen Blanchard on the bridge of the Vulpecula. He identified himself and then said, "Our communications officer is hailing Molakar Starbase, requesting to speak with its Starbase Governor."

A bit of backing and filling took place. Then a hideous exotic visage, all warts, fangs, and multiple eyeballs, appeared on the Vulpecula's big bridge display screen and a rumbling voice said, "Portitor Zela'edoo Kark responds to Commander Owen Blanchard. How may I assist you?"

"I make this formal inquiry on behalf of the Rebel Party of the Human Polity," Blanchard replied. "Please explain why large numbers of Krondak starships have assembled on Molakar."

The Portitor blinked several accessory optics. "Please wait." About ten seconds went by. Then the exotic said, "I regret to inform you that the information you request is privileged."

Blanchard's face looked infinitely weary. I recalled that he and Annushka were the very first Rebels, long decades ago when it was unthinkable for an operant human to speak out in public against the Galactic Milieu.

Blanchard posed a final question. "Does the Krondak fleet intend an interdiction and blockade of the planet Earth?"

I whispered, "Oh, shit."

Kyle, looking like a grizzly bear conked with a sledgehammer, didn't say a word.

Zela'edoo Kark said, "I cannot respond to that query. This communication is terminated." The Krondak face vanished.

Owen Blanchard said, "Initiate the demonstration."

We watched Molakar die.

It was impossible, of course, to show the activity of the metaconcert. We in the viewing audience did not even see the 156 vessels of the Rebel force gathered in attack formation. We saw what the officers on the Vulpecula's bridge saw.

For five excruciating minutes there was nothing. Then the reddish-brown clouds of the planet seemed to catch fire, beginning at the polar regions. What began as scattered pulsations of red and green light congealed into blazing waves of ionized oxygen in the upper reaches of the planetary atmosphere, surging in some arcane gravomagnetic consonance with the roiling magmatic plumes beneath the crust.

The thinner suboceanic lithosphere was the first to crack. Lava burst up through the seafloor in a hundred thousand white-hot fountains, vaporizing the sluggish seas, causing titanic bubbles to billow to the surface. The heat initiated noxious chemical changes in the complex hydrocarbons mixed with the water, breeding towering clouds of poisonous steam that clashed tornadically with the cooler air surrounding them. Deadly gases spread across the land, driven by hurricane winds. The sessile lifeforms that Molakarians call plants were incinerated in raging firestorms. Earthquakes rocked the continents.

Most of Molakar's population died then. And since the Tau-Ceti star is less than twelve lightyears away from Earth, numbers of particularly sensitive operants on our planet not only saw the Krondak world's destruction in living color on their home Tri-D sets but also farsensed the death-cry of its two billion highly intelligent inhabitants. Kyle and I, incompetent heads and bumbling revolutionaries, felt only vicarious pain.

Because of its more massive nickel-iron core, Molakar was a tougher nut to crack than Cible had been. The landmasses were not completely shattered by seismic activity, nor was the atmosphere driven entirely into space. There were no volcanic lava-bombs hurled into orbit, only rivers and lakes of seething gold, thinly edged with carmine, webbing the desiccated seabed off the continental shelves.

This took place within thirty minutes.

I have always feared the repugnant Krondaku, but that night I wept for them. They were not monsters, they were people having many of the same emotions as human beings, the first race to be inducted by the Lylmik into the infant Galactic Milieu. They were unfailingly just, but also capable of kindness. They mated for life and adored their grotesque offspring and cherished the elderly members of their race.

All the same, I decided that what Marc had done to Molakar was justified. Probably . . .

Apocalypse gave way to banality. PSS Vulpecula and her cohort fled into hyperspace and the view on my Tri-D screen returned to the studio on Okanagon, where the female astrophysicist—her face gray with shock—gave a terse technical description of how the CE metaconcert had meddled with Molakar's mantle, and exactly what had happened after that.

Annushka made a final statement on behalf of the Rebel Council. "It was with the most profound regret that our forces accomplished this demonstration. We now call upon the Galactic Milieu to insure that no additional punitive action on our part will be necessary. *Rescind the Unity Protocol.* We will give you fifty Galactic Standard days to respond. Any attack on Okanagon or Earth, or any attempt to sequester those planets by sigma-fields or any other means, will result in immediate retaliation."

Then the professor and her two companions rose to their feet and stood shoulder to shoulder, as if drawing strength from one another. The studio cameras zoomed in on their faces. Anna Gawrys said, "Citizens of the Human Polity, the Metapsychic Rebellion has shown you one way to achieve freedom. Whether it succeeds depends upon you."

The Tri-D images winked out. After a moment of silent nullity, the station logo came on. There was no commentary, only the solemn cadences of Samuel Barber's Adagio for Strings, mourning the death of a world.

[32]

SECTOR 12: STAR 12-337-010 [GRIAN]
PLANET 4 [CALEDONIA]
1 AN CEITEAN [15 MAY] 2083

A misty drizzle fell in northern Beinn Bhiorach on Caledonia's first evening of summer, tapping on the tender new foliage of the coleus trees in the garden and dimpling the placid black waters of Loch Tuath that fronted their cottage. But the droplets seemed miraculously to evaporate without getting a person wet.

"It's dry rain," she noted as they came out of the house. "Part of our Caledonian folklore. You've never been in it before, have you, love?"

"No," he admitted.

"Let's walk to the farm rather than take the groundcar," she suggested. "I'd so love to have a last feel of the dear old place before we leave."

"We'll be back after it's over," he insisted. "For a good long rest."

"And then a second vacation on Kauai," she added. "We'll have earned it, well and truly."

They set off down the narrow two-rut track, which was barely damp. The native trees in the glen and on the mountainsides were aglow with colors that were nearly fluorescent in the prolonged soft twilight. When the coleus leaves were full-grown they would be the size of handkerchiefs or even larger. Now they were like crimped, velvety cat's-ears, cerise-pink and primrose-yellow and rho-violet and magenta. Their undersides, lifting in the light wind wafting down from the extinct Forge volcano, were silvery.

They passed the docks at the end of the loch and came up the riverside road through the pastures and fields. Terrestrial grass, mingled with vivid-orange neòinean plants, grew lush in the repellor-fenced paddocks where sheep, ruddy West Highland cattle, and miniature horses grazed with their young. Long-tailed Mesozoic rinkies flew overhead. Their wild cries mingled with the bleats and whickers of greeting that the farm animals offered to the human couple passing by.

Hand in hand, Jack the Bodiless and Diamond Mask walked along the gravel road to her beloved childhood home. He wore jeans, a navy polo shirt, and a brown windbreaker. She had on her shining azure lamé hooded jumpsuit and the matching half-mask adorned with blue diamonds. When they finished their visit, they intended to embark immediately for Earth.

The airfarm seemed deserted tonight. There were no eggs or aerostatic harvesters on the landing pad and no sign of workers or ground vehicles in the vicinity of the skyweed processing plant or the other outbuildings. Over by the river, the young oak tree that had sprouted from an acorn she picked up in an Edinburgh churchyard thrust out sturdy branches adorned with monochromatic, alien green. The main house, quaintly gabled and painted Wedgwood-blue with white trim, stood on a landscaped knoll high above the other buildings like a small castle on its motte. Some of the windows were already lighted. Only the satellite dishes, the NAVCON antenna, and the fairy-critter gun on the roof detracted from the structure's archaic charm.

Dorothea paused at the bottom of the knoll's stone stairway. "I don't really know what I'm going to say to him, Jack. I couldn't refuse when he asked us to come see him, but—he's a Rebel, even if he is my father. After what's happened, I'm not willing to let him spoil our last night on Callie."

"Let's just see what he wants," Jack said. "If it's a row, we can leave."

They ascended through rock gardens bright with golden tuft and many-colored azaleas. At the slightly higher elevation the "dry rain" unfortunately regained its normal wet properties. Jack erected a metacreative umbrella until they reached the shelter of the house's enclosed porch.

Janet Finlay, Ian Macdonald's Arizona-born second wife, opened the door to them. She had declined rejuvenation, as her husband had, and her once hard-favored features had softened with the plumpness of middle age. She wore a ranch shirt in sage-green with pearl snaps, a black denim skirt, and Western boots made of Caledonian teuthis leather.

"Evenin', kids." She smiled warmly as they came into the entry hall and exchanged brief hugs. "He's holed up in his den like a sulkin' coyote, so you might's well go on along. You all come back into the library for coffee after you've had a chance to chew the fat in private. I'll wait on you."

"Thank you." Dorothea led Jack to the office wing of the big house. The workroom where Janet and Dorothea's foster sister Ellen Gunn supervised the operation of the airfarm was deserted at this time of the evening, its cluttered desks abandoned, the computer displays and sophisticated business machines devoiced but still blinking as they ruminated electronically over cuds of data.

When Jack and Dorothea reached the door of her father's inner sanctum she knocked gently. A low voice said, "Aye, come in."

Ian Macdonald slowly turned away from the window where he had been standing. Even in the rainy dusk the view to the north was magnificent, encompassing the entire farmstead and the reach of cliff-girt Loch Tuath beyond. A Celestron light-multiplying telescope was still focused on the river valley. Dorothea realized that her nonoperant father had probably been watching her and Jack from the moment they left the cottage.

"Hello, Dad," she said, when he remained silent.

He said, "Hello, Dorrie. Jack. Why don't we sit down?"

Far from being a conventional snuggery, the room was almost like the bridge of a ship with tall windows on three sides. Two huge Tri-D projection maps—one of the farmlands and the other of Beinn Bhiorach Subcontinent, which Ian Macdonald served as elected Intendant Associate—flanked the doorway. The principal pieces of furniture, occupying the room's center, were a padded swivel-chair and a massive antique Scottish table-desk crowded with reader-plaques and durafilm printouts. Near the southern bank of windows overlooking the rugged inland mountain range was a shiatsu recliner of wine-colored leather, two cabriole armchairs done in worn forest green plush, and a pedestal cocktail table made from a sawn and polished slab of malachite.

Ian perched his rangy frame rather awkwardly on the edge of the recliner while his daughter and son-in-law took the other two seats.

"I've been delegated," the farmer said without preamble, "by a certain group within the Rebel Party to ask you with the utmost confidentiality if there's any way we can stave off this war."

"A breakaway faction?" Dorothea's brow creased.

"Don't get the idea that our Rebellion is fragmenting," Ian growled. "We're all as steadfast as ever in our resolve to secede from the Milieu. But certain members of the Rebel Council wonder whether Marc might not have . . . formulated our ultimatum too rigidly. If so, I'm to let you know informally that we're still open to negotiation. We don't want flat-out war any more than the Milieu does."

"You made my brother your leader," Jack said levelly. "Why aren't you posing this question to him?"

Ian did not reply directly. "I'm going to be frank with you. The Rebel Council expected Milieu capitulation to follow the Molakar demonstration. When our fifty-day deadline came and went last week without any response at all from your side, a conference of Rebel bigwigs met to discuss new options. I wasn't there, you understand. I'm small potatoes in the Rebel hierarchy, just a body who happens to have a very important daughter. So I was appointed an informal delegation of one."

He stared at her in hopeful appeal, but the hazel eyes were coolly noncommittal above the mask of blue diamonds. Ian's sponsorship of the clandestine laser-helmet factory had never been proven, but she was morally certain of his complicity and had been deeply scandalized by it.

Jack said, "Suppose you tell us what the new Rebel options are."

"Aye, well, the majority of the magnates—including Marc—are prepared to conduct another cataclysmic demonstration unless serious negotiations for the implementation of human independence begin immediately."

"And the Rebel minority?" Dorothea asked. "Is it having second thoughts after the Molakar atrocity?"

Ian spoke with anguished sincerity. "We ordinary folk never dreamt that Marc had contemplated such a gruesome thing! We were as appalled as you. On the other hand, if it was true that the Krondaku were getting set to blockade Earth or embargo our colonies, then they deserved what they got. But . . . there's no other truly appropriate target left now, is there?" Again, he seemed to be appealing to Jack and Dorothea. "I mean, no other exotic world that just begs for smashin'. There's only innocent planets and the Concilium Orb itself. If Marc's CE metaconcert destroys one of them, it'll be naught but terrorism."

"Yes," the Dirigent of Caledonia said to her father. "That's what your Rebellion has committed itself to."

"What will ye do, Dorrie? Is there no way to put an end to it? We know that loyalist human starships of the Thirteenth and Fourteenth Fleets are zipping from hell to breakfast touching down on every colonial world, but they certainly aren't being deployed militarily. Our best intelligence guess is that the ships are just carrying bloody messages. But about *what?*"

Dorothea said, "You've guessed correctly, Dad. We haven't wanted to use subspace communication or ordinary long-range farspeech because of the possibility of interception, so our communiqués are being sent via courier. We can't risk misunderstandings at this point."

Ian's eyes lit up with hope. "So ye *do* have some nonviolent counterploy in the works!"

Jack said, "Loyalist humans are trying to find a way to resolve the matter, yes. But you can hardly expect us to discuss our strategy with you. I'll tell you this much: Every human member of the Concilium still faithful to the Milieu has returned to his or her own planet. I myself am the only temporary exception. We don't intend to negotiate with you Rebels and we don't intend to fight you. What we do intend is to end the Rebellion by a means that we hope will be nonviolent. Davy Mac-Gregor will be sending a message to Marc five days from now—but there's no reason why you shouldn't know about it and tell him to expect it. The gist of the response is this: The exotic races have agreed that the defense of the Milieu against the Metapsychic Rebellion is to be directed solely by loyal human magnates. Whichever side is victorious in . . . a certain upcoming confrontation will be granted primacy. If you Rebels win, humanity will be cut loose from the Milieu. If the loyalists win, those operants refusing Unity will be sequestered. Nonoperant Rebels will have their personal liberties restricted more drastically than they were during the Simbiari Proctorship."

"Who are the magnates directing the Milieu's defense?" Ian demanded bluntly.

Jack and Dorothea only looked at him without speaking.

Ian rose from his seat, his face agitated by conflicting emotions. "It's you two—isn't it! The only loyalist paramounts! You're going to take on Marc. But how? Do you have a CE metaconcert of your own?"

Dorothea got up, went to her father, and took his hand. "We're leaving Caledonia tomorrow morning. You'll soon know the answer to your questions. All of them." The diamond mask dissolved, revealing a plain, heart-shaped face. She kissed her father on one rugged cheek. "Goodbye, Dad. I do love you. When the time comes, make a true choice with your own heart. Don't let Marc Remillard choose for you."

The hard, sharp-edged gemstones masked her again. She and Jack left the study.

"Wait!" Ian cried. "What choice? What do you mean?"

But neither of them answered. They hurried to the front door with him following after, made a brief apology to bewildered Janet, and went away into the rain.

Ian Macdonald stared dumbly at the closed door.

"What in blue blazes is going on?" Thrawn Janet asked him.

"They're leading the counterassault. Against the Rebellion. Dorrie and Jack."

"Hellfire and double damnation," muttered Janet. Hesitantly, she added, "Wouldn't you call that sorta valuable intelligence? I mean, shouldn't we notify Calum Sorley? So's he can maybe stop the two of 'em taking off in that little Scurra starship of Jack's? If they're the leaders—"

"No!" said Ian Macdonald. He whirled about, seized her by the shoulders, and shouted, "You won't say a word about them and neither will I! Do you understand me, woman?"

"Reckon so," said Janet. Exerting herself minimally, she pried her husband's hands loose, took out a handkerchief and wiped the tears from his face, and then led him into the library where strong coffee and soggy scones with raspberry jam waited.

FROM THE MEMOIRS OF
ROGATIEN REMILLARD

Jack and Dorothée returned to Earth. They came together to my book-shop on a gorgeous late spring day and gave the Great Carbuncle back to me with their thanks.

I asked them if they knew what the Milieu was going to do, now that Marc's deadline had come and gone ten days ago.

"We're going to try to stop him, Uncle Rogi," said Ti-Jean.

He squatted on the floor of the shop, stroking old Marcel. We were in the little customer lounge up front. Tulips and hyacinths were blooming around the base of the trees along Main Street and students ambled by in shirtsleeves and light dresses. Ordinary Old World people, operant and non, had managed to put Molakar out of their minds. After all, it was far away and the victims had been nonhuman.

Dorothée was wearing an oversized red T-shirt and white shorts that looked exceptionally bizarre with her diamond mask. She said, "We returned to Earth for a brief visit to Hawaii, and to pick up Paul. In an hour or so we'll be taking off again in Jack's starship."

"Where to this time?" I asked.

"Davy MacGregor will give Marc the Milieu's response to the Metapsychic Rebellion on Monday, May twentieth. He's notifying the Rebel Council that we're coming to the space of their headquarters world, Okanagon, so they'll be able to get their armada emplaced."

"What are you going to do?" I asked, awestruck. "Will it be a space battle?"

"Every operant person will know what happens," she replied. "We'll try to arrange it so that the nonoperants will as well. But this confrontation won't be a Tri-D spectacle like Molakar. The battle will be for the Human Mind—but it will be very different from what you might expect."

"Or Marc," Ti-Jean appended. He tugged Marcel's soft ears one final time and then stood up. "We can't stay any longer, Uncle Rogi. Thank you for all you've done for Diamond and me. Be sure to hang on to the Great Carbuncle."

Before I knew what was happening he folded me in an embrace. Then Dorothée took off her diamond mask and kissed me goodbye. Her face was very beautiful.

The events I will relate to you now have come partly from my own memories and partly from information received.

The long trip to and from the Concilium session on Orb had taken a severe physical toll on Paul, and he was recuperating in the old Remillard house around the corner and down the block from my bookshop, where Lucille still lived. Jack and Dorothea found him in the sun-dappled back yard, relaxing in a lawn chair with a plaque of *War and Peace*. When they expressed surprise at his choice of reading matter he only laughed.

"I never got around to reading this and I've always regretted it. I'm about halfway through, and I figure to finish it off during the voyage to Okanagon. If there's time, I'll also try to read Milton's *Paradise Lost*. I've heard that the villain steals the show." He started to get up. "I'll be ready to go in a jiffy. I'm already packed."

Jack restrained him with a hand on his shoulder. "Wait for just a moment, Papa. I'm sorry, but Diamond must do a redactive scan of your faculties. To be sure."

Paul gave a martyred snort. "Go ahead."

She placed both hands on his head. He tensed, then cried out softly and subsided into the chair, momentarily insensible.

Jack said, "How does it look?"

"He's deeply fatigued and the psychic energy level is very low. But the neural structures are fully regenerated."

Paul stirred and snapped back to full alertness. "Well? Was I all right? All systems back on line and ready for action?"

Dorothea nodded. "Your vitality is still below par, but your armamentarium is structurally adequate for the confrontation."

"Good. I'll get my stuff and we'll be on our way." He got up and headed for the house.

"Papa, you don't have to do this," Jack called after him. "We may not even need a telergic transfer monitor."

Paul looked back over his shoulder. His face was sober. "But if you do need one, you'll need him very badly. I may not be good for much, but that's one job I still can do. Wait here." He went in through the kitchen door.

"You mustn't try to dissuade him, Jack," Dorothea said. "He loves the Milieu with all his heart and soul and he has a right to participate."

"But he looks so tired and ill, Diamond. His aura's even more diminished than it was in Orb."

"He's strong enough and it's what he wants to do."

Jack sighed. "Yes."

The back door opened and Lucille Cartier came out into the yard and greeted them.

"Everyone is ready," she said quietly. "I don't think there's a loyal soul in Hanover who isn't preparing for Saint Augustine's Day."

"Is that what they're calling it?" Jack said, his expression bemused. "How very Shakespearean! Let me see, how will it go? *'This story shall the good man teach his son; / And Saint Augustine's Day shall ne'er go by, / From this day to the ending of the world, / But we in it shall be remembered— / We few, we happy few, we band of brothers . . .'* "

"Don't be concerned about us here on Earth," Lucille said. "Your instructions will be followed scrupulously—even if we don't understand them."

"The other worlds are ready, too," Dorothea said, "hoping and praying for victory. The whole thing's a prayer, in a way."

Lucille smiled. "Denis thought so, when we were together on top of the mountain just before the Intervention. I like to think he'll be with us on Saint Augustine's Day, too."

They said their farewells. Then Lucille went off, dry-eyed, and Paul emerged from the house with a small carry-on bag, ready to go.

On 27 May 2083, Earth time, a very small starship broke through the upsilon-field superficies into the c-space of the planet Okanagon, which hung in the sky like a brilliant clouded azure lantern some 400,000 kilometers distant. The colonial world had only a tiny natural moon, Chopaka, but more than two hundred artificial satellites orbited it in a sparkling swarm.

When the vessel had achieved a synchronous orbit above the

planet's equator, it disgorged a tiny shuttlecraft, which moved off until it was 50 kilometers closer to the planet.

Paul's farspeech said: Shuttle in position.

Jack said: Very well. We're deploying the Kauai gem.

The airlock of Scurra opened and a tractor-beam thrust forth a transparent red sphere slightly less than a meter in diameter. Although the thing had no obvious orbital-correction machinery, it took up and maintained a position 2.9979 kilometers off the bow of the little ship, on a beeline between Scurra and Paul's shuttlecraft.

Dorothea said: Gem deployed.

The com display on the bridge lit up with the planetary Great Seal overlaid with a flashing WARNING notification. It said: "XSS Scurra-Two, this is Okanagon ISTC. Your vessel and its auxiliaries now occupy c-space interdicted by the Metapsychic Rebellion. Please state your intention immediately or risk a hostile engagement."

The young woman in the flying suit encrusted with diamonds sat in a command seat before the starship's navigation console. Beside her was a pedestal topped by a crystal bowl holding a disembodied brain. Her pseudovoice said softly, "Okanagon Interstellar Traffic Control, Scurra-Two requests communication with Marc Remillard, Chairman of the Rebel Party."

"Scurra-Two, say who would communicate with the Chairman."

She said, "Jon Remillard of the Panpolity Directorate for Unity and Dorothea Macdonald, Dirigent of Caledonia—designated advocates of the Human Polity of the Galactic Milieu. We are here for the final confrontation."

The traffic control computer said, "Please wait." The icon disappeared. In a moment the com screen showed Jack and Dorothea their own starship, Paul's shuttle, and a gleaming blood-red speck.

"They're not scoping us from groundside or from Chopaka Moonbase," Jack said. "The scan originates from behind us." His PK touched the pad activating their own external survey system. He commanded: "Survey, Tri-D mode, three-sixty-degree, starship analytical graphic."

The larger display above the console came to life, showing a swarm of 670 representational starship images almost entirely ensphering their own spacecraft at a distance of less than a hundred kilometers. Peripheral displays began a swift presentation of vessel classification and ID. There were 191 Vulpecula-class cruisers, 50 huge Bering-class dreadnaughts, and 429 miscellaneous ships attached to the Twelfth Sector Fleet.

The Rebel armada had exited hyperspace.

In spite of Alex Manion's deep misgivings, Marc had pushed himself to the limit in order to reconfigure the offensive metaconcert after the Molakar demonstration. He completely reorganized the executive focusing structure and also managed to modify the original monolithic generator into a more versatile tripartite design. By incorporating CE trainees, he had increased the number of 600X operators to 1900, divided into two groups that could be mobilized with great speed and agility. The third group of energizers was more cumbersome and would be held in reserve for critical situations. It comprised 5110 operators equipped with E18 helmets—virtually every Grand Master in the Rebel Party healthy enough to participate. Less than half of them were top-certified in creativity, but they did possess that metafaculty at least at the masterclass level. Marc's new design had incorporated their minds in positions where they would significantly augment the output of the GM creators in their group for very brief periods without seriously impeding the flexibility of the metaconcert as a whole.

In addition to the mental weaponry, the Rebel fleet was armed with a wide assortment of photonic projectors. Twelve of the mid-sized cruisers also carried a single robot shuttlecraft bearing an antimatter explosive device that Rory Muldowney's underworld associates had stolen years ago from the Krondak Planetary Modification Group.

On the bridge of his flagship, Marc and the members of his new prime focus team viewed the exterior scan display with unconcealed incredulity. They were all dressed in CE coveralls, ready to be conveyed to the bay where the 600X rigs waited. The operators on the other ships were already fully invested.

Marc gave a bark of cynical laughter as he studied the screen. "*This* is the Milieu's answer to our Molakar demonstration? My little brother's toy starship?"

"Evidently so," said Owen Blanchard. "How very curious."

"I don't believe this! Do you know what Scurra means in Latin? 'Clown!' And the situation is completely ridiculous."

"Perhaps," Jordan Kramer said tentatively, "Jack and Dorothea have been sent to us with a declaration of surrender after all."

"Davy MacGregor's communiqué was quite clear," Cordelia War-shaw said, shaking her well-coiffed head. "The so-called Milieu advocates are to engage us in a confrontation. If we win, Rebel humanity may secede from the Milieu without sanction. If we lose—"

"We're fucked to a fare-thee-well," said Hiroshi Kodama.

"Maybe it's some kind of diversionary tactic," Pete Dalembert suggested. "While we roll about laughing at Scurra, the Lylmik could be sneaking up on us in hyperspace."

"That's not their style," Marc said tersely.

"I don't like it," said Helayne Strangford. "Your brother has always been a wild card, Marc—no one really knows his mental potential. And that wife of his is just as peculiar, wasting her paramount metabilities dirigenting that backward little Scottish planet. Who knows what the two of them might have cooked up?"

Alex Manion and Owen Blanchard were studying a smaller display with a proper depiction of Jack's starship.

"Scurra's lifeboat is deployed," Alex said. "And there's something damned odd out there just beyond the nose of the ship itself."

"Hang on," murmured the Fleet Commander. "I'm cranking up the scan resolution." He hit a pad and a close-up of the glassy red ball flashed onto the main view-screen.

"What the hell is it?" Patricia Castellane asked, dumfounded.

Marc's eyes narrowed. "If I'm not mistaken, it's a much-enlarged version of my Uncle Rogi's watch fob. When I was a child, I called it the Great Carbuncle."

Diarmid Keogh exclaimed, "Get on with ye!" And his voiceless twin sister Dierdre transmitted a derisive trill of telepathic scorn.

Alex Manion wasn't laughing. "The thing Rogi said the Lylmik gave to him ages ago? Before the Intervention?"

"Yes," Marc said. "A very mysterious object. Rogi's Carbuncle was a red diamond polished in a spherical shape. He told me that it had saved his life several times by summoning Lylmik help. He even claimed it had something to do with the Intervention itself. Of course I didn't believe him—and I didn't bother to scan it intensively."

"Too bad," said Jeff Steinbrenner. "It might have given us a clue."

Marc turned to Owen. "You'd better have one of the comet-burner gunners get a bead on the thing, just in case."

"Very well. And not that I want to rush you—but it's about time that *you* answered Scurra's hail. All of us would like to know what's going to happen next." The Fleet Commander gestured to the command seat. "Be my guest."

Marc sat down and the others withdrew out of com-scan range. He touched the MW pad. "Marc Remillard responding to Scurra-Two."

Images of the brain and its masked spouse appeared on the big bridge screen. A dual pseudovoice spoke.

"We're here for the confrontation."

"Just the two of you?" Marc said.

"Paul is also here, in the shuttlecraft. His role is subsidiary. But we're not really alone. Every human mind in the galaxy who believes in nonaggression and peaceful coexistence is with us spiritually. There are more of them than you might think, Marc. Molakar forced a lot of people to examine their commitment to you and your Rebellion more carefully."

"What a pity these spiritual allies of yours are so scattered and so far away. Or are you expecting reinforcements?"

"No one besides the three of us will confront you physically."

Marc laughed. "Only mentally? In some grand metaconcert as diffuse and exiguous as the cosmic background radiation?"

"We may surprise you," said Jack and Diamond. "Shall we begin?"

The communication cut off.

Marc spun about and gave a sharp command to Owen Blanchard. "Blast the damn Carbuncle! Now!"

Shaken, Owen transmitted the order. The prime focus team watched in rapt fascination as the image of Scurra and its odd satellite reappeared on the big display. An instant later a golden beam of coherent light seemed to lance out of nowhere, striking the red sphere. There was a blinding flare. But when it dissipated, the Carbuncle still hung against its backdrop of sunlit, blue-and-white Okanagon—apparently unscathed.

"Shielded against actinic," said the Fleet Commander. "Try again with the X-lasers?"

"Negative." Marc was grim. "Never mind. We'll get it with the concert." His glance swept the assembled senior Rebels. "I don't know what Jack and Diamond have up their sleeves. But whatever it is, it's no match for us. Let's go down to the bay and get this thing over with as fast as we can."

.   .   .

In tight metaconcert, the brain and the woman clad in diamonds sent out their farspoken summons. It was a call similar to the one Denis Remillard had made on the night of the Intervention, appealing to human beings of good will to join together, even if only for a brief time, in a grand conjunction of peaceful and loving calmness.

The first to respond were the Uniate and coadunating children. There were millions of them by then, on every human colonial planet—even Rebel Okanagon—a silvery chorus of innocence that echoed faintly among the stars. Then the adult operants who had always remained loyal to the Milieu joined in, followed by normal minds who had never given up on the power of love to transform.

My mind's eye watched and my mind's ear heard what happened—even though I held back.

On Saint Augustine's Day, 2083, the final confrontation caught me as I was walking along the Connecticut River on a cool May evening, full of fear and torn by conflicting hopes. I sat down on a rock by the shore, blind to my surroundings, while my mind farsensed the drama taking place 540 lightyears from Earth. I desperately wanted humanity to be free of the Milieu, but at the same time I shrank from Marc's appalling tactics, praying with all my soul that there would never be another Molakar.

There would be, however—and every human being in the galaxy would be a witness to it.

Jack and Dorothea gathered that initial diffuse flow of coadunation into a concerted Song of Unity. Lucille told me afterward that operant adults experienced the transition as instant Unanimization. The nonoperants, still incapable of bonding fully in cosmic consciousness, felt suddenly uplifted by a surge of wonder, joy, and mental fellowship.

The loving metaconcert pervaded the mental lattices of the aether like the mist hovering over the surface of the Connecticut River on that calm New Hampshire night—tenuous, still relatively insubstantial, capable of being torn by the least breath of malignant wind. Of itself, this precursor to the Unified Mind of Humanity posed no threat whatsoever to the Rebellion.

Even though its joyous song was heart-stirring and indescribably beautiful, I still refused to join in.

Jack and Dorothée, strengthened themselves by the fullness of

Unity, gathered the flood of loving energy and channeled it into the huge gem he had constructed in his laboratory on Kauai, the red diamond sphere with the mysterious Lylmik machines at its faintly glowing heart. Paul Remillard helped in the telergic transfer, his mind a living conduit that helped to concentrate the lesser emanations of the nonoperants.

The Song changed.

Marc, encased in his black CE armor and interrupted in the critical task of constructing his own metaconcert, watched in disbelief as his peripheral farsight showed a slowly expanding bubble of white light that emerged from the Carbuncle, engulfed Jack's starship, and spread toward his own Rebel fleet. He had no idea what it was, and he did not intend to find out.

Owen! Abandon armada formation of encirclement retreat onehundredkayklom higherorbit NOWNOWNOW!

Very well. Armada executing maneuver.

Patricia Castellane, Dirigent of Okanagon, spoke to Marc on his intimate mode: Hit them with the antimatter bombs! All of them!

Marc said: We're too close to the planet we can't risk it.

Patricia said: The concert isn't half built. Would you rather have the fleet dive back into hyperspace like a flock of scared rabbits? Do it! It's my world.

Marc said: *FIRE ALL ANTIMATTER DEVICES AT SCURRA.*

Twelve robot spaceboats emerged from the midst of the retreating armada and streaked toward the glowing bubble, which was expanding more rapidly. When they reached the superficies there was a tiny flurry of rainbow sparks.

The shuttles seemed to vanish. An instant later, on the bubble's opposite side, sparks flashed again and the bomb-laden craft reappeared, tracing an impact trajectory toward Okanagon.

Marc roared: *Owen! Abort action recall boats NOWNOWNOW!*

After a moment Fleet Commander Owen Blanchard's emotionless mental voice replied: The boats are behind that big energy bubble and our guidance systems are unable to penetrate it.

Ti-Jean and Dorothée made certain that every human mind saw what happened. Mercifully, they did not transmit the telepathic shout of the two billion people who died when the antimatter devices ruptured

Okanagon's unstable crust and transformed the once-lovely earthlike planet into a holocaust.

Jack's mind spoke to his brother on intimode: God have mercy on all of you.

Marc said: Perhaps you'd better start praying for yourself.

At that terrible moment, when not only humankind but all of the exotic races of the Milieu watched in stunned horror, the Galactic Milieu itself faltered. Its peoples had been shielded from aggression for so long that they had forgotten its most seductive quality: the inborn instinct to take violent revenge upon one's enemies.

Billions of imperfectly Unified Simbiari experienced despair and hopelessness for the first time in their lives, knowing that their first all-important Proctorship had failed.

Even more Poltroyans were affected, in spite of Unity. Their ancient heritage of violence, suppressed for so long, began to resurface in their racial Mind in response to the perceived threat of the human Rebels.

The Gi cowered in helpless panic while the phlegmatic Krondaku tried to resist the temptation to withdraw into themselves. The Lylmik only watched, waiting to see if Marc Remillard and his Rebellion would prevail while the Galactic Milieu died.

Jack and Dorothea said: *Persevere.*

The monstrous cinder that was Okanagon glowed crimson and black inside a haze of orbiting debris.

Persevere.

Uncommitted human minds and even greater numbers of dedicated Rebels, at first stunned by the awful spectacle, began to rush into the sanctuary of the loving metaconcert. I held back myself; but a torrent of others rejected the terrible sword of the Angel of the Abyss and his remorseless demand for full mental autonomy. As humanity made its critical choice, Jack, Diamond, and Paul welcomed and incorporated the converts. The Song intensified and the great bubble of coadunate mental energy swelled and acquired a heliodoric corona. When it attained a diameter of 29,979.2458 kilometers it halted its distension, ready.

Marc's metaconcert was finally actualized. He ordered the ship carrying the secondary focus team—Adrien, Catherine, and Severin Remillard, Annushka Gawrys and her brother Valery, Masha Mac-Gregor-Gawrys, Rory Muldowney, Robert Tremblay, and Ian Macdonald's highly operant siblings Lachlan, Annie Laurie, and Diana—to execute a hyperspatial translation, penetrating the sphere of energy surrounding Scurra.

When the maneuver worked, rather to Marc's surprise, he orchestrated a titanic creative blast from the screaming generator of his own metaconcert, striking simultaneously at the great red diamond from outside and inside the glowing bubble.

Two things happened. All of us who were watching saw the first event. The second became widely known only four days later.

The enormous sphere of coadunate energy contracted like a collapsing star. I saw a woman dressed in a gem-encrusted silver flying suit and a naked brain enclosed in blazing plasma. In the aether, two voices said: *Persevere.*

Marc heard Jack speak on his intimate mode: It's finished Big Brother now you must magnify too like it or not adieu dear Marc. [Scent of white pine fading gemlight crash of silence.]

A miniature nova blazed momentarily where Scurra had been. The invading Rebel ship with its secondary focus team was vaporized by an incandescent shock wave. The shuttlecraft carrying Paul Remillard endured for only a microsecond longer before it also vanished.

I was told later that there is a striking chemical phenomenon that can be demonstrated with a supersaturated solution of anhydrous sodium acetate, cooled below its normal "freezing" point of around room temperature. A single tiny flake of the solid chemical is dropped into the supercooled solution . . . and within moments the entire volume of liquid undergoes a swift phase change, becoming a solid crystalline mass.

This, I was informed, is analogous to what happened to the Mind of Humanity, still enmeshed in its lattice of metaconcerted love, as it saw the glowing dust that had been a tiny starship named Scurra fading and wafting away on the solar wind.

The Carbuncle concentrating the Mind endured, and so did the Song, now augmented by almost every human individual. It rang from one end of the galaxy to the other, now joined by a thundering chorus of uncountable exotic voices in a hymn of Unity.

The human participants knew the third level of consciousness only for a moment before sliding back reluctantly to lower plateaus of coadunation or simple fellowship. The Song descended into diminuendo and faded away. The great red diamond remained, wrapped in stillness.

The confrontation was over.

I came to my senses sitting on my rock beside the river. It was full night, with a sky full of sparkling, enigmatic stars.

A massive wave of dysergistic flashover had struck Marc and the other nine members of his executive focus team at the instant of the phase change. They did not die, but their hyperenergized brains were severely injured, causing the entire Rebel metaconcert to collapse. The minds that had comprised the tripartite generator structure were not so lucky as the focusing agents. Every one of the E18 helmet operators was roasted alive by metacreative flashover, and many of the smaller ships that had carried them were destroyed. Those operators whose bodies were frozen solid in 600X CE rigs mostly survived, the weaker mentalities reduced to virtual imbeciles while the stronger suffered brainburns similar to those of the prime focusing team. Because of the cerametal refractive lining in the CE bays of the larger Rebel starships, their hulls did not breach. There was some internal damage to the vessels, but in most cases this was not so critical as to preclude superluminal travel.

Marc emerged from his CE rig and surveyed the scorched bay and half-melted auxiliary machinery. He farspoke the other nine members of his team, and after he had determined that they were alive and capable of shedding their armor by mental override of the ruined computer he staggered to the personnel conveyor. He had been severely injured, but his redaction and paramount creativity were already initiating repairs to his brain.

The conveyor door slid shut and Marc stabbed a shaking finger at the pad that would take him to the Vulpecula's bridge. He slumped back against the wall of the car, his soaking wet coverall dripping dermal lavage onto the floor.

Only then did he realize that he was not alone.

A tall figure stood in one corner. It was an elderly man in old-fashioned evening clothes with a neatly trimmed white beard and a patriarchal halo of silvery hair. Marc had last seen him when he was thirteen years old, in Concilium Orb, at the Inaugural Ball of the Human Polity.

Marc tried to smile. "Hello, Lylmik."

The exotic said, "Hello, Abaddon."

The conveyor was clearly not moving. Marc said, " 'We fought against the empire of heaven. We were—that I will not deny—vanquished in that conflict: Yet the great intention was not lacking in nobility. Something or other gave them victory; to us remains the glory of a dauntless daring. And even if my troop fell thence vanquished, yet to have attempted a lofty enterprise is still a trophy.' "

"I've forgotten the author," the Lylmik admitted. "Is it Milton?"

"Giambattista Marino. Have you come to haul me off to solitary confinement?"

"No," Unifex said. "The Quincunx has voted a reprieve. Your armada will go to Earth. There the injured can be evacuated to medical facilities. After they've recovered, most of them will be given the opportunity to choose again."

"Most of them?"

"I have other plans for you—and certain other grandmasterclass Rebels in the fleet who aren't too badly wounded and who choose to accompany you. Assemble one hundred of them here on the Vulpecula before you set out for home."

"What are you going to do?" Marc spoke with weary resignation. "Make some kind of example of us?"

"Au contraire," said Atoning Unifex. "I am going to let you go free. In a manner of speaking." Then he told Marc why he had to go to France, and what he would find waiting for him in a warehouse just outside Lyon Metro.

In the days following Saint Augustine's, the whole world talked about what had happened at Okanagon—not so much the destruction of the planet, nor even the heroic deaths of Jack, Dorothea, and Paul—but rather that effulgent, unforgettable glimpse of Unity that would eventually bring about a spontaneous metamorphosis of the human racial Mind.

There were still Rebel soreheads who vowed never to give in, and numbers of bloodyminded fools who insisted that Dorothée and Ti-Jean had been to blame for Okanagon's destruction. But most people knew better. The Milieu canonized Jack the Bodiless and his wife, whom the exotics called Illusio Diamond Mask, assuring their mourners that the ashes of the couple would help to bring about the birth of a new star commemorating humanity's entry into full cosmic consciousness.

But that was still in the future.

When the Rebel fleet began to limp into Earth starports four days after the confrontation, the battered crewmembers were greeted with compassion. In the excitement, no one noticed at first that one hundred and one high-echelon evildoers—including the Angel of the Abyss himself—had escaped.

After a single unobtrusive stop-off in Hanover, New Hampshire (which I did not witness), they flew in small orbiters to the tiny village of Saint-Antoine-des-Vignes in France. There, they took possession of the treasure trove of survival gear, including weaponry, that Unifex's shopping expedition had provided. Hauling the loot off in a long caravan of all-terrain vehicles, they proceeded to L'Auberge du Portail, Madame Guderian's unique establishment that provided a one-way time-gate to the Pliocene Exile, six million years in the past.

Marc took his children, Hagen and Cloud, with him. Even at the end, he refused to give up his dream of Mental Man.

The tale of Abaddon's temporal translation, his Pliocene adventures, and his expiation in the Duat Galaxy have been told in other books. My own memoirs end here . . . unless there is a new beginning.

> And the wise will shine as brightly
> As the heavenly firmament,
> And those who have instructed many in virtue
> Will be as the stars for ever and ever.
> Daniel 12:3

[**EPILOGUE**]

HANOVER, NEW HAMPSHIRE, EARTH
31 DECEMBER 2113

The old man stared at the biblical quotation on the display of his transcriber for a long time before he hit the PRINT and FILE pads.

"Eh bien, Ghost. It's done. Barely under your deadline, but I pushed myself. I hope you're satisfied."

In the night outside the little room in Rogatien Remillard's third-floor flat, the wolf wind was wailing in the doorways, the snow drifted deep along the road, the ice gnomes were marching from their Norways, and the Great White Cold walked abroad.

Rogi heard someone whistling the old college song. The sound was almost inaudible amidst the noise of the storm and the whistler was invisible, but the old bookseller knew who it was.

"What would you like me to do with the thing?" Rogi gestured at the growing stack of durafilm sheets being spit out by his printer. "Hand it over to the media?"

No, said the Family Ghost. Give it to my sister Marie. She'll know how to have it properly published. Just be certain that no one cuts anything out or alters anything.

"D'accord. Will . . . you go away now?"

Yes. But if you should ever be mortally endangered, your own Great Carbuncle will summon colleagues of mine who will assist you. There are four of them—at least for now—and they wear human bodies.

"Batège! Corporeal Lylmik. What next?"

A spectral chuckle sounded and the Ghost said: Perhaps something interesting.

The old man scowled. "Dammit, hasn't my life been interesting enough? What I'd really appreciate is a little peace for myself. And I don't mean Unity!"

You might find its merits more appealing in the months to come. Talk it over with Malama.

"Maybe." Rogi's tone was mutinous. He climbed to his feet and hesitantly stuck out his hand to the empty air. "Well, if this is goodbye, I want to say no hard feelings. It was a helluva story. There were times when I didn't even believe you were real, but . . ."

He felt a firm clasp, and then something enveloped him in a near-orgasmic rush of physical pleasure that was gone almost as soon as it began.

Adieu, mon oncle. Priez pour moi.

Rogi lowered his head and spoke in a broken whisper. "Sure, Marc. Damn tootin' I will."

Then he knew that the room was empty except for himself and Marcel, curled up in his basket beside the desk, looking at him with gray-green wildcat eyes. Rogi stood without moving for a long time.

At last he said to the cat, "Reckon that's that, old Fur-Face. Let's get on to bed."

He heard a knock at the front door.

Grumbling, he went into the parlor and then to the small entry of the apartment. He snapped the lock and opened the door. She stood there in a down-filled jacket, her strawberry-blonde hair glistening with melting snowflakes and her silvery eyes smiling. A faint scent of Bal à Versailles perfume came to him as she lifted a bottle of inexpensive domestic champagne with a red ribbon tied around its neck.

"Happy New Year! Sorry about the cheap bubbly, but it was all the supermarket had left."

Rogi stared at her, unable to utter a sound.

Elaine Donovan kissed him gently on the lips and pushed past into the parlor. "Don't just stand there, darling. We've years of catching up to do."

Rogi closed the door and got on with it.

THE END

of

Magnificat

Book Three of the Galactic Milieu Trilogy

And the end and the beginning were always there
Before the beginning and after the end.
And all is always now.

T. S. ELIOT

Julian May was born in Chicago in 1931. She has written numerous books, including *The Many-Colored Land, The Golden Torc, The Newborn King, The Adversary, Intervention* (Book One: *The Surveillance* and Book Two: *The Metaconcert*). Julian May lives in the state of Washington.

This book was set in Garamond, a type named for the famous Parisian type cutter Claude Garamond (ca. 1480–1561). Garamond, a pupil of Geoffroy Tory, based his letter on the types of the Aldine Press in Venice, but he introduced a number of important differences, and it is to him that we owe the letter now known as "old style." The version of Garamond used for this book was first introduced by the Monotype Corporation of London in 1922. It is not a true copy of any of the designs of Claude Garamond, but can be attributed to Jean Janson, a Protestant printer working in Sedan in the early seventeenth century, who had worked with Garamond's romans earlier but who was denied their use because of Catholic censorship. Janson's matrices came into the possession of the Imprimerie nationale, where they were thought to be by Garamond himself, and were so described when the Imprimerie revived the type in 1900. The italic is based on the types of Robert Granjon, a type cutter and printer active in Antwerp, Lyons, Paris, and Rome from 1523 to 1590.

Composed, printed and bound by The Haddon Craftsmen, Scranton, Pennsylvania
Designed by Virginia Tan